About the Author

Susan Delaney has worked with rescue cats since she was ten years old. Breaking away from a large well known organisation, she became the founder of the charity 'The Scratching Post', which she founded in 2004. The amount of time Susan spent with the rescue cats inspired this book to be written.

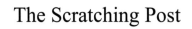

The Scratching Post

Susan Delaney

The Scratching Post

Olympia Publishers

London

www.olympiapublishers.com
OLYMPIA PAPERBACK EDITION

A CIP catalogue record for this title is
available from the British Library.

ISBN: 978-1-78830-054-4

This is a work of fiction.
Names, characters, places and incidents originate from the writer's
imagination. Any resemblance to actual persons, living or dead, is
purely coincidental.

First Published in 2018
Olympia Publishers
60 Cannon Street
London
EC4N 6NP
Printed in Great Britain

Dedication

This book is dedicated to my mother, who has spent much of her life helping cats that have been abandoned, abused and are unwanted. Also to the rescue cats, who sometimes are overlooked.

Acknowledgments

All profits from this book will be donated to 'The Scratching Post' (Rescue & Shelter appeal for cats. 1105653.)

Chapter One

'This is an odd morning,' Flick decided on waking, and after a long indulgent yawn. He unhooked himself from Comfort – a small fluffy black and white female – and climbed from the basket they shared. After giving his stiff limbs a firm shake, he stalked over to the front of the barn.

At the window that filled most of the wall, Flick took a precise leap. He landed with expert precision in the middle of the table that sat there. On arrival, he peered through the glass to study the world on the other side. Twisting his head to various positions did not change what greeted him. A spook crept through his body, causing his smooth fur to rise untidily. As his eyes adjusted focus, they assessed the many indescribable objects that hovered outside.

The ground had disappeared, replaced by a sea of swirling white mist! Flick shuddered as the spook reached the root of his tail, creeping past until it nibbled at the tip. The massive worry tensed in his head, causing his brow to pucker.

This morning, or rather last night, he had had the strangest dream. When he awoke, the insides of himself felt strangely odd. Little butterflies or moths, Flick was unclear which, must have crept into his tummy during the dream. Now they were fluttering all over and tickling him. It was the most peculiar sensation.

Spotting movement from the corner of his eye, he spun his head to look behind him. Young Pickle, a tabby and white female kitten, yawned and stretched out her limbs. She pulled back her chin so far that it disappeared into her chest. A small groan escaped her as she did this. Heaving one lid open, she twisted the exposed eye in a circle. Assured that she was not missing anything interesting, Pickle allowed it to fall. Slithering her body like a snake, she twisted upside down.

Her four legs stuck straight into the air. Then, as sleep overtook her, they sank down to a more comfortable position.

Flick's eyes darted around, to gauge any changes, inside as well as out. The six large enclosures to the left still contained the new arrivals. The doors were firmly bolted, to prevent any escapees; none of them could be seen. Being new at the barn, it would take a while for them to settle in. He scrutinised the odd-sized shelves fixed to the far wall. Little wooden ladders stood against each, making them easily accessible. Various shapes and sizes of feline lounged on each, most still asleep, snoring gently, while others were in meditation, as cats often are. More early risers were already starting to wash in readiness for the day. The whole area was utilised to create a place for stray and unwanted cats. Here they waited until good homes were found for them.

'Flick, what are you doing?' called Comfort. He jumped and looked guilty as he always did when she used that tone.

'Something weird is happening!' he answered, his eyes wide and dramatic.

Comfort, used to his drama, was not particularly alarmed. However, curiosity overcoming her, she rose to her feet. Dipping her chest to the floor, and prodding her bottom in the air, she began a long, luxurious stretch. The front half complete, Comfort pulled herself upright and pointed her nose to the ceiling. Her spine lengthened as she poked her back left leg vertically. Once satisfactorily stretched, she pushed out the right. Her ridged fluffy tail gave a slight vibration as she strained. The feline yoga complete, she strolled to the window and jumped up next to Flick, letting out a long, slow yawn as she did so.

They both stared into the gloomy winter morning, where a heavy fog had descended during the night.

'It's so weird, everything has disappeared!' said Flick, his eyes expressing the worry that hovered behind them. It was the only thing that offered a clue to his emotions. His face was so black that his other features were hard to see.

Comfort giggled, 'It's just fog, silly!'

Flick's intense expression rippled to blankness for a few moments as he absorbed the information.

'It's a heavy cloak of white stuff that comes from the sky,' she explained.

His face strained as he tried to understand her explanation.

Comfort sighed and raised her eyes in exasperation. 'Trust me; you wouldn't want to be out there. It's so cold your tail would stick to the ground.'

Leaping from the table, she sauntered over to the basket and climbed in, the spot still warm from her earlier sleep. 'Come back to bed, Flick, it's ages until breakfast.' She walked round and round before flopping on to the blanket. Coiling herself into a tight circle, Comfort lifted her tail into the air, allowing it to hover momentarily, before letting it float down and land precisely over her eyes.

Dismissing her, Flick turned his attention back to the farm. He squinted into the haze, mesmerised by the strange entities that did not seem to have any beginning or end. Odd little twinkles of light sparkled in the whiteness. He flipped his head from side to side, in order to catch one with his sharp vision, but by the time his eyes reached it, it had vanished.

In place of the enormous trees, that lined the edge of the land, hovered abnormal looking shapes that appeared to sway closer. He heard the horses in the stables opposite neighing, but try as he did, Flick could not see them.

His sight caught the movement of the black and white goat that wandered around the farm. Her legs were invisible in the heavier ground mist, leaving the fat, round body to float above the blankness. The goat stopped, and lowered her head into the thickness. He gasped with horror as she became headless as well as legless. He adamantly refused to live in a place where a ghostly goat with no head or legs glided about; it was far too frightening! It could be dangerous for his heart if she popped up unexpectedly at the window. To his relief, her head soon bobbed up again, extended with protruding lips, containing an empty crisp bag.

She stood for a while, contemplating her find, then lazily and leisurely began to chew. She bobbed again, and this time came up with a piece of cardboard hanging from her mouth. Flick shuddered with disgust at the goat's choice of cuisine!

The weak outline of the large caravan over in the far corner was vaguely visible. The man who lived there had floated past moments earlier, not seeming to mind his missing legs. With his body bent forward, hunched shoulders and pulled-up collar, he braved the onslaught of cold. He rudely ignored Flick, who had kindly blurped to inform him of his forgotten legs.

Two men stood hovering where the car park had once been, rubbing their hands and stamping their feet as they passed a greeting. Flick knew them both; one was the owner of the farm whom everyone knew as Billy Bank Robber. Retired now, but the stories of his past criminal days were still loved by most. The fine old tales cheered even the dullest day, giving him a cheeky respect amongst both animals and humans. The other lived next door. He terrified every animal; his body giving off dark, evil vibrations that made even insects move aside when he was nearby. This was often, as he climbed over the adjoining wall using a ladder that was propped there. He was bloodthirsty, and loved to slaughter and torture animals.

Flick's brother Mac sprang up beside him. 'Something's wrong!' Mac said anxiously on landing.

Flick stared back at the image of himself.

'I had the weirdest dream. Some humans came to kill us.'

Flick gave a long shudder and extended his pupils wider. 'Yes, I had a strange dream too. But surely no one would do that, except the man next door.'

'I don't know who, but I have a terrible feeling,' Mac's eyes widened with horror, 'Oh my!' he screeched, his attention darting to something out of the window.

Flick's fur, which had just begun to relax, erected again. His dilated pupils stared hard into the gloom. Horrible mental images flooded into his head: decapitated cats, and evil spirits chasing them around the cattery. His eyes darted desperately, trying to find what was coming out of the fog. He could not see anything different from what he had seen earlier, so he screeched back, 'WHAT?!'

'What on earth is that goat eating?'

'For goodness sake, Mac, do you have to do that? You scared me half to death!' Lifting one very shaky front paw, Flick licked vigorously. He pulled it down over his ear a moment later to hide his embarrassment. It was a vain attempt to calm his pounding heart.

Mac smirked and changed the subject. 'I wonder if anyone will come today to view us.'

'You say that every day. Nobody's going to offer you a home with just your nose poking out from under a blanket. You know the rules; roll over and purr as loudly as you can. Or at least run up to the humans and rub against their legs,' the wise Flick advised.

'I know, but when strangers come I go – daft. Besides, everyone knows the cute tortie in pen three will be homed next, however many rolls I do.'

It was true, people rarely chose a black cat, especially one with a nervous disposition.

Mac nudged him with his nose, and sprang on to Flick's back, biting his neck playfully before scampering away. Not being able to resist a game of chase, forgetting the dream and the hovering spirits, Flick bounded after him. Past the pens, to the kitchen area that was on the opposite side of the barn they sprinted. Both skidding on a right turn. Mac sprang on to the sofa which lay against one wall, bounced twice and flipped on to the armchair next to it.

Flick, using a different tactic, darted under a chair opposite. Only his whiskers and nose were visible from the blanket that was draped over it. He waited for a good clean attack of his brother.

As Mac reached the armchair, Flick leapt out and dived on top of him. Then the pair dashed off, scattering blankets and cushions into a disorganised array as they went. They sprang on to a shelf right over old Summer's head; she, until that time, had been asleep in her basket.

Mac landed on the corner of Summer's en-suite toilet tray. It flipped up, and the contents flew through the air landing all over her.

The old cat was so startled that her legs splayed out like a starfish, her claws pointing on the end of each foot.

'Young roughens,' she hissed, 'thugs, scallywags!' Pulling her four legs together, she lifted her paw and began the long laborious task of picking bits of grey gravel and a clump of wee-sodden litter from her coat. Having few teeth, this proved most difficult. Curling her pink lips back, she coarsely spat the grains on to the floor. Once finished, she rolled over and began the arduous task of bathing. She found many of the bathing manoeuvres difficult in her older years. Pointing her back legs together in the air was virtually impossible. Not to mention the back twist, tummy curl and ear rub at the same time. A mild melancholy flooded her tummy, so much so that in mid-lick, and with her tongue hanging out, she nodded off, to contemplate her predicament.

The boys giggled. One of the older cats, Banjo, a large ginger tom with a big head, chastised them. 'She is an elderly cat; she's entitled to nod off occasionally. You should not mock her.'

'But she is rather liverish, and besides, she looks daft,' Flick smirked. 'Every day she starts to wash her top half and falls asleep before reaching her bottom. She must have the cleanest top and the smelliest nethers in the cattery.'

Banjo couldn't help but grin himself. It was true, Summer was becoming forgetful. Her owner had brought her here because she was old, stating that she was too much trouble. The human, Sally, who looked after them, called her Summer because she said she was pretty. Banjo could not see that at all; she was just plain black. Still, he was no oil painting himself. His ears were flat, his back legs crooked, and he only had half a tail. Many war wounds scarred his face and the top of one eye. This was the result of years of living as an unneutered stray. He had always been getting into scraps with other cats.

In the winter months, he had walked so far that his feet bled and his body shook with fatigue. To stop and sleep meant a slow death from hypothermia. In the hot summer months, he was so thirsty that his parched throat would swell. His stomach constantly hurt because of the lack of food. Out of desperation, he tried to get into humans' houses. Most pelted him with stones when they saw him, laughing and calling him ugly and diseased because of the way he looked.

One day, a kind lady took pity, after he had collapsed on a pavement beside a kerb. She had brought him here to the home for unwanted cats. He was grateful as he had known that many places would have had him destroyed.

After weeks of nursing and love, he had recovered. Now he had regular food, a warm bed and lots of friends. Every day, Sally scooped him up and told him he was gorgeous and handsome, giving him a big kiss on his head, and promising that one day someone would come and take him home. He loved to hear this, even though he knew it was not true. Who'd want an ugly old thing like him? But he dutifully purred, staring up adoringly and offering the biggest grin he could manage.

Summer woke with a start, giving a slight trill. 'Scallywags,' she hissed, pointing her head and puckering her lips in the direction in which she remembered that Flick and Mac had last headed.

Banjo's thoughts melted away as he looked up at her. She drew in her now stiff, dry tongue, and moved it around the inside of her mouth to soften it.

Banjo smiled to himself. 'They went ages ago,' he informed the old cat.

'I was dreaming,' she said, once satisfied that her tongue was supple. 'My Mum came for me.'

Banjo yawned, and snuggled back into his basket. 'You've been saying that for months. Face facts! She is not coming.'

Summer looked mortified. 'Yes, she is, you wait and see.'

'Well why hasn't she come yet? Let's face it, you're no different from the rest of us – UNWANTED!'

'That's not true; my Mum hasn't come because… well… because she forgot where she left me.' With that, she turned to face the wall, to hide the sadness in her watery old eyes.

The cats sprang up and flew for the door, as they heard Sally and Candy the dog arriving.

'Breakfast!' Mac squealed, as he weaved in and out of the others. They in turn weaved back. Then they stopped and stared expectantly at the door, longing for it to open. As the key turned in the lock, a wonderful aroma of cooked fish filled the air.

Summer gave a long stretch, pointing her head so far that her tongue poked out at one end and she passed wind at the other. Embarrassed, she spun around to see if anyone had noticed.

She need not have worried, because twenty-four cats began to yowl 'FISH!' all at once – as they did on every fish day. A sea of furry bodies filled every space on the floor.

Sally picked her way through the mass to the feeding place; her loyal dog Candy trotted behind her, not showing the slightest interest in the cats.

They had long since stopped fluffing up their fur when seeing the hound. She appeared docile enough. Even so, taking no chances, they always kept a safe distance from her.

Every day she walked solemnly through the cattery, with her head lowered and brow furrowed in deep concentration. It was complicated deciding the best bed to choose. The basket had to be medium in size, with a large soft blanket, although Candy had been known to squash into a small one at times. The location must be near the radiator, with a good view of the fridge. This was essential to ensure that she not only hogged the heat, but did not miss out on the chicken treat brought out each day.

Stopping and hanging her head, Candy took painful deliberation before making her decision. She climbed attentively into the chosen bed, and proceeded to push the blanket around with her black, rubbery nose. Once satisfied with the crafted heap, she plopped down, letting out an enormous sigh.

The cats thought her most peculiar. After the long drawn-out routine, she always ended up choosing the same basket every day.

Chapter Two

An hour later, they were all lounging lazily in every available bed, their stomachs so big that they threatened to pop. Even Candy, who had consumed more than her fair share, caused the cats to give her sideward glances of distaste.

'I couldn't eat another thing,' announced Comfort, who now lolled in a basket with her back legs in the air and her front paws neatly folded over her chest, so that they did not press on her large, protruding belly.

Flick went over to her and started to wash her head. Comfort looked up at him with adoration in her eyes.

'I love you, Flick,' she trilled, rubbing her nose on his face.

'Oh please,' Mac said, raising his eyes and faking a 'sicking up a fur ball' motion. Flick threw him a look of reproach, before climbing into the basket next to Comfort.

'I had the weirdest dream last night,' Comfort told them, as she batted Flick around the ears a few times and began hissing at him.

This was a strange thing to do to a loved one, but for female cats it was a gesture of love to a partner.

'These humans came to the cattery to take us away. They wanted to kill all of us over two years old. They ran around with pole things, and were grabbing us with them. It was so scary.'

Mac's ears perked up. 'How strange, I had a similar dream.'

'So did I,' shouted Sara, a fluffy black female with a squeaky meow.

The cats stared at each other, a cold shiver creeping from ear tips to tail.

Banjo froze at the thought of such a thing happening. He shook his wide head, and tried to break the air of gloom. 'Sally and Jane won't let anything happen to us,' he said, trying to convince himself as well as the bulging-eyed others.

Relaxing, and feeling slightly reassured, they turned their attention to Treacle, another little black cat. She was dubiously approaching Candy, who was washing her undercarriage. Her nose was pushed upwards and her lips were pulled back, in order to get a good nibble at the pink skin. Treacle held her head high, and sniffed the air as she walked.

None of them had bothered speaking to the dog before; they preferred either to ignore her or, if they were bored, to hiss and fluff at her.

On reaching her, Treacle sniffed at the bushy tail. When it swished, her legs went stiff and she levitated into the air.

'You made me jump!' she huffed, on landing, and her eyes were refocused.

Candy gave a grin, which looked more like a snarl. Treacle got ready to bolt, in case she suddenly attacked.

'I won't hurt you,' said Candy, sounding a little hurt at the insinuation that she could have even contemplated such a thing.

Feeling more confident that the dog was safe, Mac walked slowly forward. Young Pickle followed closely behind him.

Her mother, Marmite, peeped out from under the nearby chair, fascinated by the whole episode. 'Be careful, Pickle!' she called worriedly.

Because cats are so curious, even when scared, more began to edge forward. Almost reaching the dog, three of them leaned their necks as far as they could, their heads slowly waving from side to side as they sniffed dubiously at her. Sensing the dog, whose eyes were darting from one to the other, was just as uncertain as they were, their bodies began to relax. Deciding she was smelly, the three of them hung their mouths open and gave her a wrinkly frown.

'Pooh,' said Mac, 'she whiffs!'

'You don't smell so good yourself,' Candy informed him.

Mac looked surprised and began sniffing under his tail.

'I come in peace,' Treacle began, glancing round at the others for support. She gave a little cough, 'I was interested to know where you go when you leave here.'

Candy's large, sad eyes clouded momentarily, obscuring the now seven cats that sat close by. She thought carefully about the question before answering. 'Well, it depends what time of day it is. As you know, every morning and evening we come here. After here, in the evening, we go to our house, where I help my Mum, Sally, work on charity paperwork.'

Seeing the puzzled eyes she explained further; 'Mum speaks to humans on the telephone, who have reported cats that need rescuing. I sit nearby, catching zeds.'

'We know what a telephone is. It's that black plastic thing that Sally carries in her pocket and talks to sometimes,' Sara interrupted, looking round and feeling very clever, 'I'm not sure what zeds are though.'

Candy threw her a brief look of annoyance at the interruption. 'On a Saturday, after we've left here in the morning, we go to work at the charity's shop.

'During the day, Monday to Fridays, I stand on the back of the sofa, peering out of the window to wait for my Mum to come home from work and walk me. I have a little shout now and again at passing humans.

'On Sundays, we come here for most of the day,' Candy finished, pleased that she had managed to answer the question correctly. It was such a lot to say, for a dog of little words.

'W… W… What's a charity shop?' Pickle asked.

Candy clouded once again; it was so difficult to explain some things, especially to cats. 'It's a building where kind humans give things they do not want. The things are sold to other humans to make money. That way there is enough to pay for you lot. My Mum set it up, and I helped her. We went every day to decorate it. Then we opened the doors and let the humans in. Sometimes a dog or two pops in with their owners.

'My Mum looked after the shop for the first year, and then arranged for another person to do that for her. Now she supervises the person, and makes sure everything is done properly. I go with her, and sniff around a bit to check corners and edges.'

Intrigued, Treacle asked, 'What does Sally do at the shop?'

Deliberating again, Candy swayed her head slightly, then laid it down, her chin propped on the plastic edge of the basket. 'Mum talks about the weather.'

The cats looked at each other, puzzled.

Candy sighed and rolled her eyes. Honestly, cats are so daft. 'Every customer that comes through the door says something about the weather. Either "it's a nice day today", "it's a hot day today" or "it's a cold day today." Mum smiles and responds. It's an important job talking about the weather. Don't you lot know anything?' Candy asked them exasperated.

'Well, how boring! It's much more interesting talking about mice, birds or worms,' said Pickle, pointing her head in the air to watch a passing fly.

Candy lifted her back leg and had a little scratch of her belly to satisfy an itch, and when she looked back, the cats had disappeared.

A few moments later seven heads popped out from behind Marmite's chair. Deciding that the dog was not attacking after all, they gingerly ventured out, this time joined by Marmite.

'Garbage gut!' shouted Summer, waking and remembering that Candy had eaten too much fish. They all stared at her in surprise. She sat bolt upright, ignoring them, gnashing her tongue and making a loud clacking noise. Then she turned to the wall and stared at it.

'What do you do in the charity shop?' Mac asked, once he had wriggled his bottom back into a comfortable position.

'My job,' Candy said proudly, 'is to sort out the soft toys and greet the customers that come in. Sometimes I take my squeaky grey rat over to them. It encourages humans to buy something. Some of them scream when I drop it on their foot.' Pausing for a while and wrinkling her nose, she added, 'They're a bit weird doing that.'

'What's a rat?' Pickle asked.

'It has four legs, whiskers and a long wormy tail. When I squeeze it, it squeaks,' explained Candy, knowledgeably.

Pickle's eyes widened. 'Oooh … Mum, can I have a rat? I like worms,' she pleaded.

'We'll see,' Marmite told her, giving Pickle's head a deliberate lick, and trying to think where she could possibly obtain a rat.

'Why do you live with Sally?' Treacle wanted to know.

'I have to, so that I can protect her by guarding her house. Almost every day, a pizza leaflet tries to break in through the letterbox. I bark and see it off. No leaflet will mess with me.' She puffed out her chest and extended her chin, in an attempt to look fierce.

The cats were very impressed, and felt safer having a brave dog around.

At least if humans come to kill them she will 'see them off', Banjo thought. He gave a long, scrutinizing stare at the old dog before shaking his wide head – perhaps not.

'If we have humans visit our house, I jump on my Mum's lap in case they attack her,' Candy was telling the wide eyes that were staring in admiration at her.

'You're very brave,' Pickle said. 'I don't think I'd attack a pizza leaflet. I would hide under a blanket if one tried to break in here.'

Sally called to Candy from the door, and the dog pulled her body slowly up and ambled off.

'Quick, trays,' Mac shouted. They jumped up and dashed off.

It was a game they played every day, and, chatting to Candy, had almost missed their chance. First, Mac dived into the toilet tray and started to scratch and strain. Seeing him from the door and sighing, Sally went to get a bag and glove to clean it. As she reached the door again Flick dived in and copied. Sally rushed back, looking flustered at her watch.

Just as Flick finished, Pickle followed, and after Marmite. It was such great fun; the cats thought it hilarious and would smirk and discuss their antics long after she had left.

'Silly game,' Summer shouted, unusually still awake and watching them.

The fog had lifted slightly, and a weak sun was periodically peering through the grey clouds, when Sally finally left the cattery.

Banjo followed and watched from the window, as Sally helped Candy on to the passenger seat of the car. The dog was old, and her back legs stiff. Noting the grey heaviness of the sky, he gave a little shudder. He turned, jumped down and went back to his basket beside the radiator for a nap. He was so glad that he no longer lived outside.

The tortie in pen three had been allowed out that day, so that she could explore. The cats were never kept confined for too long. Once they had visited the vets and had had their necessary injections and health checks, they were encouraged to mix with the others. If they did not like mixing, they were only released under supervision.

Tortie, who had been named Gracie, was young, so she adapted to cattery life quickly. The others introduced themselves by sniffing her bottom and giving a small hiss. She, in return, fluffed up the fur along her spine and tail and hissed back.

Pickle pushed herself to the front of the crowd, and reached out her head towards the new cat. Gracie lifted her paw, and patted her a few times on the nose. Pickle responded by hissing, and, lifting her front paw, tapped back.

Contact established, Pickle bounced back and forward a few times in a crab stance. This entailed arching her back and body until she was on tiptoes, hanging her head in a sideways position, with her eyes crossed, and bouncing up and down.

Gracie watched for a moment and then repeated the action. Just to show off, she added a clever, well-practised dinosaur. In the olden days, when cats as old as Summer were young, this stance was known as 'bear'. The name had long since been changed by the younger generations.

Pickle found it a very difficult move, as her balance had never been very good but, not to be outdone, she had a go. She arched her shoulders as high as possible. Then, lowering her neck until her head dangled, she lifted her front paws from the floor until reaching the full height of her back. The next manoeuvre was tricky, as it required the front paws to be waved from side to side, and a little bounce with the back paws. all at the same time. Pickle toppled badly at the bouncing point. To hide her inadequacy, she lowered herself clumsily, and spun her body, landing in another crab. Then, springing into the air, she did a double bounce, first on her front paws, then on her back. It was a move she had made up all by herself.

Gracie was so excited by the game that she did not notice her new friend wobbling too much. They both then took off, seeming to fly through the air, taking it in turns to chase each other around the cattery.

It was such a great game, hiding behind the large clawing posts, and pouncing out on each other in turn. Even though each knew the other was hiding there, they would act surprised. Each time they would spring into the air, crab-walking across the floor and bound off.

Flick and Mac, getting caught up in the exciting atmosphere, joined in. Soon the four of them were tearing around causing mayhem.

Banjo lay in his basket, grinning at their antics. He could still remember his own kittenhood when life had been so much fun, and he didn't have a care in the world.

'Keep the noise down,' Summer called from her shelf. 'Some of us are trying to sleep.' Turning her body around three times clockwise and once anticlockwise, she plopped down and instantly nodded off.

Worn out from the game, the four of them flopped on to the floor panting.

'Why are you here?' Pickle asked Gracie when she had caught her breath.

'Dunno,' she answered, lifting her back paw and splaying her toes to give them a wash.

'I don't think the male human liked me. He told the female I had to go or else. It seemed to happen after I ran up the curtains and broke a pot. Then he smacked my bottom because I ran up his back when he was getting into the shower. I couldn't help losing my balance and sliding down.'

'COR, I bet that hurt.'

'Yes it did, my bottom was sore for ages.'

'What about you, Pickle?'

'I came here with my Mummy. We lived in a garden under a pile of wood with my brothers and sisters. A big dog came and killed them.

My Mum managed to save me, but was heartbroken about the others. It was sad, I miss them so much.' Pickle hung her head for a while in respect before continuing, 'a human came one day with a big cage and caught us. She brought us here. That's my Mum over there.'

Gracie looked over to where Marmite was washing her tail. 'Your Mummy looks really young and she's black.'

'She had me when she was just seven months old. My Dad apparently was tabby and white, so I get my colours from him,' Pickle told her with pride.

'I'm getting a worm rat,' she announced, changing the subject. 'You can share it with me if you want.'

'Humans are peculiar,' Gracie said, changing the subject again while she chewed at a gritty bit on her stomach. 'They don't have much fur, well apart from a bit on their heads. They must feel cold because they walk about wrapped in cat beds.'

'I think they're scary,' Pickle confessed. 'I won't get a home because I run and hide when they come near me. A lot of us do that in here. Comfort is the worst, and my Mum. Sally says we'll be here forever, but we don't care.'

'I don't understand. Why would you want to stay here and not have a nice home of your own?'

'This is our home, we don't know any different except living outside, and that's horrible.'

'Suppose so,' Gracie mused. Thinking about her old home, she proceeded to tell Pickle all the pros and cons of having a home.

However, Pickle was no longer listening, as she had fallen into a deep sleep, gently snoring as her head fell back against a stuffed toy mouse.

Chapter Three

As February turned into March, the weather did not improve. It was the coldest winter for many years. Few people braved the conditions to visit the cattery to rehome a cat. Two big heaters were on full, to keep the barn cosy and warm. The cats could hear the cruel wind whipping round the cattery walls. The ground outside was layered with a shimmery sheet of ice, which finally assured Flick, with Candy's help, what the strange twinkles were.

The threat of snow hung in the air, waiting eagerly for the temperature to warm slightly, to allow it to fall. The older cats could feel the damp in the core of their bones; the younger ones were excited at the prospect.

Pickle ran backwards and forwards from the window several times a day, expectantly. She had never seen snow, and simply could not imagine the farm turning white, as Banjo predicted it would.

'You kittens have no idea,' Summer told the excited youngsters. 'It's terrible going to the toilet in snow. It's cold and wet and it sticks to your paws, and other bits, I might add. You mark my words, there's nothing worse.'

Banjo nodded in agreement. He remembered it well, and never wanted to face trudging along in snow ever again. The ice was even worse and colder. It seemed to dominate everywhere, making it impossible to find even a crumb of food or a bed. The thirst was dreadful, as all water sources were frozen solid. Once again, he thanked his luck that he was here in the warm. Last winter, he had barely made it through alive.

Sally came to feed them when it was dark. With her she brought Candy, her friend Sonya, and a basket containing a filthy white cat with four kittens.

In previous years, cats had only given birth in spring and summer. This was known as 'kitten season'. It was a dreaded time when all rescue charities would be at bursting point with abandoned mother cats and babies. The phone never stopped ringing with reports of yet another, until everyone felt like screaming or strangling the public, who seemed so oblivious to the problems they created by letting their cat have 'just one litter of kittens.' In recent years, the odd litter had been reported all year.

The cats had heard Sally argue many times with ignorant people, in the hope that she might just educate them to the problems of overpopulation, and the enormous stress placed on the cat, and the rescue charities that were left to deal with the aftermath of the problems they caused.

Although Banjo had fathered many kittens in his unneutered days, he could now see a different side of the argument, one he had never even considered before. This had taken many hours, and lots of naps, to mull it over. Working out complicated figures and large calculations, he had often lost count halfway through, as his eyes rolled and he had fallen asleep. He guessed it was like what humans called counting sheep.

If humans were going to allow their cat to have 'just one litter', then it was only fair to let the kittens have 'just one litter', and then permit the kittens' kittens also to have one litter each. That meant that the person was responsible for many thousands of cats in just a few years. Some of those kittens would end up in rescue centres. Others were destroyed because of the lack of homes, or were living and starving on the streets; it was so cruel and selfish, when humans themselves used birth control, and couldn't imagine having one baby after another, let alone five at a time.

He would grin at Sally when anyone proudly stated that they had rehomed their kittens themselves.

'But they were the homes we needed for our kittens,' she always answered, with annoyance at their stupidity. Now here was another litter to find homes for.

They could not resist gathering around to watch as Sally made up a special pen for the bedraggled cat. While these kittens were here, the cats knew that they had little chance of being chosen for a home. Kittens were always more popular than a grown cat.

Candy, doing her usual routine, dolefully trotted down the aisle, and stood contemplating, with her head dangling.

Sonya followed her, stroking and chatting to the cats on her way.

They liked Sonya, with her wild black hair and scatty ways. She stopped at Banjo who, while mentally debating the problems of the cat population, looked up with a guilty expression on his face. He had been caught having a dig-dag and a crafty little suck on the corner of his blanket. He felt daft, a grown cat acting like a kitten. But when no one was looking he loved to have a deep think and comfort himself while he did so. He needn't have worried; Sonya thought he was absolutely endearing.

'Oh handsome, beautiful baby,' she cooed, scooping a delighted Banjo up and giving him a big hug.

They loved the company of humans; they liked the way their mouths wiggled when they spoke, their pink tongue popping out now and again, allowing different sounds to escape. Some of the noises made they understood, but most of the time they could pick up what they were saying through reading minds. As humans made a noise, they also visualised what was being said in their head and gave mental pictures at the same time. They loved to listen, even if they did not always understand the conversation.

Cats do not need to wiggle their faces to communicate. They do it through their minds, and occasionally through meows.

They continued to watch as Sally placed a soft cushion on the floor, for the cat she had named Daisy, and her family. It would be dangerous for the kittens to have a raised bed, in case they fell. The mother cat looked totally depleted and depressed. She was underweight, and did not seem to have the strength to stand. She took no notice of her new surroundings.

'Poor thing,' Sally said, giving the little cat's filthy coat a stroke. Her grey fur was splattered with oil. Daisy did not respond and stared at the floor, ignoring the kittens that squeaked around her in confusion at their new environment. At eighteen months old, the cat was little more than a kitten herself. This was her fourth litter; she was exhausted, and suffering from malnutrition.

While Sally worked, they listened as she told Sonya the story of Daisy. Someone had reported the cat staggering along the street, as she could hardly walk.

They found out that she belonged to a lady who constantly bred her and sold the kittens. The lady did not want to part with the cat, as she had homes already lined up for the babies. Sally told her that she would report her for neglect and for starving the Mum cat, and that she would face charges. Reluctantly, the woman agreed to hand her over. It was on condition that they were returned within two weeks.

Daisy needed more than two weeks' nursing, plus spaying. However, the law gave the charity no rights to keep someone's cat. Strangely, the kittens, apart from being anaemic from flea infestation, and their bellies bloated with worms, looked relatively healthy.

'I'd love to strangle these people. I cannot understand why it's allowed to happen. They amaze me.' Sally's voice rose and fell with anger. 'When they're pregnant themselves, they eat and eat. Yet when breeding a cat, it never occurs to them to feed it extra, or to give it nutritional food to build it up; or even just to neuter the cat, to stop the breeding in the first place.'

She pushed a plate of fresh white fish into the pen; the cat's stomach would not cope with much more.

Sonya nodded in agreement, and so did a few of the female cats that had been subjected to such treatment.

Sara, for one, had been abandoned when pregnant. Luckily, she had been reported, and brought into care. But she remembered the stress of trying to find food and a safe place to give birth. The hunger and fear was imprinted in her mind forever. She had been spayed quickly, so had never faced giving birth, as Marmite had.

Daisy showed her first reaction, as her nose began to twitch at the smell of the fish. Not being able to resist, she turned her head and fell on the food. Her body shook, as she tried desperately to cram it all into her mouth at once. The plate was clean within seconds, and, after sniffing around to make sure no morsel was left, Daisy's eyes diverted to the floor again.

The kittens were still squealing. Without moving her eyes, she lifted her leg and allowed them to suckle from her. Before they had finished she turned her back, ignoring the angry protests. It was heart-breaking.

The kittens were approximately four weeks old; it was better for them to have their mother's milk for a while longer. Looking at Daisy, she had little milk to offer them. If she had still been with the owner, the kittens would have starved.

Sally, already having boiled the kettle, set about mixing a special formula to feed the kittens, hoping they were able to lap.

'It's OK, Daisy, this'll be your last litter, if you can just nurture this lot,' she told the unresponsive eyes, as she scooped the kittens one by one, and tried to encourage them to drink.

After falling into the bowl a few times, and snuffling it up their noses, three of them managed to lap at the warm liquid. The fourth Sally fed with a bottle. It sucked greedily at the teat, hardly stopping to breathe.

Sally had no intention of giving Daisy or the kittens back to the vile woman, whatever the consequences. Sadly, she knew the person would just find another to breed from. There was nothing they could do to prevent such cruel farming.

As Sally moved away from the pen, Pickle and Gracie strutted over, to have a look at the new arrivals.

'We're friends, and I'm getting a worm rat,' Pickle told them, with her chin jutting out, and her chest pushed forward importantly.

'You're too young to play with it, but I'll let you have a look.'

Eight little eyes blinked blankly at her. Then they turned in unison and began squeaking for their Mum again.

Pickle was most put out at the lack of response. She turned and strutted away. 'They are far too young to play with it anyway,' she told her companion, 'what do they know about life?'

Gracie nodded in agreement, stuck her nose and tail into the air, and bounced after Pickle.

Banjo, listening in, grinned to himself, from where he was snuggled on Sonya's lap. He had just managed to fit a piece of her sleeve into his mouth while nobody was looking. He gave a little suck and quickly looked around to make sure no one had noticed. Feeling confident that he could get away with it, he half closed his eyes and took a longer suck on the soft material. In total bliss, his paws started to join in, digging into Sonya's flesh and retreating. Then the next paw dug down and retreated. So Banjo digged, dagged and sucked; his chin slimy with glops of dribble.

The other cats, becoming bored with the human conversation, had already finished their night-time bathing ritual, and were dozing.

Sonya leant forward and patted Candy's head. The dog turned and snapped at her hand. Sonya squealed and jumped back, startled. Banjo dug his claws into her arm in surprise, his eyes opening so quickly that they were crossed. The rest of the cats shot up in alarm, and poised themselves ready to either run or attack; they could not decide at such short notice. Such matters needed careful deliberation; so they just stood, stiff and alarmed.

'Why did you do that?' Treacle snapped at the dog, as she fought to compose herself.

'I don't trust humans, only my Mum.' Candy looked embarrassed at causing so much disruption. She could not seem to help snapping at everyone lately, more so than ever. Laying her head on her front paw, a sad expression flooded her brown eyes. Closing her lids, picture images of her early life flooded behind them. She hated to remember those times; they hurt badly.

She saw herself as a little pup: brown and tan fur with large eyes, filled with innocence. A pain entered her heart as she saw her beloved first Mum smiling and calling to her. Candy let out a little moan of emotion, remembering how much she was adored. They were such good, happy days.

Candy had been a devoted friend to her Mum. When older, she had been taken to training classes. The instructor had remarked on the dog's intelligence. She had learned quickly, and could tackle the most complicated tasks.

Her Mum's partner was the only darkness in her life. He hated the little dog. When no one was looking he would kick or pinch her cruelly.

In Candy's fifth year, her Mum became ill. She had looked after her, and never left her side, except to go out to the garden for toileting. Then, one day, a white van came and took her Mum away. Candy grieved badly; all day and night she stood on the back of the sofa, waiting for her return. She whined and barked constantly, but her Mum did not come.

The horrible man hardly came home. When he did, he would smack the dog for soiling on the floor. Candy had tried hard not to, and had held on for as long as possible.

Many days passed, until a crowd of people came to the house. Food was laid out on a table. She could smell all the tasty things, her senses heightened because she had not been fed for days. How her stomach hurt and it kept making noises. A large car pulled up outside, and Candy knew her Mum was nearby. At last she had come back to her.

The little dog fled out of the opened front door and threw herself at the car. She jumped at the doors, barking and scratching in an effort to get to her. She looked through the windows but couldn't see her, just a long box.

The horrible man came out and clipped a lead on. He dragged her into the garage and tied her up. She kept barking and whining, desperate for her Mum. Panic set in that she would not be found.

Many hours passed, when eventually, a side door opened, and the man stood in the doorway. Candy cowered and trembled as she looked up at the huge figure staring down at her. He lifted his fists and began to beat her. The pounding did not stop until the little dog fell into a blissful unconsciousness.

When she awoke her body was aching and stiff; it was dark and cold. She lay there for many hours, confused and hurting.

Her Mum never came back again. It was days later, when she was near to starvation, that the man finally let her out. He lifted Candy by the collar and threw her into a basket.

For the next two years, her life was so miserable and unhappy. She became used to the man's hatred, and learned to stay out of his way. Day after day she spent cowering in her basket.

One day someone came, and, clipping on a lead, led her from the house to Sally's. She heard Sally say that she did not want a dog, as she peered at the trembling Candy. Deep pity and sadness filled her eyes, as she reached her hand slowly forward to allow a sniff.

Her back was so bruised she could hardly walk as she was led into the house. Sally and her partner had endless patience as she snapped and snarled.

Candy liked them but didn't understand that they wouldn't hurt her. Sally and her Mum, Jane, said that the dog's spirit had been broken. The hurt and pain were so deep that it was beyond repair. In time, she accepted them as her new family. However, the feeling of insecurity was deeply ingrained. Candy was terrified that Sally would leave, as her first Mum had, or that she would be sent back to the horrible man again. So Candy never left Sally's side, unless she was forced to.

The dog had found some sort of happiness again. She loved her walks, and adored a game of squeaky toy. But she never totally gave herself to anyone again.

That was three years ago, and still her back legs were stiff and ached from the beatings; a constant reminder of the past. She now thought of these as the dark days, and tried hard not to dwell on them too much.

'Why does Sally help us?' Treacle was saying.

'Dunno,' Mac shrugged, 'she's a bit weird I guess.'

'I know,' Candy said, joining in the conversation, in an effort to rid her thoughts of the gloomy past. They looked at the smelly beast.

'I heard Sally telling someone once.'

Pickle, who loved a good story, ran over to listen. Gracie ran after her, batting Pickle's tail as they went.

'Go on, tell us,' Pickle urged, once she had found a spot near the front, by edging the others out of the way.

'It's a long story, but if you want me to,' Candy said, proud of her new status as wise old dog. She wriggled, trying to find a comfortable position for her painful legs. When in an appropriate spot, Candy looked around at the expectant faces.

'A long, long time ago,' she began, 'when you lot, and myself for that matter, were not even eggs...'.

'I was never an egg, was I, Mum?' Pickle interrupted.

Marmite opened her mouth to answer. On seeing Candy's disgruntled stare she closed it again, and gave a little cough.

'Do you want me to tell you or not?'

'Sorry,' Pickle said, hanging her head and patting a piece of fluff on the floor.

Candy went on to explain to the cats how, when Sally was a little human, her Mum, Jane, had been contacted by a, then small, rescue organisation. They asked her if she would help a lady start a group in her local area, rescuing stray and unwanted cats. Jane agreed. She loved all animals, not just cats.

'What, even rats and worms?' Pickle asked amazed, 'and slugs?' wrinkling her nose.

'Jane had the greatest respect for all life forms. She felt that animals were badly treated and neglected by humans. The opportunity had now arisen for her to help cats, at least. So she travelled around the streets, gathering unwanted ones, of all shapes and sizes.

'Sally said that you could not open a door in the house without one shooting out and scaring the pants off you. The next few minutes would be spent running around, trying to catch the escapee.'

'What's pants?'

'Shut up, Pickle,' said Mac, flicking a ball at her.

Gracie giggled, and Pickle gave her a cross glare.

'Cats came and went. Most came and never went. Jane fell in love with them all, and wanted to keep them. Sally did too, and even her brother, who could not understand any of it, went to bed with a big tabby tucked under his arm.

'Despite all those cats their home was always immaculate, and never smelly. They were a poor family, as they had no money. All their items were second-hand, given by relatives who took pity on them. But Jane would scrub everywhere from top to bottom every day to make sure it was spotless.

'There were a few disasters. Bonny, a large ginger tom, ran off with Sally's potato croquettes which she was making for school.'

'What's a cro...?' Pickle stopped speaking quickly when she saw the angry glares in her direction.

Candy ignored the young cat. 'Then another cat used her geography project as a litter tray. Two years' of hard work had gone into that.

'After a year the other lady gave up, and Jane began to manage the charity; or rather, no one else wanted the job. So Jane had no choice.

'She did everything she could to raise money, including jumble sales, bazaars, and a sponsored whatever-someone-could think-of-at-the-time. She went out of an evening, checking potential cat homes to see whether the people were suitable for her rescued cats.'

'Goodness,' Banjo interrupted, 'do you mean they checked on people before they were allowed to take one?'

'Yes, indeed; Jane wanted to make sure they were serious about homing a cat. Also, she liked to know people's scenario first. That way, a cat that was suitable could be suggested.'

'Oh,' mused Comfort, pondering on how much more there was to rescuing cats than she had imagined.

'Carry on with the story, Candy,' pleaded Sara who had been enjoying it, up to the boring homing bit.

Candy sniffed at her toe to stall for time. 'Anyway, where was I? Oh, yes, I remember; the once quiet life, by now, had become very hectic. Sally loved the new activity; she was never frightened of the cats, no matter how vicious. Jane would often send her into somewhere to retrieve a fierce angry cat.

"Now", she would say, "you go in there, and put Tibbles into a basket. I'll wait out here.'' Tibbles would be a large, snapping, spitting tomcat, that would be most annoyed at being put into a basket. Sally would disappear and, a moment or two later, plus lots of swearing, (by the cat not Sally), would come out with a disgruntled, growling Tibbles, proudly presented in a white wire basket.

'When she came home from school, Jane would often call out, "Don't take your coat off. I need you to go to the vet's.'" Sally would dutifully trot off, with a blue pushchair, loaded with baskets, containing resentful looking moggies, and clutching a piece of paper with carefully written instructions. At the vet's, she would wait hours, as, in those days, they had no appointment system. It was pot luck; and Sally was always unlucky.

'Jane worked endlessly, seven days a week, even Christmas Day. She took pride in everything she did. Every cat problem that was called through on the ever-ringing phone was painstakingly sorted out. No cat was ever left destitute or homeless; every one was as important to her as her own.

'She had a certain way of making people do things which they had never even considered. Many came for a cute, cuddly kitten, and left lugging a large tomcat with protruding jowls and a chunky body. People's lips seemed to disconnect from their brains, and they would go into some sort of trance. They were no longer in control, Jane was; she would wiggle her lips at them and they were under a spell. Jane was not a controlling person; she was gentle and easy-going, but when she decided something, there was no dissuading her. She had decided to rescue cats, and that's what she did, and did well.

'The other members of the group, who worked alongside, supported her. They struggled endlessly, with little money. Most of the time, Jane paid expenses out of her own meagre income.

'Through Jane's hard work, the group has grown in size. There is now money to pay for you cats in care. Many legacies have been left in Jane's name for the charity.'

'That's great, a rags to riches story, I love a good story,' Sara said with a dreamy sigh. She did not understand any of it, but it sounded good.

Candy didn't either; she just repeated Sally's words as she had overheard them once. 'Jane and Sally don't think so. They are pleased not to have so much financial worry, but, because of their success, there are people that want to take over. Sally and Jane do not think their intentions are good. I must say,' Candy added, 'they do not smell good, and their vibrations are nasty.'

'Who are they?' Comfort asked, remembering her dreadful dream.

'Sally calls them the three witches. One is Morag, who gives out the worm pills to foster people. The other Sally calls Marge; she occasionally comes to a committee meeting to take minutes.'

'Gosh, I hate worm tablets,' Marmite interrupted with distaste. 'She can't be very nice if she gives them out.'

'The third is Marge's friend, who has just been voted in as Treasurer; I don't know her name. Sally and Jane think they're up to something, and that Marge arranged for her friend to be on the committee, so she has more clout.'

The cats looked blank and then hung their heads. The story Candy had told was confusing, and would need many good naps to digest it. But they could sense that there could be problems for them if these people were in control.

'Oh cheer up,' Banjo said with a big glob of dribble running down his chin. 'Sally and Jane won't let anything bad happen.' He turned back to the sleeve and relaxed his eyes again.

Their attention went to Sally, who was telling Sonya that, if things did not improve, she would leave, and start a charity on her own. The drone of human voices was beginning to lull them to sleep.

'But what about money? You couldn't possibly run things and work full-time!' Sonya was saying in concern. 'And what about the other half? I guess Hubbie won't be pleased, having to support you.'

'That's a problem; I've not spoken to him about it yet. I have my aunt's inheritance, and still have money from when I sold a flat some years ago. Money will be tight, but I can manage. I would have to sell my new car, and get an old banger. But who wants nice clothes and holidays, anyway?' Sally laughed. 'Besides, Candy will be elated to be with me full-time. Still, it's only a thought.'

Candy, hearing her name, gave a little wag of her bottom, making her tail fly in the air. The disturbance caused Banjo to look up, startled; and Sonya used the opportunity to wipe the wet patch away from her sleeve.

Chapter Four

'It's Easter: four whole days off work,' Sally sang, as she burst into the cattery, shivering, the doleful Candy following close by.

Billy Bank Robber came in soon after, to collect his rent. He made a few cheeky remarks, as he liked a joke or two. Sally raised her eyes to the ceiling, and laughed dutifully at his comments.

'Who've we got here then?' He ran his eyes down the line of pens, grinning at the furry faces that sullenly stared back. The permanent laughter lines crinkled at the corners of his eyes.

'We need some homes for them,' Sally explained, unnecessarily, because everyone knew that.

'What, none moving?' Billy responded, uninterested. 'Such a shame.'

Then Billy, having a few moments to spare, began telling Sally the story of when he had robbed a shop many years before. The cats, and Candy, listened with enormous interest. Sally shook her head at his bravado. He was bold, and didn't seem to care. She wondered how he ever got away with it.

There was no longer a threat of snow in the air. It was not so cold, just damp, the sort of damp that creeps into your body and clings to your bones. Sally shivered as she looked out of the window, to confirm that there had been no changes in the weather since she had entered the cattery.

'Two new cats coming today, and one person viewing. I want you all on your best behaviour. Start washing now. No using the toilet trays when they come in, either,' she chastised good-humouredly.

Summer and Banjo looked gloomy; they both hated visitors reminding them that they were unwanted.

Many people had visited the cattery over the past two weeks. A few of them had marched down the middle aisle, looking from side to side and left. One had announced that nothing inspired her. It was a comment regularly used by people more suited to shopping in a department store than a rescue shelter. Another left because none of the cats had run up to her. Well, all except black Sara who ran up to everyone for a cuddle. She only wanted a cat that chose her and not black, but would take them all if she could, as she loved cats! Sally had explained that she was opposed to running up to strangers for a cuddle too. But the woman, ignoring the comment, had shaken her head and left.

Despite this, other visitors had chosen seven cats. Most never stayed in the cattery long; they'd only just had their first vaccination and health check when they were whisked away, and now, thankfully, they were settled and happy with their new owners.

One of them was Treacle, who had been offered a home by a lovely couple. Another of the chosen cats had been Gracie, who had gone off waving to the others. She had asked if Pickle could go with her, but of course the humans did not understand.

Pickle was mortified at losing her friend. She had run to Marmite, who had tried to console her by licking her ears. The same few remained; mostly the black cats and the shy ones. It never bothered the timid cats; they always made themselves scarce when visitors came, but Banjo and Summer felt hurt by the rejection.

The first to arrive that day was the unwanted cat. The owners, a man and woman, came through the door looking upset.

'Can you tell me where you're putting the cat?' the woman asked, staring around with distaste.

'In a pen,' Sally answered, unbolting a door and pulling it open as she spoke.

'That's no good; Mitzy doesn't like other cats.'

'Well I'm sorry, but unfortunately we do have other cats here, it's a rescue cattery.' Sally's voice was flat and cold; it was the one she used to hide her irritation.

The couple stood and stared, looking at Sally and around at the cats and finally, with absolute dismay at the dog. Deciding that they

41

had no option, they walked forward with the outstretched basket, containing a ginger-coloured Mitzy.

'What will you do with our cat now?' the man asked.

'Home her,' Sally said simply, trying desperately not to raise her eyes in exasperation at the silly question.

'How will you do that?' the woman joined in.

Sally paused for a moment to observe a small hole in the fibreglass partition, making a mental note to fix it with some tape later. 'Well… I suppose, show her to people and hope they take her.'

'And how will people know she is here?' the woman asked in exasperation.

'We'll tell them,' Sally's voice no longer hid her irritation.

Banjo, who was very amused by the whole episode, had a sudden mental image of Sally running around the farm waving her arms and shouting, 'Mitzy's here! Come and get her!' He had a little smirk into his blanket.

'Why don't you want her anymore?' Sally asked, not really wanting to know the answer. She had already heard all the excuses conjured up by people.

'Because my daughter has had a baby and wants to return to work for a few hours a week.'

'Oh, I see.' Sally really did not see at all. 'She lives with you?'

The woman continued in a voice that suggested Sally was really stupid. Sally's expression did not help matters as she stared at them with a mixture of disbelief and I really have heard it all now.

'NO! – but she wants us to babysit, and doesn't want cat hairs on the baby's clothes,' she finished, exasperated, while she waited for Sally to understand the dreadful problem.

Sally did not. Her eyes turned from disbelief to coldness, portraying how she felt about people who treated life so cheaply.

'It's no good,' the woman said to her husband, 'I'm not leaving Mitzy here.'

They grabbed the basket, and both rushed down the cattery. Terrified, Mitzy wobbled from side to side as they went. Once safely at the door the woman turned back to Sally, who was still dumbly holding the pen door open.

'I really don't like your attitude,' she squeaked in her clipped voice.

Sally felt her temper boiling. 'Well, I don't like yours either. Fancy getting rid of your cat because your daughter, who doesn't even live with you, has had a baby! Why don't you home the baby? After all, Mitzy was there first.'

The couple both gasped; their eyes seemed to bulge from their sockets. Any further, and they would have rolled out, giving the cats a great game. Finally, in unison, they yelled, 'How dare you! We are going to report you!' With that, they burst from the cattery, taking Mitzy with them.

Candy went running to her Mum in a panic at the angry voices. Sally gave her a reassuring pat, and Banjo flew into her arms. Sara ran up, and reached up her black fluffy paws for a cuddle. The rest of the cats froze, wondering if they needed to run and hide or stay put.

'It's OK, the stupid people have gone,' Sally consoled them.

Flick, Mac and Pickle ran to the window, to glare rudely at the horrible people as they scurried away. Pickle wanted to poke out her tongue, as she had seen a little girl do once, but thought that was going too far. So she turned and wiggled her tail at them instead. Then she scampered off, giggling, just in case the people reported her as well.

A while later Sally received a telling-off on the phone from Jane for being rude to the people.

'You cannot tell people to home their baby,' she reprimanded. Somehow Jane always kept her temper with ignorant people.

Sally told the cats that she would never manage to be like her Mum. She just did not have the patience.

'Honey catches more flies than vinegar,' Jane repeated, not for the first time.

The next cat to find its way to the cattery that day was Trevor, a peculiar-looking tabby. His body was long and sleek, and his face pointed. One of his fangs jutted from the side of his mouth. This caused his lip to get stuck on the tooth, giving him a permanent Elvis curl.

'Well, you're a strange looking fellow,' Sally told him. He blinked at her and yowled in response.

'Got any grub? I'm starving.'

His owners had moved, forgetting to take him. New people had come to live in his home. When Trevor had returned for his dinner, he was shocked to see strangers there. The new owners had a cat phobia, and started shouting when he appeared.

'It's a tiger!' the lady screamed, holding her two terrified children protectively against her breasts. The quick-thinking man threw a cup of tea over the confused cat. When the startled Trevor didn't run away, he threw the cup as well. He sprinted out and huddled under a bush. Cold and hunger caused him to venture in again the next day. He was met with the same response, so he waited patiently under his bush for his owners to come back. They didn't, so, eventually, not knowing what to do, he moved into a derelict shed in a neighbouring garden to wait.

Out of desperation and hunger over the next few weeks he caught a mouse. Trevor had lived in the shed for the next two years. Every so often he would return home, hoping his family had remembered him. Each time he was pelted with stones or water by the screaming humans.

Eventually, the owners of the tumbled-down shed became fed up with him hanging around. They called the rescue charity to take the cat away. It took two months to trap him in a special cage, earning him the name of clever Trevor.

The skinny cat dived on to a plate of food, containing a carefully disguised worm tablet. Giving a long yowl he begged for more, he was so hungry; but too much food would make him ill, after severe hunger for so long.

Sally went off to deal with a lady and man who had come to choose a cat. One by one, the cats ventured over to Trevor's pen to sniff the newcomer. Not used to friendly cats, he hissed at them. He saw them as a threat, thinking they would attack. Worse still, pinch his precious food.

'Hi, my name is Sara, pleased to meet you.'

'Bugger off,' Trevor snarled rudely.

Sara walked sadly away.

'Charming,' shouted Summer.

The people choosing a cat could not find anything that 'inspired them,' so they left. Sally sighed as she shut the door, and childishly stuck up two fingers at the letterbox. Feeling better, she went to the sink to mix up a special feed for Daisy's kittens, which were now eating on their own, and soon due to go to new homes.

Daisy was looking much brighter. She had groomed her coat, and had put on weight. Sally had received several threatening phone calls from the owner, but had still refused to return the cat and kittens.

'Another week or so, and you can be spayed, Daisy,' she told her. Then she looked around the barn, wondering why the cats were standing up and staring at the door.

'It's Morag worm tablet,' Candy whispered dramatically. 'I can feel her dark vibrations from here.'

Pickle's wide dilated eyes darted from one to the other, 'wh … who...?' She pulled up the corner of a blanket in order to hide.

'She is the one from my dream, who emanates evil vibes,' Comfort said, staring at the door, while debating whether she could squeeze under the blanket with Pickle. 'I can feel it.'

It was a difficult decision, so she flew under a chair with Mac and Flick instead. Their three bottoms got stuck, wiggling in desperation to achieve their goal.

Marmite did follow her kitten, Pickle, under the blanket, and Banjo ran to the top of the pens, cowering in a corner. Even the unresponsive mother cat, Daisy, seemed to shrink on the spot, and not a squeal could be heard from her four kittens. The cats, from their various places, strained their ears so that they could listen.

Sally looked up, thinking it was another potential home. Her eyes narrowed, as the figure darkened the doorway, and Morag stood there.

'What brings you here?' Sally asked, trying to sound pleasant. It was difficult, as hiding her feelings of dislike was not an easy task.

'I just thought I'd pop in to see the cats,' Morag said in her sickly sweet voice, as she looked around. 'You've not got many in?'

'Twenty-seven at the moment. The waiting list, for the first time ever, has almost been cleared. Six months ago we had over one hundred and fifty cats waiting for help; now there are only thirty. This is our best figure on record; it's so much easier with a premises,' Sally glowed with pride.

'That's fantastic,' Morag gushed, a little too pleasantly. 'You're doing such a wonderful job. The place looks clean, and, although a little scruffy, is great.'

'Mum finds homing much easier now that the cats are in one place. Most of the time they just come and go. I cannot get them vaccinated and spayed quickly enough,' Sally told her. 'It's certainly easier than having one or two cats in each foster home.'

Morag strolled down the length of the cattery, with her hands neatly folded behind her back. 'Splendid... super... splendid.' She stopped at Trevor's pen door and the tabby gave a long, loud yowl.

'Got any grub?'

'Do you not think this one should be... well... you know... he looks a bit rough.'

Trevor's head snapped up so quickly that he got cramp in his neck. Despite the pain he managed to give Morag a hurt stare.

'Of course he looks rough; he has been living outside, starving for two years. I'm sure you'd look 'rough' if you had to,' Sally snapped, irritated for the second time today.

'Yes... yes, of course. So what do we do then?'

'Do? We send him to the vets to be neutered, vaccinated and health checked. Then we feed him up and rehome him. That's what we do with all the cats.'

'Really... splendid... good job... fantasti ... so he should make it then?'

Sally raised her eyes to the ceiling to express Morag's stupidity. 'Why shouldn't he make it, he's OK, just a little undernourished. Most strays are skinny when they come in,' she snapped.

'Of course, yes... splendid. I'm so glad we agreed to rent this cattery; it seems to be working so well.' On reaching Summer's shelf, Morag stopped to study her.

Fear filled Summer's eyes.

'This one is old. Do you think it's a good idea to keep her here?'

Sally's eyes narrowed, 'What's that supposed to mean?'

'Oh… emm… nothing. I was just saying, that's all.'

Sally's cold glare followed her, as she left the frightened old lady, and made for the door.

'Don't forget the committee meeting next week.'

'It's being held here,' Sally told her, putting a protective hand on Summer and scratching under her chin. As the hand reached a particularly good spot, the old cat started to wiggle her back leg in ecstasy, her fear forgotten.

Morag gasped, and wrinkled her nose in disgust. 'Here? But I thought we were going to that nice hotel.'

'You want to pay for a 'nice' hotel with charity money?'

'It doesn't cost much. Besides, it's a relaxing atmosphere, and they serve coffee and cakes.'

Sally looked at her with distaste. 'That money belongs to the charity; the people donate it to be spent on the cats. It's not for paying for 'nice' hotels. Besides, it's about time the rest of the committee took notice of the cats we rescue. Most have never even been here. It'll be good for them to see some of the work that takes place.'

Morag's eyebrows sprang up with surprise. 'What on earth do you mean by that?'

'You all turn up at committee meetings, throw around a few useless ideas and float off again, leaving Mum and me to do the work. We could do with some help.'

'Oh gosh, I just couldn't.' Morag's voice wavered, and her legs wobbled a little. 'I would lose sleep seeing the poor unwanted things; it's far too upsetting.'

'Do you not think we feel the same? Is that not why we do this work in the first place?'

'Yes but… I do what I can; someone has got to give out supplies to the foster homes. Marjorie is far too busy to help, with all the committees she sits on. We should be honoured that she shows an interest in our group, with her being a magistrate.'

With that, Morag flounced out of the door, leaving Sally's lips wiggling with words Morag did not hear, and the cats did not understand, but they sounded offensive.

'Good grief, that woman's stupid. It amazes me that she's on a cat rescue committee!' Sally told Candy, whose attention was firmly fixed on the fridge, willing the treats to come out.

Not getting a satisfactory response from the dog, she rang Jane, to let off steam. Putting the phone on loudspeaker, as she did when alone, and balancing it on the side, Sally busied herself with washing up while chatting.

This, as always, intrigued the cats. They could hear a voice, but could not see the face making it. It was difficult to pick up the conversation without the person present.

Mac had previously looked behind it and tried to see underneath. He had decided that it was one of those phones which Marmite had talked about.

'Do you think you'll be well enough for the meeting next week?' Sally was saying, knowing that her mother's bad health prevented her from doing so much these days.

'I'm sorry, but I don't think I will; but I'm worried. There's something going on.'

Mac and Pickle were dabbing the phone with their paws. When it spoke again, Mac twisted his head on one side.

'Can you ring Mrs Pooper?' Jane was asking.

'Who? You are joking?' Sally's voice was filled with disbelief. 'You surely don't expect me to call someone and ask for that name. Last week it was a Mrs Porker, and the week before Mr Legless, who turned out to be Mr Legit? I felt a right prawn, asking for the wrong person.'

Jane burst out into a fit of giggles, and then more giggles. This caused both cats to twist their heads so far that they almost toppled into the sink. Eventually Sally began to laugh too.

'At least I feel a bit better,' Jane confessed, when she had finished.

Mac batted the phone so hard it fell into the washing up bowl.

'Bloody hell, Mac, what have you done?' Sally despaired as she retrieved it from the soapsuds; it took hours, and a hairdryer, to dry it.

Chapter Five

Later that day, after Sally had left, the cats gathered to talk.

'It's our responsibility to welcome new arrivals,' Comfort said decisively, 'so I vote that Banjo, being the biggest male, should go and welcome him.'

'Sara tried,' Banjo protested, not wanting to face the unneutered tomcat. 'He made it clear that he doesn't want to be friends.'

'I know you're talking about me,' Trevor yowled.

Ignoring Trevor, Comfort gave Banjo one of her determined glares. He lowered his eyes.

'OK... I'll do it,' he mumbled.

Comfort smiled, as Banjo slunk dubiously to the pen, taking deep breaths to enhance his bravery.

Trevor, seeing the tom approaching, arched his back until he stood on tiptoe. He turned his head sideways, and fluffed up his coat. On such a skinny body, he did not look much fluffed at all. He flattened his ears and crossed his eyes, wagging his lowered head slowly from side to side, in readiness for battle.

Banjo was so glad there was the protection of wire between them. 'I... I... come in peace,' he began, a tight feeling of nervousness entering his stomach. 'W... we just want to welcome and reassure you.'

Trevor snarled and hissed, not listening to the words. Banjo looked round at Comfort, who waved a paw indicating he should continue. He turned back to the pen just as Trevor launched himself at the wire. Banjo ran for his life and dived into the nearest bed. He was a large cat, so he did not fit entirely. His edges sagged over the small basket sides.

'Well, really!' Summer shouted at Trevor, 'how rude! He came to welcome you, and you treat him like that!'

Trevor, dropping from the wire, looked a little shamefaced.

'He was after my food,' he said guiltily, as he stared down at the bowl.

'What food, you've scoffed it all.'

Trevor scrutinised the bowl for the hundredth time just in case he had missed some. Then he gave it another lick, just to make absolutely sure he hadn't left a morsel. Finally, he looked across at all the eyes directed at him. 'Sorry everyone,' he shouted over.

By the afternoon he was a fully-fledged member of the home. He spent the rest of the day entertaining them with stories about his earlier days. He was a very brave cat, and had fought off animals as large as horses, and, once, even a tiger. Eventually, worn out by his drone, they began to nod off. Trevor was still waffling on when they awoke for their late day wash. The funny tabby cat had had so many adventures that he did not know where to begin.

'Have I told you this one?' he said after a short pause.

'Yes!' shouted Flick, a bored tone to his voice.

'Well, what about this one then?'

'You told us,' Mac answered, his voice flat and uninterested.

'Oh,' said Trevor, disappointed. Then he brightened, 'have I told you this one then?'

The cats groaned as he began a long tale about the day he had fallen down a well.

'Trevor,' Summer finally said, for once awake, and when the cat was in mid-flow, 'if you don't shut up, I'll throw my water bowl over you.'

Goodness knows how she would have managed such a task; but Trevor did stay quiet for a while.

'Thank goodness he's going to the vets tomorrow for his operation,' Sara whispered conspiratorially to Marmite. 'He'll sleep for ages afterwards, and we can get some peace.'

'Have I told you the story of when I worked in the theatre…?' Trevor suddenly piped up, while sniffing at a flaky paint spot on the floor, thinking it might possibly be an overlooked food crumb. They all pulled their paws over their ears.

The day of the meeting arrived. Although the cats were not looking forward to Morag's visit, they were excited to have other visitors. They took great interest in the people who came through the door late in the afternoon; except Banjo, who felt safer on the roof of the pens, his damaged ears hanging near the edge, so that he could listen.

The first lady who arrived made them shudder. She marched along the cattery aisle in a smart, black suit, clutching a brief case and looking important, which made Sally smirk. Candy told them this was magistrate Marge.

A tall woman arrived soon afterwards, who they guessed was 'no name' the treasurer. Morag came next; she bustled along, kissing everyone on the cheek, and God Blessing them as she passed. The three of them stood huddled together giggling and whispering, throwing sideways glances towards Sally.

The cats hated the devious vibrations; and judging by Sally's face, so did she.

'Did I tell you about the time I was involved in a committee meeting?' Trevor shouted across, his nose developing a crisscross pattern as it pressed against the wire door.

'Shush!' the cats hissed from various hiding places.

There were three other female humans who arrived soon afterwards. After it had been agreed that Marge would chair the meeting, it began.

Summer sat in her bed, her chin jutting out, and her pink tongue visible between her protruding lips.

Marge looked over to her shelf. 'She's an old cat, isn't she?' Her voice held a hidden meaning, and Sally gave her a glower. Then she spotted Trevor in his pen, who was staring out dolefully at the group of women. She laughed at his protruding tooth. 'What's his name, Fang or Goofy?' she said, and all the ladies burst into nervous laughter.

'Oh Marjorie, you're so funny,' Morag giggled.

Sally glared at them. 'We don't use derogatory names in here,' her voice was cold with distaste. 'It would be like calling someone Fatty or Ugly; and we would not do that, would we?' She directed this comment at the overweight, plain-looking Marge, with her glasses propped on the end of her nose.

Marge's face reddened at the insinuation in Sally's voice; she gave a little cough and quickly looked down at her notes.

Sally started the meeting enthusiastically, telling everyone how successfully the cattery had been running. 'In the last few months we have homed over sixty cats, and rescued...'

'Splendid,' Marjorie interrupted in a monotone, dismissive voice, finding the nib of her pen far more interesting than Sally. 'Anyway; moving on, I think it's time we had a little treat. I've decided to arrange a trip to the Houses of Parliament in the spring.'

'Oh, Marjorie, what a wonderful idea,' Morag cooed, clapping her hands in excited glee.

The cats found the meeting which they had so looked forward to extremely dull. They longed for the people to go, so that they could stretch their cramped limbs.

'I think someone should do more car boots,' Marjorie was saying in her cut crystal tone.

'Brilliant idea, Marjorie,' Morag said smiling and clapping her hands again with delight, then clasping her cheeks with them.

Sally put on her best exasperated expression and shook her head. 'We need events that will raise large amounts of money for the veterinary expenses,' she said.

'And what do we suggest?' Marjorie sneered, raising her eyes at Morag and smirking at Sally's stupidity.

'What about trying to find someone to run in the London Marathon for us?' Sally offered, trying to ignore the distaste directed at her.

'How ridiculous!' Marjorie spat. Morag and Marjorie's friend, no name, sniggered.

'Anyway, I think it's about time we gave the shop manageress a large pay rise, plus a bonus at summer and Christmas,' Marjorie suggested.

'But if you do that, the shop won't be making any profit for the charity. We already only just make ends meet,' Sally explained. 'You'll be spending more than we're taking, and the charity will go broke.'

Marjorie had the grace to look silly at her own ignorance. Despite this, she was determined not to lose face in front of the other women. 'Well, I disagree.'

'I disagree too,' Morag added.

'So do I,' sang no-name Treasurer, who until now had stayed quiet.

'Well why don't you look at the figures before you decide,' Sally suggested.

It was the new Treasurer's turn to look silly, as Marjorie looked to her for backup. She suddenly found a little mark on her skirt, and scratched it with her nail.

'Or even,' Sally continued, 'visit the shop and meet the manageress. I can give you directions to where it is.'

Judging by the reddening face of everyone, it seemed that none of them had ever been there.

The meeting droned on and on. The cats started to drift off, in order to blank off from the voices. Suddenly they heard Sally's voice snap, when she had finally lost patience; and their eyes shot open again.

'We need to talk about the fosterer, Janet, who is continuing to over-cram cats in her pens. These are cats we know nothing about; goodness knows where she finds them. They are not cared for adequately, and the cruelty that goes on there has to stop.'

'That old chestnut,' Morag yawned under her breath.

'What on earth are you on about? What rubbish,' Marge snapped.

'Absolutely! Janet is an adult. You cannot stop her taking in cats. It's nothing to do with us,' Morag added.

'Of course it's to do with us. We are supposed to be rescuing cats, not making them suffer. The foster people must work to our guidelines. Even Janet's friend René is allowed to foster. The woman knows nothing about cats. She's terrified if any spits at her, and classes it as wild. Then she locks it into a small, dark pen and pushes food in with a broom. Most cats spit when they come into care, they're afraid. It doesn't mean that they're wild. Plus, she's a cruel, hard woman, and needs to be stopped from fostering. As for Janet, she sends us her expenses; we need to withdraw her funding. Then she will not be able to rescue cats without supervision. Failing that, we should report her.'

'Report her?' Morag screeched, 'that's dreadful.'

Sally looked to the others for support, but they diverted their gaze. It was clear that they were too intimidated to back her. 'It has to stop,' Sally said in a low meaningful voice.

They began to whisper amongst themselves, ignoring her. Apparently, Morag was going to a wedding in a few months, and still had nothing to wear.

'Well if you're not interested in taking action as a committee, then I'll report her myself. We shouldn't be supporting people who keep cats in such terrible conditions. It's diabolical. We work using cat care standards and guidelines. The guidelines are written by Head Office, to protect cats whilst in our care. If they knew what was happening here, they'd close us down.'

'Oh, you mean the guidelines your Mum helped to write,' Morag sneered.

'That is exactly what I mean.'

'Thank you, Sally, for your useful input.' Marge looked at her watch. 'Anyway; moving on, I suggest we have a little trip to Kew Gardens as a social gathering.'

'Splendid, Marjorie,' Morag said. 'Gosh, what a clever idea! We could take a picnic, and if we make a small charge we could raise some money at the same time.'

'From now on we should have meetings in a hotel, where we can have cakes and coffee, plus sandwiches, so that we can have a little nibble. I mean it's lovely to see the cats once in a while…'. Marge flapped some fur from her skirt.

'Oh Marjorie,' said Morag, tears of delight filling her eyes. She clasped her hands together gleefully. 'You're so clever! What a delightful idea!'

'How much will that cost the funds?' Sally asked.

'Well, I... it shouldn't cost too much. Don't be such a wet blanket,' Morag said. 'We deserve a little treat now and again. All this hard work, we should have some perks.'

'I guess so,' Sally said sarcastically. 'Giving out worm pills and writing up a few minutes must take it out of you.' Giving up, she said no more.

Sally began to pat Candy, who was squashed on her lap. She was a little large to do this, and her legs stuck out in four directions.

The dog responded by pushing her nose into her Mum's hand, grateful for the reassurance.

Morag, sitting next to Sally, smiled at the dog, and reached over to pat her too. Candy bared her teeth and snapped at her. Morag squealed and quickly pulled her hand away, clasping her fingers. Sally grinned, her eyes showing that she did not mean the apology she offered.

Over the next week or so, Trevor was freed from his pen. He was now neutered, and his vaccinations were all complete. He loved being out with the other cats, and delighted in telling them more about his adventures.

Once the cats were used to him, and when in the right mood, they loved his stories. But being in the right mood became rarer as time went on. Trevor talked nonstop, and his tales soon became extremely tiresome. Especially when his adventures seemed very far-fetched, or 'far-stretched', as Candy pointed out.

For instance, at one time he had helped to build a house. His job was to check the guttering. He would wee down the plastic pipes to make sure there were no leaks, and the water ran the right way.

Another time, he was filmed in a famous soap opera. He was the star cat, and would be seen often in shots walking over the sets and spraying up trees.

A few years prior to that, he had helped the police force to uncover a mystery surrounding the disappearance of some cat food from a warehouse. With his sensitive nose, he was able to sniff out the trail. For his cleverness in catching the thieves, the police had allowed him to sample as much evidence as he was able. Trevor had been and done everything.

'How old are you?' Banjo asked him one day.

'I don't know,' Trevor said, having a hard think which involved lifting his paw, and giving his toe a vigorous lick. 'When I was on the stage…'

Four rattle balls came hurtling through the air, and one hit him on the ear.

'Well, really!' Trevor said, from under the safety of a chair.

'Trevor, you are a blagger!' Comfort told him; and they all turned their backs and ignored him.

'Fibber!' Summer shouted, and flicked a biscuit in his direction. It was supposed to hit him, but landed near his chair. Trevor, never one to turn down food, rushed out and gobbled it up.

'Gannet,' Summer shouted, and wished she had not flicked the greedy cat a biscuit after all. Lifting her tail and nose, she turned away.

'Never mind, Trevor,' kind-hearted Sara said. 'You really must try not to annoy everyone, or you'll make more enemies than friends.'

Trevor looked downcast. 'I just wanted to be part of your group,' he told her with a wavy voice. 'I've been so lonely, I wanted to join in.'

Sara smiled at him. 'Silly, you are a part of our group. Stop telling stories, and everyone will be your friend.'

The new leaf lasted a few days. Until, not being able to resist, Trevor began to tell everyone about his farming days, and how he would sit on the end of the tractor and give directions to the farmer. They raised their eyes and looked from one to the other. Trevor shut up and went to sit alone, fearing an onslaught of cat toys again.

Waking from a deep sleep, Summer spotted Trevor skulking in a corner. 'Tale teller,' she shouted, before her face disappeared into a food bowl.

Trevor stared glumly back at the old cat. It was true, well sort of. He had seen a tractor; well he had thought it was a tractor. It was a big wheelie thing, and the man driving it had a cap on. He would have sat on the back if he had been closer. Trevor sighed. Laying his head on his paw, he felt very down in the dumps. Suddenly, he felt someone looking at him. Twisting his head, he spotted eight little eyes, looking out of one of the pens. He ambled over to take a closer look.

'Well hello, little 'uns,' he began.

Daisy's kittens blinked at him. The larger one moved slightly forward, edged on by his siblings. Then the others copied, and moved to the pen door. It was his cue; off he went with a stream of stories, starting with how he had used his first litter tray, and moving on to his days as a stowaway on a sea liner.

The little eyes widened with fascination at the stories. Daisy did not mind; the drone of his voice sent her to sleep, and it kept her babies quiet. The dull grey coat had now turned white, and the stress lines had smoothed out from her face. She began to look her young age again. Her kittens, now ten weeks old, were going in pairs to their new homes over the next few days. The following week, Daisy was to be spayed; as Sally had promised, no more kittens for her. How she looked forward to a new life where she could enjoy her missed youth.

In four months' time, the owners of the kittens would be contacted with a gentle reminder that they were due for neutering. They must not be allowed to breed. Life was good, and Daisy felt really light hearted.

Chapter Six

'Reported!' Sally screeched at the phone. 'What for? What do you mean you don't know? Who on earth would report me?'

She clicked off from the caller and stared, dumbfounded at the phone, before calling Jane.

'Now, don't fly off the handle! You always get into trouble when you have a strop. It's bound to be a mistake. No one would report you, you've done nothing wrong,' Jane reasoned.

The anger subsided. Her Mum was right; it was just an ignorant person, being spiteful. They usually pop up here and there.

'I'll just ignore it; the Head Office knows we're a successful, hard-working group. Our annual report proves that.' Sally put down the phone and continued cleaning.

Having a second thought, she called Sonya to offload on to another willing ear.

'How strange! Why would anyone do that?' Sonya puzzled. 'You haven't done anything wrong. Maybe it was those Mitzy people?'

'What does "reported" mean?' asked confused Sara, wondering if she needed to have a worry.

No one could answer; they didn't know.

It was a few days later when Banjo, from where he crouched on the pen roof, could hear angry voices. Wiggling forward, he twisted one flat ear to the direction of the noise. Morag was in the cattery, talking to Sally.

'Headquarters are angry that you have rented premises without either the committee or their agreement. The three of us have met with the Area Manager to decide what action to take,' Morag was saying.

'She has handed control of the charity to Marjorie and myself and instructed that the cattery be closed. The cats will be removed by Headquarters. You are not allowed to know the location. Any over two years old will be destroyed.'

Banjo swallowed and trembled.

'What's happening?' Summer called, sounding cross. 'Why is everyone shouting?'

'Shush… we're gonna be killed!' Banjo hissed and edged closer.

Summer fell silent and hunched her body, as a sickness flooded her tummy.

Sally's voice sounded bewildered. 'But we all voted and agreed to rent a premises. You and another committee member came to view, months before we voted. We talked about it for hours,' Sally stammered, before the realisation flooded her eyes. 'What do you mean, you've had a meeting? You don't even know the Area Manager. Every contact from them goes through the Coordinator.' Her voice grew angry, as several different emotions rippled across her eyes. 'You had a secret meeting and lied, to gain control of the charity.'

Banjo could see Morag's red face before it lowered to her feet.

'And because Marge is a magistrate they believed you...?' Sally was saying. 'So as punishment for 'being a naughty girl' you're going to take the cats to a secret location and destroy some. Who do you think you are – the secret service? You must have been planning this for months. Do you think it's glamorous running a voluntary cat rescue charity? Or is it the bank balance and credibility that interest you? Anyway, the committee minutes will prove you are lying.'

'What minutes?' Morag smirked, 'I don't recall agreeing to anything.'

Sally glared at her. 'That's true. Marge has 'conveniently' forgotten to send them out for the last three meetings.'

Morag's smirk widened. 'Don't call her Marge. She doesn't like it. It's disrespectful.'

'Neither of you knows how to run a charity. You know nothing about cats. I guess you forgot to mention that to the Area Manager,' Sally shouted, clenching her fists with emotion. 'My mother struggled for almost forty years, virtually on her own, to build this charity. Now you want to steal her success. GET OUT!'

'You have one week to empty this place, or we'll do it for you. Don't bother to tell people; they'll never believe the likes of you over us.' Morag's victory showed in her stride as she left.

Sally sank shocked on to a chair. Banjo appeared first and threw himself into her arms, pushing his face into her long hair. The other cats ventured out and gathered around.

'Are we going to die, Banjo?' Sara asked, her little black face looking up in desperation.

'You'll be OK, you're young,' he consoled, trying to hide his own anxiety.

Flick reached out and touched Comfort's paw; she was eight years old.

'What's happening?' Summer called, 'has she gone?'

'You're going to die, 'cos you're old,' Pickle shouted.

'PICKLE, HUSH!' Marmite scolded, as the old cat's head and body jerked up with shock, and then sagged down into a deflated heap.

'It's true,' Sally told the trembling Banjo, 'no one will believe me …I knew they were up to something. I don't know why I'm telling you this.' She kissed his head, and gave him a reassuring squeeze.

After Sally left, the cats sat looking gloomy.

'I don't understand why humans want us dead when they claim to be helping us,' Banjo said, a great weight of sadness filling his stomach and resting next to his fish.

'It's to do with power,' answered Comfort.

Everyone stared at her in admiration; she was such a smart cat. She looked at the expectant eyes studying her, making them wait in anticipation before continuing.

'Managing a large, wealthy charity is a status symbol. Control, power and image are important to many humans. They'll do anything to achieve this, even lie and hurt others.'

'B... b... but why?' Pickle asked, her eyes wide with disbelief.

Comfort combed her whiskers with her front paw, deep in thought.

'Why won't people believe Sally?' Marmite asked, confused.

'Because they follow wealth and status; they do not question it. Humans have a strange hierarchy; those lower in the line are ignored or dismissed as unimportant.'

'But that's stupid,' Mac said with a furrowed brow, 'where are we in this h.i... archy?'

'We don't even meet the bottom line. Some humans consider themselves owners of the earth. We are just here for their use. Few understand that we are intelligent, have feelings, and as much right to life as they have.'

They fell silent, deep in their own thoughts. A sudden knock on the window made them jump with fright. Marmite hissed and arched her back at the long, grey wiggly thing tapping on the glass.

'There's a snake knocking on the window; it's trying to get in.'

'Stupid!' Summer said, wrinkling her forehead in irritation, 'it's not a snake; it's that silly goat's horn. Go away, goat! We're having an important meeting,' she shouted, and was surprised, when turning back, to find an empty cattery. Gradually, hairy heads popped out from every direction.

'We knew that,' Mac said in a deep voice, as he lifted his shoulders and swaggered back to his position.

'What are we going to do?' Marmite asked despondently, once they had settled again.

'All we can do is hope that Jane finds us homes before next week,' Comfort added doubtfully.

What else could they do? They were at the mercy of humans; they had no choice in their fate.

'How do you know this, Comfort?' Banjo finally asked.

'Because I listen and work it all out.'

With heavy hearts, they fell asleep. All except Banjo, who stared at his blanket. He knew that no one would choose him. He was ugly and, in one week's time, was to die.

The next morning the sun streamed through the large window. The sight of it helped melt some of their troubles away. Flick and Mac were filled with excitement as they fought over one particular sunbeam, even though there were many more to lie under. Both were nudging the other out of the way to gain the best position. The argument was eventually solved amicably. After measuring the patch, they both lay flat out, back-to-back, in the centre of the beam. Only their toes and whiskers poked over the edge, not being able to fit into the space.

Comfort and Sara giggled at the two, and then laughed more when the sunbeam moved, a short time later.

Over the next few days, a friendly fight for homes began. Sara ran up to the next person who came through the door. She reached her paws out to the lady for a cuddle. The human flicked her away.

'I don't like black cats,' she stated, walking past, leaving Sara deeply hurt. 'Oh, I would take them all if I could.'

'All except the black ones,' Sally muttered.

The woman ignored her and burst out laughing as she stopped near Banjo. 'What an ugly cat; look at his face.'

Sally glared at her. 'There are no such things as ugly cats, only ugly humans,' she told her, pointing towards the door. 'GET OUT!'

Banjo hung his head in humiliation. He went to his bed, staying there for the rest of the day. He had once been a handsome cat, with a home of his own. When his people drove away, he remembered sitting on the pavement watching. He still sat there waiting months later – they never returned.

The next person started to stroke Summer, who was so delighted that she almost toppled from the shelf. When the lady was informed of her age, she recoiled in horror and rushed past. Summer did fall off the shelf when she stretched too far to stop her going.

'Come back,' she mewed, but was ignored.

'I can't see any I like,' the woman announced. 'I'll come back when you have different ones.'

'Where have I heard that before?' Comfort said sadly.

Trevor went into a deep think, taking on a particular stance to help his body receive useful information from the recess of his mind. His tail was erect, back legs stiff and ears flattened, showing the seriousness of his think.

Two people were due the next day; they both wanted fluffy cats.

'I've got it,' he burst out after a few moments. 'When I was a stray,' he began, ignoring the groans of protest. 'Please, you've got to listen! This is important.' His voice strained with urgency. 'The lady at number nine had short blonde fur; and the next day, she had long red fur on her head.' He wiggled excitedly; everyone stared at him as if he was mad. 'No, really…she added fur to her head. She called them 'extensions'. We could have fur extensions,' he garbled, looking around eagerly, waiting for everyone to be overwhelmed by his cleverness.

'And how on earth do you suggest we do that?' Banjo said, raising his eyes and shaking his head at the silly cat.

'Well… we could put fur on ourselves; we could even change colour if we wanted to.'

'And?' Banjo smirked incredulously.

'We can gather fur from cat beds. When Sally grooms everyone tonight, we'll hide the wads; and when she has gone, put them on.'

'It's worth a try,' Marmite added, with growing enthusiasm.

They all nodded in doubtful agreement. People were due the following morning, so there was not much time to prepare. That night, while Sally was grooming Daisy, Flick sat close. As she dropped the loose fur into a rubbish bag, he stuck in his head, grabbed it with his mouth and ran off.

Sally, intent on her task, did not notice. Summer, who was in excellent condition, had little excess. Pickle waited patiently under her shelf, but little came her way.

Comfort squirmed and pulled faces, as she hated to be brushed. She was long-coated, so did not need extensions; but maybe different colours would help. A little ginger and grey would brighten the black and white coat, making her a popular tortoiseshell.

Later that night, after Sally had left, the cats gathered their trophies. More were added by scraping excess from the blankets in the laundry basket.

Banjo sat on his bed; he would not take part in the silliness.

Mac lifted a tabby clump and pushed it on Flick's head, then laughed at his brother's new quiff. But as Mac moved, the fur rolled off, and floated under a chair. Pickle dived under to retrieve it. She gave it a back kick, before raising it in her front paws and giving a brisk shake.

'Pickle, stop mucking about; this is serious,' Comfort scolded.

Pickle carried the fur out and adopted the same glum expression which everyone else had.

'We need to stick the fur on somehow,' Flick stated.

'I know!' Sara squeaked. She rarely had good ideas, but all of a sudden one had popped unexpectedly into her head. 'We could use that sticky stuff Sally puts in her drink.'

'Honey,' Banjo shouted, not being able to resist adding to the madness.

'Yes!' Sara shook with enthusiasm, 'Sally keeps it in the cupboard, and I know how to open it.'

They rushed over, and Sara pulled the corner with her paw. It opened; she pushed the jar and it smashed on the floor. They stared despondently at the gooey mess amongst the broken glass. Marmite stuck in her paw and wrinkled her nose at the feel of it.

'It's sticky,' she announced, attempting to flick it away.

'Roll in it, and cover your bodies as much as you can,' Trevor instructed.

They stood and gaped at him. He tutted and raised his brow when no one moved. It seemed that he was to be the first. He gingerly went over, suddenly unsure of his idea, but not wanting to lose face.

'I'll go first then,' he announced hesitantly. 'I've always fancied a fluffy tail.' He lowered his thin tail into the honey and rolled it about, careful to avoid the glass. Then he went to the mound of fur and dabbed at a ginger piece – it stuck. 'See,' he said in triumph.

The other cats, feeling more confident, copied. Watching the fiasco, Banjo smirked.

When Summer woke up she stared in disbelief. Pickle had a brown fur ball stuck on her nose, and a black lump on one leg. On her right ear hung a piece of torn paper, and some fluff from a red blanket.

Trevor, who had been caught short in the middle of the project, had bits of gravel stuck the length of his paws, and a large piece of newspaper on his behind. A worm tablet that had been missing for a few days was wedged on his brow, and a key ring on his flank. Not to mention the strange ginger lump on his tail.

Flick and Mac were covered in different coloured fur balls, one of which was stuck over Mac's eye. No matter how hard he tried, he couldn't remove it. The fluff, covered in honey, was completely flat, and his eyelid firmly shut.

Marmite had a blue blanket covering her body, from when she had flopped into a basket while trying to remove a stuffed mouse from her foot. Around her nose and face was cat food, complete with dried biscuits.

Comfort's fur was absolutely flat. From her tail hung a tea bag, and two human sweets. She waved it from side to side, trying to dislodge them, but, to her distress, her tail kept sticking to a scratching post. On her stomach swung a ball with a bell and an envelope. A long piece of kitchen roll was wedged to her forehead, making it impossible to see.

Out of them all, Sara came off worst. Having run out of fur balls, she had rolled in the laundry basket to scoop up leftovers. Every colour imaginable clung to her body. Not one part of her coat was visible. A fur ball someone had sicked up dangled from one ear, and a long strand of yellow wool trailed along behind her. Pickle had tried to chase it, and her paw kept sticking to Sara.

Summer just gaped at the sight. She must either be hallucinating or dreaming; she could not decide. She turned to Banjo, who was rolling on his back, holding his stomach trying to gasp for air. He had laughed so much he could not breathe, set off again by Summer's expression. The old cat scratched her ear in confusion and tugged at a claw.

'Don't ask!' Banjo managed to say.

Summer didn't; she couldn't. Turning away she nibbled at her few remaining biscuits; turned three times and went to sleep.

When Sally opened the door the following morning, she came in with the lady who wanted a fluffy cat. They both stared in horror at what greeted them. Their bottom jaws hung and their eyes widened. Even the doleful Candy did a double-take.

Banjo, who had waited all night for this moment, collapsed again.

Summer sat bolt upright looking extremely pensive. Her bottom lip stuck out and for once her tongue was not on show.

Trevor!' Sally called out, 'it can only be you,' as she spotted the tabby nose and fang sticking guiltily out from under a chair, a piece of pink blanket stuck to his flat ears.

'I think I'll come back another time.' The lady reversed and disappeared.

It took Sally all day and most of the evening to clean up. The soggy cats, worn out from their long night and scrubbing, slept the rest of the next day.

It was the first time Sally had ever bathed a cat. With Sara and Comfort there was no choice. The usually gentle Sara became a ball of teeth and claws when the hair drier was turned on. There was no choice but to leave them to dry naturally. Since they were long-coated, it took hours.

Chapter Seven

'Only twenty-four of you left,' Sally sighed as she opened the door to a sudden tapping. On the other side stood a man. She stared at him, her eyes flicking from his face to the carrying basket he was clutching, and to another, a few feet away.

'Yes?' she snapped, having the whole scenario sussed in her head.

'Err...I'm going on holiday tomorrow, so I can't keep these kittens. I err... don't want them.'

Sally adopted her best intimidating glare, which was difficult, as she had not brushed her hair that morning, having rushed out late. 'Whose kittens are they, and how old?'

'They're mine. My cat gave birth to them; I couldn't afford to get her spayed,' he said, pushing the basket forward.

'Sorry, did you say you are going on holiday?' The sarcasm was clear, even to the cats. Sally peered into the basket. 'They are too young to leave their mother,' she snapped, having one of her mental images of producing a machine gun and shooting him.

'Oh, they're OK; they eat and everything.'

'They're too young to leave their mother!' she repeated in a no-nonsense tone that warned that he had better not argue, or she might just bob him on the head with the litter tray she was holding.

'I'll give you money for the trouble.' He groped in his pocket, and produced a five pound note.

Sally looked from the money to the man. 'We'll take the kittens with the mother!'

Grinning, he pushed the basket forward.

'As I said, when you bring the mother, I'll take the kittens,' Sally reiterated, having another mental image of launching through the air and slapping the man's smug face. 'So, what's in the other basket?'

The man turned and shrugged. 'Nothing to do with me.'

As he walked away, Sally picked up the abandoned basket. It was filled with a large, unneutered tabby cat. His big jowls jutted out from his head, making his eyes look small and narrow.

'Who dumped you? There's no room in here for an unneutered tom.'

The tabby hissed and snarled in response. He smelt dreadful, as unneutered toms tend to do, once over the age of two. With a sigh, Sally placed him in a pen and locked the door. He glowered at the other cats with a killer expression.

The man appeared an hour later with a skinny black mother cat in tow. Sally put her in a pen with the five kittens. Scribbling his details on a form, he rushed away. She read that he was going to Barbados for three weeks. On returning, he wanted the Mum and a male and female kitten. He also requested that someone deliver, as he would be tired from the flight.

'He didn't even leave the five pounds,' Sally said as she ripped up the form, and went to flea and worm the Mum, Obama, and the black and white kittens.

Obama was eight months old, and very undernourished and depleted.

After Sally left, the tomcat threw himself against the pen door, yowling and snarling.

'I'm going to kill you lot when I get out of here!' he hissed.

Even Banjo, who was a big strapping tom, shrank to half his size.

Brave Comfort went over to attempt calming him. 'Please,' she began, 'you are frightening the babies.'

They both glanced at the pen where Obama was trying to cover her kittens' ears against the swearing.

Comfort spoke again. 'It's OK – you will be safe here once you have your… well... your… you know.' She gave a small cough. 'When your whatsits are taken away, you'll feel different. Isn't that right, Banjo?'

From under Banjo's blanket, a muffled 'yes' could just be heard.

'I'm gonna kill you all!' Tabby snarled. 'You first, Long-Fur!' His eyes narrowed, and Comfort slipped away.

'Thug, bagabon!' Summer shouted from her shelf, before washing her tail.

Tabby looked up at her. 'You're next, old lady.'

'Huh!' said Summer, twisting on to her back to wash her belly. She promptly fell asleep with her tongue hanging out.

It was a long, noisy and smelly night.

It was rare for Sally to have a day off, but one of the volunteers, Rose, insisted she have a break. Rose cleaned the cattery and fed the cats for her the next day.

Tabby kept shouting obscenities, and Summer shouted back.

'Shut up, Big Chops,' she called.

'Die, Black Stuff,' Tabby retaliated.

A moment later Flick screamed, 'CRUMP.'

'What?' said fourteen cats in unison, jumping in fright.

They followed Flick's bulging eyes to Tabby's pen. Rose hadn't bolted it properly.

A look of contempt glowed in Tabby's eyes. 'I'm going to rip you all apart later, starting with…'. He pointed to Summer who was still snoring, her extended tongue vibrating as she exhaled.

After a long, terrified pause, the cats ran in all directions, each trying to find a suitable hidey-hole. Flick, Mac, Comfort and Pickle squashed into one igloo bed, with not a space between them. Flick had an elbow in Comfort's ear, and Pickle was on top of Mac's head with her legs in between Flick and Comfort. Clever Trevor took himself to an empty pen and knocked the door closed behind him. Then he cowered behind the big plastic bed at the back. Not even his long thin tail or ears could be seen.

Obama lifted her kittens one by one, and carried them up the ladder to safety. She dug out five little holes in a blanket and buried them. She was tired; it was so hard being a young Mum. The kittens were demanding, and Obama was little more than a baby herself. Life had been hard and cruel. She knew that an unneutered tom could kill her babies so he could mate with her. Even though she was locked in a pen, she was taking no chances. 'Hush,' she whispered to the squeaking babies before returning to recheck the door.

Daisy was so glad that her babies were now safe in new homes. Having just been spayed, she was still safely shut in a pen. Banjo rushed to the top of the pens to squash himself into his dark corner. He nudged Summer as he passed.

'Quick, old lady – HIDE!' he yelled.

'Err... what... who did that? Speak up... I can't hear you,' said a lisping Summer. Her tongue was so dry it had stuck to her lip. She drew it into her mouth, gnashed it a few times and promptly fell back to sleep.

Once Rose left, Tabby pushed gleefully against the door. With a dangerous glint in his eye, he strutted along the aisle of the cattery and into the large communal unit. Not one cat could be seen. He raised his tail and sprayed; a foul smell ensued. Lifting his heavy brows, he looked around, taking in every detail.

'Come on out, wherever you are, and die like cats,' he snarled.

A little black head popped up from the shelf. 'What on earth is that horrible smell?' Summer wrinkled her nose in disgust.

Then her eyes bulged and she screamed, as the large tabby body launched itself through the air, landing on top of her. She screamed and screamed as the vicious teeth sank into her tail and legs.

She tried to fight back, lashing out with her paws, but it was in vain. The tabby was far too strong as he punched and clawed at her. Her screams died when she fell from the shelf, landing with a sickening thud on the floor. After a long pause she painfully, and with great effort, pulled herself upright and crawled into the communal area. Dragging herself behind a toilet tray, she crouched low so that only the tops of her ears were visible.

Tabby laughed with glee, waving his large head slowly from side to side. 'Come out, Long-Fur,' he shouted, 'it's your turn.'

Comfort cringed in her hiding place. Flick tried to squeeze her paw for reassurance, but he was so condensed he could not move. Tabby jumped on to a scratching post, and groomed his sharp claws. Deciding that there was no one brave enough to take him on, he began to doze.

As soon as one of them moved, to ease their cramped position, Tabby's eyes shot open and he glared around the cattery, his cold, slanted eyes scrutinising every inch.

Comfort tried mentally to will Sally to hurry and come. But humans were hopeless at picking up telepathic signals. They were not as clever as cats, who communicated so brilliantly.

Marmite stuck her nose out from under a chair, to check Pickle was safe. Tabby's eyes sprang open, so she slunk back into the darkness and safety.

The night felt more like a week, as each minute ticked deliberately past; until, thankfully, they heard Sally's key in the door.

The tabby stood up and hissed, flattening his ears to his head and puffing out his body, which rippled with muscles.

Realising something was wrong, Sally's eyes scanned the large room, resting on the snarling Tabby.

'Oh no,' she cried, going to the cupboard and pulling out a large green towel. She approached the vicious, snarling creature. When he realised that his swearing had no effect, he backed away and ran. He sprang up on to the wire of Obama's pen. She and the kittens screamed. He hung there suddenly looking very vulnerable and small. The towel was thrown over him, so that he could not bite, but he freed his head enough to sink his teeth into Sally's hand. She determinedly kept her grip, pulling him from the wire and locking him back into his pen.

Slowly the cats started to appear from their hiding places. Comfort ran over to where Summer lay, crouched behind the tray. At the same time Sally spotted her. She lifted the old lady. After checking for wounds or breakages, she wrapped her in a blanket and made a hot water bottle.

'Poor old thing,' she soothed.

'It was terrible,' Summer told everyone. 'He came at me from a southerly direction. But I told him – big chopped… rogue! He won't try that again… hooligan!'

Sally pushed food into the tabby's pen with a very swollen hand. He snarled and sprang at her, but she slammed the door shut and bolted it.

'You're a mean cat,' she told him, 'but it's not your fault. It's the irresponsible person who thought it clever not to neuter you,' then she added, 'and the person who left your pen open.'

After phoning Rose to explain the importance of keeping an unneutered cat separate from the others, Sally took Summer to the vet for an extra check. Apart from her war wounds, she was OK.

At three o'clock, a young couple came to view the cats. Sally looked very white and unwell; her hand was swollen, and every movement caused excruciating pain.

The cats did their best to look 'cute'. Comfort rolled on her back with her legs in the air. Sara ran up for a cuddle, and Flick and Mac, trying to swallow their nerves, and desperate not to be left out, purred loudly and kissed the nearest scratching post in unison.

Trevor was still hiding behind the plastic bed, and not even food had tempted him out.

Despite the great show they gave, the young couple walked past them. Imagine everyone's surprise, especially Banjo's, when he was lifted from the floor and handed to the couple.

'Oh,' said the lady holding out her arms, 'what a beautiful cat.' Banjo leapt at her and rubbed his nose into her hair; his purr was so loud that it sounded more like an aeroplane taking off. Everyone in the cattery just stared.

'Go for it, Banjo,' Flick shouted.

Comfort smiled, and Marmite had delight twinkling in her eyes for the big, soppy tom.

'We'll have him,' said the man, 'he is the loveliest cat I've ever met.'

The cats cheered and wiggled their tails. Flick and Mac did fives, which means jumping up and over each other five times.

Then Sally gave Banjo a big hug. Sinking her face into his soft fur she had tears in her eyes. 'Be good, sweetheart,' she whispered to him.

'Oh I will!' replied Banjo with conviction. Then in a teary voice he shouted, 'Bye everyone, I will miss you so much.'

Off he went in a 'designer' basket to his new home. They waved from the window until his orange face disappeared from sight. Wiping the tears from her eyes, Sally painfully took chicken out of the fridge, and they had some, to celebrate Banjo's good luck.

The next day, Sally did not appear. A man called Alan and a lady called Margaret came to clean the cattery. The cats heard them tell Billy that Sally was ill because of a bite. They were dreadfully worried; only a few days to go, and now there was no one to save them.

Tabby, ignoring the tension, was singing and licking between his splayed toes. 'I'm getting out of here,' turning his bottom he sprayed.

'How's that?' asked a disgusted Comfort.

'I'm going tomorrow to be chopped.' Then, twisting his lips to one side, he added, 'what does chopped mean?'

Everyone burst out laughing.

'At least it cheered us up,' said Marmite as she washed Pickle's ears.

'Gerroff, Mum,' objected Pickle, 'you're making me all soggy.' She pulled her paw over her ears to dry them.

The next day Tabby was taken in a basket.

'Good riddance, Saggy Chops,' shouted Summer.

Obama put her paw around her kittens, and pulled them into her breasts. 'Don't look at that horrid tom,' she told them as he passed.

After he had gone, Pickle went to see the kittens. 'I bet you can't do a crab,' she boasted.

'Course we can!' And to prove the point, five kittens arched their backs and crab-bounced around the pen. Then, just to show off completely, two of them performed a perfect dinosaur. Another did an iguana, followed by a springy twist and bounce. They all finished with a perfect meerkat.

Pickle was very upset when she saw the performance. She turned and left the kittens, who had forgotten she was there, bouncing around the pen. Pickle found a place under Summer's shelf and sat alone.

Summer stuck her head over the side. 'What's wrong, young scamp?' she asked.

'Nuffink,' Pickle sighed. Sticking out her chin and bottom lip, she turned away.

Summer shrugged, and began washing her front paw. She paused, remembering she had done that one the previous time. Placing it down, she lifted the other one.

'Actually,' Pickle began, 'I'm fed up. I'm no good at dinosaurs or iguanas, and my crabs are terrible.'

'Ehmmm,' Summer uttered, 'That's a big problem for a young cat. If it makes you feel better, I cannot do any of them either.'

'Really?' said Pickle, cheering up a little, and looking up at Summer.

'No, in fact I think if I attempted any of them, I'd topple off the shelf and fall in a water bowl.'

Pickle giggled at the thought of the old cat's back legs sticking out of the large brown bowl. 'I'm due to be spayed soon to stop me having kittens,' Pickle went on, changing the subject. 'I want to be a mummy.'

'Trust me, Pickle, you wouldn't want to be. Look at how many unwanted kittens and cats there are. Sally and Jane struggle to get them all into care because of the numbers. Then, when they do come in, it's a struggle to find them homes. How do you know your kittens, once homed, won't end up as rescue cats? It's a hard life. Why would you want to bring more into it? Look at poor Daisy and her brood, and Obama.'

Pickle thought for a while about how her Mum had struggled to care for and feed them. There had been five kittens. She always looked so worried and stressed. 'Yes, I guess you're right. Does it hurt being spayed?'

'It stings a little, but it's OK. You'll be fine a day or so afterwards.'

Seeing a ball move, Pickle lowered the front half of her body and stuck her bottom in the air; wiggling her back end four times, she bounced off.

Summer smirked after her, before deciding she had washed both front paws earlier; she twisted on to her back, grasped her tail between her front paws, and gave it a vigorous wash.

That night they sat in silence. It was their last together.

Tabby, who was now named Gerald, had returned from the vet's, and was in a deep sleep. He had woken once and groaned. 'What happened? My bottom hurts.' He went back to sleep again.

They knew that in a few weeks he wouldn't smell so bad.

'I will miss you, Comfort,' Flick sniffed. 'I love you.' And he nuzzled his face into her neck.

'I love you too, Flick,' she sobbed.

'At least Banjo is safe,' Marmite added glumly.

The man who lived in the caravan staggered past the window. He stopped and looked in, then gave a detailed sermon to the cats. They did not understand what he was saying, as his lips moved too fast. He held up his hands and began to conduct an orchestra. He finished the piece by falling in a heap on the floor. After picking himself up, he staggered off, tripping many times as he went.

'What was that about?' Mac mused.

'Dunno, maybe he was telling us about tomorrow,' Marmite guessed.

Remembering the enormity of their worries, they fell silent again. None of them even felt in the mood for their evening bath.

Early the next morning, a large van pulled up outside the cattery, and a man and woman climbed out. Sara watched them from the window, unloading baskets. She relayed the details to the trembling blankets containing heaps of furry bodies.

'It's locked,' the man announced, pulling at the door.

'Morag's here,' Sara told the blankets.

'Hide,' Comfort hissed, 'or they'll get you.'

Morag unlocked the door, using the spare key she had taken from Billy, who had handed it over after hearing that Sally was ill.

The baskets were carried in, along with an evil-looking pole with a vicious loop of wire at the end.

'What's happening?' shouted Gerald, then let out a shriek. 'Who stole my...my what-sits?'

The first to be caught was Sara, who had frozen with fright. The wire was lassoed around Comfort's neck; she hung in the air before being dropped into a basket. Flick ran out to help her, so was caught next. The vile-looking magistrate, Marge, came in. Following her was the lady who had arrived in the van. The three women stood in a corner talking and laughing, ignoring the distress of the cats, as each was looped and lifted by the neck until secured in a basket.

Even old Summer, who wet herself in terror. 'I don't want to die,' she cried.

'She hasn't even bothered to show her face,' the women jeered. The cats took her to mean Sally.

'Oh, I wouldn't miss this for the world!' a voice said.

The cats looked to the doorway and were relieved to see Sally standing there, her bandaged hand held upwards. Behind her stood two other women, one holding a camera and the other a note pad.

'This,' Sally said, pointing first to Marjorie, 'is Magistrate Marge and her friend Morag. The other is the Area Manager from the Headquarters of the large cat rescue charity. They have come to destroy these cats. The reason for their doing so is that they want to control the branch, because there's one hundred and twenty five thousand pounds in the bank account. That's money which people have given in good faith, to buy a sanctuary for rescued cats. Some of the funds came from legacies given in my mother's name for the charity. The rest was fundraised by hard-working volunteers and me. Isn't that right, everyone?'

The Area Manager stared at her, then at the two people with Sally. Marge and Morag's faces reddened, they looked at the floor. Both shuffled one foot each around the other.

Sally pointed to the lady scribbling frantically. 'This is Rosemary from the newspaper; she's going to print this story.'

The Area Manager spoke. 'These are our cats, and you cannot stop us from removing them.'

'This cattery is in my name, so I can,' Sally said holding out papers. 'Here are twenty-five forms sent by my mother. They are signed by people offering homes for these cats.'

'They're fake,' Morag spat, teeth gritted, her eyes slanted and narrow.

It was Sally's turn to smirk as her lips turned into a sarcastic smile. Dismissing Morag with great satisfaction she waved another piece of paper. 'This is my charity registration paper. "The Scratching Post (Rescue & Shelter appeal for cats)" is now an official charity.'

Sally snatched the baskets and began releasing the cats. 'I have enough courage to start a charity from scratch. I do not need to steal someone else's hard work. My charity will never be corrupted by shallow-minded social climbers, who are so powerless in their own lives that they have to use the guise of others' achievements to gain power. It will be a great charity, one that sets out to do what it claims: rescue and rehome cats. It will never become embroiled in sick politics,' she stated, throwing the baskets out of the door.

'You and your mother will pay for this. No one will back you, not after we have finished. Your mother's name will be deleted from the records of the branch. We will humiliate her by throwing her out. If she tells anyone we will disgrace her further,' Marge snarled, making her fat face even more distorted and ugly.

Realising there was nothing more they could do, they walked towards the door.

Morag turned one last time before she disappeared. Her face screwed up in bitterness and hatred. 'You've not heard the last of this. We will make sure your name is mud for the rest of your days.'

Sally said no more. She thanked her friends and closed the door behind them. Only she and the cats were left. Looking around at them, her heart was pounding and her hands were shaking. Despite her bravado, she felt sick at the enormity of what she had done.

'Where now? No money, no support, and a cattery filled with homeless cats!' she said out loud.

Summer rushed back to the shelf, desperate to clean herself.

Comfort, Flick and Mac performed fives with extras. This was far more difficult than normal fives. It required a good deal of accuracy and timing. They jumped over each other in turn. On landing each weaved in and out of the other, with their tails vibrating.

They managed the sequence twice before Pickle joined in. She got into a dreadful muddle with her weaves. Being short, instead of jumping over Mac, she leapt into him. The four of them ended up in a tangled heap of legs and tails. Exhausted, they lay on the floor, happy and relieved.

Gerald, who had not only escaped the ordeal but had been oblivious to it, was twisting round and round, trying to see under his tail.

'What'll happen to Sally and Jane? Marge and Morag were very cross,' asked Marmite.

'I don't know,' Comfort panted, 'but I've a feeling they'll be OK. There is an old human saying: a firm tree does not fear a storm!'

'Do not steal a mountain or you could end up with a mole hill!' Pickle added looking very pensive. They stared at her in amazement.

'Where did you hear that?' Marmite asked proudly.

'I made it up,' Pickle giggled.

Mac cuffed her playfully around her ear.

Chapter Eight

The following weeks were difficult for Sally. Having broken away from the large organisation, she was alone, Candy explained, as she pushed a blanket into the usual unruly heap with her nose.

'What does it mean?' asked Pickle, bored, as no one wanted to play. She lay on her back, trying to catch her tail between her legs.

'There's no money. No way of paying vets' bills, buying cat food or other necessities. Or paying rent for this cattery. The other charity is large, well-established. Many people help them. Few people support small charities like Sally's. Especially as the three witches are spreading horrible lies about her.'

'What lies?' Marmite pulled her whiskers forward with worry.

'Sally says that she prefers not to know. There's no point, as she can't put people right if they won't listen,' Candy told them, settling into her basket, the signs of stress furrowing her brow. She was so upset that people were hurting her Mum. If she had the chance, she'd sick her dinner over them. She wished she had at the meeting.

'What are we going to do with no food? I simply couldn't survive without my dinner,' Trevor added, his legs weak at the thought.

'I know!' Daisy piped up, as she treadled a blanket. She had now been released, and resided in a bed she had had her eye on for weeks. 'We could sell some of our dinner to the animals on the farm. That way there will be enough money.'

Trevor's head snapped round, his eyes large in their sockets, making his face appear thinner than ever. 'W ... we ... can't do that. I need my food. I'll die if I don't eat the right amount.'

Flick gave him a strong, hard stare.

'It's no good; no one will buy it. The horses eat hay, and the goat, crisp packets and cardboard,' he told them despondently, still glaring in Trevor's direction.

The cats listened to the phone calls over the next few weeks. They sensed the stress, which made them worry about their future. Sally had even been banned from her shop. The locks had been changed so that she couldn't go and retrieve her personal belongings.

Candy, knowing this had hurt Sally, tried to comfort her by sitting on her lap more. She even offered her precious squeaky snowman, that had been her Christmas present. This way, Sally could let out frustration by squeezing it. Candy always felt better when she had a squeak. But nothing helped. Candy despaired, not knowing what to do.

'It's so difficult,' Sally told her Mum over the phone; her job now given up, she worked full-time developing the charity and rescuing cats.

Jane was devastated that her group had been stolen by people who knew nothing about cat welfare. Marge and Morag had arrived at her house unexpectedly a few days previously. They announced that she was to leave the charity from that day. They had decided to tell the members and supporters that Jane had resigned. If she told anyone the truth, they would make her pay, in so many different ways.

One of them had rung the telephone exchange, pretending to be Jane, and had her phone disconnected. It was a personal line but, over the years, had been used for charity calls. She had to pay for her phone to be reconnected with a new number.

'After all her years of hard work and dedication, people would believe that Jane walked away,' Candy informed the cats, later that evening, as she nibbled her paw.

'Why would people believe the witches?' asked Sara, looking very sad.

'As Comfort said, they have status. People will believe a magistrate who lives in a big house.'

'But it's not true!' puzzled Mac, as he washed Flick's back.

The cats, not understanding, felt sorry for kind, gentle Jane. She had cried at the betrayal and deviousness.

'They'll squander the money we worked so hard for. It'll never be used to buy a rescue shelter, or even be spent on the cats,' Jane sobbed.

'We can start again, Mum. We'll have the best rescue centre ever built. I still have the database of members. I've already sent a letter to everyone saying that we have left and started on our own. It's a start.'

'You'll get into more trouble,' her Mum said worriedly.

'I already have. I had a very cross letter from the Headquarters,' Sally laughed. 'Come on Mum, cheer up. We'll not be beaten and, just think, we'll not be a part of their corruption any more. We'll be an excellent charity and do as we state – rescue cats.'

'But how will you manage?' Jane asked, unsure of her daughter's boldness.

'I have been offered a shop. I'll take it to help towards finances. There are lovely people that support you; they will see through the politics and support our new charity. We can do this. Truth will out,' Sally finished, trying to convince herself as well as her mother.

'But how will you afford to start the shop?' Jane asked.

'Goodness knows, but I'll do it and hope for the best. If I waited for things in life to be possible, I'd wait forever.'

Trevor was bored with the goings-on. He had a plan, and it took precedence over all else. Lounging in a basket near the radiator, he'd worked on it all day, his paws tucked in, and his face screwed in concentration. He had hardly said a word. The others had given him sideways glances, thinking that he was ill and that they might be at risk of catching it.

'It's probably a stomach-ache; the greedy cat never stops eating,' Summer surmised, scratching her ear with a back paw, and examining the toe afterwards.

It was late that night when the young tabby moved from the basket. Taking on an 'iguana' and then a 'snake', he slunk across the floor. His legs splayed out so far that the fur from his underneath almost scraped the concrete. Every so often he stopped to listen, hearing the deep breathing of those sleeping around him. Reaching the ladder, he stopped and looked once again. Not a sound could be heard, except the soft snoring of cats in their slumber.

Satisfied, he stepped up the first run. As his head poked through the hole in the shelf, he stopped abruptly. He could hear a scraping of litter, followed by a slight trickling, as a cat was completing its ablutions. Holding his breath, he lowered his head.

He could make out the shape of Marmite on the other side of the room, her tail straight and her head poised in concentration. The next few minutes felt like an hour as he waited for her to finish. At last the scraping of litter was heard again. Bouncing from the tray, Marmite hopped back to bed.

Trevor breathed a sigh of relief, and continued to slither up the ladder. At the top, he listened again and took a glance around. It was safe; the cats were still sleeping. He continued his pursuit across the ledge, until he reached Summer's bed.

She was snoring gently, her pink tongue vibrating as the breath came away from her. Trevor couldn't resist giving it a flick. It stuck on poor Summer's nose, making her look very silly. Trevor smirked and, confident that she wouldn't wake, he shimmered past the old cat.

Reaching his destination, he breathed a sigh of relief. He lifted the corner of the white blanket that was Summer's spare bed. It was just as he suspected. The crafty old cat hid her fish under it, in readiness for a midnight snack.

He grinned to himself for his cleverness, before wriggling his body under the blanket. Within seconds, Trevor had consumed the contents of the bowl. He gave a quiet belch, and studied the bowl to make sure that no morsels were left.

Freezing with horror, Trevor could hear a dreadful noise, muffled through the blanket that covered his ears. As he realised that the horrendous noise was screaming, his fur stood on end. His eye found a small hole in the blanket to look through. The screaming became louder, and to Trevor's horror he realised it was Summer.

'IT'S A GHOST AND IT'S GOT AN EYE! AGHHHHHH.'

Trevor bristled even more as he scanned the room frantically, to see the ghost with an eye. The overwhelming fear caused a scream to escape him too.

'AGHHH! THE GHOST'S SCREAMING!'

Trevor's one eye jiggled from side to side. Cats were running everywhere, seeming to be flying through the air in their desperate flight to hide.

Obama and her kittens bravely stood stone still, on tiptoes, with their fur erect, ready to fight the entity. Seven cats were piled on top of each other, creating a mass of fur balls. Mac and Flick were face down in a basket, with their bottoms pointed in the air, and bits of Pickle and Comfort were sticking out from under them.

Trevor's eye bulged at the chaos and settled on Summer, who was still hysterical.

'ITS EYE IS GETTING BIGGER. AGHHHH! IT'S FLOATING!'

Summer was staring straight at him. His heart sank, and the realisation dawned along with it. He, with the blanket draped over him, was the ghost with an eye.

Trevor backed slowly out, wiggling his body to shed his disguise. It was all too much for poor Summer, as the ghost wiggled towards her. Her legs buckled, and she collapsed in a heap. Trevor's head popped out and, with bits of fish stuck to his lips, he tried to explain to the eyes that bore angrily into him.

'Trevor, how could you!' Comfort chastised, as she wriggled free of the tangle of bodies.

Pickle, Mac and Flick, recovering their composure, burst into fits of amused giggles.

Comfort gave them a look of disgust. 'It's not funny. We have plenty to eat; there is no need to steal.' She turned back to Trevor. 'You're no longer a stray. You gobbled more than your fair share of food today, including everyone's leftovers. You'll get an upset stomach if you're not careful. Apologise to Summer.'

Trevor hung his head with shame, and twisted it from side to side, in an attempt to look endearing. 'Sorry, Summer,' he stammered to the heap of old cat.

'I think you need to revive her first,' advised Gerald, who was peering over the edge of his basket. Now that his hormones were settling, he was becoming a loving, affectionate cat. Soon he would be released to join the others.

The next day the cats waited eagerly for Candy, to see what was happening to Sally.

Trevor was still in disgrace; no one spoke to him. They kept their backs towards him. Poor Summer, still shaky from shock, shouted obscenities at him all morning. She had run out of derogatory remarks so had settled for 'lizard lips' and 'skunk bum.'

While Sally cleaned the cattery, the cats gathered around Candy, eager to hear the latest events.

'Sally has had a fantastic response to her letter; there are people who want to support the new charity. A few have offered to help by volunteering their time. Her mother-in-law, Shirley, who has experience in accounts, has offered to become the Treasurer. A lady called Maria will visit potential homes, to make sure that they are OK for you. She has also offered to help with administration. Another, called Fiona, with the help of her Dad, has set up a website for the charity. Mum is very proud of it, and there has been positive feedback already from humans about how excellent the site is.'

Candy finished, and then pondered why humans were proud of such things. If she had known what a website was, she might have felt proud, too. But all she knew was that Mum spent time staring at a bright square thing. Sometimes she prodded at a black thing, beneath the bright thing. Candy thought that, one of these days, she would go blind from staring.

She glanced at the cats' glazed expressions. It seemed that they didn't understand either. But to appease the dog, they tried not to glaze too much, and even added a few encouraging nods here and there.

Injected with Sally's enthusiasm, she carried on. 'And others have come forward, eager to help,' the dog told them. 'My Mum Sally is so pleased.'

'But what happened to the old charity?' Comfort asked, throwing Trevor a look, as she had forgotten for a while.

'Oh, they're angry. Apart from spreading more horrible stories, they have sent out a letter too. It tells people to ignore Sally. But some are smart enough to see through it, plus they know Jane, and what a good person she is.'

As Sally cleaned, she was deep in thought. Noticing the unusually quiet Trevor, she stooped and gave him a stroke. He opened his mouth to yowl, but, as eyes bore into him, he thought better of it. He sank down into his basket with a firm plop, and looked at Sally with a dismal watery gaze.

'Are you ill?' she asked him, concerned. 'It's not like you not to be in some sort of mischief.'

Trevor took offence at the remark. Even Sally was being rude to him. He was fed up. Every time Gerald looked his way, he burst out laughing, making Trevor even bluer. It was not fair; he was just hungry that's all.

'Blaggard,' shouted Summer.

Sally left Trevor, as the door of the cattery opened. It was Margaret and Alan, two loyal supporters who had left the old charity to join with Sally; or, rather, Morag had dismissed Margaret, climbing from her car and shouting back, as she hurried off, 'We don't want you in the group anymore.'

Margaret had been shocked, mortified and deeply hurt. She, like Jane, had worked for many years rescuing cats. Shortly afterwards, Morag's and Marge's husbands had turned up at their house to remove the six cat pens which they had in their garden. The once derelict pens had been paid for and renovated by Alan.

'We want to help the new charity,' Margaret told her, smiling and nudging Alan.

He held out an envelope. Sally gasped; inside was a cheque for £20,000.

'The money is to pay for the shop.'

Sally was lost for words. What could she say? The money would certainly help.

'Sonya was called by Morag and asked to stay with them as she was more "one of them" and not like Jane and Sally,' Candy was saying, watching Comfort contort herself in the middle, to wash a difficult bit on her back.

'Goodness,' Marmite looked shocked, 'that's dreadful. It's like saying that you can only sit with me because you purr as I do!' she pondered thoughtfully.

'Is that not what happens?' added Flick equally as thoughtful.

They fell quiet, to absorb the information they had learned from Candy.

Another visitor arrived that day. A plump woman barged breathlessly through the cattery door. Slamming it behind her, she lent panting against it for support. Then, almost treading on Sara, she hurried to the window. With terrified eyes she bobbed up and down, examining every inch of the farm before she was satisfied.

'Are you OK, Daphne? Is someone after you?' Sally looked out of the window, to see what ailed her. 'Has the goat frightened you? She won't hurt you. She's really all just horns and beard.'

Assured she was safe, Daphne turned to Sally and laughed nervously.

'I talk to who I want. No one dictates to me!' She pulled back her shoulders to prove her words with gestures. Then, just to be extra safe, she had another bob up and down at the window.

'Who?' Sally asked, taking another peep outside.

'You won't tell anyone I came, will you?' Daphne's brow was creased with worry. 'I mean, not that I care of course.'

'Of course you don't care,' Sally answered, realising Daphne's predicament. 'After all, we've been friends for years and you've never met Marge, or liked Morag. I care for your cats while you go on holiday, and we are neighbours. Why wouldn't you talk to me?'

Sally attempted to divert them both from the awkwardness that hung between them. 'Do you want to buy a raffle ticket? I'm trying to raise money.'

Daphne looked at the tickets with a horror. 'I will, but you won't tell anyone if I win, will you?' She fumbled in her bag for a pound coin and, with trembling hands, gave it to Sally. 'Keep it. I'm in a hurry.'

She opened the door and ran to the car park, leaving Sally gaping after her. The feline world mafia had now dissolved their twenty-year friendship.

Sally rang Sonya and told her what had happened. 'Surely people have not been forbidden to talk to me?'

'I'm afraid so; I didn't want to tell you. You're also not allowed to receive a newsletter either.'

'But that's unbelievable. I don't understand how friends I have known for years are listening to gossip. Most of them have never even met Morag and Marge,' Sally repeated as she did most days.

'It's like something out of MI5,' Sonya laughed.

Sally laughed too; it was more a shocked disbelief. It was so ridiculous that she didn't know what else to do.

Over the next few weeks, the charity shop was underway and being refurbished, Candy told the eager cats. They went with Sonya every day, to decorate, sort items and make ready for the grand opening.

The new charity now had its own helpline number. It wasn't long before it was ringing with reports of abandoned and unwanted cats. Jane managed the incoming calls.

The lack of neutering was taking its toll, and there was an explosion in the cat population in Britain, an explosion which threatened to worsen every year if people did not listen, and did not neuter their cats.

It did not take long before Daisy was chosen for a home. The couple were retired, so they were around all day.

The once scruffy white cat now glowed with health. Daisy had become exceptionally vain, giving herself an extra-long bath twice a day. Long after the other cats had finished theirs and fallen asleep, she still sat grooming. Her ears and nose shone because of their pinkness. Daisy's green eyes sparkled with happiness.

Sally explained that, because Daisy was white, she needed sun block on her nose and ears if outside in the sun too long. Daisy didn't like the sound of that, but was elated to be a special cat to someone.

The couple promised Sally that she was to be spoilt rotten. They had a new pink basket, complete with fluffy cushion waiting for her, plus fresh chicken for her dinner and supper.

'We give an oath that this cat will be treated like a princess,' the lady assured.

Everyone was pleased for her. The little cat had suffered so cruelly in her early years. Now, hopefully, her life was to be happy.

Daisy could not wait; how wonderful that she would never see her vile owner again.

Chapter Nine

The cats were excited, as Jane was coming to visit. Her poor health had prevented her coming before. They had heard her voice many times, when Sally had had her phone on loudspeaker. She sounded nice and gentle; they longed to have a sniff, to assess vibes.

After breakfast on the day, they had extended baths. Summer was desperate not to fall asleep in mid-wash. Listening to Candy, it seemed that Jane was a sucker for an old cat. If she was extra clean then she might take her home with her. Try as she did, Summer could no longer reach all her body parts, her underneath and back being the trickiest. Not prepared to admit defeat, she lay on her back and attempted to lift her head for a chest wash. Every time Summer tried she rolled to one side. That was bad enough but once she rolled, it was so comfy that her eyes closed, as sleep overtook her.

The younger cats giggled, making it more frustrating. Kind Comfort, feeling sorry for her predicament, jumped on to the shelf and washed her chest and back for her.

'I'm so glad I've not got long fur like you,' Summer told her.

'It is difficult,' Comfort agreed. 'It gets twisted in my teeth and it takes an age to clean. And the knots, don't even mention them. If Sally sees them she cuts them off. Then I end up with a wonky bald patch. She says it's because I make such a fuss at being groomed.'

'Thank you,' Summer sighed gratefully, feeling clean.

Later that morning, Jane arrived with Sally's stepfather, Eddie. Worn out from the difficult wash, Summer snored away, missing the visit.

Many of the nervous cats hid under various chairs. Only their noses and whiskers could be seen poking out.

Gerald, who was trusted out of his pen, found it amusing, after watching them spend so long preparing. 'You're daft,' he told them, walking over to see what the fuss was about.

Jane smiled at him, stretching out her hand to allow a sniff.

Trevor, now forgiven, also wandered over; he loved company and gave a long, piercing yowl. 'Pleased to meet you; my name is Trevor,' he greeted Jane, in his flat tone, giving Gerald a firm shove with his bum.

'Goodness, what a loud noise,' Jane laughed, and stooped to stroke the long, thin tabby.

'I know,' Sally said, 'I think he has some Siamese in him; he is rather piercing.'

After making a cup of tea, Jane sat on the chair that Comfort, Flick and Mac were hiding under. Gerald leapt on to her legs. He had decided that he rather liked a warm lap to snuggle on. It was a new experience for him. Once in a comfy position, which required a lot of wiggles and spins, he settled down to meditate. With his eyes half-closed, he dug and digged on Jane's soft jumper. Soon, a bulb of dribble appeared on his lips, showing his contentment.

Sally gave Eddie a list of repairs that needed attention. He was hyperactive, and hated sitting still. That way, the two women could gossip in peace. He was in his element, as he produced a toolbox from his car and went about the tasks.

Sally sat opposite her Mum, with her legs curled under her. Reaching into the basket, she absently stroked a delighted Trevor, who was tired after escorting them around the cattery, chatting all the way to tell them about his stray days. It was important to have the details correct. The tabby cat welcomed a nice rest and rub. He twisted himself in different directions, to make sure every inch of his body received a good fondle. Careful not to disturb the rhythm of the hand, he edged on to his back until his legs were in the air. This allowed his stomach to receive attention.

'I can't understand how people can be so cruel and nasty and get away with it,' Sally was saying. 'All that work you did, and they have put different names to it. Even the shop I opened – everyone believes it was someone else. Your name exists nowhere, Mum; all those years of hard slog!' Sally moaned, feeling very sorry for herself and her mother.

She lifted the mug of steaming tea, and took a sip. Trevor's head snapped up, and he let out a wail. Sally smiled at him, and continued to rub his stomach. He lay back, closing his eyes contentedly.

'Does it matter?' Jane reasoned. 'You know what you've done, and so do I. All those years of work can never be erased, because of the thousands of lives saved from misery. It doesn't matter what people think. I gave up my life for animals, not people.'

It was true. Jane had saved over twenty thousand cats' lives.

'People,' she continued, 'may seem to get away with the bad things they do. But believe me, life has a funny way of coming back to haunt you. The truth will come out one day. In the meantime, we have a charity to run, and a lot more cats to save.

'People will believe what they want to. Just hold your head high, ignore it, and say nothing. We still have a lot of support, so not everybody believes them. The Scratching Post is already an excellent charity. That'll shine through, and people will see. Never stoop as low as them because you're better than that.'

Sally sighed. 'You're right, let's forget them. They're not worth our energy. But what about cats like him?'

They turned to a pen containing a large ginger tom, cowering on the concrete floor. Jane looked at the dull eyes, which were diverted down.

They had heard about his having been rescued by the old charity. Having been petrified when taken to René, he had spat, and lashed out. Assuming that cats that spat were feral, she was frightened of him. Not knowing what to do, she shut him in a tiny, dark pen for months. He had had no human contact, just his food, pushed in daily, using the famous broom.

When Jane heard, she had arranged for someone to go there, and to pretend to offer a feral cat a home. Now the cat lay on the floor, too scared to move, because of the trauma he had suffered.

Much to Trevor's annoyance, Sally went over to the pen and opened the door. The ginger cat cringed in an attempt to make his body smaller and blend into the concrete.

'It's OK,' she said gently, and reached out her hand.

He sniffed delicately at the fingers, and lowered his head again. The fear and desolation that dominated the green eyes was heart-breaking.

Sally stroked the full length of his body, and then scratched under his jaw. Jacob responded slightly by lifting his chin and stretching it forward.

'It's terrible,' Jane's voice was filled with sadness. 'That's the thing that worries me most. What about the cats they rescue? Now I'm not there, there's no one to keep an eye on them. They don't understand cat welfare at all.'

'Well… all I can think is: the more we save, the fewer they do. Our biggest problem is money,' Sally worried.

Once Jane and Eddie had left, Summer sprang up. 'When are they coming, then? They're late. Typical, after the trouble I went to! You'd think they would have the grace to be on time,' she spluttered indignantly.

Everyone stayed silent, because no one had the heart to tell her. That was all except Gerald.

'They've been and gone. You were so sound asleep they thought you were dead.'

Comfort gave him a sharp nudge and one of her 'shut up' glowers.

Summer looked dismayed, and turned to the wall. She had missed her chance of a new home. She was sure that Jane would have fallen in love with her if she had been awake.

Sally spent many hours gently talking to and coaxing Jacob. He gradually began to trust her, and often rubbed his nose on her hand. His confidence grew daily.

One day Sally went to the pen and there he sat. Bolt upright, looking proud and majestic as he had once been. He trilled a greeting to her and Sally smiled.

She scooped him into her arms and gave him a big kiss on his head. He purred as he snuggled into her.

'We'll find you a lovely home, Jacob. With people who love and care for you,' she told him.

'But I want to stay with you!' he cried, devastation filling his eyes.

Sally seemed to understand. 'I love you all, and wouldn't let any of you go. But there are many others that need help. So I have no choice. We'll find you the best home we can. But one thing Jacob, I'll never forget you. Not any of you,' Sally told him; his sad eyes full of love and trust. She gave him another kiss on his lovely silky fur.

Over the next few days three old cats arrived. The first was Sky, an overweight grey female, who was bewildered by the environment. She could not stop trembling as she hung her head.

Comfort went over to reassure her. 'It's OK, you'll be safe here.'

'I w… w… want… my D… dad!' Sky let out a long ear-piecing howl.

Comfort looked at the other cats, for support. But they stared back, nonplussed.

Except Summer, who for once was awake, sitting bolt upright in her basket. 'Well,' she shouted over, 'that won't get you anywhere. I want my Mum, but it's no good shaking. You've got to get on with it.'

Comfort gave Summer a harsh stare to quieten her. 'Where is your Dad?' she asked.

'I… don't… kn… now. He wasn't… well. Someone took him away. He… never… came home,' the cat stammered, and howled again.

'Bet he's dead then,' shouted Summer.

The grey cat let out three more howls, and pushed her head under a blanket.

'For goodness sake, Summer, will you be quiet!' Comfort scolded.

'Huh!' She turned away.

Sky needed an urgent diet. Because of her weight, her health was at risk. As much fat as was outside, was also in; her organs were being crushed.

Next came two brothers, Bernard, a small ginger, and Bertram, an enormous black and white. Their owners no longer wanted them. When they rang the helpline, they said that they were moving. They called again the following week to see if a space was available, saying that they had both developed asthma.

When the cats came into care, the people confessed that they were going on holiday, forgetting the other excuses. Sally guessed that it was because they were old.

They hid under their beds, despite Comfort trying to make conversation.

'Have you told them they're here for life?' Gerald asked Comfort as she left the pen doors.

'No, I haven't!' she answered, backing it up with one of her famous 'shut up' looks.

'Well, nobody offers homes to cats as old as them, do they? Look at Summer.'

'Shush,' hissed Comfort, 'They may hear you.'

Within the next few weeks, the three new cats had been vaccinated and had had their teeth cleaned. Feeling braver, they were allowed into the communal unit. The two brothers found themselves a shelf to live on, away from the others, particularly the younger ones, who were boisterous. They kept to themselves, only whispering to each other.

Sky found herself a basket with a red blanket, and daintily climbed in, looking nervous in case she was told off for doing wrong. They watched the obese cat slump down trembling, with eyes diverted and shoulders hunched, showing her depression and rejection. When another cat approached she looked up and trilled in greeting, then quickly looked away in case the cat was aggressive.

Comfort, feeling sorry for her, sniffed her head and washed her ears. 'Don't worry, Sky. You'll find a new home, with people who adore you.' In her heart, she knew it was not true.

'I wish we could go out,' Pickle sighed, as she watched Sally and Candy leave from the window.

'Speak for yourself; I had enough 'outside' when I was a stray,' Gerald shuddered. 'Anyway, I heard Sally say that she is having an outside enclosure built, so we can.'

'That'll be ACE!' Pickle wiggled to show her enthusiasm.

'What on earth does ACE mean?' Marmite puzzled. 'Pickle, really! Where do you get these terms from?'

'I dunno,' she shrugged, 'I think it means good.'

'Well then that's ACE,' her mum laughed.

Over the next few weeks, the enclosure was added to the back of the unit. The cats were delighted, as they watched log climbing frames carried through. A small Perspex door was inserted into the wall. It took time to realise that, if they pushed it with their nose, they could dart out.

Comfort adored the garden the most; even when the weather was cold, she was outside watching the activity around the farm. Each morning Flick, Mac and Comfort would sit out, waiting for Sally's car. On seeing it, they would weave in and out of each other's bodies in their excitement over breakfast.

On warm days, the back door was left open; next to the door was Summer's shelf. She never ventured out, but she watched the others while sniffing the fresh air.

Bertram and Bernard congregated on another shelf, near the garden. They didn't go outside either. From where they sat, they could catch sunrays that streamed in through the door, making the dull building warm and inviting. Although they grieved for their home, they gradually accepted cattery life.

'I can't understand why we can't go home?' Bertram often said, in fact every day, to his brother. He ignored the question, because there was no answer, and he felt just as gloomy about it.

Flick and Mac found a new game, leaping from one log to another. Pickle always tried to join in, but soon gave up, as she never made it to the next post without wobbling and falling.

How exciting it was to watch the birds every morning, coming down to peck and scratch for worms! Ten cats, including Trevor and Gerald, would line up at the fence. Their heads stretched stiffly, and their jaws juddered in excitement. It was a strange thing to see, as the cats made no noise with the jaw movement. Juddering was a difficult move to learn. It required opening the mouth as wide as possible and vibrating the bottom jaw with exact precision. What a peculiar sight to see a line of cats of all shapes and sizes juddering. Pickle, somewhere in the middle, never got her vibrations right. She over-juddered, making her teeth knock together. The others laughed at her, and poor Pickle always ended up going off for a sulk.

'It's OK, sweetheart,' her Mum reassured her, 'I wasn't good at judders when I was your age. It'll come, just keep practicing.'

So Pickle would sit for ages, vibrating at the wall; well, that was, until she was bored, or something else caught her attention.

Sometimes Trevor, being fond of young Pickle, would judder with her. They sat together, facing the wall, and juddered a few times, turned to each other and did a few more.

For variety, they did two judders facing each other, two left and two on the right. They made up a rhythm, and Trevor would tap his foot to the beat and wiggle his bottom, making Pickle giggle.

A tiny grey kitten, two weeks old, was found outside the door one morning. Sally picked it up and wrinkled her nose. So did the cats, and Candy.

'What's that diabolical smell?' shouted Summer, tucking her nose under her tail to prevent the odour penetrating her nostrils any more. Trevor sniffed around the other cats' bottoms, and Comfort twisted her lip while looking around, as did the others.

'What's that horrible smell?' Sally said to the squawking kitten. She recognised it, but couldn't think what it was.

Boiling a kettle to mix up special milk, Sally fed the kitten. It sucked hungrily at the teat, and promptly fell asleep. Tucking it in a blanket she called the vet.

'I've never bathed a tiny kitten, but it smells so bad I need to,' she explained.

Leaving Candy behind, Sally drove to the nearest shop to buy baby shampoo. The cats felt sick with the stench.

'Poor mite,' the motherly Marmite cooed, going to the basket to mew at the bundle.

'Poor mite! Good grief, it smells like someone's innards have fallen out,' Trevor grumbled. 'How can something so small smell so bad?'

'She can't help it,' Marmite defended, 'it's what a human has done to her.'

When Sally returned, grasping the shampoo, the cattery was empty. Even Candy had her head out of the cat flap.

The protesting kitten was bathed three times before it smelt reasonable.

'Gosh, you have a temper,' Sally smiled as the kitten screwed up its face with annoyance. 'You're a girl,' she cooed.

'Well that's even worse. I thought girls smelt better than boys,' Trevor remarked, venturing in from the garden.

'Stale human urine!' Sally burst out, with her nose pressed against the kitten's head.

The kitten jumped, and screwed its face again.

'Urine and toilet chemical. Someone has been peeing over you and keeping you near a portable toilet. Must be a mobile home.' Then she remembered the traveller park, not too far away.

They had a big notice outside twice a year, '*Grey kittens for sale.*' The mother must have died, leaving new-borns. Probably bred to death, she thought angrily.

The kitten's skin was raw from chemical burns. Sally said some rude words about the people. Drying her off, she rubbed cream into the sores, before poking her down her top for warmth. Exhausted from the activity and exertion of temper, she fell asleep. The kitten, who Sally said looked like Marty Feldman because of her eyes, went home with her – still down her top. She slept happily and didn't notice the change of residence.

Each day she came back with Sally, so she could be bottle fed, in between cleaning the cattery. The kitten was constantly hungry. Instead of two hourly feeds she screamed every hour.

'Even when she's driving, Mum has to stop and feed her with a warm formula made-up ready in a flask,' Candy told the cats, raising her eyes upwards to the ceiling to show irritation. 'It drives me mad, all that squeaking. We get nowhere fast. Stop start, stop start, can drive a dog to distraction.' She looked around for support, but everyone was asleep.

Except Trevor, who was giving the food bowls a last lick. In concentration, he had heard none of Candy's moan.

Now that Jacob had been released, he took a shine to Sky. He adored the chunky grey cat. After he had trilled at her for a few days, she agreed to share her basket with him. Once the batting around the head ritual, complete with a few hisses, had finished, they both squashed in together. There was not much space between them. Bits of each hung over the edges of the basket. They looked so uncomfortable that Sally offered them a larger one; but they preferred Sky's residence, so did not budge.

As Jacob washed her head, Sky purred in ecstasy. Both fell asleep in a mass of large cat bodies.

The month turned to July, and the weather was hot. The shop was now open to the public. After cleaning the cattery at 5 am, Sally went to work there every day, coming back after it closed to feed them again. Soon she began to look extremely tired.

Candy explained that when they got home at seven p.m., Sally typed letters, answered emails, and worked at charity administration. She often fell asleep at the computer in the evening.

The shop, not yet established, took little money, so Sally paid out of her own income to keep the charity afloat. On Sundays, when the shop was closed, she spent all day at the cattery. It was when visitors came, and she hoped that she could rehome cats.

Candy told them about a fête that Sally was organising in the garden of the shop. It was to take place on the first Saturday in September. The preparation for the event took even more of Sally's time – gathering items to sell, pricing and advertising. Jane helped her, and, after the cattery each night, they went to the shop to prepare.

The cats were excited to hear about it, and wanted to know all the details. They had never seen such a thing before, so struggled to imagine it.

Jacob thought that he had been to one in his stray days. He remembered the smell of food cooking, and had wandered in to see if any scraps were dropped.

Trevor told them that he knew what a fête was, because he had helped organise one. He had run around the streets telling people about it. That way, money could be saved on advertising.

'We could tell everyone, couldn't we, Mum?' Pickle suggested.

Gerald had an inward smirk, as he imagined them running round the farm telling the goat, horses, rabbits and foxes. 'I'm not sure Sally would want a herd of animals turning up,' he tactfully explained, so as not to deflate the youngster too much.

As Sally left the cattery that day, Flick was dozing in the window with Mac. He opened his eyes as Billy walked over to Sally. He was studying her chest with great interest; it appeared her boobs were moving. Billy moved his head closer for a further inspection. Assured that his eyes were not playing tricks, he moved away a little. He had seen the film 'Alien', where something popped out of someone's stomach.

'Do you know your breasts are moving?' he asked Sally, when the pause became awkward.

Suddenly, a little grey head popped out of her cleavage, and blinked at the man. Ignoring him it screamed, 'bot!' as her food was now late.

After staggering with surprise, Billy turned, scratched his chin, and went off chuckling.

It was not long before Sally rented two other units from Billy. The first was his old cattery, no longer in use. This contained nine pens. When new cats came into care, they were to be placed there until health checks were complete. They were then transferred to the main unit once declared healthy.

The next unit was a large barn adjoining the main unit. Beds, boxes and clawing posts were carried in. The intention was to use it for feral cats. With so many abandoned, unneutered females, numbers of colonies were developing fast. If in a safe environment, the cats could survive adequately once neutered. Sometimes it became necessary to move them. Few charities entertained, or had the facilities for, wild born cats.

'What's a feral cat?' Marmite asked, on hearing the humans talk.

'Well...' began Comfort as she knurled at a knot on her stomach, 'it's an abandoned female cat, whose kittens are born and grow up never having been socialised by humans. They're frightened and cower when people are near them. They are better suited to farms and stables.' She paused, while giving the knot another grinding pull, then vacantly said, 'I'm a semi-feral. So are Pickle, Flick and Mac and yourself. None of us want to live close to humans, because they make us nervous. We never go to someone for a stroke, or sit on their lap.'

'Oh,' Marmite said, thoughtfully, 'What's to become of us then?'

'I'm not sure. I guess we'll be homed on a farm.'

'It sounds scary,' Marmite shuddered.

'From what I hear, Jane, who sorts out the homes, makes sure we are fed twice a day, and have a lovely warm place to sleep. We have freedom to walk around the land, and are never homed alone. We are homed in groups. Wouldn't it be fantastic if we were homed with Flick and Mac, and stay together?'

'That doesn't sound bad. I couldn't bear being separated from Pickle.'

Comfort did not answer; she had given up on the knot and fallen asleep.

Chapter Ten

Finally, after many months, a lovely lady and man came to the cattery and chose Sara. They adored black cats, and were delighted with such an affectionate one. Sara reached out her paws for a cuddle and rubbed her nose on the lady's ear. The other cats were pleased for Sara, who desperately wanted a human to love her.

'We'll miss you, Sara!' Comfort shouted, as the basket containing the little black cat left.

Sara couldn't speak, she felt too emotional. How she had longed for this day to come. Now it was here, she was frightened of leaving her friends, whom she might never see again, and of going to a place with humans she didn't know.

A week later, Jane called the owner to find out how Sara was settling. They adored her, and took it in turns to cuddle her. They even allowed her to sleep on their bed.

Two weeks after that, photographs arrived and were stuck to the cattery wall. There was Sara, blissfully happy on her own yellow bed. Another showed her playing with a toy mouse, enjoying various cat cuisines, and even one using her litter tray. The last two showed her juddering at the birds through the window, and finally lounging on her owner's bed on her own, very soft, red blanket.

The little grey kitten Sally had nursed was growing rapidly. She no longer fitted down her top.

Furby, as she was now called, was so fluffy that it was hard to see her face. The Marty Feldman eyes now fitted into her head. It was only her ears that were far too big, making her look like a bat.

The other cats called her Snobby Princess. They found her embarrassing, as, at her large size, she still wanted her 'bot-bot' as Sally called it, demanding it as and when she squeaked. In the middle of whatever she was doing, Sally stopped and mixed up the special milk. Furby would climb up her leg and lie backwards like a human baby, holding the bottle with her paws as she sucked away.

The other cats giggled, as her eyes crossed and the bat ears wiggled with the sucking effort.

Furby gave them dirty looks, not knowing why they laughed at her. What was wrong with having bot-bot?

It was also sometimes difficult for them to understand what she was saying. She came out with strange words. For instance she was telling them one day that she sat in Sally's 'orifices'. It took them a while to realise that she meant 'office'. Then she went around telling them she was 'abedoned' and that 'Nelly kept chasing her around the house.'

'Why does she use funny words, and who's Nelly?' Pickle asked Candy one day.

'It's my Mum's and Dad's fault; they use silly words when they talk to her. Now she comes out with kitten talk and thinks we understand. She calls me Candy Coo, which is daft.' Candy felt her face go hot as she confessed this. "Abedoned" means abandoned, and Nelly is the vacuum cleaner. Sally sings a stupid song to her as she cleans the carpet.' Candy began to sing to demonstrate, *"Nelly the Elephant packed her trunk."* She stopped abruptly, on seeing the cats' horrified stares. Lifting her back leg, she hid her face in her groin to avoid further disgrace.

Because the other cats laughed at Furby, she rarely spoke to them, preferring to jut along with her nose held high.

Comfort, who was always so welcoming, tried to be friends. But Furby would just ignore her.

'Stuck up snob,' Summer called, whenever she spotted the youngster.

This made the relationship between them even worse.

The only cat Furby ever spoke to was Trevor. Well, at least Trevor spoke to her. He never noticed whether she spoke back or not.

After a few weeks of one-sided yowls, Furby walked over and sniffed his nose. Then she bounced up and down a few times, in an effort to play. Trevor, who was not into games, made a big effort by wiggling his bottom slightly. His thin tail looked like an anorexic rattlesnake as it followed. Delighted at the response, Furby sprang on to Trevor, throwing her paws round his neck and biting his ears. Soon bored with the game, and not wanting to offend the young princess, he stood and endured the assault. When his ears were nibbled and chewed enough, he lifted his paw and pushed her to the ground, holding her as she struggled to move.

'See, young pup, you'll have to grow more before you can get the better of me,' he told her.

'Un-paw me!' demanded Furby, looking boss-eyed in frustration.

Trevor laughed and let go. Young Furby sauntered off, leaving Trevor to dry his ears. He flapped them around slightly before going off to search for food.

Because Furby still required 'bot-bot,' she went home with Sally each night. After she reached six months, she stayed at home full-time.

'Sally will keep her now. She says she can't part with her after hand-rearing Snobby,' Candy told them, not pleased. 'She keeps chasing my tail,' she moaned.

Soon, with the help of an advert, feral homes were offered through the helpline. Sally or Jane completed a phone interview. Then Sally, taking Candy with her, would visit the premises, to make sure it was suitable.

Ensuring a safe environment, she would then transport the required ferals to their new home. Usually the homes were a long distance away, where farms and stables were more abundant.

One day Jane rang with exciting news. 'There's a feral home on a farm in Puckeridge. It sounds lovely. The people adore cats, and if they become domestic they can go into the house. There are two barns, one already prepared with cat beds and boxes. There's no road nearby, just fields and other farms,' the voice of Jane told Sally. 'What do you think?'

'It sounds great. How many do they want?'

'That's the drawback; they only want two. What about the black brothers?' Jane suggested.

Flick and Mac froze in horror on hearing this. They met Sally's eyes, which were staring at them. She hated letting them go. They had lived with her a long time now.

'I don't know; they're close to some of the others. It's a shame they can't all go together.'

'Well have a think about it, and visit, to see if everything is OK.'

Before Sally left that night, she told the brothers about the home, trying to convince them and herself it was for the best.

After she had gone, they all sat looking very gloomy, except Gerald and Trevor, who were having a deep discussion about who had caught the biggest mouse when they were strays.

'Mine was as long as my tail,' Trevor was saying, giving his back end an exaggerated jiggle, to show the enormity of such a large mouse.

Not to be outdone, Gerald stood up and puffed his chest. 'Mine was bigger than me, and so heavy that I had to drag it rather than lift it.'

'Huh! I think you're exaggerating,' Trevor said, looking at him with disbelief. 'You're a taleteller.'

'Will you two shut up?' Comfort shouted, from the middle of the little group. 'We're upset, and you're making it worse.'

The two cats fell silent; sticking their noses up, they twisted their backs to each other.

'What are we going to do?' Marmite said, turning away from the silly males.

'I don't know,' Comfort answered. Her heart would break if the brothers left, especially Flick, whom she loved so much. Who would wash her ears and whiskers? Who would cuddle into a basket with her? It was too much to contemplate.

Neither Flick nor Mac spoke that night, as they wallowed in their own thoughts of sadness at leaving their home.

Flick walked over to Comfort and waited, while she batted his ears in affection. Once that was over, he sank into their bed and washed her. She washed him too, both caressing each other's cheeks with their tongues.

'Oh Comfort, I'll miss you so much,' he told her, looking at the fear and sadness in her eyes. 'But if I go, I won't stay. One day I'll come back. You must wait and not be homed.'

'I promise, Flick. I'll wait, for the rest of my days.'

They spoke no more; both fell into a fitful sleep, filled with sadness and longing.

Maybe it won't happen, Comfort consoled herself.

The gloomy thoughts were forgotten the next day, when Candy told them that Sally's friend had been for a visit. How they loved Joy; she was bright, cheerful and very funny.

Trevor, who had never met her, thought she sounded mad. But he kept this to himself, because the other cats seemed to love her so much.

Sometimes, at night, they would talk into the early hours, telling each other 'Joy tales'. They loved the stories that they knew so well, but enjoyed hearing them over and over. Even Trevor, with his fantastic tales, could not compare to Joy's.

Human women loved her; she was funny and eccentric. The men were terrified of her. They felt intimidated and scared by her boldness.

One day, she offered to mate with a stranger if he bought her a sandwich. The stranger had scuttled away in fear, leaving Joy with a twinkle in her eye and a smirk on her lips. Goodness knows what she would have done if he had said 'Yes'! I guess Joy would have been the one to run.

Every day they had asked Candy if Joy had been to Sally's house, eager for new stories to add to their already long list.

Most of the time the dog shook her head. 'Joy has not been seen for ages. She rescues dogs, including me, so is often busy with them.'

Wherever Joy went, so did her rescue dogs, barking away in her large estate car. They were delighted that she had been to the charity shop for a visit.

'What happened?' excited Pickle asked, in hopes that it was a good one.

'She didn't stop long,' Candy began, taking her usual deliberation in telling them. 'Sally was distressed to see that Joy had not parked her car. Most people find a parking place before going shopping.

'The road outside the shop is busy with traffic. For fear of her six dogs being stolen Joy wanted to keep an eye on her car. She stopped outside, in the middle of the road.

'Sally, hearing cars beeping, went to see what was wrong. To her dismay there was a long traffic jam, plus three stationary buses, as far as the eye could see. Joy's car was sitting at the head of the line. A large Labrador sat in the passenger seat, and a Pug in the driver's. All the cars, except Joy's, contained very red-faced people, waving and cursing.'

'Goodness,' Marmite said, padding on Pickle's stomach, and trying to picture the scene of angry-faced humans, with bulging neck veins. She couldn't, so gave Pickle a cuff round the ear for biting a red spot on her paw instead.

'Mummmm, you startled me!' Pickle protested.

Candy watched the little scene before continuing. 'Sally scolded, "For goodness sake, Joy! Could you not find a parking space?" "Certainly not! What if someone tried to pinch my dogs?" she answered anxiously. "There are few brave enough to climb in your car with six growling, barking dogs,'' Sally retorted.'

Comfort and Gerald giggled at the thought. Pickle joined in, not knowing what she was laughing at. She had lost the story in concentrating on the red spot. It was OK, though; it would be told again, many times.

'Silly woman! Smelly dog!' shouted Summer, with her mouth full of cat food, which splattered out as she hissed.

The weather for September was exceptionally hot, even more so when wearing a fur coat. Although the cats had long since shed their winter fur, what was left was still too much. It was hard to move in such heat. They lay flopped wherever they could find the coolest spot, or on any shady bit in the garden. The discovered patch kept disappearing as the sun moved, much to their annoyance. This made the cats irritable. It was time-consuming finding a good position. They argued over the biggest and best shady one. Once this was established by careful debate, which involved lots of paw batting, hissing and shoving, and sometimes even a long sulk, the winner would try and settle down, exhausted. After wiggling and tucking body parts into the cool, they would attempt to nod off. In such intense heat, this was difficult. Once the operation was complete, the shady spot would then move to another area. The process would start again, with a lot of frustrated, worn out cats.

Summer was the most sensible, remaining on her shelf where it was cool. The odd sunbeam shone through, which she enjoyed for a few moments, twisting her face into the sun, before moving to various positions to absorb the rays on other parts of her body. When she had covered all areas, she moved away, shouted a few rude words at Trevor and Gerald, and fell asleep.

Poor Sky, still overweight, found the heat unbearable. She puffed and panted so much that Sally became worried. Her weight loss was slow, because her heaviness made exercise difficult.

Sally rubbed her with a cool flannel, which helped slightly, and made a water bottle with ice-cubes.

Sky wasn't happy about this but it helped to cool her.

One warm evening, Marmite twisted her head to one side and lifted her ear.

'Did you hear that?' she nudged Comfort, who was lying on her back, holding a toy mouse with her front paws and giving it cycle kicks with her back.

She stopped kicking, and twisted her radar ears to listen. 'Naa, can't hear anything,' she said, and went back to her mouse.

'There it is again, surely you heard it that time.'

Comfort sighed as she lifted her head and had another listen. 'Naa, nothing.'

Then, suddenly, Comfort sprang upright, her fur bristling. The toy mouse launched through the air, and hit Marmite on the head. The strange noise, Comfort's spook and the added bump of the mouse scared Marmite so much that she took off, so high she landed on top of Sky.

Sky, startled by Comfort, plus a flying Marmite, squealed so loud that the others went on red alert.

Composure regained amongst the muddle, Comfort turned to Marmite, who was gingerly climbing from a cross Sky, 'Yeah, I heard it; it's scratching, coming from the door.' Bravely, she dashed over and sniffed.

'Psst, psst... hellooo, can you hear meee?' said a voice.

'Who's there!' hissed Comfort.

'It is I, goat.'

Comfort turned to the crowd of bristling cats standing behind her. 'It's that weird goat. What do you want? We have no crisp packets in here,' she shouted to the door.

'I came to warn you that there's a fox on the farm. She's looking for food, and I'd hate to see you eaten.'

'Goodness,' cried Comfort in alarm! 'Do foxes eat cats? I didn't know that. I've met many foxes in my time, and I've never seen that happen. I thought they were scared of us.'

'Take no notice,' Jacob said, trying to calm Sky's frayed nerves, 'foxes don't eat cats. It's that silly goat, spreading rumours. I always thought she was dodgy.'

Summer shouted from her shelf near the back door causing them to erect at once. 'Go away, fox,' she spat.

The cats ran to the garden to look. The fox was sniffing at the back fence. She was skinny, her coat thin with weeping sores on her skin. The expression on her face was desperation and despondency.

'What do you want?' Mac shouted.

So intent on sniffing, the fox had not seen the crowd staring at her. Startled she jumped and looked terrified.

'I... I'm... so sorry,' she stammered. 'I'm looking for food to feed my babies. We're so hungry, we've not eaten for days.'

The cats were surprised by the fox's politeness. They were sorry for her. She looked so hungry.

'But I thought foxes found food easily?' puzzled Flick, his neck stretched out and nose twitching.

'We used to when people put bins out each week. But now that they have large bins with lids, we hardly find any food. Thousands of foxes die of starvation every year. Humans hate us; they do not want us to live any more. They take our homes to build their own, then say we are a nuisance.'

'That's terrible,' said Marmite, 'the planet belongs to us all. Not just humans.'

'Yes,' the fox answered, a look of sadness flooding the already troubled face. 'You try telling humans that. A lot of animal species don't exist anymore, because humans decided they shouldn't.'

They hung their heads, because they knew it was true. One day they would all cease to exist because humans wanted the planet for themselves.

Comfort broke the heavy atmosphere. 'You must go, fox. If the man next door sees you he'll shoot you.' She looked around to make sure he was not nearby.

'I know. I'm here out of desperation. So many of us have been shot because of him. He hangs food in a tree. We're so desperate with hunger that we take the chance and go to it. No one has ever survived. A special light comes on as soon as we reach the tree, which alerts him that we are there. That's when he shoots us. But what can I do? I'm so hungry, and my babies are starving to death.'

'I wish we had food for you. But there's none here. Not with Trevor and Gerald about.'

The two of them had the grace to look guilty, as the fox scurried away.

'How sad!' cried Marmite, knowing how terrible hunger pains were.

Chapter Eleven

They told Candy about the fox the next day. She looked melancholy as she listened.

'Everybody has a right to food and kindness, animal or human. We all have a right to share the earth in peace. Life is hard enough, without hunger and fear added. Humans should never take life. It is so wrong.'

'But isn't that what we do?' Comfort questioned.

'We've no other means to survive, as humans have. They pride themselves for being more intelligent; they hold the power on the planet and have a choice, we don't. But some choose to abuse and ignore that privilege, and take advantage of it,' Candy explained, laying her head on her paw, to think more about her spoken words.

Pickle found the conversation boring, and wondered if she could politely slope off and find something else to amuse herself, without offending Candy.

'Some of the human cultural beliefs dictate that they must not hurt or kill others,' Candy continued after a long pause. '"Others," to them, means only human others. They do not consider us included, because we look different. They believe that God created us for their use. But if God had done so, he would not have been so cruel as to give us emotions such as fear and love, or pain, so that we die in agony, for food and for experiments.

'Is that why they break our hearts by taking our babies, because they believe we don't feel?' Marmite asked.

'Yes,' Candy told her, 'They don't believe it hurts us, so they dismiss it from their minds. I really don't think some of them understand that there is any cruelty involved in some things. For instance, milk is produced from a cow once it has given birth. The calf is taken once born and slaughtered, the corpse is then called 'veal', and enjoyed on a dinner plate. The cow is milked daily for humans to drink. Their teats bleed dreadfully as the metal contraption extracts the milk. Sometimes they become infected from constant extraction. The cow is not only in excruciating agony but grieves terribly for the loss of its baby. Once it stops producing milk, it's made pregnant again and the process is repeated. But humans think that the cow does not suffer, and really don't give it much thought.'

'That's barbaric. They eat babies! And why would humans want to drink a calf's baby milk? Why don't they drink their own?' Comfort looked horrified at the thought.

'Naivety,' Candy answered. 'They think it's good for them. But the only thing it is good for is baby calves. Some of the cows try to fight back when their baby is taken. Then they go into a depression; some cry for days. It's interesting though, because if you asked most humans if they would sacrifice one small thing in their life to stop some of the horrific cruelty in the world, most would reply, "Yes, of course". Then suggest that they stop using milk in their drinks, or don't buy a lipstick, or hair product: they would recoil in horror at the suggestion.'

'So most would not even share their food with us, because they believe we aren't important?' Comfort said dismally.

'Some people do. I know Jane shares what she can with everything possible, even slugs in her garden,' the dog explained.

'Goodness, why would she do that?' Trevor shuddered. He did not like slugs; their slime got into the most awkward places. It could cause problems if animals accidently licked it.

Since meeting the cats, Candy had grown to love telling them stories. Every day she looked forward to coming to the cattery, having a sniff around the grounds and shouting a few rude words at any strangers, and then a long rest while her Mum worked. As she rested, she told a story or two. The cats were always so inquisitive, wanting to know everything.

'It's a long story, but if you want to hear it I'll tell you.' Her eyes sparkled, hoping that they did.

'Wait for me,' Pickle called. She had wandered away, and had got her claws tangled in a crochet blanket. As much as she tried to free herself, she became more tangled. Desperate not to miss the tale, she wriggled and fought to get loose; but, in her desperation, she became more knotted. Now four legs were stuck through holes, and she was tightly wrapped in a ball of cover.

'Pickle, for goodness sake stop messing around! You'll miss the story,' Flick called, looking round. 'How odd, she's gone.' He scratched his ear in confusion. 'I'm sure she was there a minute ago.'

'I'm here,' Pickle mewed. But because her head was covered, no one could hear.

Marmite looked around. 'You know what she's like; she has the attention of a gnat. She's probably in the garden, playing with a fly. Go on, Candy, begin without her.'

'Well,' Candy began, looking round to make sure they were paying attention, her eyes clouded as she thought through her words carefully.

'It started when Jane placed food in her garden every night, to feed any hungry animal. Smelling the food, a stream of animals came. They waited in line for each to feed. The cats ate what they wanted, and after them the foxes. The hedgehogs went forward next, and finally the slugs and snails finished the leftovers.

'Soon afterwards, Jane noticed that the slugs had stopped eating her plants. They were so well fed that they didn't touch them. The hedgehogs and birds ate the slugs, so were, and still are, well fed too – thus creating a healthy, natural food chain.

'Jane told Sally, and she began feeding her slugs too. She was surprised at how intelligent the creatures were. Every night at nine p.m., they all gathered outside the back door. Any food scraps were thrown out. By the morning, they had disappeared. Sally has a beautiful array of flowers and a family of hedgehogs in the garden.

People laugh at her and Jane, saying that they're quite mad. But my Mum says they're just ignorant, choosing to destroy, rather than to find a solution. Using poisons to destroy slugs in turn kills the birds and hedgehogs that live off them.

'Mum says that if farmers fed foxes, they wouldn't destroy their chickens.'

Mac looked very guilty, as he remembered the moth he had eaten the previous night.

Gerald, who had been listening intently, suddenly spotted a wriggling lump on the other side of the room. He lifted his coat, flattened his ears and sprang from his chair, landing right on top of Candy, who let out a big yelp.

The startled cats sprang to their feet and pushed out their fur. Their legs stiffened and stretched as much as they could. All stood on tiptoe, their heads waving about, trying to assess the direction of danger.

Even Summer, unusually awake when a drama occurred, stood and fluffed. 'What's happening?' she called, squinting round the cattery, 'why are you on guard?'

No one spoke; they stared at the large lump rolling around the floor. Comfort thought it was Trevor up to his tricks. But she spotted the tabby licking a piece of trod-on cat food from the floor.

He looked up, surprised at the scene of both large and small cats standing stiff. The funniest was Sky. She was twice the size, with her fur sticking out. Because of her large belly it was difficult to point her legs vertically. They splayed out sideways so far that her stomach hung on the ground.

Trevor, feeling spooked, felt something roll into his back legs, making him jump a whole chair-height into the air. On landing, he took off and fled behind a basket. The jump was enough to start them all off. The cats sprinted round the room, knocking bowls and tins everywhere. The clanging noise startled them more, and caused them to dash faster. One leapt up Sally's body. Sally had just walked back through the door after speaking with Billy; the cat used her head as a springboard, and bounced to the top of the pens. She dropped a pile of carefully balanced newspapers in her fright. Looking around at the chaos, she spotted the heap of blanket rolling around the floor.

'What are you doing in there, Pickle? Honestly, you really are a woo-woo,' Sally told her.

When the young cat was finally released, it took ages to calm everyone down; but the cooked chicken helped to settle delicate nerves.

A few nights later, the fox appeared again. The goat, taking pity on her, offered her an empty paper bag she had been saving. Out of desperation, the fox tried to eat it. Wrinkling her nose, she gave up, spitting out the now soggy paper.

Her legs were weak as she still struggled to find food. The little she had managed to scrounge was fed to her babies.

'Still no food?' Comfort enquired, dreading the answer.

'No,' the fox told her, desperately. 'Soon I'm going to have to take my chances next door.'

'You can't!' squealed Pickle, 'you'll get shot. We hear his gun almost every night.'

'He has so much food in there though. If I'm quick, I can grab some and run without him seeing me. I have no choice, my babies will die if I don't do something.'

Comfort's eyes widened as she sensed the evil vibes of the approaching figure. 'It's him, he's in the yard and will kill you if he sees you. Quick, goat, do something!'

Goat looked startled, thought for a second, and rushed over, lowering her head. Once she reached the fox, she unceremoniously butted her under a nearby bush.

The startled fox gasped with shock.

'Be quiet!' hushed goat.

The man from next door walked past, glancing at the goat; she grinned at him, lowered her head and tugged at a piece of grass.

Once he had gone, they breathed a sigh of relief.

Goat stuck her head under the bush, and eyed the fox. 'You can come out now, he's gone.'

The fox crawled out and slunk off, her stomach close to the ground as she looked from side to side. Pausing a few times to catch her breath, she disappeared through the hedge.

They had forgotten about the potential home for Flick and Mac. It was such a surprise when, the next morning, a car pulled up with two baskets to take the boys. Sally had a dreadful job catching them as they sprinted up the pen doors, and sat on top, looking down at her, petrified. It took a while but eventually, secure in a basket, they were taken. The people were kind and gentle, as they cooed at the terrified faces that stared from the front of the basket.

Comfort was distraught as she watched in horror; running to the baskets, she pawed at the wire and Flick pawed back.

'Don't forget, I'll be back for you, Comfort. Wait for me!' he called, as the baskets were carried to the door.

No words could describe the pain inside her stomach at her loss. She stayed in the garden and watched the two baskets being loaded in the car. She still stared hours after the car had pulled away, longing for Flick to escape. At midnight she went indoors and had some water. She vowed never to leave the cattery; she would wait for Flick till the end of her days.

Comfort waited and waited, but Flick did not come. She stopped eating, because her stomach was painful as it twisted into knots of despair. She sat in the garden, staring at the car park day after day; transfixed on the last place she had seen Flick. The cats tried to help; she did not respond to their pleas and coaxing. Nothing lifted her spirit.

They missed the black brothers terribly. The cattery was so quiet without them. Eventually Comfort became ill, and Sally found her one morning lying lifeless in the garden. She lifted her up and took her to the vet's. When she came back, Comfort was put into a pen and covered in a blanket to keep her warm. Sally syringed fluid and runny food into her mouth, talking, and trying to encourage her. But the cat's spirit had been broken; she did not want to live, not without Flick.

Sally had no idea what had caused Comfort's illness. Humans do not understand cats' emotions. If she had realised, Sally would have gone and brought them home.

Even Trevor, who was fond of Comfort, tried to explain to Sally. He followed her around the cattery every day yowling away.

'Please, Trevor! You are driving me mad!' she told him in frustration.

'But I'm trying to help Comfort,' he yowled, in his monotonous tone. Eventually he had to admit defeat; Sally did not understand.

Pickle tried to make her laugh, taking on different cat stances. Her inadequacy made her wobble and fall. Usually, Comfort would smile at her. But now she turned her head towards the wall, her back hunched and her tail straight out. It was clear that if something were not done, Comfort would die.

Each night, just before dusk, the fox came. The cats were always pleased to see her. They rushed to the window as she skulked out of the hedge. As the fox passed, she always nodded a greeting before disappearing.

Sometimes she came to the wire to chat. 'I don't suppose you've any eggs?' she asked on one visit.

'Eggs, goodness me, do you eat eggs?' Pickle screwed up her face to show distaste.

'Foxes love eggs, and it's difficult to get them. I want to teach my cubs how to lift them without breaking them.'

'I'm sorry, we don't have any,' Marmite told her.

It was a week later when they realised that she had not visited for a while. The cats waited for her, and then worried when she did not appear.

After a few had nights passed, they spotted two little fox cubs, running frantically out of the hedge.

'Have you seen our Mummy? She's been missing for ages,' they whined. 'We've looked everywhere for her. We're so hungry and frightened.'

Marmite could not speak, because of the emotion in her throat.

'I'm sorry, we haven't,' Pickle choked, wishing there was something she could do.

The cubs ran off to search further away.

The fox did not show the next night either. Sally, on her way to the cattery, was stopped by the man next door.

'I shot six foxes the other day,' he boasted.

'Wow, how brave and fearless you are!' Sally responded flatly, her narrowing eyes showing her hatred of him.

'It's kinder to kill them. I done 'em a favour; they were half starved, so I put them out of their misery. One of them was a vixen. My dogs had a great feast,' he laughed.

'So, what if she had cubs?' Sally walked away, not bothering to wait for an answer.

'Don't tell me you like foxes; they kill everything, even cats,' he shouted after her.

'What rubbish. They don't hurt cats. They're hungry because their entire habitat has been taken over by humans. They have no homes. I think you will find that it is hypocritical humans who kill everything, not foxes.'

The next night, the cubs returned. Their bodies were skinny, and their eyes frantic with distress.

'Our Mum hasn't come yet. We don't know what to do. Please help us.'

The cats could not meet their eyes; they didn't know what to say. After that night they were never seen again. The two gunshots told the cats that the cubs had suffered the same fate as their mother.

'It was better that way,' Candy consoled the cats. 'Starvation is a worse death.'

The following Friday, Candy told them that the local paper had reported fourteen animal corpses hung by the neck in the man's tree. Most were foxes; there were two baby cubs and a few deer. People walking down the footpath near his land had reported the bodies. Nothing could be done; the man was within his rights to kill what he liked.

A few weeks after Comfort had become ill, something happened to lift her out of her depression. A big battered orange cat turned up at the cattery, in a plastic basket.

Both Pickle and Marmite ran over in excitement. 'Banjo,' they both called, 'it's Banjo.'

Comfort lifted her head weakly, and surprise rippled her dull eyes, as she glanced at the basket containing her old friend.

'Hi, everyone, I'm back!' Banjo shouted, using his loudest meow.

'Oh, I see,' Sally was saying to the embarrassed people.

'I'm sorry, but, with the new baby, we just can't manage to look after him anymore.'

Sally snatched the basket, and gave them a look of reproach. She put him in the pen next to Comfort, to allow him time to settle. Many new cats had arrived in the unit since he left. He would need to get used to them all over again.

For the first time in weeks, Comfort got out of her basket and wobbled over to the Perspex screen between the pens. 'Oh Banjo, I'm sorry. But it is so good to see you again. How I've missed you!' She sat exhausted from the exertion.

Her eyes were so full of pain and sadness that Banjo was shocked. The once beautiful, silky coat was now dull and greasy. He looked at her with questioning sympathy.

Comfort told him about Flick and Mac. 'Oh, Banjo, I miss them, so much.'

'I'm sorry, Comfort. That is sad. The only thing I can say is that he will come back for you one day. He loves you very much. Many of us go through life never having been loved as much as you were.'

It was true. His owners had not loved him enough to keep him. He'd done nothing wrong. He loved the baby and had tried to protect her while his owners were busy. Banjo was always on the look-out for intruders. When the baby was in her cot he purred to lull her to sleep. How he would miss his home, with his own basket and garden to lie in.

'You owe it to Flick to be happy and find a new life while you are waiting.'

Comfort sat quietly, trying to absorb Banjo's words and find some reassurance in them. She looked at the sadness in her friend's eyes. He had lost his home again. He so wanted to be loved and wanted. Well, at least by humans: all the cats loved Banjo once they got to know him.

'It's so good to see you,' Comfort meekly smiled.

She bent her head, lifted her paw and began to wash. Banjo smiled; he was sad and gloomy, but seeing his old friends again lifted his spirit.

From that day, Comfort was going to live again. Not only for Flick, but also for her old friend Banjo, who was so brave and good.

It was about a week after Comfort's return to health when Trevor got chosen for a new home. He yowled all the way down the cattery, and they could still hear him in the car park. The cats watched from the window, and then smirked, as they could hear him telling his new owners about his adventures. They did not understand of course, but the cats did.

'Have I told you this one?' he was screeching.

'I'll miss him,' Marmite sighed.

'It'll be quiet without his endless stories,' agreed Comfort.

'Yes,' shouted Summer. 'We can all catch up on some sleep; in fact, I'm going to have an early night.' With that, she lifted her tail and began her bath in readiness.

They need not have missed Trevor, because two days later, he came back still yowling in his basket.

'I don't understand; I was only giving him a gift to make friends,' he was telling his now ex-owners.

'What's wrong?' Sally asked, surprised at the quickness of his return.

'He ate our budgie,' the man explained, near to tears, 'or rather, most of it. He took the remains and ... and ... left them on my son's bed. My son is still traumatised.'

'Oh, dear! I didn't know you had a bird. I would have warned you not to leave him with it. Cats will kill birds.'

'Well,' the man reasoned, 'I guess it was our fault for trusting him. But we wanted to make him feel at home, so we left him in the room with the bird all night.'

Sally opened the basket. Forgetting his disgrace, Trevor sprang out and went to check the food bowls.

'Mum, can we get a budgie to play with?' Pickle asked Marmite.

'We'll see.'

Luckily, Pickle had forgotten the rat. A budgie created a new problem.

Chapter Twelve

'Sally!' it was Jane on the phone with the tone she used when promising a good nag.

'Now what have I done?' she grimaced.

'I bet you've not finished the newsletter, have you?'

Sally, never good at keeping up with paperwork, thought about the metre high pile that waited at home. 'Almost,' she appeased her Mum, crossing her fingers at the lie.

'That's a fib,' Candy said, while prodding her blanket. She had lost a piece of fish earlier, and was sure it was there somewhere.

Trevor and Gerald sat close by, both looking innocent. They had seen where the fish had gone. Not wanting to let on, they kept their eyes diverted. Trevor stared at a lump of fluff on his cushion. Then deciding he was causing suspicion by staring, he gave it a dab with his paw. Gerald, not finding anything to stare at, had a poke at Trevor's fluff too. They both hoped desperately that Candy would not spot the fish first.

'Sally has only just typed the heading,' Candy betrayed.

'What's a newsletter?' asked Pickle and Marmite together, wondering why the two males were poking fluff.

'People send a small amount of money each year, and Sally posts a letter, every so often, telling them about you lot and things happening in the charity.'

The two male cats both looked crestfallen when Candy found the fish, and swallowed it in one swoop.

'Huh, didn't even touch the sides,' Gerald grumped.

'Appalling,' Trevor huffed.

'I've not stopped,' Sally was telling Jane in her defence. 'I had a break last night to watch a film, and fell asleep at the peak bit. I can't keep working these hours,' she moaned.

'I know you're tired. But the newsletter's important; without it, you won't get support. I was thinking,' Jane continued, 'why don't you arrange a sponsor scheme for cats that you can't home? I'm sure people will contribute a small amount each month to help with their keep.'

Sally stared at Comfort, who stared back, and then behind her, to see where the line of sight was directed, hoping that it was not another prospective home. Swallowing, she started mentally planning ways to avoid it.

'That's a great idea, but I have no spare hours to fit any more in.' Sally's voice held the exhaustion her body felt.

'Well, I thought about that too. Why don't you ask Alice to help? She's good at writing letters, and is so supportive of the charity.'

'Okay, I will,' Sally brightened, knowing that Alice was a dear friend of both Sally and Jane, a friend who loved cats, and would do anything she could to help.

A new resident came that day. He was the strangest cat they had ever seen.

'He has dreadlocks,' Banjo whispered to Marmite.

She looked confused, as she had never heard of them. Banjo explained that they was fur or human hair that was twisted so much that it formed mats.

'Oh,' Marmite said. 'Why would anyone want to do that?'

The cat was large with crossed eyes. Still, they reasoned, he seemed pleasant enough. He sat in his pen, staring out at them. As they passed he chirped a greeting.

'Smelly sack,' Summer shouted rudely to him.

She slept more than ever these days. Sometimes she slept for so long that when she was awake she would throw in a comment only appropriate for an earlier event. Like 'stinky pants,' four hours after Candy had left the premises. Or 'sewage bum,' which was referring to an earlier toilet event.

The cats got used to it; most of the time they ignored her. She never noticed, as she nodded off into her own little world.

The strange chirping cat went off to the vet's early the following day. He returned that evening, and slept all night.

'Stinky sack coot,' shouted Summer, on seeing his now-shaved coat. He received the name 'Mathew'. As he was so accepting of the other cats, he soon joined them.

'Where are you from?' Pickle asked, intrigued. 'Why do you look so odd?'

Mathew's eyes appeared more crossed now that he was bald. 'Well I … I'm not sure. I had a long car journey to get here. But then again, I did nod off for a while. So it may have been shorter. Do you live here?'

'Yes,' Pickle answered, muddled by Mathew's reply. 'Did you live with humans, or outside, like Mum and me?'

'Well I …', began Mathew again, having a think. 'I lived with a family. One day they vanished. I was having a long nap in the garden, and when I woke up they'd gone. Some new humans were there instead. As I strolled down the garden they threw stones at me. I don't know why.'

'That's terrible, similar to Trevor. You'll meet him soon.'

Mathew glanced across the cattery to where Pickle had nodded. 'Yes, it was not very pleasant. I was very hungry and waiting for my cuddle; they would not stop throwing. It hurt so much when one hit me on my head and back. Then a child ran over and kicked me in my stomach, so I ran and hid.'

'What happened then?' Pickle asked in disbelief.

'I went back and the same thing happened; and again every day for weeks. I was so hungry my legs began to wobble. I'd never caught my own food before and didn't have a clue how. My beautiful coat became knotted, because I didn't have the strength to groom it. It was very painful; every time I walked, the knots pulled at my skin. There were branches and leaves tangled up in the mess, not to mention a piece of yoghurt pot and a sticky sweet wrapper. A lady picked me up, I thought it was for a cuddle, but she brought me here.'

'Poor you, don't worry, we'll look after you. Can you do a crab?'

'Well I… I think so. At least I haven't for many years. I'll give it a go though.'

Mathew stood up and arched his back. He glanced at his behind to make sure his tail was erect. Satisfied, he turned his body to one side leaving his face towards Pickle. With his boss eyes he looked most comical. She started to giggle as Mathew raised himself on tiptoes and began to walk sideways around in large circles.

The other cats popped up their heads like meerkats at the strange sight.

'What's wrong with him?' Gerald asked, nudging Trevor.

'Dunno,' he replied and, after watching the peculiar Mathew for a while, went to investigate. Not wanting to approach such a strange cat he stopped a safe distance away. Crouching low, so he didn't look so conspicuous, Trevor stretched out his body to full length. With his neck and head pushed out, he looked like a long tabby caterpillar. He felt safer this way; after all, he'd never seen a large cat crabbing before. He might have been mad, or worse still – dangerous.

'The toilet's in that direction if you need to go,' he suggested to the strange cat.

Mathew stopped in mid-crab and glanced at Trevor.

'Thank you,' he replied, 'but I went earlier.'

He lifted himself again and continued his crab.

Summer, catching sight of the cat, stopped washing, her tongue touching her chin as she stared.

By this time, Pickle was upside down in fits of uncontrollable giggles that shook her body so much that her toes vibrated.

Trevor's face was a picture as he gaped with his mouth open and his wonky tooth protruding. He began waving his head from side to side in confusion.

'Mathew, you're hilarious,' Pickle gasped.

He sat down to catch his breath for a few moments. Then, standing up, he began crabbing again. Trevor, still long and rigid, slithered closer, in hope of a sniff. This might help to understand what was taking place.

Mathew turned and batted him on the head in greeting. Trevor sprang two cat-leg heights into the air and ran off, hiding behind the usual basket.

When Candy came that night, the slow, deliberate Mathew suddenly became all-dynamic. He sprang from his bed in a blink, fluffed the meagre fur that was left on his body, and pulled back his lips to show large, threatening teeth. Examining his claws to make sure they were sharp, he was ready to attack.

'Dog alert, dog alert!' he shouted. 'Make ready. Trevor! You take the rear; Gerald: the side! Girls, the other. I'll go north!' he commanded, to the surprise of the cats.

'It's OK, it's Candy, she's a friend,' Marmite reassured him.

The dog, unaware of the threat, plodded solemnly past. Mathew followed her path by jumping around in little jerky moves as she progressed, his body arched, and his head again turned sideways ready for battle.

Pickle, only just recovering from the earlier fit of giggles, started again.

Surprised, Banjo lifted his head so quickly that he forgot to let go of his blanket, as he watched the cat jiggering past.

Trevor, ignoring the peculiar Mathew, wandered over to Banjo.

'Can I have some of your blanket? I'm starving,' he asked.

It took time to convince the large cat that the dog was OK. Pacified, Mathew sat back on his bed while the cats rushed to the window crying, 'It's Joy!' as they heard a car.

Sally walked over, wondering what they were looking at. As Joy climbed from her car, six barking dogs flew at the windows. It was usual for her to wear long dresses or trousers. But this time she was wearing a man's shirt. Her legs were bare and there was nothing on her feet.

'Well I never,' Sally said, her voice full of alarm.

Joy was talking to Billy and the man next door.

'I've got no clothes on under this,' she was telling them.

'Yeah,' said Billy, sounding unsure and frightened.

Joy lifted her shirt to prove it. From the cats' and Sally's view they saw her naked backside. A full frontal was seen from the men's, who froze with shock. Once snapping from their trance, they ran away. A big cloud of dust was left as Billy drove panic-stricken from the farm. The man next door pole-vaulted over the wall to the safety of his home.

Once they had gone, Joy came bounding through the cattery door. Her eyes settled on Trevor, who didn't mind in the least that Joy had no fur.

'Strokes are strokes,' he told the cats later. 'It doesn't matter in what guise they're delivered.'

'Who's this handsome fella?' Joy enquired of a delighted Trevor.

'Yes, I am rather handsome, aren't I?' he yowled, forgetting his earlier opinion of Joy.

'That's Trevor,' Sally told her. 'Full of mischief and he never shuts up.'

The other cats smirked and nodded at the description of the long, thin tabby.

'Well, really!' Trevor was most indignant. 'I don't think that's fair.'

Joy laughed, and asked if he was mischievous.

'No, I'm not. Don't listen. She's telling exaggerated fibs,' he yowled, and swung his body to allow his back to be tickled. 'I might get into the odd scrape or two, but that doesn't warrant a label of that description.' He gave Sally a severe stare.

'Joy?' Sally asked, 'Why are you naked?'

'Well...' she began; and, at that point, Sally knew it would be one of those stories that could leave her scratching her head for some time after.

'I took a friend out for lunch. We went to a pub with a beer garden so that I could take the dogs. I left my friend in the garden with them while I went to get a menu. The only one I could find was a large chalk board stuck on the wall. It was so heavy, that as I dragged it across the garden, I tipped over it and went sprawling, tearing my dress. All my other clothes were in the washing pile.'

'Oh, right, makes sense,' Sally said, realising she was right in her assumption.

'How are things? Have you heard from the black witches?' Joy asked, changing the subject.

'I've heard rumours that they're so angry that I have started my own charity that they want to have it closed.'

Joy laughed. 'They don't matter. Truth will out. You look tired, though.'

'It's a hard slog. But with Fiona doing the night feed on a Sunday, things are looking up.

'Also, Margaret and Alan have offered to clean the cattery on Mondays, and take the cats to the vet's each week for me. I can go straight to the shop and have a lie-in till seven a.m.,' Sally laughed. 'They have been so kind in helping me.'

'I wish I could do more for you, but with the dogs, I just don't have any free time.'

'Well, it's good to have your support, Joy, even if you are naked. It's encouraging that not everyone believes the terrible things they have spread about me. I want to buy a rescue centre, but it's so far in the distant future.'

'If I know you, Sally, it won't be that long,' she laughed.

Sonya arrived late that morning, so the three of them sat to have a gossip. She didn't mind either that Joy was almost naked.

Gerald and Trevor had a fight for laps. Mathew ambled over to find a lap too. Trevor chose Sally's lap, but was jealous, because Mathew was heading for Sonya's. He quickly leapt on. Mathew, taking it in his stride, turned to jump towards Joy's lap. Gerald, noting his movement, rushed there first. As Mathew jumped on to Sally's lap, Trevor changed his mind and, quick as a flash, jumped towards her, knocking him flying as they met in the air.

'Trevor! Stop being mean!' Sally told him, noticing his behaviour. She put Trevor on the floor and picked up Mathew, who gratefully put his arms around her neck.

Trevor gave him a glare of jealousy as he settled on Sonya, then proceeded to throw Mathew a penetrating look of displeasure every so often.

The rest of the cats, enjoying the company, lay dozing. Pickle, not feeling sleepy, batted Candy's tail for something to do. The dog, unhappy with her tail being batted, kept sighing and swishing it out of the way. The delighted Pickle batted even more.

Sally told her two friends how the charity was developing. She injected a buzz of enthusiasm into her words. 'We've had more volunteers come forward. Many of the hands-on workers have left the other charity and joined us. They are good people, whose only intentions are to rescue cats.

'I think we have the diamonds amongst the stones,' she told them proudly. 'With more volunteers, it allows me time to spend with cats that need more attention, and also on other areas of the charity, like fundraising and trapping,' Sally groaned.

'Trapping can be a demoralising job when you're out all night freezing.

'More people have offered help with the cattery. With eighty cats in care, I must admit it's a struggle on my own before going to the shop.'

'Sally, you must be shattered,' Joy said.

'Well, I knew it would be tough. It was hard enough working long hours for the other charity. With only Mum and me, the hours are more horrendous.'

'Well, I know the trapping is terrible,' Sonya added. She had done it for years. 'If only people realised the problems they cause by abandoning an unspayed female. A colony forms within a year.'

'Yes, we had a call the other day,' Sally looked cross. 'The lady confessed that she had a small problem. She allowed her cat to breed in her garden, because her children loved watching the kittens. That was years ago; now she has over fifty cats there. She thought it was a joke when she asked us to pop over and remove them. Because they're not socialised, they're wild.

'So while I'm out trapping all night in the cold, and paying for their neutering, she'll be curled up with the television on and a hot drink, not a care in the world.'

They nodded in agreement; so did the cats, hoping that the fifty cats were not moving in.

'What'll happen to them?' asked Joy.

'They'll have to go back after neutering. She caused the problem; she must pay for it, by feeding and providing shelter. After a strong lecture, she agreed.' Sally smiled grimly before continuing to tell them the developments of the charity.

'I'm so lucky to have Shirley, my mother-in-law. She's great and takes so much weight off me. She keeps the accounts impeccably. What would I do without her? And of course Mum, who spends hour after hour, day in day out on the phone line, dealing with abandoned and unwanted cat calls. It's terrible listening to yet another report of abandonment, or some silly excuse, because someone is bored with their cat.'

'And of course giving you a good nagging,' Sonya laughed.

'She certainly does that,' Sally agreed. 'But she keeps me on my toes; my Mum's a perfectionist, and, after managing her own charity for all those years, an expert on cats and the mechanics of it all. And of course, she is clever with her learned knowledge.' Without her, Sally knew that she would never have coped.

She continued to tell them about three new volunteers who had joined them. The first was a lady called Stella.

'She will help Mum with the phone line. It's the worst job in the charity, with endless calls. The phone line can be transferred to any number, so it's not a problem. She's such a good person, who's passionate about cats and is experienced, having worked for many years with another rescue. Stella will foster kittens for us, too, and help in any other way she can.'

'Great, who are the others?' asked Joy, pleased for Jane and Sally.

'They're a married couple called Angela and Terry. Again, they are wonderful people with heaps of experience. They don't seem to mind what they do to help. Bless them; they often go out in the middle of the night to rescue a cat or help at fundraisers, and transport goods to and from the shop. We're delighted to have such wonderful people on board.

'Like attracts like,' Joy smiled.

In the early hours of the morning, a few days after the social meeting, Sally came into the cattery, carrying a basket. Inside were two timid four-month-old kittens. It had taken weeks to trap them. Their mother had disappeared, which was unusual. She must have met some dreadful fate, Banjo surmised, bleary-eyed and yawning.

'Or gone to have more kittens,' Marmite added.

They were named Annie and Twix. It was not a good place for them to be, because they needed a home environment, with constant human company to socialise them. But there was nowhere else for them.

They huddled and hissed at Sally, their eyes full of fear and suspicion.

The cats tried to reassure them, but they were terrified. They had never been to, or seen, anything but the garden they had been born in.

The only cat they responded to was Comfort. She went over and poked her nose through the wire of the pen. The kittens rushed up and kissed her by rubbing noses with her.

'It's OK,' she consoled, 'No one'll hurt you, you're safe here. But if you don't calm down you will live here forever, like me.'

'We don't like it here,' the bigger of the two told her. 'We want our Mum.'

'I know, but you're here now and you'll soon settle down.'

Pickle wandered over next. 'Hello,' she said, putting her paw on the wire of the pen. 'Can you do a crab and an iguana?' she asked.

The kittens were too frightened to demonstrate their moves so just stared at her.

Pickle, not understanding their fear, thought they probably did not know how to do them. Feeling grown-up and knowledgeable, she started bouncing at the pen door to show off. Her moves were still inadequate to cat standard, despite constant practice. Not to be put off, she demonstrated an unstable iguana and a crab. Encouraged by the kittens' open mouths, Pickle finished off with a shaky snake, which looked more like a squashed worm, and a new breed of monkey that had never been heard of.

The kittens were intimidated, and, thinking they were under possible attack, began to spit at her.

Pickle looked dismayed as the biggest kitten launched himself at the wire. Feeling out of her depth, she made her excuses and skulked away more depressed than ever.

She went to Marmite and told her what had happened.

'They're babies and very frightened,' Marmite explained. 'Give them time, and I bet you'll be great friends, once they settle down.'

Pickle nodded, trying to understand; then, dismissing the kittens from her mind, she proceeded to tell Marmite how bad her moves were.

'They didn't even recognise them, Mum; they thought I was attacking them.'

'Never mind, Pickle,' her mum cajoled. She herself was so good at moves that she could have been a cat ballerina. 'Some cats take longer to get their moves right. Look at silly Gerald, and your Dad, who was always a bit clumsy. You probably inherited it from him.'

Pickle sighed and felt fed up for the rest of the night.

Banjo had given up on ever having his own home. He resigned himself to thinking that he would stay in the cattery forever, like Comfort.

She was determined that there was no way she was leaving. Just as she had promised Flick, she would wait for him. If forever was what it took, then that's how long she would wait. Once, when Sally had suggested her for a feral home, she had cleverly pretended to be ill. When Sally had come to collect her, Comfort had lain on the floor, rolling her eyes and panting. As a consequence of her action, she was taken to the vet and given a week of antibiotics. But it was worth it to lose the home.

Banjo did not have to pretend like Comfort; he just never got chosen. To save his feelings of rejection and hurt, he tried not to ponder on it too much. However, sometimes, without thinking, his mind drifted back to his old home: the lovely basket and soft-sucky blanket that had been left behind; how he had loved lounging on his owner's lap while they watched television. His new Mum had cuddled and kissed him every day. He missed them dreadfully, and the baby, who by now must be crawling. These thoughts hurt him so much that he cast them from his mind.

Sometimes Comfort, sensing his sadness, would come and lick his ears. She never seemed to mind that he was ugly.

'Never mind, Banjo,' she would purr. 'I think you're beautiful, and I love you.'

Despite her love, Banjo became very depressed. He never ventured far in the cattery, preferring to stay in his bed. He hardly ever integrated with the others; every night he sat alone in a corner, sucking his blanket to soothe and lull himself to sleep. He didn't even bother bathing anymore; there was no point. If people thought him horrible to look at, then why try to make himself handsome?

'You can't make a silk purse out of a pig's ear,' he reminded himself, constantly.

Sally worried about him, and gave him extra cuddles every day. But he no longer smiled or purred at her.

One day, Jane sent her friends, Julie and Robert, who were looking for a kitten. They were lovely people and Julie cried when she saw the unwanted cats.

'It's so sad. I couldn't do this work; it would upset me too much.'

Although Sally liked them the comment, often said, annoyed her. She always had the urge to say: 'Oh, it does not bother us! We never give the abuse and unjust treatment of animals a thought! We only do this for amusement!'

But instead, she politely replied, 'I don't know why people think we do this work without emotion. We lose sleep over the animal, and get upset, just like you would. It affects us badly. But putting our own emotions aside, at least we are doing something to help them.'

Julie, realising she had said the wrong thing, apologised. 'How can we help?' she asked trying to make amends.

'You can offer Banjo a home and not take a kitten,' Sally smiled hopefully.

Banjo, hearing his name, turned his head and pricked up one deformed ear. Sally walked to his basket and scooped him up.

'Oh my goodness isn't he handsome,' Julie gushed.

'He needs a loving home, with people who appreciate such a fabulous cat,' Sally told them. 'The majority of people, who visit, choose a cat or kitten under two years and with 'pretty' coloured fur. Rarely do people want a cat like Banjo. He's depressed, living here.'

Julie's eyes flooded with compassion as she took the surprised Banjo and cuddled him. He instantly liked her and her vibes were good.

'We'll have him,' Julie smiled kissing his head.

Robert smiled too, 'I think he's fantastic. He looks like he needs spoiling.'

'Oh I do,' agreed Banjo and the first purr for a long time burst from him.

Comfort smiled through her sadness. How she'd miss her beloved friend. But he deserved the best in life. She was so happy for him. Before Banjo left they touched noses.

'I'll miss you so much. I'm so pleased you'll now be happy,' Comfort choked.

'Never give up, Comfort! Flick will come back one day.' Banjo's words were full of emotion.

The people promised faithfully to send photos. They did, a few weeks later, and they were hung on the wall with the others. In each photo, the big orange face glowed with contentment. An enormous cat smile crinkled his eyes. One of the photos, Comfort knew, was a message for her; she could tell from the way he held his paws, curled his toes and bent his head.

The message was: 'Don't give up on happiness. It will find you one day if you wait long enough. I am so happy.'

If Comfort could have cried tears, she would have. Even Summer's throat caught with emotion. Her time for a home would never come. But how glad she was that dear old Banjo had managed to find one.

Chapter Thirteen

The weather for November, was surprisingly mild. So much so that the back door was left open and only closed at night, when the air turned damp.

Twix and Annie were declared healthy by the vet. After being wormed and flea'd, they joined the group. More relaxed now with their new friends, they adored each other. Whenever you spotted one, the other was never far behind.

If it had not been for the fact that Twix, being a boy, was slightly larger, it would have been difficult to tell them apart. They became known as the twins or, when mischievous, the terrible twins, which was often, with Pickle's influence.

'It'll soon be Christmas,' Sky told them, one evening.

'What's that?' asked Pickle, her ears pricking up with interest.

'It's a human celebration. They do odd things at that time of year. My Dad loved it, and so did I.'

A little lump formed in her throat, as she thought of her Dad. Jacob, feeling her sadness, rubbed her face with his nose. She smiled at him, and cast away her thoughts.

'What odd things?' Pickle asked, trying to imagine anything odd that sprang to mind. A lot of things did, but she couldn't imagine humans doing them.

'They hang things on the ceiling, and plant a tree in their house. They hang balls and glittery things on it,' Sky continued.

'How peculiar,' Marmite added. 'What for?'

'No idea,' Sky shrugged.

'That sounds fantastic. I hope Sally puts a tree with dangly things in here,' Pickle wiggled her bottom with excitement.

Annie and Twix thought so too, so wiggled with her.

'Oh I loved the tree when I was your age, Pickle. I used to run up it and pull off the balls. It always fell over. Once it was picked up, I did it again. Don't think I'd manage that now, not with my big thighs.' Sky looked at her hips to confirm that they were still large.

'We have nice things to eat at Christmas,' Comfort told them, climbing into the basket with Jacob and Sky. The limited room meant that she had to lie on top of them.

'Last year we had chicken, turkey and salmon. It was bliss.'

'Oh wow! This gets better,' Pickle squealed, not containing her excitement.

She ran off to tell everyone about the tree. Trevor, Mathew and Gerald weren't interested. They were lounging in a large basket, discussing food.

'I ate a whole ostrich to myself once,' Trevor was saying.

'That's nothing. A few years ago, I ate a whole crocodile,' Gerald claimed.

Trevor flicked his eyes, and then had a think.

'That's nothing,' he piped up. 'I hunted and killed an elephant. I ate it for a whole month.'

'Now you're being kittenish,' Mathew told them, exasperated.

Pickle tried to interrupt, giving a garbled detailed description of the tree. None of them looked even mildly interested. Trevor and Gerald were having a hard think, trying to imagine what could possibly be bigger and better than an elephant.

'Ah.' Gerald sprang up, making them jump. 'I hunted a whale once…'

Pickle was deflated when they ignored her. She ran off to find other cats to tell. Bernard and Bertram stared at her as though she was daft, and Summer had fallen asleep, having done so upside down. Pickle shook her head and went to the pens. They appeared empty, as the new cats were hiding.

'Oh I give up,' she huffed, and went back to the little group by the radiator, batting Annie and Twix around the heads in frustration.

Every day after that, though, she waited for Sally to pull out a tree from her car.

Among the people who came forward to volunteer was a young lady named Lola. She spent hours with the cats. They loved her gentleness; she was not afraid of the ones that spat and snarled. She was brilliant in covering for Sally, so that she could have an occasional day off from the cattery, to catch up with other things. This should have helped, but Sally seemed to spend her life 'catching up'.

Getting near Christmas was horrendously busy; it was a good time for raising funds.

By December, the weather turned freezing, seemingly overnight, so Jane and Sally tried to bring in as many stray cats as possible.

Most nights Sally went out trapping. She had given up any thoughts of Christmas. With cards to send to supporters and the newsletter, and a stream of letters thanking people who kindly donated, it was impossible.

'It's very odd,' Gerald puzzled, eyeing up a family with two children. But I thought I heard a helper say, rescues don't home animals near Christmas, because irresponsible humans sometimes buy them for presents and become bored soon after. The animals have either been dumped or ended up in rescue centres. So, if that's right, why are there people looking today?'

'Mum and Jane say that many people have a long holiday at Christmas, giving them time to spend with a new cat. Not everyone has a jolly time, some just a quiet time at home. People who come forward are visited at home, as they are all year. They're not allowed to arrange surprise presents,' Candy explained.

'So why is Christmas different from any other time of year?' Marmite puzzled.

'That's what my mum says, it's not; people dump cats all year, not just at Christmas,' Candy sighed.

The family with the two teenage children wandered over, escorted by Trevor, who, as usual was showing them around. Candy lowered her head, and most of the others bolted. Only Mathew and Gerald remained. They both put on a big show. Gerald rolled upside down and purred, which was the homing rules. Mathew reached up his paws for a cuddle. The family could not decide between them.

'It's so difficult to choose; they're all lovely,' the young boy said.

Sally was pleased; it was what she loved to hear. She walked away and left them talking, coming back a short time later.

'It's been a difficult choice, but we're choosing Gerald. He's so lovely, they both are. And Trevor. But isn't he loud,' the mother said, giving him another stroke.

Sally nodded and laughed, 'Yes he is rather vocal.'

After answering a stream of questions and giving cat homing advice, Sally prepared Gerald. He was flea'd, wormed and microchipped all at the same time.

'Good gracious, I feel like I've been through a mangle,' he complained, grinning because he had a new home.

Everyone was sorry to see him go. They had grown to love the big daft tom. But they were pleased that he would no longer be living the hard street life.

He waved his tail as his basket was placed in the car between the two young people.

'Hope you have a big tree there,' Pickle shouted as she watched him go from the window.

Christmas drew nearer; Sally and a few of the volunteers had been making strange wailing noises.

'Christmas carols,' Candy explained.

'Well,' grumbled Mathew, 'I hope it's over soon; they sound worse than Trevor.'

Pickle was growing more and more despondent, as no tree had appeared.

A heavy frost lay on the ground every morning, making Comfort dream about Flick and his twinkles, and miss him all over again. She still watched the car park, hoping to see him wandering along the driveway. In her mind, she often saw him with his flag held high, chirping a warm greeting. The vision would fade, and only an empty space could be seen; there was no Flick.

Sally promised every day, five cooked chickens on Christmas day. They did not care about the special day, but they cared about the promised chicken. They waited eagerly, wondering when the day was arriving.

The volunteers disappeared a week before, with a promise to return two weeks after. Sally waved them off despondently, as most wished her a happy holiday.

At seven a.m. one morning, Sally drove into the car park. She climbed from the car, followed by Candy. With them was a man who carried several large plates.

'It must be Christmas day,' sang Mathew, eyeing the plates piled high with the promised chicken.

'Who's that man?' Pickle asked, expecting the rest to know.

'I guess it's her mate,' Trevor said uninterested, dribble wetting the corner of his lips and his eyes dilated with excitement.

The weather outside was so cold that Sally, the man and Candy were shivering. While Sally unlocked the door, the cats began to weave.

Even Bertram and Bernard climbed tentatively to the floor, leaving the safety of their shelf. Finding a spot away from the others, they began to weave together. Summer, from her shelf had no one to weave with, so she went round in a circle instead.

Mathew, who was not used to weaving, and really did not feel he was a conformer, did a dinosaur.

The cats grew impatient when the door didn't open. Pickle ran to the window to see what was happening.

'The door's stuck!' she called to them.

'Oh no,' they wailed together, 'what are we going to do?'

Then all became so quiet that you could have heard a grain of litter gravel fall.

'It's the weather, making the door stick,' they heard Sally say to the man.

'Come out of the way. Let me do it!' he demanded, his voice impatient.'

Suddenly, much to the cats' amazement, the door sprang open, and the man came crashing through backwards. He staggered, before falling straight on to his back. The plates he was holding flew into the air. Time froze as the cats' eyes rose to the ceiling to follow the trail of chicken.

Trevor had already mentally inscribed his name on his bits. Time thawed, and it came hurtling down, landing everywhere, mostly all over the man who was still lying flat out.

Luckily the plates were plastic, as one hit him on the head. There was a slight pause before the herd of cats rushed forward. Even Bernard and Bertram gave an almighty leap through the air, landing straight on the man's belly and knocking the wind out of him.

Trevor, not to be outdone, was like a bullet from a gun as he arrived with precise negotiation on the man's chest, gaining, as he saw it, the best place.

Mathew looked from side to side before springing into action. He jumped over the furry bodies, and plonked on the man's head. With one paw in his eye, and another in his moving mouth, he gobbled the chicken.

The timids, including the twins, lost their shyness and rushed forward to join in the feast.

Sally stood in the doorway, tears of laughter running down her face. 'Don't move,' she gasped, 'I don't want more to go on the floor.' She ran to the kitchen area, grabbed a pile of plates, and ran back with Summer tucked under her arm.

'I don't want her to miss out,' she told him as, finding a gap, she placed the old cat on his leg before picking bits of chicken from him to fill the dishes.

The man obediently lay on the concrete, ranting about his mishap. He tried to get up but Sally put her foot on his forehead to stop him.

'Really, Sally,' he moaned, 'you are the limit.'

But he dutifully stayed where he was. He was cross with Sally, who did not seem to care if he was hurt or not. She was more interested in the waste of food and in the traitor Candy, whose head was pushed in the middle of the cats, wolfing gulps of chicken.

Once Sally and the ranting man, now known as 'Chicken Man', had gone, they had a long nap. Soon a strange happening awakened them.

'Pssss… hello… psssss…' a voice called.

'The wall's talking!' shrieked Pickle, making ready to bolt for the nearest chair.

She stared at Trevor for an opinion. But he was standing stiff, pointing towards his hidey bed.

'Hello wall,' called Mathew, most indignant at being woken from such a deep sleep. His comfy head had plopped down as Trevor's sprang up.

Marmite and Comfort, the bravest, stalked towards the wall for a closer look.

'Any brick suddenly moves, girls, run,' advised Mathew, blinking sleep from his eyes.

Comfort and Marmite were now standing on Summer's shelf and sniffing towards the wall.

'Go away, wall,' Summer shouted, most put out by the intrusion on her shelf.

'Is anyone there?' the wall said again.

It was too much for Marmite. She leapt six cat-leg heights in the air and sprang from the shelf, running to the safety of the chair which Pickle was now hiding under.

Comfort felt vulnerable standing alone, with only Summer for protection. What if the brick flew at her without warning? Both she and Summer were at critical risk. Keeping her legs stiff and ears alert, she looked back at the others for support. They stared, eyes round, and necks stretched to their full potential. The most support they offered was their twitching noses.

Comfort looked to the wall hesitantly, 'I didn't know walls could speak.'

'I'm not a wall,' the indignant wall replied, 'I'm a cat.'

'Really?' said Comfort curling her lip in puzzlement. 'Well you look like a wall. Are you stuck in it?'

'No silly, I'm on the other side. I hear you every day, and wondered who you were.'

Comfort looked up and saw a small hole in the brickwork. She smirked and turned to the others.

'It's OK,' she reassured them. 'It's a cat on the other side of the wall.'

They relaxed. Mathew was especially relieved; maybe he could get some sleep now.

'Ask if they have any spare food they could push through,' Trevor called from behind the bed.

Pickle's head popped out from under the chair. 'See if they have a tree?' she shouted.

'Now how are they gonna get a tree through such a small hole, not to mention lift it?' Jacob grinned.

'Well I dunno, do I?' Pickle stuck out her white lip in a sulk.

'Who are you?' Comfort asked, sniffing the hole.

'My name's Pansy. Who are you?'

Introductions were established, as most of the cats jumped up to have a sniff and hiss, much to Summer's annoyance.

'How am I supposed to nap with you lot standing on me?' she moaned, particularly at Trevor, who was squashing her tail, craning his neck to see into the small hole.

Pansy was a feral; she had lived on a farm and was encouraged to breed constantly. Her kittens were sold at four weeks old so that she could give birth to more. She was worn out, and her last kittens, so undernourished, had died both after being born and before. Her angry owner had refused to feed her. Fed up with her hanging around, she rang the charity, pretending that Pansy was a stray.

Sally had known the fate of the cat just by looking at her. She always knew a cat's history by its condition. 'I think you've almost bred her to death,' she told the woman, not disguising the look of disgust in her voice and eyes.

'How dare you? She is a stray!' Despite her tone the woman's face reddened.

'I think people who breed animals like that should be shot. I wonder if you've had baby after baby. Or do you use birth control? I hope so; we don't want more people like you walking the earth,' Sally, snapped at her.

The woman looked agog at such rudeness. She stomped off, hurling rude words at Sally.

Sally was not in the least intimidated. She shouted that she would be reporting her; that way her farm could be checked for more 'strays'.

Pansy, who had never been socialised, or even shown any kindness, was released into the feral unit. It had taken time before she was strong enough to be neutered. Only now had she found enough strength to be aware of her surroundings. She heard the cats on the other side of the wall and wondered about them.

Comfort told her about their life there and Candy, the dog that was OK.

'Cor, the dogs where I lived chased me. I can't imagine one that doesn't.'

'Oh, Candy doesn't. She can't run anyway, she has stiff back legs.'

After that, the cats often jumped up for a chat when Summer was asleep. The old cat never knew that her shelf had been invaded.

A few nights after Christmas, when they were all having their groom, ready for bed, Summer sat bolt upright. Straining her eyes towards the window she screeched, 'She's here, it's my Mum; she's come for me.'

Several hanging tongues could be seen dangling from interrupted mid-licks. The startled cats, with their paws stuck in all directions, stared at the window. Through the darkness, they strained until Trevor announced, 'She's bonkers.'

'Stop it,' Comfort glared at him, before turning to Summer who was still squinting at the glass.

'How do you know it's your Mum, Summer?'

'Well I…' the old cat stammered.

All eyes turned to her, making her most uncomfortable. How did she know? Her eyesight was not good, so she could only make out a blurry shape. Was it her Mum? It must be: who else would call to her?

'It's my Mum, she's come for me,' she said decisively. 'You must be able to see her.'

All eyes and dangling tongues turned back to study the window again; no one was there.

'Silly old cat,' Trevor said shaking his fur into place.

Summer ignored him. 'She looks such a nice lady, so kind and gentle, it must be her.'

'Your Mum wasn't nice getting rid of you,' Trevor said spotting a piece of missed chicken squashed on the floor.

Summer did not say any more; she turned away. Comfort jumped on to the shelf and washed the old lady's neck.

'Don't listen to him; what does he know? I'm sure it was your Mum,' she consoled.

'Do you think so?' Summer said, feeling a little better. 'She looked so nice and kind. She was definitely looking at me.'

'Maybe it's a lady wanting to offer you a home.'

'Who would want an old black cat like me?' she said sadly, unusually curling herself into a ball and tucking in her tail.

'Lots of people would want a lovely cat like you. I would, if I was a human. In fact you'd be the first one I'd choose.'

'Would you really?' With her warm thoughts, Summer went into deep sleep with a lift on her lips.

That is how Sally found her the next day. Her body stiff in death. A look of peace on her lovely face, with her pink tongue protruding out of her black lips.

Tears filled Sally's eyes, as she gave her a kiss on her head. 'Sleep peacefully, old lady. This cattery will never be the same without you.'

Comfort looked on and swallowed; the other cats were sad. They would miss the funny old lady who had left this life for, hopefully, a better one.

'She was chosen,' Trevor's voice was full of compassion. 'An angel came and took her. That must have been who she saw.'

Comfort stared at him, amazed by the hidden depths of the cat who only seemed to think of food.

Chapter Fourteen

Sally felt ill with exhaustion; the ground spun every time she looked down, and her legs felt weak. She became snappy with people, particularly her Mum. The long hours were taking their toll, and wearing her out.

The more well-known the charity became, the more work piled in. The phone never stopped ringing, from early morning till late at night. Sally desperately needed more help. She confided in Sonya on one of her visits.

'You need a break,' Sonya concluded.

'How can I have a break? Who will take over?'

The cats worried about Sally. If she was ill, who would help them? They asked Candy about it. The old dog was slower these days. Her legs wobbled as she walked.

'Sally keeps taking me to see the vet,' she told the cats, 'but I bite him, so he can't examine me.'

Jacob thought this amusing, as he washed Sky's stomach. 'I did that too,' he confessed.

'But that's naughty,' Sky scolded, and bit his ear. At last she was slightly thinner. Some days she strutted along, showing off her new figure.

'He tried to stick something in my bottom,' Jacob justified. 'I went stiff with shock. So I turned and bit him to teach him a lesson. How would he like it?'

'That's right,' Candy agreed. 'I saw him reach for the long thing and bit him too. There is no way I'm having that stuck there.' She lifted her nose and pointed it to the ceiling to show how undignified that would be.

The others nodded in agreement, all having suffered the same assault.

'Well I didn't mind in the least. He gave me biscuits when he did mine,' Trevor confessed, without any shame.

'Honestly, Trevor, you'd do anything for food,' Comfort shuddered.

'What are we going to do about Sally?' Marmite asked, reminding them of the conversation.

'My Mum's put an advert in the local paper, asking for help both here and at the shop. She's worried about the expense but there's no choice; she can't keep working so many hours,' Candy informed them, standing up and twisting around a few times, before sinking down with a big sigh. She couldn't get comfortable today.

'Does that mean we'll have someone new here?' asked Comfort, unsure whether she wanted different people around.

'I guess so,' the dog said, seeing Comfort's worried face. 'Don't worry. I'll help Mum do the interviews. She can ask questions, and I'll sniff their legs to make sure they're OK.'

A week later Candy told them that twenty-eight people had applied for the jobs.

'We've selected a few to see,' Candy informed them.

It was not long before the 'chosen ones' came to the cattery for interviews. Some of the cats bolted and hid, while the boldest took great interest in them. They helped Candy have a sniff, and Trevor, who was an expert interviewer, went over and yowled questions to them.

'Will you bring treats in every day?' he asked. When they didn't answer, he thought them not much good.

It was a hard decision, but eventually Sally chose two young ladies. Sarah was to work three mornings a week at the cattery and Abbey five days at the charity shop. Sally would still cover the other days.

When Sarah started work the following week, she seemed OK, so the cats relaxed. She cleaned the cattery from top to bottom. Working over the agreed hours, she was still there when Sally came to feed in the evening.

'Goodness, you're still here?' Sally looked round at the gleaming barn.

'I thought I'd do a spring clean,' Sarah told her, pleased that Sally had noticed her work.

'You've worked so hard,' Sally was impressed.

That evening, while the cats had their evening bath, Mathew strolled over yawning, having woken from a long nap.

'I've been mulling things over, and my conclusion is that Sarah is strange,' he announced, intently.

'Why do you say that?' asked Marmite feeling a worry creep inside her tummy.

'Well, she spent the whole day cleaning, and didn't once speak to any of us. I went over for a cuddle, and she ignored me. Everyone knows that I require a fifteen-minute cuddle every morning,' he told them indignantly.

'Well,' added Trevor, 'she ignored me when I asked for treats. So I think Mathew's right.'

'You boys aren't being fair. After all, it was her first day. She probably wanted to make a good impression,' Comfort reasoned, attempting to dispel the worry they were causing.

The next shift, Sarah pedantically cleaned again. This time she arranged the beds and clawing posts at precise angles against the wall.

'Are you OCD?' Sally laughed, finding Sarah still hard at work that evening.

'Errr, what's that?' asked Sarah.

'Obsessive about cleaning. Everything looks so pristine.' Her eyes diverted with concern to the carefully arranged, empty baskets around the wall. The cats were huddled on the concrete floor by the radiator.

'The cats like to lie by the heaters. I know it looks scruffy, but they don't mind,' Sally said, as she put the baskets back.

Sarah did not look pleased, but said nothing.

One evening, a month after Sarah had started work, Sally and Candy arrived at the cattery and stared around in dismay. The baskets had been removed; only two remained. Candy was most disgruntled on seeing even her bed had gone.

With nowhere to lie the cats wandered around despondently. Jacob and Sky stood looking forlorn, as their bed had been tidied away too. Sally sighed and went to the store cupboard, dragged them out, and placed them in a disorganised array on the floor. The relieved cats gratefully climbed into their beds.

The next day a note was pinned to the wall.

'I spend a lot of time cleaning here. Please leave beds as I have left them. Sarah.'

'Told you,' Mathew said. He had always been a good judge of character.

Sally, cross, ripped it down and threw it in the bin before pinning up her own.

'Please remember this is a cats' home, not human. They need beds to sleep in. Concrete is not sufficient. **Baskets are not to be removed!***'*

Sarah was annoyed, but didn't argue.

After a few months, she settled in OK. She still, however, did not have time to cuddle the cats, not even Mathew or Trevor who had tried to make friends.

'She's not interested in my adventures,' Trevor moaned. 'The cleaning is her only concern.'

'At least Sally always has time for a cuddle and a chat,' Comfort consoled them.

When summer arrived, and the weather was warmer, Candy made an announcement.

'I won't see you for a while, because Mum's going away for a few days with Sonya. I'll be responsible for looking after my Dad.'

The cats looked worried, especially Trevor.

'But who'll feed us in the evening? I won't survive on one meal a day.' Tension stiffened his skin at the thought.

'It's OK; Lola is coming in the evening to look after you. It's only for two nights.'

The cats breathed a sigh of relief. They liked Lola, and knew she would feed them well. They guessed they could survive two nights.

Mathew, not joining in the conversation, was in meditation. He sat bolt upright, with his head hanging almost to his chest and eyes distant in concentration. Although an odd stance to humans, it was a typical cat-pondering pose. He lifted his head for a moment, because his neck was aching and he needed a ponder break.

'Why are decisions so difficult?' he said out loud, to no one in particular. Then lowered his head again to continue. Weighing up the pros and cons, he made a mental note of each on a separate imaginary list. At the end, he was still no clearer about what to do.

Seeing that he was in a dilemma, Jacob wandered over. He sat down and lifted his paw; splaying his toes to reach the bits in between, he began to nibble.

'What's wrong?' he asked, spitting a piece of cat litter accidentally in Mathew's direction. He watched it absently, as it landed on his eyebrow. Dismissing it, he carried on gnarling at a claw, and ruthlessly pulling out lumps which he had accumulated from an earlier scratch.

'I just can't decide.' Mathew's voice was distant and thoughtful as he stared at Sally, who was sitting down on one of the armchairs having a rare break with a cup of tea. 'Should I leave this cushion and opt for Sally's lap, or stay here?'

Jacob stopped licking and stared at him in disbelief.

Mathew's coat had grown back beautifully, making his crossed eyes no longer look crossed at all. With his magnificent mane and bushy fur, he was enormous.

His cushion was so comfy, all soft and warm from his body heat. It had taken hours to find the right spot, a lot of twisting and turning, plus long concentrated digs. The lap would be warm also, but it would take some time to find a good position. Sally moaned at him when he dug his claws in too far, as it made her skin bleed. Much maneuvering would be required to find a good niche. He just couldn't think what to do. With so many difficult thoughts swirling in his head, he fell into a deep sleep.

When he awoke, both Sally and Jacob had gone.

While Sally was away for her short break, two new cats were moved from the isolation pens to the main unit.

The first, because she squeaked rather than mewed, became known as Squeaky Molly. She was completely black, and, although fully-grown, she was very small. Her owners had bought her from a pet shop as a tiny kitten. Being only four weeks old when sold, Molly had been too young to leave her mother.

The people had soon become bored with her, so she went to live in their garden. Here she stayed for two years. Being unneutered, she had given birth to many litters of kittens. Most had died, as Molly struggled to feed them. The owners sold the ones that did survive.

A lady, who lived nearby had watched the struggle of the young cat, and took pity on her. She called the charity to take her away.

The owners were angry that she had been taken, and had called requesting her back. They already had clients lined up for her next lot of kittens.

Sally agreed they could have her. She had no choice; the law prevented them from keeping someone's cat, even if it was neglected and badly treated.

The cats smiled as they heard the conversation when Sally spoke to the owners.

'I'll get her ready for you to take,' she told them, her voice cold and emotionless. 'I'll have the invoice from the vet's ready for you to pay. As she is your cat, I don't expect the charity to pay for her.'

'What invoice?' the surprised voice asked.

'The neutering of course, plus she was ill, undernourished and extremely run down. It has cost time and money to nurse her back to health. Plus good food and antibiotics, etc. it all adds up. The bill is approximately over £200 so far. But I'll add it up properly. When are you coming?'

Sally would have smiled as the phone clicked off, but she was too annoyed. The cat was useless to them now she was neutered. As a consequence, Squeaky Molly stayed until she was ready to be re-homed.

Despite her hard life, she was a very loving cat. When anyone went into her pen, she stuck one of her claws up their nostril and reeled in their nose so she could wash it.

The next was a grey stripy kitten called Minnie. She had been bought as a present for the children of a family to play with. The three-year-old child, not knowing any different had thought her a soft toy, picking her up by either her tail or her head.

Minnie endured many traumas and had once been flushed down the toilet. The man of the family had luckily retrieved the distressed kitten.

Minnie suffered terribly, as she was pulled from one child to the other. Several times she was trodden on when they had been running about playing, causing terrible injuries.

The family never took her to the vet's, so she suffered a lot of pain.

The final straw came when the children had slammed a door. Minnie had been going through it at the time. Her head had crunched between the wood. The kitten screamed in pain, the injury so excruciating that she was hysterical.

Spinning around on the floor, she bit and scratched anyone who went near her. The father of the family became worried for his children's safety. He scuffed the kitten and threw her into the garden.

Minnie stayed there for many weeks, cold, frightened and in agony from her throbbing head.

The children were too scared of her to go into the garden. So eventually the mother grabbed the kitten up and took her to a vet, to be destroyed.

The vet could not bring himself to kill one so young. He called the charity to ask if they could take her.

She now sat in a pen, staring dismally out, not responding much to any coaxing. The extent of her injuries was unclear, as no one could examine her. She hit out and scratched at anyone brave enough to try.

The cats tried to welcome the new arrivals. Squeaky Molly spat as they went to her door. She was not used to other cats, having lived alone in the garden for so long. Every time she saw one, which it was difficult not to, she let out a long, piercing screech. The loudness made them cringe and grit their teeth. They soon learned to avoid her, or creep by on tiptoes.

'I hope she gets a home quickly,' whispered Trevor. 'I don't think my ear-drums or nerves can take much more,' he moaned, at least three times a day.

Minnie told them all to 'bugger off' when they went to her.

'I've never known such bad language coming from one so young,' Comfort said, as she attempted to wash that difficult bit on her back which she never could reach. It was at times like this that she missed Flick even more.

In the end she went to Mathew and asked for help. It was so difficult with long fur. Having a long coat too, he understood the problems, as he licked away at Comfort. Then he wrinkled his mouth as he tried to rid himself of the loose bits, which came away.

'The poor little mite has been through hell,' Marmite reasoned. 'We need to give her time.'

Pickle wandered over to the pen to take a look at Minnie. 'Hello, my name is Pickle, what's yours?' Pickle knew full well what her name was, but needed an opening line.

Minnie turned her head away from Pickle. 'Go away,' she hissed.

'It's OK, you're 'Nothing's wrong with it. But safe here. Sally will never let you go to a home with children again,' Pickle told her.

But the kitten did not respond.

With Sally away, Sarah had a great opportunity to clean. She collected up the baskets, turning out the resentful cats.

Again Jacob and Sky stood watching despondently as their bed disappeared into the cupboard.

After a few hours of standing, they had no choice but to settle on the concrete. Only two baskets remained, which they all fought desperately for.

Mathew was very down in the whiskers. He so loved his cushion, which had been taken and placed in the wash basket. 'Where am I supposed to sleep?' he asked the others, hoping that they would offer an answer.

They couldn't; they were as dumbfounded as him.

Bertram and Bernard, who still said little, looked on.

'I hope she doesn't take our bed,' Bertram worried.

'She'd better not. I'll spray on her if she comes too near,' his brother threatened, shaking his shoulders and pulling them back to make himself look more threatening.

Twix and Annie smartly had the perfect idea to resolve the problem. They went to the linen cupboard and pulled the corners of the door. While Sarah went to clean the isolation pens, they jumped in and started to push out blankets and towels.

The others looked on, thinking the kittens exceptionally clever. The blankets were too heavy to drag anywhere, so they marched over to the growing pile.

'Well we'll sleep here,' Mathew decided and climbed to the top of the mound.

The others followed, until not one blanket could be seen for bodies as they settled down to doze. It proved difficult, because the pile was so high that they kept rolling into each other. Soon a tangle of fur balls could be seen, as legs and bodies intertwined in one big heap. It was most uncomfortable, but they had little choice. It was that or the hard floor.

When Sarah came into the main unit, she was really cross to see the mess. She turfed them off and tidied the cupboard. Annie and Twix scampered off, as a large folded towel was thrown on top of them.

After everything was in a satisfactory order once again, a chair was pushed to hold the door shut. The cats did not know what to do. They tried to pile in the two baskets that were left. But the bottom ones kept getting squashed, especially when enormous Mathew was the top cat. He weighed so much that little Comfort and Marmite almost suffocated. They had such a miserable night huddled on the concrete. They longed for Sally and Candy to come.

While Sally was gone, Sarah kept ringing her up with complaints. When Lola arrived to feed in the evening, the two girls took an instant dislike to each other, and kept arguing. Sarah called Sally in floods of tears, as she poured out Lola problems.

The cats heard Sally on the loudspeaker, trying to pacify Sarah as best she could from a long distance.

Things turned worse for the cats the next evening, when Lola brought her little boy with her. Some of the cats cringed because, although Lee was gentle, many of them had been pulled about by children.

Minnie eyed the child with suspicion, ready to attack if he came to near. She became jumpy when he 'brromed' his car on the concrete floor.

Their opinions about naughty children were confirmed when Lee began pelting them with cat biscuits.

Comfort ran in terror as a handful hit her on the head and one landed in her ear. She was grateful he only had little hands.

Pickle and Marmite ran and hid when they saw what had happened to Comfort.

Jacob bravely threw his body over Sky to protect her.

Squeaky Molly began to break the sound barrier with her screams of fright.

Only Trevor thought it a great game, as he ran around with his mouth open, trying to catch the raining biscuits.

'LEE!' Lola shouted as she walked in on the scene, 'what on earth are you doing?' She grabbed the tin from him and began chastising the surprised child.

'But, Mum, you told me to throw some biscuits down,' Lee protested, his bottom lip jutting out and beginning to tremble.

Lola, realising that she might not have been too clear with her instructions, relented, and gently tried to explain. 'What I meant was "put biscuits in the bowls, and place them down nicely for the cats." Not "pelt them like hand grenades!"'

At ten p.m. on the Sunday night, Sally came into the cattery with Sonya.

'Was it worth the stress of going away?' Sally moaned.

Sonya didn't look happy. 'Do you realise I counted over fifty-four phone calls in two days?'

'It can't be helped. You have to realise I run a charity,' Sally retaliated.

'Yes, I realise that. But almost all the calls were stupid niggles from Sarah.'

They both stopped and stared at the immaculate cattery and at the cats, who were milling around looking miserable. Sally was furious as she opened the cupboard door and pulled out baskets and beds, laying them on the floor for the grateful cats. As she worked, her phone rang. It was Sarah, in floods of tears again.

'I can't talk now, Sarah. I have just got home and am very tired. I'll come to the cattery tomorrow morning and we'll talk.' Her voice was calm, holding none of the annoyance she felt.

After the beds were in place, and the cats looked more settled, they went home.

At nine o'clock the next morning a very annoyed Sarah walked into the cattery. She picked up the phone and called Sally.

'Where are you? I expected you here first thing!' she screeched down the phone, her voice shaking in temper. She hung up and set about clearing away the beds. Banging them into the cupboard, the cats ran, terrified, and hid.

An hour later Sally arrived.

'I expected you at nine o'clock!' Sarah raved at her.

'Do you not think I have other work? I had phone calls to catch up with. I'm also exhausted from travelling,' she explained with a cool calm which threatened to explode any minute.

'HOW dare you go on holiday!' Sarah ranted, her eyes blazing. 'I work hard here to keep it clean and you make a mess like this.' She threw her arms about to highlight the disarray of cat beds.

Sally's eyes flashed with temper as she fought to keep it under control. 'No, Sarah. How dare you! It was my first two days off in years. How many days do you work without a break? I work seven a week, even Christmas day. I've told you before, this is a cats' home, NOT a show room. Get out, NOW!'

Sarah froze with surprise.

Sally pointed to the door, her teeth gritted and eyes still flashing. 'I said get OUT!'

With that, Sarah grabbed her bag, which Trevor was just about to wee on, and walked out, slamming the door behind her.

'Oh well,' Sally said, calming down, 'so much for getting help.'

They were so glad to see the back of Sarah.

Chapter Fifteen

'Things are going missing at the shop,' Candy told the cats, a few months after Sarah had left.

'What, you mean a ghost?' Marmite asked bristling.

'Someone's stealing and Sally keeps finding empty bottles of alcohol hidden.'

'What's that?' Twix and Annie asked together.

'It's like catnip; it makes humans daft,' Candy explained, confused at why cats went silly over catnip, or humans over alcohol. She had had a sniff of both, and neither had done much for her.

They knew what catnip was; Sally gave it to them and the new cats; it helped them to settle down.

Trevor, Mathew and Jacob adored catnip. They dribbled on it for ages, making it wet and gooey and then acted daft, rolling around the floor. The females moaned and raised their eyes at their silliness. Some of the girls didn't take to it. Pickle did, but she had to have a sneaky rub when no one was looking. And only then when it was second-hand. She longed to have some new, with no dribble, but her over-protective Mum didn't like her having substances.

'Your Dad rubbed it regularly. He would wobble past singing, "Chill cat"', Marmite told Pickle.

'I don't see what's wrong with catnip,' Pickle said, pushing out her lip and giving her Mum a harsh stare. 'It keeps squeaky Molly quiet.'

It was true; whenever Sally gave her some, the black cat would rub it into her cheeks, then throw herself upside down with her four legs in the air, and stare at the ceiling. No one heard a peep from her for hours.

'Nothing's wrong with it. But alcohol's different. It's not a herb, and can be dangerous to humans,' Candy explained.

'See, Mum, there's nothing wrong with catnip,' Pickle glowered again at Marmite.

'I don't care. You're still not having any. I'm your mother and what I say goes.'

Pickle stood up, and, after flicking a ball at Marmite, went off in a strop. 'I 'ate it 'ere,' she shouted back.

Pickle jumped up on to Bernard and Bertram's shelf. They were her new friends. They liked the young cat and welcomed her visits. She made them smirk with her antics.

Pickle complained about her Mum, while they washed her head and ears to console her.

'Never mind. When we get some, we'll let you have a rub and a dribble on it,' Bernard assured her.

'Only after you two have made it soggy,' she grumbled.

'That's true, but it'll be cool to lie together with our legs in the air,' Bertram grinned at the image. Pickle was slightly cheered by their offer; she curled up with them for the rest of the night.

Once Pickle left, and Marmite had finished batting the ball, Candy continued. She was unwell, but was still adamant that the vet was not examining her.

'Sally and Sonya suspect the manageress, Abbey. But there's no proof. There's a room upstairs in the shop where items are placed to sell elsewhere for the charity. Many of them have disappeared.'

'Like what?' Comfort asked, concerned, 'not cat food surely?'

'No, but other things. A Victorian wedding dress is one of them and some Ray-Ban sunglasses and many others. They were donated by people to help raise money.'

'Well that doesn't sound too bad,' piped up Trevor, not understanding what the fuss was about. If it wasn't cat food what did it matter?

'The items were to be sold to make money for cat food, rent here, and vet bills,' Candy told them. 'Sally has been told that Abbey leaves with bags full of items. And a relative of hers visits and takes more away.'

Trevor nodded, as he could see the problem.

'What a horrible person she sounds. It makes you wonder how she sleeps at night. I guess the catnip helps,' Comfort agreed. 'Candy, why don't you let the vet see you?' she asked concerned.

Candy ignored her. 'Abbey keeps pretending that she doesn't know how to bank the shop takings. Every time Sally adds it up it's not right.'

'Goodness,' exclaimed Marmite, her worry multiplying.

'My Mum constantly worries about money. It's a struggle to keep things going. For someone to steal is devastating. There are so many good, kind and giving people who support the charity. There is always one to spoil things.'

'But why doesn't Sally tell her to go?' Comfort queried.

'She needs to catch her doing it, and even then Abbey may make a feasible excuse. Constant reports from people are not enough. It could make her liable, and be in trouble, to accuse her. It's not easy when you employ someone, whatever they do,' Candy explained.

Sally called from the door, and Candy gradually eased her body from the basket. The cats could see how sad Sally looked as she watched the old dog. They sensed that her time in this world was not long. They also sensed that Sally knew too, and her heart ached at the thought of losing her dear friend.

After she had gone, the cats stayed gathered. They had lots of problems to ponder: the shop, and Candy; also Sally, who, after losing Sarah, was working long hours again. Trying to cram in the work was too much. Not having enough waking hours, she was getting behind.

'Candy said that Sonya was working at the shop, job-sharing with Abbey. At least that's a weight off Sally,' Comfort said.

It was one of those days when Sally, late as usual and in a flap, rushed in with Alice, who now managed the sponsor scheme and often helped at the cattery.

With so many cat problems, Sally's head swam and her heart raced too hard.

One of the charity's good supporters, Rachel, arrived for a visit. Late with the cleaning, Sally was still mopping the floor when she walked in. Rachel walked around looking at the cats and greeting the ones that appreciated a greeting.

'Who's this cat then?' Rachel asked peering at a large ginger that peered mournfully back.

Sally told her that he had been abandoned when his owner had given birth.

Rachel, who had stopped listening, pointed at Trevor. 'What's that one? Why has he got a funny tooth?'

Sally proceeded to explain. Before she had reached the middle of the explanation, Rachel had blanked off.

'Why's this one here?' she asked pointing to another.

Sally, irritated, explained. Rachel moved to the next before she had begun the second sentence.

'Who's this cat? Why's he here?' she asked, reaching out to stroke Mathew.

Sally opened her mouth and closed it again, giving up. 'We're busy today, Rachel, why don't you come back another time?' she offered instead.

Rachel, ignoring her, pointed to Jacob, 'Why's that one here?'

Sally looked at Alice, who was giving an irritated expression with her eyes.

Rachel, who had run out of cats to point at, walked over to Sally and Alice.

'I'm here because I'm cleaning,' Sally quickly said.

Missing the joke, she told them about a cat she once had named Billy. Sally never minded hearing cat stories but when it stretched to a detailed description of his toilet habits and use of the cat flap, it was mildly boring. The story of Billy droned on and on. How he once slept upside down. The food he liked, his adventures in the garden. The way he balanced on a fence one day looking at a neighbour. The meows he produced, with different sound effects.

Rachel demonstrated various cat stances to prove that he actually did them. Both Sally and Alice cooed and laughed in the right places, as Sally attempted to maneuver the mop about Rachel's feet.

She wondered how old Billy had been when he died. It appeared that, after an hour of the story, he was still only two years old, and a long way from death.

Finally, after another hour and a half, he passed away, at sixteen years old.

'Oh that's sad,' Alice and Sally dutifully remarked. Then they both looked horrified to learn that that was in 1962, and Rachel had got another cat.

By the time the story reached the 1970s, Sally's and Alice's, Candy's, and the cats' brain cells had wilted.

Sally still moved the mop from side to side, but was no longer aware of her hands. Eventually, by the 1980s her legs began to buckle, and she sat down. A vivid mental image flashed into her mind of the film *Aeroplane*. A man had hung a rope to commit suicide because the person next to him talked and talked.

By the 1990s, Sally's image changed, she was now running round the farm screaming hysterically, flailing her arms uncontrollably. A van drew up and tied her in a straitjacket and locked her away in an institution. Now she sat staring vacantly out of barred windows, her eyes completely dead and deeply disturbed.

'Did he do a reverse walk into the toilet tray or go in front ways?' she heard herself asking.

Alice who stood behind her was now threatening to burst from suppressed hysteria.

Rachel never noticed the comment; she carried on relaying Duncan's life story. The end of the 1990s saved them, as the cat was still in residence.

The next day was Sunday. It was a homing day, when people came to view the cats. They were always on their best behaviour on a Sunday. Sally and Candy stayed all day. Many ladies also came to 'meet'. While Sally rushed around with a mop and bucket, trying to clean, the ladies would stand having a chat and a cuppa. The cats could tell that Sally got flustered, trying hard to have everything clean for the first visitors.

The lady gang would lift their legs as Sally cleaned around them.

This day she was extra tense. She was tired, near to tears and could not cope. Hearing the ladies' babble she threw down the mop.

'I need help,' she flopped down. 'I'm exhausted.'

The little group stopped talking and stared at her.

'Well you should get yourself some help then,' one of the ladies, Tricia, said.

Sally got up and looked at her cup of coffee. Tricia had not even made Sally one. Without speaking, Sally walked out and went into the feral unit.

'Well, how rude,' Tricia remarked.

Pickle poked her head out from behind her chair and had a quick look around. A blanket that was flopped over it kept her safely hidden.

'I'm bored,' she complained to Marmite who was behind her.

'Not long now, and they should be gone,' Marmite consoled.

Pickle sighed and pushed her paw out. She could just reach Sky's bottom, if she stretched hard enough.

Sky, dozing peacefully with Jacob, felt someone tap her; she lifted her head and opened her eyes to see who it was.

Pickle quickly pulled her head behind the blanket.

Sky, not seeing who could have tapped her, shrugged and settled down again. Closing her eyes, she began to doze.

Pickle stuck out her head again, tapped Sky's bottom a second time, and quickly hid.

Sky felt spooked as she squinted around. Spotting Mathew in the next basket, she decided it must have been him.

'Mathew! will you stop touching my bottom,' she snapped.

'Err,' Mathew turned surprised and looked at her, 'I didn't touch anything.'

'I don't like it. If you do it again I'll bat you.' Sky turned in a huff and shut her eyes.

Pickle, having a great time, pushed out her paw and tapped again. Sky, really cross now, got out of the basket and walked over to Mathew, who had just fallen back into a doze. She batted him around the ears. He was so surprised at the assault, he shook his head and stared at her.

'What was that for?' he asked on the final bat.

'You know exactly what it's for.' Sky stuck her nose in the air, and stomped back to her basket very cross.

Jacob, oblivious to what was happening, groaned as she got back in.

Mathew was confused, thinking that Sky was having a nightmare of some sort. He closed his eyes, but left one lid slightly ajar in case she did it again. He spotted Pickle's paw coming out from behind the blanket and tapping Sky.

Sky flew over to Mathew, with her paw at the ready.

Mathew leapt up. 'It's Pickle!' he shouted.

Pickle stuck out her head giggling.

'Pickle! I might have known!' said Sky, feeling guilty at blaming poor Mathew.

'I'm sorry,' Pickle apologised, not looking sorry at all.

'Huh!' Mathew huffed, and climbed back into his basket, turning his back on Sky and Pickle for the rest of the day.

Ten minutes later, the first people wanting to home a cat came through the door. They looked round at them, or at least the ones they could see. Sally came back into the main unit, still fed up. She pointed out prospective companions for them.

The lady pointed to a black and white tom in a pen. 'I like that one. But he would be better if his patch was the other side.'

The family nodded in agreement. 'Have you any more with different patches?' they enquired hopefully.

Sally, not daring herself to speak in case sarcasm escaped, turned to see another couple who had arrived.

'Have you any grey males?' they asked.

'No, but we have other beautiful cats. It's probably better to choose them by personality rather than colour,' Sally said, attempting to keep her voice level.

'We fancy a grey one,' they stated.

The next potential home came. It was an older lady who walked with a stick.

'Please just look around, and I'll be with you soon,' Sally said, grabbing the mop to finish the floor.

'Have you any kittens?' the older lady asked.

'I don't think a kitten would be advisable. They are very boisterous. With walking difficulties, one could easily trip you up; they constantly get under your feet. They also have a habit of running up legs and sliding down. When your skin is older it does not heal so quickly. Would you not consider an older cat, that would be more company for you?'

'No!' the lady exclaimed, horror masking her face. 'I've had cats all my life. I lost my last one at seventeen years old, and now want a kitten.'

'Then your memory must have dulled as to how lively your cat was when it was a kitten. I know mine has. I'm sorry, but I cannot recommend one for you,' Sally gently explained. 'Cats can live to twenty years old. Do you think when you are a hundred you could manage a cat?'

'I want a kitten and that's that,' the stubborn woman stated.

Sally walked away, thinking how selfish and silly she was. How many young cats had they taken after the owner had died? Or, worse, the family cleared the house, and the cat was abandoned in the garden.

She looked over to the ginger they had recently taken. He had sat on the doorstep of a house for three years after his owner had died. Not knowing how to survive, he was found eating cardboard and drinking oil. How many phone calls had they received from family members, saying that their elderly mother or father could not cope with the kitten they had recently bought for them because it was too lively?

Sally's mobile rang; it was Jane. 'There is an emergency. Someone has just called in: an injured cat,' she told her worriedly.

'But we have no room …'.

'Excuse me,' the man from the first couple interrupted, 'I want to know about this cat?'

'Sorry,' Sally apologised, 'I won't be long.'

The man huffed at her, and stomped off to moan to his wife.

'Excuse me,' said the lady of the second couple. 'Have you any more cats we can see? We cannot see anything inspiring.'

Another couple arrived, followed by two more families. Sally hung up the phone to her Mum with a promise to call her back.

'Have you any kittens?' one of them asked.

'No but we have a cattery full of beautiful cats that are desperate for a home,' she repeated.

They glanced around with distaste and left. They were a young couple, so Sally guessed it was what they called a 'baby substitute'. Youngsters that had moved in together – their first addition being a kitten. A puppy, not being house-trained, was too risky to leave all day. The lone kitten was then left on its own for long hours while they went to work, and possibly in the evening, if they went out. It was very cruel to the kitten that needed stimulation, feeding throughout the day, and company. The kitten usually became depressed and lonely. Of course the couple would never notice as they would not be there. The charity would eventually receive a call from one or the other. Either the lady would be pregnant, or the couple would be splitting up – either way, the kitten or cat had to go.

The last couple was more reasonable. Feeling sorry for the rejected black and white tomcat, they chose him. More people came wanting kittens. It seemed to Sally that, by now, they were all talking at once and making her head spin. Answering questions about the cats, she went from one to the other. The older lady with the stick was still grumbling about wanting a kitten. Sally went to her as she spotted Minnie sitting in her pen.

'I'll have that one,' she pointed with her stick.

'But you don't even know what her personality is like!' Sally pointed out.

'I like the colour, so I'll have her.'

Sally had a mental image of letting the lady go in the pen and Minnie, who always lashed out, tearing her legs.

'She isn't for homing,' she told her instead.

'When will she be ready? I want her.'

'I'm sorry, but it would be irresponsible of us to allow an eighty-year-old lady to have a boisterous kitten.'

The lady's daughter looked annoyed, 'That's discrimination.'

'No, it's not, it's realistic. Do you think Social Services would allow your Mum to adopt a baby? An older cat would enjoy keeping her company, and would be more suitable.'

They left saying they would complain and go elsewhere.

The last potential home, to everyone's delight, chose Squeaky Molly.

'Thank goodness for that,' whispered Trevor.

'Out of ten homes, only two cats went,' Sally moaned to Jane. She told her about Tricia's unkind comment. 'I don't understand why she comes every Sunday, and all she does is wash up. And then makes herself a coffee and stands chatting. There are eighty cats here to care for. I can't manage alone any more. I rush around trying to clean three units, then streams of people turn up, all at once. At least Lola comes some Sundays to help now and again.'

'You must learn, Sally, to be thankful for any help offered. People will never see what you do; only what they do for you. Tricia comes because she believes she is helping. She also donates money to the charity.

'One day, people will come to help with the workload. But for now, just carry on. I know you're tired, but it will get easier. The charity is fast becoming one of the best,' Jane advised. She was always so wise and knowledgeable.

It was true; Sally expected too much. They did not see how hard it was for her: how much she struggled to balance a fast-growing charity, or how difficult it was to make ends meet financially. She did have help. It might only be a few hours here and there, but without that, her work would be harder. She must always remember to thank people.

Glad everyone had gone, the cats could have a long-awaited nap.

'I'm not sure I like the intrusion,' Matthew grumbled, stretching out his legs.

'You slept through most of it,' Comfort laughed, creeping out from behind a chair, with Pickle and Marmite close behind.

165

'Yes, but I kept waking up with the noise. And Sally never gets time for my cuddle on a Sunday.' Leaning his head against the edge of the basket, he gave an enormous tongue-vibrating yawn, and fell asleep.

Pickle was still bored, so she went off to find Annie and Twix. They were skulking in the garden, watching, with relief, the last car drive away.

'Thank goodness they've gone,' Twix exclaimed. 'I was beginning to think that we would never get any peace.'

'Do you fancy bird-juddering, Pickle?' asked Annie, spotting one land in the field nearby.

Pickle's judders, although she had been practising, were still not up to scratch. Not wanting to show herself up, she declined, and sat on a log, to watch the twins.

Winter crept up, and before they knew it, snow threatened again.

'It's my Mum's biggest dread,' Candy told them, one evening. 'Her car, having big wheels, is like skis in the snow and ice. It gets stuck everywhere on the farm. She spends hours digging it out. The road outside was too narrow to park there. Snow meant that she would have to walk the two miles from home. And I won't be able to come with her, as I can't walk very far, especially not in snow.' She shivered, to show her own dislike of it.

'I've never seen snow,' Twix told them, trying to imagine what it was like.

'It's horrible,' Comfort added. 'The pipes freeze, and there's no water, sometimes for days.'

'Yes,' agreed Candy. 'Mum has to carry water containers from home. It will be easier when we have our own premises, and can live on site. Then I can guard the place.' She wobbled her body, to show her responsibility as a dog.

The little group scrutinised her, wondering how she would chase off intruders. But they didn't say this, as it would have hurt her feelings.

'Why doesn't Sally just buy somewhere, then?' Jacob asked.

'I don't understand it myself,' Candy admitted, 'But I heard her say that building societies and banks don't want to lend charities money. She has tried over seventy so far. One agreed, but they expected too much interest in return. Mum is always writing to rich people, in the hope they might help, but no one wants to know. She never gives up, and still looks for suitable places,' Candy told them.

'Oh,' Jacob said, his expression glazing and wishing he'd not asked.

He washed Sky's head, waking her from a deep sleep. She stretched out her legs and bit his nose.

'Do you think we'll move, then?' asked Comfort, with new worries creeping over her. If they did, Flick wouldn't know where to find her.

'I don't know. But I know Mum's desperate for somewhere which can be purpose-built, with adequate facilities.' The old dog, looking gloomy, laid her head on her paw.

Matthew sat close by. He had just woken from his pre-nap. It was a necessary thing before a major nap, after he indulged in a waking nap. So many naps were sufficient for a day. He stood up and stretched out his limbs, before wandering over to a food bowl for a nibble at some biscuits. It was hungry work sleeping. It was too late; Trevor had hoovered up any leftovers.

'Well, really, Trevor, you could have saved me a munch.'

'Sorry, but I was hungry.' He let out a slight belch.

'I'd be careful if I were you. If Sally sees you eating too much, she will worm you again,' Matthew pointed out.

'That's OK; she hides them in tasty food,' he grinned.

Mathew despaired as he walked over to Sally for a cuddle. She scooped him up, giving him a big kiss. He put his paws around her neck and purred contentedly.

Sally was cross, and Matthew helped to calm her. A new lady called Morgan had offered to help with the cleaning.

Sally arranged for her to come along at ten a.m.; after feeding and some of the tidying, the lady had turned up at eight-thirty a.m.

As Sally was running late, Morgan was at the door waiting for her. She walked in, and sneered at the dirty litter trays. When she left, she reported Sally to her friend at the RSPCA, stating that she could not work in a place with dirty toilet trays.

'Well, I will either have to put corks in the cats' bottoms so they don't go in the night, or stay all night cleaning them as they go. What an option,' Sally ranted, angry at the stupid woman.

Her friend laughed, 'Take no notice; people are thick at times.'

Staring at the snarling Minnie, Sally made a decision to take her home. 'I don't think anyone will home you, Minnie,' she told the kitten.

'Bugger off,' Minnie hissed. So that day Minnie went to live with Sally, Candy and Chicken Man.

Candy was none too pleased, as the cat shouted rude remarks to her all the way home, such things as 'baboon face'.

Candy, puppyishly, stuck out her tongue at her.

'Muck mouth,' snarled the kitten, turning her back on Candy, who in turn turned her back on the kitten.

When Sally came back that evening so did a lady looking for a cat. Her eyes focused on Jacob, who was squashed in his usual spot with Sky. She was purring and digging his tummy in contentment. Jacob, enduring the ten needles, washed Sky's head, they looked so happy.

'How old is he?' the lady asked.

'He's young, but I don't know exactly; he was a stray.'

'Oh, so you don't know how old then?' the lady prompted.

Sally, who had had a rough day, wanted to reply: 'We got him, but left his birth certificate under a bush', but she refrained from doing so.

'We can only tell you that he is a young cat, probably about three or four. Does it matter?'

'I want a ginger.'

'He loves Sky, so it would be lovely for them to go together,' Sally suggested hopefully.

'Goodness, I don't want the fat one!' said the lady before adding, 'I would take them all if I could.'

'Except the blacks, black and whites, tabbies and tortoishells, not to mention the overweight ones,' Sally smiled, trying to make it sound like it was a joke.

'How sad it would be if we chose our friends and family that way. Only accepting those with certain colour eyes and hair. Dismissing the people who are overweight,' she added, scrutinising the none-too-thin lady. 'Sky is a beautiful, loving and gentle cat.'

'Sorry, but I want a ginger, and she looks old.'

'We will not separate them,' Sally told her firmly. 'I would not take you away from your family either.'

'They don't understand,' the woman objected.

'Of course they understand. They have intelligence,' Sally snapped. How I wish I were tolerant like my mum, she thought.

The lady was not pleased. Not liking anything other than gingers, she left, thankfully, because Sally had decided she was not having one anyway.

Sky and Jacob felt relief; they had taken years to find each other; to be forced apart would be unbearable.

Soon, Candy reported Sally had sacked Abbey from the shop for swearing in front of customers. Sally refused to pay her last week's wages. She used them for the funds, to claw back some of the missing money. However, a furious Abbey arranged for one of her friends to go to the shop, pretending to deliver something for Sally. The person stated that two hundred pounds had been left outstanding on the item. The volunteer who was serving gave over the shop takings. So Abbey got her money, and the charity lost out. The volunteer also left the charity.

'That's stupid,' Trevor looked horrified, 'I wouldn't hand my biscuits over for anyone.'

'We know that,' said Mathew, giving him a knowing stare.

Chapter Sixteen

After Sally had re-advertised the cattery position, two carefully chosen ladies came for interviews. Again, many people had applied, but not many of them seemed to know anything about cats.

The first lady was called Sylvia. She seemed so willing that Sally thought her ideal. Neither the cats nor Candy liked her.

'She just doesn't smell right,' exclaimed Matthew.

'She seems pleasant enough,' added Sky, who was such a gentle cat, and loved everyone.

While Sally and Sylvia chatted away, Pickle took a long sniff of her bag. Lifting her nose, she allowed her jaw to hang open.

Trevor watched her. 'Shall I wee in it?' he offered. Being fond of young Pickle, he was always ready to help her in any way he could. 'I can do a really long spray if you want.'

'I don't think that's a good idea,' Pickle said, clasping her teeth together again.

Shrugging, Trevor went back to his biscuits. He had eaten his wet food in record time today, but he did that every day, finishing just as the others were still giving their food a sniff. Biscuit elevenses were Trevor's second biggest event of the day. Crunching the last one he looked again. Having forgotten about Pickle and the bag, he was surprised to see her still lurking. 'You sure you don't want me to spray?'

'This lady doesn't smell good,' Pickle shared.

She looked at Trevor, but he had wandered over to the other side of the room, to check everyone else's biscuit bowls.

The next lady that came for the position was Leonie. She was pleasant and jolly. Having previously worked in a veterinary practice, she was ideal.

It was agreed that the two would job-share, as they each only wanted a certain number of hours. Between them they would cover six mornings a week. Sally would cover the evenings, and Sunday, homing day.

They started working the following week. How grateful Sally was to have time for other charity work, which she was struggling to manage.

Sylvia was OK, so the cats stopped worrying. She worked hard at the cleaning, and fussed them nicely. That night, when Sally came to feed them, she was still there.

'Are you spring cleaning?' she asked suspiciously, remembering Sarah, as she glanced apprehensively at the baskets and clawing posts. They had not been moved so she relaxed.

Sylvia made them a cup of tea, and they sat chatting for a while, before Sally started the feeding. It became a pattern that, on the three days she worked, Sylvia stayed waiting for Sally.

The cats sensed that Sally did not like it, and was confused as to why someone would start work at eight a.m. and still be there at six p.m.

Sally missed the quality time spent alone with them. Sylvia was intruding on that, but Sally dismissed it, assuming that Sylvia might be lonely, as she lived alone.

The cats were confused too; they did not take to her. Sylvia's vibrations were strange, but they could not work out why.

Trevor thought them all silly. 'I think she's a nice lady. She loves hearing about my adventures, and doesn't mind that I follow her chatting.'

'Guess not,' stated Jacob. 'At least we get some peace while you're chatting to her.'

Leonie was OK though; they got on with her. Even the timid ones relaxed and accepted her.

'My Mum's confused about why the volunteers are leaving,' Candy told them one day, a few months after the new ladies had started.

'We know why,' Jacob told her, 'Sylvia is so rude to them.'

'We don't understand why,' the twins said. 'We liked the last lady that left. She pulled fluffy snakes for us to play with.'

'But why do they tell my Mum different excuses for leaving then? Why don't they tell her that Sylvia is nasty to them? Mum has rung and asked if there are any problems.' Candy wrinkled her brow, and twisted her black rubbery nose.

'I guess they don't want to cause trouble,' Comfort surmised. 'Or maybe they think Sally knows.'

'Sylvia is so friendly and nice to some people. Maria and Jane never have problems with her. I wonder why?' Marmite puzzled.

'I know why,' Mathew said having just woken up from a nap.

They looked at him waiting for an answer.

'It's obvious. They are closer to Sally, so would tell her.'

'Oh,' said Candy, 'I get it. Poor Mum, at this rate she'll have no volunteers left.'

'Sylvia absolutely hates Leonie though. I hear her telling Sally all sorts of things about her, none of them good.'

'What are we going to do?' Comfort was worried.

'That's easy,' Trevor said, having wandered over after giving the empty bowls their fourth lick.

'How?' Pickle asked, scratching her ear and studying her claw. She nibbled off some debris, and received a clump from Marmite for being disgusting.

'I'll tell her. She listens to me.'

Candy looked doubtful. 'You tried that before, and she didn't understand. What makes you think this time will be different?'

'Of course she'll understand. I'll try a different approach and keep speaking until she does,' Trevor reassured confidently.

'Well... I'm not so sure,' Mathew looked doubtful, before having one of his famous yawns, which scrunched his forehead into deep lines. 'I try to talk to humans all the time, but they never understand me.'

'That's because you don't know how to yowl; you only ever manage a barely audible croak,' Trevor dismissed.

'Mmmm…' Mathew mused, 'maybe.' He turned a few times, before flopping back on to his cushion.

'Go for it, Trevor,' Comfort said. 'What harm can it do? Sally is due in tomorrow morning so it's your big chance.'

The next morning, when Sally arrived, Trevor prepared himself for his big moment, while the others looked on encouragingly. It was important to get things right and not lose face.

Eyes bore into him as he organised himself. He began by coughing to clear his throat of a fur ball. Sticking out his tongue as far as it would reach, he rolled the corners into a half tube. Lowering his body to a crouch position, Trevor stretched his neck as far as possible. Being a long, thin cat, his neck stretched rather a long way. With his chin almost scraping the floor, he began to clear.

Satisfied, he sat bolt upright, and, using his best most pronounced yowl, began to explain to Sally, who simply ignored him.

After a while, she looked down at him with annoyance. 'For goodness' sake, Trevor, will you be quiet?' she said, covering her ears with both hands to demonstrate the annoyance. 'It feels like a cheese grater is attacking my ear drums.'

Trevor, encouraged that Sally was listening, continued to yowl. He followed her around the cattery screeching and even ducking with her, as she dipped to scoop out the litter trays.

The others watched, willing her to understand, until Candy shook her head despondently and sighed.

'It's no good. I guess my Mum will just have to find out herself. We can't help her.'

'We have a potential manageress at the charity shop. A young lady has come forward who is confident she can manage the position. I'm giving her a trial to see how she copes. Her name is Kelly, and I really like her,' Sally told Jane over the phone.

'That's great news. It'll certainly help you out, if you're sure she can do the job,' Jane was pleased.

'She has no experience, but is eager to learn,' Sally enthused.

Sally liked Kelly, and felt that everyone deserved a chance. She was young but with guidance, would cope.

The cats had not seen Sonya for a long time. One night she came to the cattery with Sally. With them, they brought a bottle of wine and a take-away. It was Sally's birthday, and what better way to celebrate than with the cats?

'How are things going with Sylvia?' Sonya asked.

'Well, the loss of volunteers is difficult,' Sally confessed. 'I'm a bit suspicious, as it's only the ones who work with Sylvia who leave. The only one left working with her is Leonie, on a Wednesday, and Sylvia hates her. The rest of the time, she's alone. Every Wednesday, a new disaster seems to happen, which is very odd.

'Sylvia is extremely supportive, and helps in so many different ways. Nothing is too much trouble. Even taking the cats to the vets at odd hours. I can't tell you how much stress that has eased from me. I don't think I could manage without her,' Sally fell quiet and thoughtful.

'What's wrong, Sally?' Sonya asked, seeing her friend's expression.

'I don't know, something about her makes me uneasy. I can't explain what it is. But there is something odd about Sylvia.'

Sonya walked over to the twins and Pickle, who were crouched in a circle with their heads together. She picked up a long, fluffy string with a toy mouse on the end, and began to pull it along the floor. The delighted youngsters sprang into a line, lowering their front halves and sticking their bottoms into the air. After a few wiggles they rushed forward and chased it.

Pickle, being the biggest, nudged the smaller two out of the way to attempt a dinosaur followed by a perfect crab. She was elated, as she had not faltered in the moves. She stopped chasing and, leaving the other two, ran off to tell Marmite.

Marmite was having a bath when Pickle pounced on top of her. 'For goodness' sake, Pickle, you made me jump.'

'Mum, Mum... I've got something to show you. Watch me, Mum... watch!'

Marmite was in mid-flow, and did not want to lose her place, so was not happy with the interruption. But to please her daughter she obliged.

Sadly, Pickle's moves were a disaster, muddling a dinosaur with a crab, and falling in a heap on top of Sky. She was in a deep sleep, when attacked, leaping up so fast that she knocked Jacob out of the basket. He was shocked as he thudded on his back. Quickly flipping over, he flew into the air, spinning in a semi-circle, with his legs sticking out.

Marmite tried desperately not to laugh. Mathew, for once not asleep, felt sorry for Pickle, who looked mortified. He went over and rubbed noses with her.

'Come on, cheer up. Let's go to the corner and practice. If you say you did it perfectly once you can do it again.'

'Thank you, Mathew. That's very kind of you,' Marmite smiled.

Jealous Trevor followed too. He wanted to show that his moves were the best.

'What about the other girl?' Sonya asked.

'It seems she's making a lot of mistakes. Sylvia tells me that she doesn't fill the water bowls, and at times she's forgotten to feed the cats in pens, and has let them out when they're not ready. Apparently she's also rude to people, losing us many homes, and is always moaning about me.'

'That's terrible,' Sonya exclaimed. 'I hope you tell her off. In fact you should get rid of her.'

'Well that's the thing. I've had discreet words with Leonie. She's adamant that she hasn't done these things. I've even been up to check while she's here. Nothing ever appears out of order.'

'That's odd,' Sonya puzzled, coming back over with Trevor tucked under her arm. He was not pleased, as he was just in the middle of showing Pickle his snake.

'Sylvia has told Maria, and another lady, Irene, the same about Leonie; and they think I should sack her too.'

'What stops you, then?'

'Admittedly, she's a slow worker. In fact I've never known anyone take four hours to clean nine pens, especially with volunteers to help her. But, generally, Leonie seems OK. After what happened to me with the other group, I've learned never to listen to gossip. Unless I catch her out, I have no proof.'

'Mmmm,' Sonya rubbed Trevor's belly and chest.

Forgiving the interruption, he lay on her lap, purring loudly, with his legs stuck in the air.

'Trevor!' Jacob exclaimed, after settling back down and calming his heart. 'You can be so embarrassing at times.'

'Good job she didn't have to clean the cattery alone, like you did, before going to the shop,' Sonya laughed.

It had been a week since Candy had visited the cattery, when she came in with Sally. They had missed her dreadfully, and longed for news of the outside world. However, she did not look well as she plodded down the aisle and sank into a basket. Not even the blanket was rucked by Candy's long nose.

'Something's not right,' Comfort whispered to Marmite.

Sally was so quiet that she hardly spoke to the cats.

'Candy, what's wrong?' Sky asked concerned.

'I don't feel good. Mum has been trying to give me tablets, but I keep biting her. She took me to the vet's again. But I bit him again too.'

'Oh Candy, they may be able to make you well,' Comfort told her, hating to see the dog suffering.

'They can't make me well, I know that.' The old dog looked sadly into her blanket.

Jacob's head snapped round to where Sally was making a phone call. He heard what she said and swallowed. Comfort and Marmite heard too.

Sally had her head turned away, and Jacob guessed that it was to hide her tears from the dog. He looked at Candy, who was staring back at him, her eyes full of sadness and fear. She knew, as he did, that it was the end for her. He lowered his gaze, emotion rippling in his chest.

The vet turned up a few hours later, and Sally went to Candy. She knelt beside her and gently kissed and stroked the dog's head.

'It's OK,' she told her, 'You'll be fine. Your old Mum will be waiting for you, Candy. I'm going to miss you so much, but I've got to let you go...' Sally stopped speaking; she was unable to go on.

Candy looked at her, defeated and beaten; she knew it was time. She was tired, and her life had been long and hard.

Tears streamed down Sally's face as she nodded to the vet, who walked forward with a long needle.

'Cand... Candy...'

The dog lifted her head in surprise. It was her first Mum calling her. She looked around trying to see her, but couldn't. She felt the prick of the needle go into her paw, but took no notice. The excitement of her Mum's voice dulled the pain. Then there she was, holding out her arms and smiling. Candy leapt from the basket, wagging her tail and spinning in happy circles, whimpering with excitement.

Her body no longer hurt; she was young and able to move easily. She ran to Sally and the cats to introduce them. How shocked she was to see Sally cuddling a brown and tan dog. Its head was forward and its body limp. She scooped the dog on to her lap, sobbing and kissing her head.

'Come on sweetheart, it's time to go,' her old Mum said, smiling sympathetically at Sally.

Sally stayed for over an hour, rocking the body, unable to speak. The vet had long since gone, leaving her alone with her grief.

The cats sat near by, feeling the loss.

'I'll miss her,' Trevor confessed, before diving into a bowl of chicken.

'So will I.' Comfort's voice was choked with emotion. 'I miss them all.'

'You've still got me.' Marmite nudged her and began to wash her head, trying to ease the sadness which she knew her friend felt.

Chapter Seventeen

It was many months later that Sally was working and looking very pensive. 'Sweeping the floor and nursing are hard work,' she told Mathew, as she lugged him around with her.

Deep in a trance, he did not acknowledge the comment. He purred contentedly, streams of his dribble running from his lips and down Sally's neck. His claws were digging in her skin. She lifted the needles to give herself relief, before calling Jane on her phone.

'Items are being taken from the shop without being paid for again. I feel so let down,' she told her Mum.

'What are you going to do?' Jane asked, her voice sounding as devastated as Sally felt.

'I've informed the volunteers and Kelly I'm aware of it. So let's hope it resolves itself. How can people take from animals?' Sally asked. 'It is not me they are hurting, but them.'

'Do you know who it is?' Jane asked.

'Yes. I lost a gold ring in the shop. I asked Kelly to keep an eye out for it, but it never turned up. I mentioned months later how odd it was that no nice jewellery had been given for some time. The next day Kelly gave me a small box with gold in it. She said it had come in that day. Inside was my gold ring. I guess she had taken the jewellery home and then got worried when I had noticed. She must have forgotten that it was my ring. Another of the rings inside had her initials on. So she took that too. It was a man's ring, so I know it wasn't her own.

'To confirm my suspicion, I arranged for someone to hand in a gold ring to her as a donation. It disappeared. Soon afterwards, I was working upstairs late one night, when Kelly came in. She took some items and left. I took a photo with my phone, but never confessed I'd seen her. I asked the next day if she had ever been into the shop at night and she swore she never had.

'There's more proof than that. It's terrible, when I gave her the chance of the job, and supported her so much. Kelly has handed in her notice, feeling uncomfortable with the situation,' Sally finished.

The door opened, and Chicken Man walked into the cattery. Mathew looked up, startled at the interruption.

'Sally, we need to talk; as you're always working, it's difficult at home.'

She rang off the phone to her Mum. The nosier cats twisted their ears, because he looked so serious.

'It's Chicken Man,' hissed Pickle making sure she was hidden close by to listen.

Sally put down the broom and sat on Pickle's chair, positioning Mathew on her lap.

Not happy, he sprang off and looked around for his cushion. 'It's disappeared,' he griped. 'It's probably been rudely snatched and has gone in the washing yet again.' He felt cross, and most put out. Looking back at Sally's lap, after a short think, he jumped back on.

'I don't want to move,' Chicken Man was saying, sitting opposite.

Trevor, not to be outdone by Mathew, ran up and leaped on to his lap. He began cleverly dig-dagging, with four paws.

This was an advanced move for a cat, and took great precision. It entailed four paws' being placed in the correct position. Even a millimetre out could cause an overbalance or wobble. The front paws in place began to dig and dag. Once a rhythm was established, the back paws joined in. Swapping paws systematically was essential. Front right with back left and visa versa. Trevor, satisfied that his paws met perfection, closed his eyes in concentration.

Pickle stared out from under the chair. When everyone had gone she would try this. Her crabs and dinosaurs were coming along great. She had done four now, without toppling once. She felt more than ready to try something more complicated.

'You know it's been my dream for years. I've suggested so many potential sites for a shelter to you. Every time I try to discuss them, you find fault and walk away. You're adamant that you'll not move.

Now I've found the ideal property, and you're still finding fault. I won't be put off this time,' Sally was saying.

'But Sally, the property's a heap. The house is falling down and needs a colossal amount of work. Our house is almost perfect, and the mortgage is paid,' he added to the carefully planned speech he had obviously gone over many times.

Sally looked at her shoe. Despite her optimism and stubbornness, it was a huge project.

The land for the shelter consisted of dilapidated barns and stables. When she had gone to view it, she found the yard used for dreadful animal abuse. Pathetic dogs looked out from steel cages. No bedding was offered on the concrete floor; it was the middle of winter.

A cat ran around, obviously used for breeding, in search of her kittens. The vile man had grabbed her by the back legs and thrown her into a metal box, slamming the lid. What she saw sickened and upset her. Sally reported the cruelty, but nothing was done.

The site itself required a complete rebuild or demolition, and a fresh start. Chicken Man was right: the cottage attached was dilapidated. The heating and hot water did not work adequately; the place was filthy and uncared-for. Water leaked in from everywhere, and the roof was bowed, threatening to cave in at any minute.

The interior of the house had depressing brown walls. Horrible hunting ornaments littered the place. Even a deer's head had hung dismally from the wall in a small hallway, making Sally shudder.

The atmosphere in the house was one of death and gloom. Used to more comfort, it was not a home she would have chosen. Their lovely house sold, and the equity ploughed into a ramshackle site. Still, she thought, her usual optimism returning, 'I'll make do; the charity needs an adequate rescue centre.'

The atmosphere could be changed from the dark cloud that hangs over it to a happy place full of love and hope.

'I'm sorry; I cannot carry on the way I am. This place has no proper facilities. We need an isolation unit, somewhere for kittens, and a feral unit. Plus, I need to live on the premises. Making do is no good. I either move with or without you.'

He stood up and walked to the door, turning before leaving. 'Then I have no choice or say in it.'

Sally kept her eyes diverted to Mathew. After he left she stayed there for a long time. Had she just ended her relationship?

'Are Jacob and Sky married?' asked the twins.

'Yes,' Pickle told them, very knowing, while giving Twix a back kick and biting his front paw at the same time. All three were feeling fed up, having no game to play. They had suggested several to each other and none had gripped as yet.

'We need new ones,' Twix sighed; releasing himself from Pickle he put his head on his paw. He batted a piece of paper with the other.

'I know one,' Pickle said. 'I've been working on it for ages.' It was a fib, as the idea had just come to her.

'What?' The twins felt excited. Pickle came up with good ones at times.

'Well...' She recalled the memory of the time Trevor had been a ghost, scaring poor Summer half to death. 'We could drag some white cloth from the rag bin and put it over our heads, then creep up on the others and pretend to be ghosts.'

'That's daft,' said Annie, sinking deflated and letting out a sigh.

'No, it's not.' Pickle told them about Trevor's ghost. They giggled as she acted out the moves to enhance her story.

'Okay, let's give it a go,' Twix agreed, once Pickle had finished.

They wandered over to the rag bin, and Twix, being the boy, leapt in. Sinking his head amongst the material, he hooked out a very suitable white piece. Flicking it over the edge, he stuck over his head to make sure it landed OK. Satisfied, he dipped again, and found two more pieces.

Once his task was complete, he jumped down to join the girls. Annie lifted the corner of one piece of rag, while Pickle pushed her head under.

They giggled as she walked in a circle. 'Wooo... wooo...' she wooed.

Annie did the same for Twix, who was really enjoying himself.

'Who shall we scare first?' he asked.

'What about the new cats?' Pickle suggested. 'There's a Mum and kittens in pen six.'

Thinking it a good idea, they went off to the pen. It was a difficult journey, as they could not see properly, and kept bumping into things. Arriving the short distance, they hid, one on each side. Annie stood and watched, giggling, as she had a mental image of the Mum and kittens springing into the air at the sight of two ghosts, or fainting as Summer had done.

They were so disappointed when it did not go to plan. The kittens, at the learning stage, were used to seeing new things and absorbed every detail. They blinked at the white heads wooing at them. The mother became cross at the distraction, because she was trying to feed and wash her kittens. She got up and strolled petulantly to the pen door. Sticking out her paw through the wire, she batted Pickle and Twix on the head and hissed. Satisfied, she went back to her babies.

'Well that didn't work,' Twix huffed. Discarding his cloth, he batted a strand of loose cotton hanging from the edge. 'Your games are silly,' he told Pickle, who felt so upset that she went off to see Bernard and Bertram. They didn't think her game silly, as they geffuffed while she demonstrated the details.

Later that day, a new cat arrived. He was a large black and white male, named Sylvester. He had been living on the streets for many years. His coat was filthy and full of gravel. Stray cats never washed themselves. Their main priority was food; if they were not fed, they neglected their coats.

A very irate man had reported the stray, as he was trying to get into his house, frightening his own cat.

'He's hungry, possibly starving. Could you not feed him?' Sally suggested when taking the phone call.

'Feed him!' the man shouted, appalled. 'I want him gone. If I feed him it will encourage him.'

'He's already encouraged by hanging around your house. If you were cold and starving to death, what would you do? Because I'm guessing you would break in somewhere to get food. If you feed him he won't come inside to steal,' Sally advised. 'It'll make it easier for us to trap him if you feed him at a certain time. Otherwise we could be running about for weeks trying to find his location.'

'No, I won't feed him. I want the cat gone; it's not my problem,' he snapped.

'Whose problem is it then? Someone has abandoned the cat, and he is obviously suffering the consequences. I hope for your sake you never starve, because it's a horrible and painful death.' How selfish people were, with no compassion for a starving animal, Sally thought.

She tried to check herself, and give more of an explanation, instead of losing her temper. 'The cat is frightened, hungry and scared. People have probably shouted at him, chased and thrown things. We have to gain his trust to catch him. We cannot run round the streets for days in hopes of grabbing him. It will be almost impossible without your co-operation.'

The man slammed down the phone in disgust. As a consequence, it had taken weeks to trap the cat because he was never at the same place for long. His long rampage for food took him over a wide radius of distance. Once caught, Sylvester was found to have damaged ears and a terrible leg injury, not to mention the malnutrition that could have been prevented by the man who reported him.

'His leg was broken, and had reset itself crooked. The cat had been in excruciating pain, having had to walk on it to find food. No doubt he was someone's abandoned kitten,' Sally said sadly.

'What will happen to him?' Sylvia asked.

'I guess the leg will need removing,' Sally surmised.

The vet confirmed that there was no way of fixing it. Too damaged, the back leg was amputated. Sylvester also had broken teeth, needing a dental operation, and his ears were infested with mites.

'Another one thousand pounds,' Sally sighed.

Sylvia kindly transported the cat to the vet in the morning and collected him the next day. He was put on cage-rest while he recovered. Although frightened, it was obvious he was a loving, gentle cat. Despite the pain he chirped at the females, but felt threatened by the toms.

He took to Pickle straight away, calling out to her to come and chat. 'It's so lonely in here.'

So Pickle, feeling very sorry for him, sat and chatted. 'Why are you in such a small cage?' she asked.

'I've had my leg cut off,' Sylvester answered worriedly. 'I heard them say that I had to stay in here for a few weeks.'

Pickle cringed. 'Does it hurt?'

'It does, but I've lived for a long time with pain. This is nothing compared to when I first injured it. It's strange, though, 'cos I can feel my missing toes and claws.'

'How odd!' Pickle tried to see the place where the missing leg was, but he was lying on it. 'From here you look like you still have a leg,' she told him.

'I've such an itch on my cheek and neck. I can't scratch it. It is driving me crazy. I want to scream,' he told her frustrated.

'If you weren't in a cage I'd scratch it for you,' she offered unhelpfully.

At that moment Sally walked over with his food. Because of his ordeal, she served him chicken, which he gobbled in seconds. Pickle watched as Sally knelt before the cage and put her hand to the cat's nose. He gave a hiss and pushed himself backwards with fear, scared that the woman would hurt him.

'It's OK,' Sally cooed and moved her fingers to his cheek.

Sylvester forgot his nerves, as Sally scratched his head and neck.

'Ohhhh, Ooooo…' Sylvester cried in pleasure. He wiggled his bandaged stump, imagining that he was scratching himself, moving his head to make sure that all the itchy bits were accounted for.

How strange, Pickle thought as she watched. Sally must have heard our conversation.

'I bet that's been itching for a long time, hasn't it?' Sally grinned at him.

'You bet,' he answered, stretching his neck towards the ceiling. 'For years. It's wonderful!' Lots of dried skin and gravel fell from his fur. It took some time before he was satisfied.

'I guess people don't realise that three-legged cats need scratching on the parts they can't reach.'

'They certainly don't,' Sylvester agreed, his head rotating in large circles.

'I heard that there's a new manageress at the charity shop,' Comfort told them, as they gathered in the garden. She gave a stifled yawn, wiggled her tail and laid her head on a log.

'What's she like?' Marmite asked, resting her head back on her friend's belly.

'Sally told Jane that she's excellent and very experienced. It seems that she has finally got it right at last. She's honest, caring and handles things wonderfully. Jane predicted that Pam would turn out to be a loyal and trusted friend.'

'I'm pleased,' Mathew grinned, stretching his legs and squeezing his toes together. He laid his head on Marmite's back legs.

The movement disturbed Trevor, who gave a small protesting yowl, as his head was on Mathew's flank. 'Well, hopefully, we won't get any more shop worry.'

They nodded before sinking back into their own world of dreams.

Pickle, still keeping Sylvester amused, shot up, startling him.

'The mop's out,' she yelled. She spotted Twix and Annie darting in from the garden. Riding the mop was a game they loved. Sally pulled it along the floor, while the three of them dived on for a ride. It was even more fun jumping from a shelf as it passed.

Once on top, the mop could be killed by biting at the loose strands and ripping them. If it was stationary, a good back kick usually helped kill it. Sally was forever moaning about how many mops she bought.

At one time, all three of them got on the mop and rode the full length of the room. Well, they were sort of on it. Annie was at the bottom, Twix on top of her, and Pickle on top of them both. Pickle's legs hung over both their heads and bodies.

Mop-smacking was another usual activity in the cattery, if one was having a bad day. Giving the mop a harsh smack helped crossness to subside. For instance, when Mathew's cushion was removed to be washed, he went to the mop. Standing in the corner, the large cat smacked it at least fourteen times.

'Naughty mop, bad mop,' he chanted while batting.

Pickle was more often mop-smacking than any of the rest, particularly when her moves went wrong.

A new mop was brought out that day, as the old one had only one strand left.

From Sally's conversations with Sylvia, the cats learned that plans were going ahead for Sally to buy the property that would become the new Shelter.

'I'm not going,' Comfort announced at their evening bath.

'Why not? It sounds so much nicer than here,' Jacob reasoned.

'Well I agree with Comfort,' Sky nodded, giving Jacob his bat around his ears, before biting the tips and nibbling them. 'It will be frightening moving. I like it here, now that I have got used to it.' Biting and nibbling finished, she washed the sore ears.

'I need to be here to wait,' Comfort said.

'For Flick?' Marmite said looking dreamy, 'how sad.'

'He'll come; he promised,' Comfort told them decisively.

'But Comfort, it's been so long. If he was coming, he would have, by now,' Trevor said gently.

Comfort did not answer. She went into the garden to stare longingly at the car park. The emotion at the back of her throat was so large that it threatened to burst. 'Oh Flick, where are you?' she said out loud.

Trevor followed her, and washed her face, to offer some understanding.

Chapter Eighteen

The black mother cat and five kittens that arrived a few weeks later were pitiful. Everyone was shocked when they saw her. The mother had had some chemical thrown over her. Her skin hung from deep wounds that blistered and bled. One kitten must have been in the line of fire, as it was scalded too.

They named the cat Elsa. She was a fabulous Mum who washed her babies intently, taking care of their every need. The wounds, after being bathed and having cream applied, looked marginally better. Her face had taken the brunt of the assault.

Elsa was a cheerful soul, purring and chirping at anyone who spoke to her. Not bitter or angry with humans even though one had inflicted such horrible abuse.

'What adorable babies,' Marmite cooed as she went to see Elsa in her pen.

Elsa looked up, pride glowing from her burnt features. 'Yes, they are adorable, aren't they?' she purred and bent her head to lick them.

Marmite felt sad; she knew that the black kittens had little chance of a home. There were too many more desirable colours in foster homes; the charity had over sixty in care. She refrained from saying this.

The weather was remarkably hot again. But then it was July, they reasoned, which was usually a hot month. The windows of the cattery, and the back door, were left open. The cats flaked out in the garden, grateful when the night air cooled.

How they missed Candy, telling them information! They listened in the evening when Sally talked to Sylvia. This was OK but, without the dog explaining in animal language, it sometimes became terribly muddled.

Sally was due to move to the new property within weeks. Comfort was worried, and could not be pacified.

'If Flick comes, I'm sure someone will tell him where we are,' Mathew consoled her, after hearing the story quietly whispered by Trevor.

'But I hear it's miles away,' Comfort objected dismally.

'I've walked miles before, and with a broken leg,' Sylvester shouted from his cage.

'I completed whole marathons in one day,' Trevor informed them, 'I'm sure that Flick will do the same to find you.'

'We can tell goat; then if Flick comes, she can direct him with her horn,' Marmite suggested helpfully. It was a stupid idea, because goat would have no clue where they were. But it calmed Comfort slightly.

Although Sally was outwardly friendly with Sylvia, she was becoming increasingly more suspicious of her. It seemed that Leonie could do nothing right. Every day Sylvia gave her a rundown of more incidents.

Sally did not take the complaints lightly, but she had yet to prove any of them.

'She was swearing at a person who was a potential home,' Sylvia reported that day.

The cats looked at each other. None of them had heard rude words. Sally had no doubt that there was some truth in the accusations, but she suspected that the truth had been somewhat twisted, into something more sinister.

Sylvia also had become incredibly possessive. If any of the volunteers, or rather one of the few who were left, called Sally, Sylvia demanded to know why.

'I've told people that you're busy, they mustn't interrupt you.'

It was the anger in her voice that worried Sally.

'But I want people to come to me. It doesn't matter how busy I am. I'm always available to talk,' she protested worriedly.

Sylvia didn't look pleased at this answer. 'Leonie needs to be sacked. She let four cats out the other day. Something terrible is going to happen, you mark my words.'

'But I asked her about that, and she said it's not true,' Sally reasoned. 'Without proof, I can't sack someone. You keep telling me you don't want me to confront her on the issues you tell me about. How can I deal with them if I'm not supposed to know? I cannot just sack someone without good reason,' Sally told her.

The cats agreed they had not seen any of the incidents which Leonie was accused of.

'What if it gets worse?' Mathew worried. 'Every time Sylvia reports something it's more disastrous than the last.'

'Yes, but they have not happened. They're make-believe,' Comfort justified.

'I have a niggle,' he told them, yawning, before his head fell forward in sleep.

Sally, stressed with the potential move and work overload, put her thoughts to one side for now. There were too many other things to contend with. It was just a jealousy thing; she did not worry too much.

'Could I offer Gus a home?' Sylvia asked Sally on the phone one day. 'I'm so taken with him.'

'Of course,' Sally laughed, 'I know you love him.'

The cats had only recently met Gus, a fluffy ginger, as he had been moved from the isolation unit to the main unit earlier in the week. He did not get on well with the others, but related to Sylvia who spent a great deal of time with him.

'You'll need a home visit. I know it's strange as you work at the cattery, but it's just a formality, and I can't visualise any problems,' Sally assured her.

'That's OK, I expect that.'

Home visit complete, Gus went home with Sylvia a few days later.

'Well she can't be that bad,' Trevor decided, 'if she fell in love with him.'

Comfort nodded thoughtfully in agreement.

Both Sylvester and Elsa were charming cats. They were soon freed to join the others. Sylvester adapted with ease to his disability. He hopped around, and even managed to climb on to shelves and up the side of pens. He rejoiced at his new life, food came regularly, and there was always a cosy bed for him to sleep on. He painstakingly cleaned his dishevelled fur, just as the other cats had once done, washing away the rejected stray days and bringing new hope into their lives.

Now that her kittens were older, Elsa was spayed. Her burns had healed, but no fur grew over the ugly scars. Some people who visited cringed or laughed at the sight of her. This hurt Elsa dreadfully. Sally reprimanded them for their ignorant behaviour. A few people recoiled, blanking off, not wanting to believe such cruelty existed.

The burnt kitten had luckily healed, with no signs of scarring. The kittens had been vaccinated, and were now charging around the unit without a care in the world.

Pickle, Twix and Annie loved to play with them. They were great fun, and so entertaining. Hide and seek was the favourite, especially as the kittens did not know that they were playing. One of them hid behind a chair or post. As a kitten passed, they leapt out on it. The small kitten, petrified, would jump and twist into the air, landing with its fur bushed up and claws out, ready for attack, spitting and hissing to frighten the enemy. This amused them, seeing something so small becoming so threatening.

The older cats did not like the disturbance.

'They're so boisterous,' complained Comfort. 'I was lifting my tail to wash it the other day, and there was one hanging on the end. I wondered why it was so heavy. As I lifted it, the kitten flipped off and flew through the air. It's a good job it landed on Sky, or it might have been seriously hurt,' she grumbled.

'Everyone lands on Sky,' Marmite giggled.

'Yes,' said Sky, 'it could have had my eye out, flying through the air like that.'

'I agree,' said Trevor, 'They're such a nuisance. It had taken me months to work out how to remove the lid from the biscuit tin. I finally managed the other day. I looked away for a second to check that no one had seen, and didn't notice one bury itself in the tin. It gave me a real start when a black head popped out. I had to go and lie down, because my heart was pounding so hard that I felt faint. I could have bitten off its head.' He was none too pleased. 'I got no biscuits, either, as Leonie heard the commotion and confiscated them.'

They shook their heads and tutted.

'Serves you right,' laughed Jacob.

'Well, that's nothing,' Mathew griped. 'I was washing my belly for ages the other day. I was completely stressed out when I found a large numb lump. Then I was flooded with relief to find it was a knot. I began to pull at it, and soon realised it was not a knot at all, but an attached kitten. Gave me a right turn, I can tell you. Especially when it dug its claws into my tongue.'

'But surely you noticed the colour? You're tabby, and the kittens are black,' Marmite queried.

'I was concentrating so hard I had my eyes closed,' he frowned.

They all agreed that the sooner the kittens were homed, the better.

Trevor looked up to Bernard and Bertram's shelf; they were sitting crouched, facing them, and listening in as usual. The two brothers, having recently started making small talk with the others, looked most disgruntled.

'Bernard, do you know you have a black kitten attached to your head?' Trevor shouted.

'Well of course I know, you tabby twit, I can't get the blimming thing off, can I,' he raved.

He looked ridiculous, with it standing straight up on his head, pawing his whiskers. Bertram sat next to him, looking straight ahead, not seeming to notice his brother's distress.

Pickle and the twins ran in from the garden in a game of "chase and petrify a kitten". Pickle ground to a halt, and stared at the brothers. 'Bernard, why have you got a kitten standing on your head?' Pickle asked, and then wished she hadn't, when reams of rude words were hurled at her. Shrugging, she ran off to find the twins, who were hiding from her, ready to pounce out.

'That Mum's weird,' Jacob said.

'Hush, she'll hear you,' Marmite hissed.

Jacob lowered his voice. 'She was standing in the washing-up bowl yesterday. It took Sally ages to dry her, and she drinks from the tap. The ladies leave it running for her,' he told them, aghast. 'And to top it all, she doesn't stand to eat. If she's lying in a basket when she's fed, she sits on her bottom like a human. The other day, I saw her lift her back legs in a 'v' and eat through them. It's the strangest sight I've ever seen,' Jacob finished, retracting his chin to express the oddness.

Comfort wrinkled her nose and curled her lip on the left side 'How peculiar!'

'I think she's lovely. So polite and good-natured. To think what pain she suffered, being burnt like that,' Marmite shuddered, adding emphasis to the cruelty.

At that moment, Elsa wandered over, with a line of black kittens following. The last one climbed down from Bernard and joined them. Elsa chirped in greeting, and they chirped back.

They changed the subject and stared in various directions, so she didn't realise that they were discussing her. Elsa climbed into a basket, and the kittens followed. She began to wash them one by one, making sure that every ear and tail was soggy, but clean.

At twelve weeks old, they were too old to feed from her, but they sucked happily, Elsa lifting her back leg to allow them. She had no milk, as it had long since dried, but the kittens took comfort in the action.

'I'm finding humans stranger and stranger,' Elsa announced, once her kittens were thankfully asleep.

The cats turned their furry faces questioningly towards her, grateful for peace.

'The more I'm here, the stranger I think they are.'

'You've only just noticed?' Jacob pulled forward his eye whiskers to study her.

'I've seen several people come and state that they want to re-home a cat that no one else wants. Several are suggested, Sylvester and myself included. The people have then chosen the prettiest, youngest cat here. It seems that they say one thing but mean another,' she puzzled.

'It's guilt,' Comfort explained. 'They say that because it makes them sound caring. No human likes to appear shallow.'

'But it's so hurtful,' Elsa confessed.

'You get used to it,' Sky assured her, 'Jacob and I were recommended to the same people. They looked at my fat, and hurried away. I agree, it is hurtful.' Her eyes clouded, proving just how hurtful it was to be considered a reject and no longer appealing. When Sky was a kitten, many people had wanted her. She was grey with peach stripes, and was considered beautiful.

'So humans say one thing and mean another,' Elsa concluded, trying to understand.

'But my kittens have been suggested to people, and they walk away without one. What is wrong with my beautiful babies?'

No one wanted to mention that it was because they were considered plain.

Trevor, sort of, saved them from any answer. 'Too disorderly for people,' he grunted.

'Too disorderly? Of course they are; they're kittens.'

'Yes, but those things are monsters.'

'Trevor!' Marmite gasped.

'Well, it's true. People don't realise how lively kittens are. They think they're such cute little bundles. They are when asleep. But oh boy, are they unruly when awake.'

Elsa looked hurt, before a long smile overtook her scarred but endearing face.

'Yes, I guess they are little rascals – love um!' She began to wash them again from ear to tail tip.

To everyone's horror their eyes sprang open, and they woke.

Chapter Nineteen

One hot day, in fact the hottest of the year, Sally moved to the new premises.

'The house is in a terrible state, worse than I even realised. It needs so much work done. Still, it'll have to wait; the shelter is priority,' she told Sylvia, the stress lines etched on her face.

'How will the charity manage financially with running expenses and building the shelter?' she asked.

'With lots of begging and fundraising, I guess.'

'I admire your optimism. I wouldn't be brave enough to take on such a large challenge.'

Sally didn't feel brave. 'If I waited until things were easily do-able, I'd never do them. Sometimes you have to 'plunge' and hope you don't drown. I'll just pray and keep my fingers crossed that people will help. It may slow progress, though.' She made a mental note that, when things got tougher, she should remind herself of her own words.

People did help; they sent money for the charity to build a sanctuary for the rescue cats. More was always needed, but what was sent kept them going. Life deteriorated further for Sally, as many builders started and then disappeared without a word. She stood looking in despair at the crumbling barns and stables, not knowing what to do.

Her father turned up one day, and, taking pity on her, began repairing and converting the dishevelled mess into a suitable site. He was a retired builder so knew what to do. Sally, picking up tools, helped, and Chicken Man, when he had time, kept the accounts, which Sally hated doing.

Liking an early start, her father, much to Sally's dismay, turned up at six a.m. every morning. It was usual for her to oversleep, so she jumped out of bed and flung on the first clothes to hand. Long gone were the days when she was smartly dressed in clothes that matched and were fashionable.

The shower leaked, and there were no other washing facilities. Her clothes, make-up and jewellery were packed away; she lived in the same things every day. There was even less time for anything other than work.

Sally purchased thermal underwear and thick suitable clothing, for when the winter came.

'Not the most attractive, but necessary when building in the cold,' she laughed, as she confided the day's developments to Sylvia.

One day began to blend into the next, without any gap in between.

'I always fancied myself as a labourer. It's amazing what you learn about building,' she told Sylvia, rushing into the cattery, yet again, in a late panic.

Sally was puzzled as to why, when Sylvia went out of her way to help, she never offered to feed the cats in the evening. What a relief it would have been, to have a break now and again and not drive the twelve mile round trip in rush hour traffic, after such a gruelling day, saving her some sanity. After all, Sylvia was there anyway. But she never questioned her about it, even though she struggled to cope.

Only once had Sally ever asked her to do the feed, when some tragedy had befallen. Sylvia hadn't been pleased, claiming that her daily meetings with her were crucial. The topic of the agenda was always Leonie's downfall.

The strain on Sally was phenomenal, especially trying to keep up with the running of the charity, on top of everything else. Her stress levels rose to past breaking-point, and she operated on adrenalin. Sometimes she dreamt of running away. But not being a quitter, she never gave up.

'The stray cat that came in today doesn't look well,' Sylvia told her one evening.

Sally went to look and came back, white-faced.

'It's flu,' she confirmed, trying not to panic.

It is a highly contagious virus, especially in a cattery environment, where there are so many. One sneeze, and the germs would be sprayed through the air and contaminate every cat within a small radius. Even the vaccinated ones were at risk. As the virus went from one cat to another, it would become stronger and more lethal.

'Oh no,' Sylvia gasped, 'what should we do?'

'We can't be beaten; the pen must be barricaded on the sides. I will call the volunteers. No one must go into the infected cat and then to any other; nothing must be taken out either. Any dirty bedding needs to be tied in a plastic bag, inside the pen and dumped in the waste bin outside. Everyone must disinfect themselves as they leave each unit,' she instructed.

She took rehydration fluid and antibiotic to the sick cat.

'How is he?' Sylvia asked on her return.

'His throat's sore and his nose gunky, he can't breathe. But I got him to take a tablet and some fluid. He needs to go to the vet tomorrow.'

'I'll take him,' Sylvia offered.

'Thanks. We must be so careful,' Sally reiterated.

'OK. Don't worry, we will be,' she reassured.

The cats in the main unit sat cringing as they listened to the conversation.

'I've had it,' Mathew told them, relieved, 'I should be OK.'

'The isolation unit is not near us, so we should be safe,' reassured Comfort, attempting to dispel the tension that hung in the air.

'I'm so glad my babies have gone to lovely homes and are safe,' Elsa said with relief.

'So are we,' several said, and others nodded, Bernard included.

Elsa looked at them, but didn't speak.

She escaped the threat of flu, as that day a kind supporter came and took her home.

The next day, Sylvia took the sick cat to the vet. Before she left, she came into the main unit, carrying a pile of bedding and dumped it on the floor. Delighted, Pickle bounded over, followed by the twins, in anticipation of a new game. In no time, the three of them were hiding under the pile and pouncing on each other.

The cats, most in meditation or daydreaming, absently watched the three, smiling at their antics.

Sylvester, settling in, hopped to a basket near Sky and Jacob. He contorted himself into a comfortable position and started to doze. Changing his mind, he decided to rub his itchy neck on the hard plastic edge instead.

Sky watched, a wave of sympathy flooding her eyes. How dreadful to lose a leg, she thought.

Sylvester picked up on the thoughts. 'Don't be sorry for me. I'm happy now. After years of pain and struggle, I have somewhere I belong. I think, one day, someone will come and offer me a lovely home. We cats must never give up hope,' he told her.

'It's true,' Mathew said. 'I think being secure is the best.'

'Don't you think we are rejects, though?' Marmite pondered.

'Goodness!' Comfort lifted her head, surprised. 'What a statement!'

'Well... I've heard many people say things that insinuate that we're here because something is wrong with us,' Marmite added.

'But that's not true. We're here because of ignorant people.' However, despite her objection, Comfort was despondent after the remark.

'I heard Sally row with a vet a while ago. He apparently told people off who had homed a rescue cat,' Marmite continued.

'But why?' Trevor asked miserably.

'The cat was poorly after it was homed, because it had recently been vaccinated. Sally always explains that this can happen. But the people panicked and took it to the vet. He told them that it served them right for homing a rescue cat,' Marmite explained.

'That's terrible, there's nothing wrong with us. We're just unwanted. Bought as kittens on a whim, and then discarded. It doesn't make us rejects,' Mathew argued.

Trevor pulled back his shoulders and stuck his head in the air, to show fight and defiance at such a horrible assumption. 'There's nothing wrong with me.'

Marmite was just about to answer when something caught her eye. She sprang to her feet, alarming them.

'What's wrong?' Comfort leapt up too, and looked anxiously around.

'Where did that dirty bedding come from?' Marmite burst out.

All the cats froze in horror as they stared open-mouthed at the three youngsters.

Trevor was the first to speak. 'She wouldn't.'

Marmite ran over to the pile of blankets and sniffed. 'It's flu; I can smell it,' she was, horrified. 'Pickle, Twins, come away at once!'

'Oh ... Mum ...,' Pickle, having a fine game, whined.

'Come away now! the bedding is infected.'

Pickle and the twins did not understand what infected was, but Marmite's tone alerted them to the seriousness of what she had said.

The cats felt a coldness creeping across their fur, bleeding through to their skin, causing a shiver to spread over their bodies.

The door opened and broke the spell, as a cat in a carrying basket was brought in.

Marmite, still near the door, gasped. Sylvia was back with the sick cat. She placed the basket near the radiator, where they congregated. The cat was too weak and ill to notice its surroundings much. It sneezed, and blood flew from its nose.

They all flew for the cat flap.

Sylvester looked around; he didn't understand what was happening. 'What's wrong?'

'Run!' shouted Trevor as he flashed past.

He hopped out with the others, still not knowing why.

The cat was removed a few hours later; but it was too late. The unit was infected.

Within days, Sally was in despair, as twelve cats in the isolation pens were sick. The virus was vicious, and even the vaccinations were not protecting them. She spent hours syringing water, and trying to encourage them to eat, sometimes staying at the cattery till eleven p.m.

or midnight, nursing them. On top of all the other work, she was ready to collapse herself.

Five days later, three cats had died, and sneezing was heard coming from the feral unit. Sally prayed that it would not reach the main unit.

One week after playing in the blankets Pickle became ill.

'Mum, I don't feel well,' she told her; sounding like a small kitten, she snuggled to Marmite for comfort.

Marmite was so anxious. If she lost her last baby she would never endure the pain. Not after losing her other kittens. Pickle was so hot, and couldn't eat her breakfast. Washing her head and face, Marmite hoped it would pass. By the next day Pickle had deteriorated further.

Later that day, Sylvester and Trevor became ill. Sally knew it was flu when Trevor did not come for his food. She made them both warm beds and hot water bottles.

'I don't understand how the virus spread to the feral, and this unit?' she said anxiously to Sylvia.

'I didn't want to tell you this. If I do you must promise not to say anything.'

Sally looked stressed, worried and very pale. 'What?'

'Well, a few days ago I found the pen door of the sick stray open. Then I noticed Leonie not using disinfectant when leaving the unit. Plus, she brought bedding in from the isolation to the main unit. You mustn't let on that I told you though. She definitely needs sacking now,' Sylvia finished.

Sally looked like she would burst into tears. She studied Sylvia's eyes hard trying to read her. 'Then I must sack her, and I need to tell her why.'

'You can't. I don't want her to know it was me who told you.'

'Then I'll say I saw it for myself,' Sally knew there was no way she could do this, but needed to see Sylvia's response, 'this is far too serious to let go.'

'Please, no. Just sack her.'

After Sylvia left, Sally called Leonie.

'Do you disinfect your feet when leaving a unit?' she asked.

'Of course. I worked for a vet; I know how serious cat flu is,' Leonie replied puzzled at the question.

'Have you ever let a sick cat out of the pen?'

'Sally, I'm not stupid, and I'm always careful.'

'What about dirty bedding?'

'For God's sake! I dispose of it like you told me, using a plastic bag. Are you blaming me for the spread of flu?'

'No, I'm just checking and being paranoid. Sorry.' Sally put down the phone and stared at it. 'What the hell am I going to do?' she asked the black plastic. 'The only thing is to check more regularly: keep turning up unexpectedly until I get to the bottom of it. It's difficult with the building work, but there is no alternative.'

Pickle was so ill that she hardly moved. Marmite was sick herself, and beside herself with worry – her little Pickle was dying.

'If I lose my little baby, I will die myself,' Marmite croaked with a sob in her voice.

Trevor was too weak to point out that Pickle was far larger than her tiny mother.

Annie and Twix, extremely poorly, were snuggled in a pen, hardly moving.

Sally shook her head sadly, as she lifted Pickle up and took her to the vets. Marmite howled all that night, calling for her.

The ferals, luckily, had a natural immunity. They showed signs of flu for a few days, and then shook it off. It would be near-impossible to treat them. Cats only ate if they could smell food. So any tablets were always disguised in a strong smelling pâté. With flu, if they stopped eating, it would be impossible to administer a tablet.

Sally was exhausted, spending all her time at the shelter. Sylvia helped with the care by driving them to the vets. Eight were now hospitalised, to be given intravenous fluids and antibiotics. The vet sent more antibiotics, which Sally locked securely in a cupboard.

By now, Sky was so ill that she had to be put in a pen to be monitored. Jacob was not too bad, although his throat was sore and his eyes runny. He sat outside the pen door, watching Sky. Eventually

Sally relented, and let him in to be with her. It didn't make much difference as they had already mixed.

'How are you, Sky?' called out Comfort every so often.

'Not good,' Sky rasped her voice, weak and barely audible. Comfort shook her head at the others.

The next day, Sally asked Sylvia if she could take her to the vet's. The vet called later that night, stating that there was no hope. Her kidneys had packed up due to the dehydration. He advised that Sky should be put to sleep.

They held their breath when they heard the conversation. Sally looked over at Jacob, tears falling from her eyes. He looked up hopefully, seeing the tears he knew. He lowered his head, and his body shrank as his heart broke.

'OK,' Sally agreed.

The unit fell into an even worse depression. Comfort and Marmite lay helpless in a basket. Marmite had lost the will to fight now that Pickle had gone.

Mathew and Trevor lay in a basket next to them, cold and shivery. Trevor gave a weak cough, his nose and eyes streaming. Mathew, like Jacob, was not too bad. His throat was sore, and his head thumped, but he had escaped the other symptoms.

They were distraught over the loss of Pickle and Sky, wondering who was next.

Trevor had another cough and laid back his head on Mathew's stomach. Keeping his head raised helped with his breathing.

'I feel so ill,' he mumbled, as he did every few minutes.

'Well, go to sleep, then, and you won't know you feel ill,' advised Mathew.

Comfort looked over at the two friends. She didn't have the strength to go to the litter tray, as urine ran from her.

The worry over the cats went on day after day, as one after the other became ill. Nine cats had now died. Sally thought it would never end. All she could do was nurse them and pray.

Christmas loomed once again, and a thick blanket of snow lay on the ground. It was relentless, as it fell again and again, becoming thicker and more treacherous every day. The water had frozen in the pipes; Sylvia and Leonie, who managed the journey, brought in water containers, helping Sally as much as they could. She could no longer walk from home, as she lived too far away.

'Building in the snow is dreadful,' she told Sylvia. 'My hands and feet freeze and cramp. I live in thermal underwear constantly as the house is freezing; it's even too cold to undress to go to bed.'

Thoughts of the Christmas holiday for Sally were, as usual, forgotten. There was no time; the volunteers had disappeared for their three weeks' celebrations. Only Sally, Sylvia and Leonie remained, and soon Leonie would be gone for her Christmas.

Sally and Sylvia were sitting having a cup of tea mulling over the illness. It was a week before Christmas.

'I did some shopping on the way here,' Sally told her, 'I bought my Mum a necklace.' She lifted a small box from her bag to show her. Inside was a silver chain with an oblong pendant and several glittery, coloured stones.

'That's lovely,' Sylvia exclaimed, 'I'm glad you got something for your Mum.'

'It wasn't easy, as I only had an hour. The snow fell in the biggest lumps I'd ever seen. I was covered in seconds.'

She looked out of the window watching the white, fluffy clumps float across the fields, as they sparkled and gleamed with tiny crystals. How can something so beautiful be so dangerous, she thought, like a rose with hidden thorns.

'I bet I get stuck,' Sally said miserably.

'Don't worry, my car never gets stuck; I'll wait for you and give you a lift home if yours does.'

'Thanks Sylvia, I'm so grateful,' Sally smiled.

It got stuck, and Sylvia, as promised, gave her a lift.

The next day Sally called her at the shelter. 'I wondered if you've seen the necklace I bought my mum. It's disappeared. I wonder if it fell out of my bag in your car,' she asked.

'I'll look, but I haven't seen it.'

'It's odd because I definitely saw it in my bag when I was in your car. When I got indoors it had gone.'

'How strange!' Sylvia told her. 'I'll try the car park too, just in case. I've something to tell you,' she announced. 'You won't be pleased. But when I got here this morning the medication cupboard was wide open, and the antibiotics were gone. It could only be Leonie. Because she was here before me today and it was locked last night when we left.'

There was a long pause while Sally tried to digest what she was being told.

'Oh no. What am I going to do?' she finally raved down the phone. 'The cats will die without them.'

'You've got to sack her now, Sally. Don't stress too much; I've some at home. I'll bring them in tomorrow. They'll keep us going until you get more,' Sylvia pacified.

'But what am I going to tell the vet? He will never give me more. There were ten courses in the cupboard.'

The next day, when Sally came into the cattery, Sylvia handed her the antibiotics she had brought from home. Sally took them and stared at the foil packets. Then she glared at Sylvia.

Sylvia, noting Sally's expression, explained that they were tablets she had left when her cat was ill once. But it was too late, Sally knew. There were two complete courses of antibiotics. They were in new blister packs. It was unusual for a lay person to have these at home, and even more unusual that none had been used. They were an antibiotic rarely prescribed for minor cat ailments.

'She knows,' Trevor croaked thankfully.

'Knows what?' Comfort groaned.

'That Sylvia took the tablets to get Leonie into trouble.'

'Thank goodness,' huffed Comfort, 'but she doesn't know she spread the flu.'

The next day Sally came to the cattery and told Leonie everything she had kept to herself for so long.

'But I don't believe it. Why does she hate me so much?' Leonie was devastated.

'I don't know. But I need to watch her. In the meantime it's best you never work together. She's better alone. It's only when you're together these incidents happen.'

Most of the ferals had recovered from the illness without the help of tablets. This puzzled Sally, and she marvelled again at how their immunities were stronger than those of domestic cats.

Sadly, Pansy was not one of these cats. Already weak from cheap food and too much breeding, she was dreadfully ill. Sally moved her to a pen in the main unit.

A few days later Fiona found a young, black cat hidden in a box in the feral unit. She had obviously crawled there when she fell ill. Badly dehydrated, and her nose and eyes ulcerated, she was taken to the vets and kept in for treatment.

Marmite grieved terribly for Pickle. How she wished that Candy had been here, to give them news.

Just as things could not get any worse, they didn't. Each day the cats improved in health. Trevor was the first; he managed to eat a mouthful of fish. Sally smiled with relief as the tabby gave a small croaky yowl. Sylvester was next, as he attempted a little too.

Later that day, Sally came into the cattery clutching a basket. She opened the lid, and Pickle leapt out. Marmite was as happy as she could be while near to death's door. She climbed from her basket and wobbled along to meet her beloved daughter. She washed her head and nose as the others smiled.

Twix and Annie were let out of their pen. While they were so ill they had forgotten to spit at Sally when she syringed a special liquid feed into them. They had even enjoyed a comforting stroke, and endured a hot water bottle pushed under their blanket.

The young black cat was brought home from the vets. She was left with a weakness and was at risk of re-occurring ulcerated eyes and nose. Being a feral, the vet advised that she should never be homed to a farm or stable. She was also moved to the main unit, as she was to stay in care for the rest of her days. The cats soon learned that her name was Domino.

Once Comfort was feeling better, she went over to the pen to meet Pansy, the 'wall cat', face to face.

'You're so pretty', she told her. She had a cream-coloured body and a brown face. 'No wonder your kittens were sold.'

The two, along with Domino, became firm friends.

Six weeks after the illness erupted, all the remaining cats were back to health. However, fourteen cats had lost their lives.

Chapter Twenty

Sally kept Sylvia and Leonie separated. She asked Sylvia if she would cover the evening feed on a Wednesday. Leonie worked the morning shift, so their paths only crossed for a short while. After Sylvia left, every Wednesday night, Sally went to the unit to check. At times she waited a close distance by and watched while she worked. No incidents happened.

She spoke to some police friends and asked their advice about Sylvia.

'There's nothing you can do without proof. You can't accuse someone of stealing unless they are caught red-handed. The only incident that is illegal is the missing medication,' one of the officers told her.

'I can't think what to do,' Sally told Jane on the phone.

'I don't know either. You can't just sack her or accuse her.'

'I've a horrible feeling she spread the flu virus to blame Leonie. And the necklace I bought you for Christmas just vanished,' she told her worriedly.'

'Maybe you lost it in the snow,' Jane reasoned.

'If I had, it would still be there. I remember checking my bag when I was in Sylvia's car. I was dropped right outside the house. Why would she take it? Surely she doesn't hate you too?'

That night an older lady came to the cattery to choose a cat. Her husband had recently passed away, and she was lonely.

'I need a companion to keep me company,' she told Sally. 'One that will cuddle me and sleep on the bed.'

'I've just the cat,' Sally smiled knowingly, and she led the way to a sleeping Mathew. She gathered him up, and he went gladly to the lady's waiting arms, not caring that she was a stranger to him; he was just delighted to have a cuddle.

'Oh, he's lovely!' The lady wrapped her arms around his big fluffy body.

Trevor looked sad to see his friend chosen; he would miss him dreadfully.

'I'll take him,' the lady smiled.

'I'll give you an accident card. If anything happens, or you need to go into hospital, then someone can call us and we'll take him back.'

'You mean if I die, dear?' the lady nodded, understanding.

'It'll give you and Mathew protection,' Sally told her.

'I understand. I love cats, and don't want him to be left destitute.'

Mathew left that night, happy to have his own home with someone who would spoil him.

His place was soon taken by Roly, a skinny, tall black cat. He had been reported as sick, wandering around a high road amongst traffic. The man who reported him hated cats, Jane told Sally on the phone. He had been hanging around for weeks, crying for food. Eventually, through malnutrition, he lay on the floor, his legs no longer strong enough to support him.

The disgusted man demanded that the cat was removed instantly as he had children, and they might catch a disease.

'Charming,' Sally remarked before leaving to collect him.

The man had looked in disbelief as Sally scooped the cat from the ground. He reached out his paws offering a weakly purr.

'It's a shame that no one thought to feed him,' she moaned to the man.

'Certainly not, I have children.'

'Let's hope you feed them, then. Or if they collapse, I hope someone has enough compassion in their heart to help.'

Once healthy, Roly turned out to be a massive character. He was always into mischief, even worse than Trevor, which took a lot.

When the ladies cleaned the pens, he would rush into the run and leap for the nearest clawing post, where he hung upside down smiling. As the broom swept past, Roly attached himself to it for a ride. He took great delight in sitting on the mop bucket until it tipped, flooding water everywhere.

Roly was painfully thin, and unneutered as usual. Some people were reluctant to neuter males. But if they saw them fighting with other males, or the dreadful mating process, they would, hopefully, change their minds. How many female strays had the charity taken with ears ripped off or bleeding neck wounds through mating, or the viruses that passed from one unneutered cat to another?

When Alan and Margaret came to transport the cats to the vet, for their check-ups, Margaret blinked at Roly in disbelief.

'Good grief, he has the biggest … balls I've ever seen.'

'About time they came off then,' Sally laughed.

Once he was well enough, he was moved to the main unit to join the others. He had endless energy, as he charged around with Pickle.

Sylvia still raved to Sally about Leonie, demanding to know why she had not been sacked for stealing the antibiotics. Life between them was more amicable now they only briefly met on a Wednesday. Relieved, Sally relaxed, as no more incidents had happened.

Sylvia was a fantastic help, and willing to assist in any way to ease the pressure from Sally. How grateful she was, as by now Sally was exhausted, mentally and physically.

The following Wednesday as Sylvia came into the cattery, Leonie was just leaving. They chatted for a while before Sylvia fed the cats. None of them ventured near her anymore; even Trevor kept a safe distance away.

'What's she doing?' Comfort asked seeing Sylvia stand up and walk to the cupboard.

Bringing out a carrying basket and a large towel, she headed towards Twix. Startled and afraid, he leapt from the floor on to the wire of a pen. Sylvia, who had seen Sally catch cats many times, lifted the towel and threw it over him. She pulled him from the wire, and dumped the struggling kitten into the basket. Once locked, secure and free of the towel he called to Annie. She ran panic-stricken to him pawing at the wire.

Sylvia looked out of the cattery door; no one was there. She grabbed Twix and left. The cats rushed to the window and watched as she shut him in her car boot.

'What are we going to do?' Annie cried.

As Sylvia came back into the unit, they ran and hid. Remembering the last time people had done something similar, she picked up her phone and called Sally.

'I can't find Twix,' she told her.

Sally paused at the other end. 'What a surprise, he's disappeared on a Wednesday. Don't tell me, Leonie must have let him out.'

Sylvia, missing the sarcasm, replied. 'Yes that's exactly what I think. I've searched everywhere. He's nowhere to be found.'

Just as Sylvia drove away Sally turned up with Chicken Man, hoping to search her car.

'Why's she searching round the farm for him?' Pickle asked, watching from the window as Sally climbed into the large bin and ripped opened the filthy rubbish bags.

'Goodness knows,' replied Marmite.

'He's lived here too long to go far. Besides, he would never leave Annie,' Sally told Chicken Man as she returned.

'You know she's taken him, so why are you looking?' he asked, giving Trevor a scratch under the chin.

'I guess it's just to make sure I'm right,' Sally explained worried. 'I want to be wrong, and Twix is here somewhere. What am I going to do now?' Sally looked from him to Annie, who was sitting by the window. 'I don't think she'll hurt him, but what if she doesn't bring Twix back?'

'I don't know what to suggest. Try talking to the police again.'

Sally called them. There was nothing they could do without proof.

She rang Leonie. 'Was Twix here this morning?' she asked anxiously.

'Yes, he was there for breakfast and when I left. Why?'

'Sylvia has taken him, to make out that you let him out.'

Leonie was shocked, as Sally was, at the extent of Sylvia's hatred. 'Don't worry, she won't hurt him. Despite her madness, she loves cats,' she reassured.

The next day she went to the cattery while Sylvia was working. She looked around, surprised to see Sally there, who had a tape recorder hidden to catch her out.

'Isn't it strange that these incidents only happen on a Wednesday, when both you and Leonie cross paths?' Sally scrutinised her eyes for a clue.

'Thank goodness,' Trevor breathed, Sally's going to sort it out.

'I… hadn't realised it was always a Wednesday,' Sylvia replied, her voice slightly shaky.

'Twix has been taken, and I want him returned,' Sally's voice sounded menacing and held no waver, her anger not far from the surface.

'I don't think he's been taken. Leonie let him out. I've searched everywhere. I even climbed in the bin and ripped open the sacks before I left yesterday,' she innocently told Sally.

'Is that right?' her eyes penetrated deep into Sylvia's. But she needed Twix back before she could confront her. 'Well, I'll repeat, Twix must be returned straight away!'

A man turned up that night with his young son, wanting to rehome a cat. Sally was not in the best of moods. As the child ran round the cattery screaming and knocking water bowls flying, she showed the father the cats. She felt cross at the disruption, and wondered about their homing a cat.

'That's why we don't like homing cats to families with young children; they're far too boisterous and scare them.' Sally gave the man the best 'keep your son under control' look she could muster with a headache.

'I don't think that's the case,' the father laughed.

Sally looked around and burst out laughing. Roly was tearing around the unit, chasing the little boy, knocking everything flying in his excited game. The boy squealed in delight as he ran from Roly. He turned and began to chase the delighted cat. Roly skidded to a halt and galloped away. Round and round they went, causing absolute mayhem.

'You have to take him; he will love your son.'

'No way,' the man laughed, cringing at the mess.

Twix was not back the next day, or the next. Sally was becoming more anxious. She spoke to the police again.

'Is there nothing we can do?' she asked in desperation.

'I'm afraid not. You have no proof.'

'But I know it's her.'

Sally did not go to the cattery the next day while Sylvia was there, allowing her time to return Twix. Sylvia called her during the morning.

'I can smell burning,' she told her.

The cats sniffed; they could smell nothing.

'She's going to set light to the unit,' Trevor gasped. 'We'll be stuck in here and burn to death.'

None of them spoke, as fear ran through their bodies. They could hear the dread in Sally's voice. She came later and sealed up the letter box. It was in vain. But she didn't know what else to do.

Lola helped by hiding on the farm to watch the cattery, so that Sally could have a break.

The snow was melting at last. Grey, dirty sludge now lay on the ground, making everything even duller.

Sally kept reiterating to Sylvia that she wanted Twix returned. She confided in her close friend Maria and told her what had been happening.

'But that's unbelievable,' she gasped, 'how could someone do such a thing?' She was shocked. 'It can't be true, Sylvia's so nice. Maybe Billy took Twix,' she said in disbelief at what Sally was saying.

'How? Leonie was there all morning. She was still there when Sylvia arrived. Besides, the door is locked and he has no spare keys as I had the locks changed some time ago.'

'Well I still think he did it. I can't believe Sylvia would.'

'Me neither, but she has.'

Four days after Twix disappeared, Sylvia brought him back. It was five a.m. on a Sunday when she came into the cattery. Twix was calling from inside the basket.

'Thank goodness,' Annie breathed and ran to him. 'Twix, are you all right?' she called, as Sylvia went to the garden door.'

'Is that you, Annie? I'm OK. I don't know what happened. Sylvia took me to her house. Thank goodness I'm home.'

Sylvia went outside, taking Twix, and closed the door behind her. Annie ran up, and waited for him to come in through the cat flap. But it was locked, and she could not see Twix through it.

Soon Sylvia came in and went to the linen cupboard. She pulled out a pile of towels and went back into the garden. The cats were mystified at what was happening. It was a long time before she came back in again. Twix still did not appear. After returning the basket, Sylvia left and drove away.

They waited staring at the cat flap hoping to see his tabby face on the other side, but there was no sign of him. Annie kept calling through the Perspex door. They had no choice but to wait for Sally.

It was four hours later when Lola came into the cattery. Not long afterwards, Leonie joined her; she had, unusually, offered to cover the shift for Sally, allowing her a break.

Annie, losing her shyness, ran to Lola mewing. 'Please go into the garden,' she begged, running to the door.

'Twix isn't out there, Annie, we've already searched.' Just to satisfy the kitten, Lola opened the door.

Annie tore outside and she followed. There was no sign of Twix in the garden. The melting snow caused puddles of grey muddy slush.

'How odd,' Annie mewed to the others, 'Twix isn't here.'

A few of them ran out to check.

'He's disappeared,' Pickle exclaimed in confusion.

Lola went to go back inside, as she noticed the clean towels piled high in one of the plastic igloo beds.

'Strange, towels outside in this weather?' she puzzled. 'Even odder that they are clean,' she called to Leonie who came into the garden to look.

'How odd,' Leonie agreed.

Lola pulled at the towels to take into the cattery.

Annie had just left the garden when she heard Lola cry out. She ran back, stopped and stared in horror. Among the pile of towels lay Twix.

He was dead, his legs curled into a grotesque position. The expression on his face showed he had died an agonising death. She wailed, causing the other cats to run out. Marmite nudged Annie away. Lola was crying as she stooped to stroke his head.

Leonie called Sally, and she arrived a short time later. They stared at the body which was still warm, suggesting he had died recently. Not one of them wanted to believe someone could do that to Twix. The twisted body was imprinted in their minds forever. Once Sally had taken photos, another volunteer took his body to an emergency vet, where Sally paid the money for an urgent post-mortem.

As Sylvia was at the cattery the next day Sally turned up at the same time.

'We found Twix,' she told Sylvia, the tape hidden once again.

'That's fantastic,' Sylvia's voice was flat and emotionless.

'He was dead. An urgent post-mortem showed his stomach had burst through being kicked or punched to death. He died early yesterday morning, just before he was found. But he suffered excruciating pain before dying,' Sally kept her voice as cold as Sylvia's. She tucked her shaking hands into her pocket to hide them.

'Really?' Sylvia exclaimed, not looking the least bit shocked. 'How horrible. He must have been injured outside and climbed back into the garden.'

'How do you think he managed that?' Sally asked raising, her eyebrows in sarcastic amazement.

'He could have found a gap in the wire.'

'And where's there a gap?' Sally asked again. 'Only I'm sure one of the thousands of cats we've had here would have found it before now.'

'I don't know but there must be one.'

'Well let's look then, because I've never seen a gap.'

'It's the only explanation.'

'I don't think so,' Sally said, her voice hiding hatred. 'So, let's say he did escape. He would have come for his breakfast. But no one has seen him for four days. So he injures himself by … falling from a height on to a boot or something similar. He then comes back. Climbs, in pain, up the wire and finds this hole that appears. He then drops through and blocks it up. After which, 'injured', he heads to the linen cupboard. Opens the door, drags out a large pile of laundered towels. Closes the door, in agonising pain, drags the towels to the garden. Then lifts them above his head so that they don't get wet and muddy. Because, let's face it, the towels were dry and clean, which is odd, because the garden is filthy with slush and mud. But, back to his movements. He then has a wash. Oh, I forgot to mention, his body was pristine. In fact he was so clean not even a toe had touched the ground. So he washes himself, gets into a plastic bed, pulls the pile of towels over him, and dies?'

'Sarcasm doesn't suit you,' Sylvia eyes were narrow. Although she was exposed, she did not waver. 'I think it's better I leave.'

Sally said nothing as she fought to calm herself.

Sylvia walked away from the cattery, her head held high.

Within days Maria called her. 'How could you get rid of Sylvia? She's devastated.'

'She murdered a cat,' Sally told her, trying to remain calm.

'She said she didn't,' Maria defended.

'Oh well, that proves she didn't do it then.'

Maria grasped for an explanation. 'It must have been Billy.'

'I'm sorry, Maria, but I have trouble with that explanation. So you think that while Leonie and Sylvia were in the cattery Billy walked past them, and took Twix who, being timid, would run away if anyone approached him. He then kept him locked up somewhere, kicked him to death, broke through the locked door at five a.m. on Sunday, and put Twix in the garden.'

'Well, it's possible,' she said and taking a deep breath continued. 'Only first there was Kelly at the shop, and now Sylvia.'

Sally understood the insinuation. How hurt she was that Maria doubted her. They had been friends such a long time.

That day Sally received a phone call from Jane.

'I've just heard something so horrible. It has really upset me.'

'Please don't tell me, Mum. You know how those animal things give me sleepless nights.'

'It's Mathew. The lady let him out, and a gang of blokes kicked him in the face.'

'Oh no! He's so friendly, he must have gone to them for a cuddle. How can anyone do something so dreadful?'

'It's upset me so much. His nose was a mass of blood and his jaw pushed to one side, one eye sunk into his head.'

Sally felt the sickness rise in her stomach. Who could hurt such a lovely, gentle cat that was so inoffensive and loved everyone?

'He's since been having epileptic fits. The lady can't cope with his care. She's heartbroken; but he needs to come back.'

Mathew returned that night. He was subdued as he sat crouched in a basket. At every little noise, he jumped and shrank in fear. The other cats felt devastated for their friend who was hurt both emotionally and physically. Trevor snuggled next to him, trying to ease Mathew's pain. His beautiful face was now distorted, with a big boot mark denting his skull.

After the burning threat, either Lola or Sally stayed to guard the unit until late into the night.

'It's no good, ready or not, we have to move the cats to the new site,' Sally announced. 'It has large security gates and cameras. They'll be safer there.'

Chapter Twenty-One

Comfort, Domino and Pansy sniffed each item in their new home. Domino wrinkled her cheeks and lowered her jaw, 'It smells new and clean.'

Comfort pushed her nose against the wire of one of the three introduction pens that covered the back wall. Her whiskers squashed against her cheeks in a horizontal pattern. 'They're bigger than before,' she said, observantly.

A large enclosure sat next to them, for cats that did not want to mix with the others. Pansy wandered in to inspect it. A large climbing frame dominated one side. Lots of shelves with little ladders lined the other walls at various levels.

'Wow,' she grinned, imagining the fun they could have in there. Just to demonstrate, Roly rushed past and threw himself on to one of the roped posts. He hung for a while, before cleverly leaping into the air, twisting his body and landing upside down. Throwing back his head, he winked at Pansy.

She flicked her eyes to the ceiling. 'Show off,' she thought.

Bernard and Bertram had found themselves a shelf, with a cosy bed to live on. It was by a window on the opposite side of the unit. After they were comfortable, Bernard jutted his neck forward and stiffened his body.

'What is it?' Bertram whispered urgently, feeling spooked by his brother's rigid composure. He squinted his eyes toward Bernard's line of vision, straining his neck to see.

'Dunno,' he hissed back. 'There is some sort of bristly animal over there. It has an enormous tail.'

'Do you think it's dangerous?' Bertram asked, the spook creeping and stiffening his tail before rippling over his spine and settling into his ears.

They both fell silent while they contemplated the situation. The distance, and their worn eyesight, prevented them from adequate risk assessment.

Bernard, making a brave decision, climbed from the shelf. 'I'll get closer,' he whispered, from the corner of his mouth. He did not want to give away their position and alert the animal to attack. 'You back me up from the rear.'

Small Bernard had always been a warrior, never afraid of danger.

However, large, cowardly Bertram, instead of following, lifted his hind leg over the back of the basket, not once taking his dilated eyes from the strange animal. Once the leg was positioned over the lip of the bed he lowered it to safety, carefully following with the other. He then pushed himself backwards, desperately trying to keep his neck and head in the same spot. This, he figured, would prevent the animal from suspecting anything suspicious. Satisfied that his body parts were in place, Bertram began to move his front legs. Drawing in a deep breath, he sank, until perfectly positioned. Aware that his ears were on show, he flattened them against the sides of his head, making him, as Sally always said, 'a Fred with a cap.' Just to check that he had been successful in not arousing suspicion, he poked his head over the basket; with half-moon eyes on show, he observed Bernard's progress.

Now that Pansy was no longer an audience, the post soon grew tedious. Roly leapt off and rushed away to find something else to feed his attention. He stopped in front of the girls to have a chase of his tail.

'It's great here,' he puffed, with his usual enthusiasm for life.

'I want to go home,' Comfort announced, ignoring Roly, and feeling strange and odd. It had been a long time since she had lived anywhere but the old cattery.

'Give it a chance, Comfort, it might be OK,' Domino looked to Pansy for dual reassurance.

The three of them went to the large window that dominated the front of the new unit. It stretched from floor to ceiling. Next to it was a patio door.

'We can see all round the shelter,' Pansy pointed out, unnecessarily, because they could too.

To the left of them stood a large portable cabin, with steps leading to an office. Next to the office were two enormous electric gates. Opposite them was an isolation unit. It had a small outside enclosure built on the front.

'No more risk of cat flu,' Comfort stated, feeling sad at the memory of those dreadful days, not too long before.

Noticing movement at the corner of her eye, she flipped her head round and did a double take.

Bernard was stalking a broom that leant against one wall. His head was outstretched and his nose was wrinkling, as he moved cautiously towards it. One front paw was held ready to hit on attack. He let out a long, piercing war cry as he crouched his body, before he rushed forward. With the outstretched paw, he thumped away at the animal. The broom shook menacingly from the beating. Seeing it as a counter-attack, Bernard leapt into the air, spinning and screeching to protect his rear.

On landing, he went in for the kill; this time, lifting both front paws, he boxed the brush into submission.

Bertram, still peeping over the basket, looked on with his wide eyes full of admiration for his brother's bravery. He held his breath in concentration to send mental encouragement to help him beat the brush. Comfort watched for a while, shrugged, and turned her attention back to the window.

The next unit along were stables that were converted into nine pens. New cats would be staying here while they awaited health checks and vaccinations. Opposite was another building with another nine pens.

'It looks like there's more room for cats to be rescued,' Pansy said. 'I can see the feral unit at the far end.'

They looked to the large enclosure with a garden. The sides were layered, with wooden shelves at various levels. Cats of all sizes lounged on them in various positions.

'There's Marvin in the garden,' Pansy said excitedly.

'Which one?' squinted Comfort.

'The handsome, big, fluffy, white and black. Youuuu hoooo, Marvin,' Pansy called wiggling her tail tip at him. 'He was my friend,' she proudly told them.

'I think Marvin has a new friend now,' Domino smiled, seeing the large cat cuddled up with a small ginger.

'They seem contented in the new feral unit, but I guess, having been here a few weeks, they have settled down,' Pansy smiled.

'I'm so pleased that the kittens will be in a separate unit. Thank goodness we will no longer be plagued by them,' laughed Comfort. She was far too old to have a kitten swinging on her belly or her tail for that matter.

Domino went through the back door into the garden, giving a long sniff on her way.

'Come and see out here,' she called, and the other two followed. They walked past Bernard who was thumping the broom, and Roly, thinking it looked fun, thumped with him.

The garden was larger than the last. Plastic beds, baskets and tree logs to scratch were already in place. They looked up the sides of the wire to the various shelves with access ladders and bridges.

Sylvester was already perched on one. 'I can see the forest,' he called excitedly.

Roly, his paw aching from thumping, flew past in a whirl. He dashed up the ladders, and was at the top in seconds. 'Did you see me, didn't I fly?' he boasted.

They looked the other way to make out that they hadn't.

Disappointed, Roly pushed his nose between the wires. It slotted securely into the hole; he stared across at the trees. Never in his life had he seen so many clustered together. How he longed to climb up them.

Domino made for the nearest ladder, and climbed up beside them. 'It's true there are millions of trees. I can see for miles, or at least to the trees.'

Pansy followed, and went to one shelf with a window above. 'It looks into the office. We can see the humans,' she called to Comfort.

Then she galloped back beside her again. 'I like it,' she nudged Comfort, and washed her ear. 'Give it a chance, Comfort, it might be OK.'

'I can see Sally's house,' Domino shouted. 'I wonder how the boys are getting on.'

Both Mathew and Trevor had gone home with Sally a few weeks before the move. On hearing his name, he appeared from nowhere. The five of them sprang around.

'Trevor!' shouted Comfort.

Behind him stood Mathew.

'Welcome to your new home,' Mathew grinned, his damaged face not spoiling his handsome looks. His fits had subsided, and he looked much better. But his confidence had plummeted, and any sudden noise startled him. He clung to Trevor as much as possible, and now only ventured out when his friend was close by to give him support and encouragement.

'Oh, it's so good to see you both. What's it like here?' Comfort felt happier now all her friends were around her.

'It's great! There's lots of food and it's much more fun than the other place. You'll be fine once you settle in,' Trevor reassured them. 'How's Annie?'

They looked over to where she sat in a basket, her head hanging.

'She's still grieving for Twix. She hardly noticed the move,' Comfort told them lowering her head in sadness.

They stayed silent, not finding adequate words to express their thoughts about what had happened to the lovely Twix.

'Where's young Pickle and Marmite?' Trevor asked looking eagerly around longing to see them. They could practise some great judders here, he grinned.

'They went to a new home,' Comfort explained. 'Jane found it for them. Apparently, they have a heated room to live in with a cat flap. The place is in a stable where other cats live too.'

Trevor was glum; he would miss them both so much. 'I think Pickle will be happy living at stables,' he concluded, pleased that they had found happiness and freedom. 'She may even find the worm rat she was always on about.'

'Pickle didn't want to go; she screamed all the way out of the drive,' Comfort told the boys. 'But we heard Sally say that, after a few weeks, Pickle was in her element. She even jumped on a horse's back. And Marmite has a boyfriend, a massive black cat who follows her everywhere.'

'I'm so glad they're happy,' Mathew said. 'What about Jacob?' As he asked, a lump entered his stomach as he thought of Sky.

'A lovely lady came and took him. She was kind and gentle. Sally explained how he pined at losing his partner. Since Sky had died, he'd hardly spoken. He preferred to sit alone in their basket, with his memories of her. Sally sent his basket and blanket with him, hoping that it would help with his loss. It's so sad,' Pansy exclaimed.

'Jane called the lady, and he's happy. He's going into the garden, and has made friends with the neighbourhood cats,' Domino finished.

Within a few days, they had settled. Comfort decided to give the new shelter a chance, and found she was happy there. How could she ever forget Flick, though? She had waited so long for him. He must have forgotten her, and made a new life himself. All she could do now was build a life with her friends; hanging on to memories of him, which sometimes flooded her day and night dreams.

A large basket had been placed by the front window. This was where they now congregated for their evening bath. It was Comfort, Pansy and Domino's favourite place. Roly and Sylvester sometimes joined them. There they sat, and watched people and cats come and go. They took bets on how quickly a cat would be homed, the stake being biscuits.

Comfort usually guessed right. She would lift her head, glance at the passing basket and state: 'Two weeks; three days; four months.' If the cat was young, and a pretty colour, it would be chosen straight away. Plain cats, black, black and white or timid cats were always destined for a long stay. Raggy old toms usually stayed the longest.

Every night, Comfort went to Annie and encouraged her to sleep in the basket with them. She understood loss, and tried her best to soothe the pain the kitten felt. Curling herself around Annie, Comfort washed her. The kitten laid her head on Comfort's tummy, staring into space until the lulling of purrs sent her into a peaceful sleep. Her dreams were filled with Twix. Sometimes they were so real that she woke and looked for him. When reality hit her, it was like a knife twisting in her stomach, and she sat and howled.

It was exciting for the cats when, over the next few months, new volunteers came forward to help, even people to play with them, and welcome new arrivals.

Comfort was not too sure that she liked people chatting to her. When they pulled a long wiggly thing around, she gave them a dark glare.

'Am I supposed to chase that?' she asked Pansy, when one persistent person wouldn't give up.

Pansy laughed. 'You have to humour humans. I do, it's fun when you get into role play. Make out it's a mouse or a snake.'

'Huh! If it was a snake, I'd leap to the ceiling and stay there,' Comfort snorted.

'Me too, but it's pretend, to please the people.'

When a lady named Rochelle started work at the shelter, a few of them sized her up from the window.

'She looks OK,' Roly decided.

'Guess so,' Sylvester shrugged. He cared little who worked there, as long as they were aware of his neck scratch.

'I remember her from the old cattery; she volunteered for ages, she's nice. Trevor said she is to become the shelter manager,' Comfort told them, taking Candy's place as informer.

'Really?' Pansy sounded surprised. 'Has Sally been sacked then?'

'Pansy, you are dim sometimes. How can Sally sack herself? Rochelle will take over from Sally, allowing her time to run the charity. With Pam managing the shop, things are slightly easier for her,' Comfort explained. 'She will cover the days Rochelle doesn't work, feed us in the evenings and spend time with us.'

'Oh.' Pansy felt daft.

'Besides, according to Trevor, Sally wants time to make the house liveable and unpack her belongings. He told me that he's sick of the place. He has to use the litter tray in the cold, because there's no heating. Plus, they live in just two small rooms, as the rest are not habitable. Sally has no money. Her father, taking pity on her again, will help to renovate the house.

'Another thing,' Comfort lowered her voice, 'Trevor believes the place is haunted. Things keep going missing or moving about. He often hears people upstairs, and the cupboards and doors keep opening and shutting on their own.' She paused, looking around for effect, but only Annie was there and she was not interested. The others had wandered off into the garden.

'Charming,' she grumped, giving a loud sniff and washing her bottom to hide her embarrassment.

The cats soon grew to love Rochelle, and looked forward to seeing her each morning. She was an excellent manager, clever, efficient and ran things methodically. Trevor thought her great, as she always gave him little treats. He sat in the office, listening to Rochelle talk about fundraising ideas she had thought of. He had already worked out that that meant more money, thus more food.

'She's rather nice, but peculiar,' he declared one day, joining in on the gossip with the main unit while scanning the garden through the wire.

'I thought you liked her,' Pansy asked, alarmed as Sylvia's oddness flashed through her mind. 'Why is she odd?'

'Oh I do like her, she gives me extra breakfasts. It's just I heard her say that she was going out with another lady to hold a bucket. Apparently, they do it in a shop every month for hours, dressed in disguise. I'm guessing it's so that no one recognises them. After all if I was going to stand holding a bucket I wouldn't want anyone to recognise me either. Sometimes they rattle it a bit to relieve the monotony. If that's not odd, then what is? Any food scraps in there?' Trevor finished, as his sharp vision hadn't spotted any.

'I think they go to collect money and food for the charity,' Comfort told them. 'There are a lot of ladies who do that now. They stand for hours in all weathers, just to help us. The coins they collect help pay our expenses and vet bills.'

'No, we have no food scraps,' Domino said in disgust. 'You're so greedy.'

Trevor skulked away, offended. 'Well, it's silly standing with a bucket,' he called back, sounding more like a kitten than an adult cat. He kicked at a loose pebble with his toe, his bottom lip pushed forward as far as possible to show how big his sulk was. Then he regretted it, because his toe hurt as it scraped on the concrete.

'Even with the collections, I heard Sally say that it's still a struggle financially to keep the charity running,' Comfort told them, as she watched Trevor ambling down the yard, hopping around a bit and then ambling again, hissing.

'There are so many abandoned cats, and each year the numbers grow. I guess people can control their own breeding, but we have to rely on them to help with ours,' she pondered, then turned upside down and began washing the knot she had been trying to untangle for days.

'Those poor cats. How terrible to give birth to one litter after another. I've seen cats so sick of having kittens that they walk away from them after a long labour. I can understand it. I've considered it many a time,' Pansy shuddered.

'Years ago, female humans had one baby after another. Many of them died through overbreeding. I guess they must have forgotten how horrible it was for them, when they allow us to breed constantly,' Comfort frowned 'How cruel!'

Another new lady soon began working with them. Again the cats sized her up and decided they liked her too. Her name was Chrissie; she was kind and gentle, with always a nice word for them.

'I wonder why she digs in those plant pots?' Domino said one day as she watched Chrissie tending them, hours after everyone else had gone. 'She even puts in greenery, and pours water in.'

'Goodness knows why, 'cos Trevor and Mathew dig them up again,' Pansy shrugged. 'I think it looks pretty though.'

'I can't understand why that Chrissie takes home our bedding,' Roly said, looking perplexed. 'It's weird; but maybe she likes lying on it too. I guess blankets used by us are cosier than her own. Even one I weed on, Chrissie took it for herself. Maybe she wanted to wee on it too. When bored with the blanket, she brought it back again. When I looked my wee had disappeared. Goodness knows why she would want to keep my wee?' he puzzled.

'You're as daft as Pansy,' Comfort laughed, 'she probably washed it off.'

'Washed it off, how? Do you mean she grooms it until it has gone?' he had never heard of such a thing, so he ran off to chase a leaf that blew past the door. It was far more exciting than his wee.

As he dashed past, he chirped a greeting to Bernard, who was again tackling the broom. This time he was taking a different approach. He stood behind the open back door. Every time he thought the strange animal was not looking he ran out, gave it a thump, and ran back to hide before it wobbled at him. It was too much, having dangerous animals in the unit. If it wasn't dealt with, he and Bertram would be forced to leave the premises.

More and more people came forward to offer help, some to take photos of them, much to the disgust of Comfort, who hated the strange object pointing her way.

'It won't hurt you,' Mathew reassured. 'It helps with homing you all. The photos are for publicity. I personally love to be photographed, and have done great model work.'

'I don't care what pub they go in. I don't like it, and I don't want a home anyway. I always look strange in those photos. They're nothing like me. My fur stands on end, and my lip gets caught on my tooth. I look deranged,' she objected.

'Besides, we know that with groups of people, unlike cats, you get the ones ready to criticise and spoil things. I heard Sally say the same. I don't want people talking about my fur being crooked.'

Mathew smiled, 'You're a funny cat, Comfort. What would we do without you?'

Chapter Twenty-Two

There was much excitement one Sunday, when Sally and Chicken Man were standing in the yard, having a heated discussion. The cats, hearing the commotion, ran into the garden to listen.

Sylvester, gaining the best view, watched from a higher shelf. Roly ran up the side of the wire to sit beside him.

'What's happening?' he panted.

'I don't want hens,' Chicken Man was saying. 'I do despair of you, Sally, whatever next? Do you not think we have enough problems with this lot?' He waved his arms around the buildings; this not only stressed his point but also released some frustration towards Sally.

She straightened her shoulders, not wavering in her determination. Then she raised her eyes upwards to express annoyance at his objection.

Comfort felt it was more a look of 'here we go again'. She smirked, knowing Sally would win the argument as usual.

'They are ex-battery hens. They need people to offer them homes and give them freedom. If people don't help them they will die, after living a life of evil cruelty. It is far easier to be an ostrich and bury your head in the sand than to help,' she told him firmly.

'What are battery hens?' asked Domino, 'I thought hens were alive.'

'Goodness knows, I think it means mechanical, like toys,' shrugged Comfort.

Sally grabbed the car keys from Chicken Man. 'Well, if all you can do is stand there ranting, I'll go to Norfolk alone.' She opened the car door and eased into the driver's seat.

Knowing he was defeated and wasting his breath, he relented and climbed in.

Sally was grinning in triumph as she reversed the car.

Chrissie had been spending time with Annie, talking and coaxing her. The little cat responded well, much to everyone's relief.

'I'm going to ask Sally if I can take you home,' Chrissie said to the delighted kitten. She picked up her phone and sent a text.

For the first time in months, the young cat climbed from the basket and began batting at a rattle ball.

How pleased they were to see a glimmer of cheerfulness, after all this time. Comfort could not wait to tell Mathew and Trevor of the progress that Chrissie had made with Annie.

After they had said their farewells to her, the cats waited in the garden for the car to return. They were dying to see what mechanical birds looked like. Roly couldn't begin to imagine what a hen was, let alone one you wind with a key. The excitement of a large sparrow, as Sylvester had explained, was causing his jaw to judder every time the image popped into his head.

Sylvester, seeing his judders, kept running to the wire in anticipation of a bird in the yard. His chin was vibrating on the way to warm up and gain a head start. How disappointed he was, on arrival, to find no bird in sight.

'Will you stop that, Roly?' he grumbled, feeling a mixture of foolish and disappointed at the same time. 'I get all built up, and feel so let down when there isn't anything to judder at.'

'I can't help it; I'm so excited,' Roly burst out, his tail wiggling and mouth moving as the latest image burst unexpectedly into his head.

Much later that day the car drove into the yard. Four baskets were lifted from the back. The cats tore into the garden in anticipation of what was inside.

Standing in a line, with their noses pressed to the fence, they watched as Sally carefully lifted the lid of one basket. Inside was the oddest-looking creature they had ever seen.

Roly and Sylvester were ready in judder stance, complete with jaws hanging and tails in perfect erection. When they saw the strange birds, their tense mouths flopped and erections slackened, floating down like lowered flags.

'Those aren't chickens,' Pansy said. 'I've seen chickens and they're nothing like that.'

'Where are the big sparrows with feathers?' Roly's jaw trembled as a heaviness of disappointment grew in his chest, so large it sank to his toes.

The six birds were bald, with raw skin and bleeding sores. Their eyes were staring vacantly, and they were full of trauma. The crowns that usually sat, red and proud, on chickens' heads, were white and swollen. The weight caused them to flop over one side of their faces. The wattle that hung from their chins was also white and swollen. Their bodies were painfully skinny, with bones protruding from them. Their beaks had been cut at the tip, making them flat instead of pointed.

Not being able to understand what they were seeing, the cats gaped in amazement.

Then one fell over and lay on its side without moving, bumping into the others that shuffled along to make room for it to fall.

'I guess they need winding up,' decided Pansy, fumbling for an explanation.

'Yeah,' Roly and Sylvester nodded, bewildered.

'Now do you see why they need our help?' Sally was telling Chicken Man.

He stared at the pathetic sight, not speaking. Maybe he was as disgusted as she was for the sins inflicted on them.

Sally carefully carried the hens one by one to a large shed next to the gates. She placed them outside the opened door; not a sound could be heard. They stood leaning into each other, not a flicker of life in the depleted eyes.

Coming back to the car Sally brought out the last basket. Opening it, she put in her hands and brought out a very small, beautiful, black cockerel. As he turned his coat shimmered with greens and blues. He flapped his wings and pecked at Sally's skin.

'That's more like it!' Roly's tail began lifting and his jaw stiffening in anticipation of a good chase.

'Unhand me at once,' the bird screeched.

Sally placed him on the floor, and he bushed up his feathers, pushed out his chest and pulled back his head.

'Goodness gracious, how terrible, he has no legs,' Pansy gasped.

Domino quickly averted her eyes; she could not stand to see such horrors.

'Don't be silly, of course he has. It's his feathers; they're so bushy, they're covering them,' Comfort explained, exasperated. 'In fact, he looks like he has a dress on.'

It was true. The small cockerel's feathers fanned out so much that he looked legless.

'Phew,' breathed Domino, giving the cockerel a hard stare in an effort to see the missing legs.

As the cockerel ran, he wobbled from side to side in an effort to gain speed. Running around in a circle, he tried to peck Sally's ankles, paying her back for the disgrace of being handled.

'It's not much of a harem for you, Bungay,' Sally told him, laughing at his annoyance, while hopping from one leg to another to avoid his beak.

He seemed to understand, and strutted off to meet his ladies. Not impressed with their lack of response he disappeared into the shed to take a look at his new home. Giving his approval he came out again and ushered his ladies inside.

Trevor suddenly ran up to the unit. He looked at the line of cats with their noses pressed to the wire.

'What's going on? Why is dinner so late?' he moaned, skidding to a halt in front of them.

'Sally's gone and got some mechanical birds,' Comfort told him nodding towards the shed.

'Birds, birds, where? Excellent! 'Bout time we had some sport round here.'

'They're not real,' Pansy shouted, as he raced off, 'they're battery.'

'Trevor, be careful,' Comfort called.

He did not hear her in his eagerness to reach the birds. They all watched as his skinny bum disappeared through the door; only the tip of his tabby tail could be seen poking out, wiggling like a rattlesnake.

It took only a few seconds before Trevor came flying out again like a ball from a cannon, his feet not even making ground contact. A very cross Bungay was flapping behind him.

They could not help giggling at the distressed Trevor, who disappeared in a cloud of dust and was not seen again for at least an hour. Hunger finally dragged him from his hiding place behind the store cupboard.

'Hhhhas he gone?' said the tabby, his eyes so huge in his head they filled most of it.

'Serves you right, Trevor,' called Mathew, moderately amused, as he had watched the whole episode, napping in between, of course.

Seeing the size of the chickens, even with no feathers, he had already made a decision not to venture near. Even more so as Bungay had already flown over and pecked his nose earlier. He strongly objected as, at the time, he was minding his own business. The cockerel had then chased him three laps around the car before relenting and going back to his ladies.

'Is he a battery, too?' he had asked Comfort, who had sat watching the whole episode with her curled lip.

'I'm not sure. He certainly is a feisty little fellow. Especially as he is only half the size of the mechanical birds.'

The next day the cats, on waking, had a quick wash and rushed into the garden. They were desperate to see the birds again; Mathew had told them that Sally had put little coloured knitted jumpers on each one to keep them warm. They could not wait to see what they looked like. How disappointed they were to find that the birds had not ventured out of their shed.

The interest was soon lost when they heard a loud meow from outside the gate.

'Put me down at once. Where are you taking me? I demand to know. I can't see.'

'What's all the noise?' Sylvester cocked an ear to one side.

Roly and Pansy ran to the office window to see what was going on.

'Goodness,' Sylvester screwed up his face, 'I don't think that cat wants to come in. What a row.'

Comfort twisted her head, and pointed her ear towards the office. 'I recognise that voice.' She climbed up the ladder to join them, and peered through the window.

'Take me home at once. I demand that you let me out of here,' the cat screamed. Then a small, frightened voice said, 'Please, I don't like it. I want to go home.'

'It's Squeaky Molly,' Comfort whispered to them, as they strained to see what could possibly make so much noise.

'Who's that?' Roly asked.

'She was at the other shelter years ago. They must be getting rid of her. She must be about twelve years old now. Poor thing!'

'Poor thing!' Sylvester exclaimed, 'I hope she doesn't come in here. Her meow breaks the sound barrier.'

Comfort giggled, and looked back to the window.

The owner was explaining that the cat was aggressive, so she could no longer keep her. Rochelle peered into the basket and looked back at the owner. She was always far more polite and diplomatic than Sally.

'She is very overweight; no wonder she's grumpy.'

That was a slight understatement. When Molly came into the main unit and was put in a pen, she proved to be not just overweight, but obese.

The once petite cat could hardly walk, her legs buckling under her weight. She could not climb up the ladder to her bed part, or even lie down. Her distorted face was unrecognisable as the pretty, black female Comfort had once known. Molly was in danger, not only of a heart attack but also from her organs packing up.

She certainly was not pleased to be back in a pen after all those years. Especially not surrounded by other cats, which she hated. Feeling really miserable, she shouted obscenities all night: long, whining ones that eventually caused Sylvester to go to her pen and hiss at her. That made things worse, as Molly retaliated with louder hisses and screams. They all spent the night with their heads under blankets.

When they awoke the following morning, she had finally fallen asleep. They tiptoed around, careful not to make any noise that would wake her. They needn't have worried because she was out cold; even the ladies cleaning did not disturb her.

When Bernard woke that morning, he was horrified to find that the strange animal had moved closer to their bed. He caught its image in the corner of his eye. It was almost underneath them, having sneaked up during the night. He sprang from the bed and stiffened his body, his tail a long, thin rod at one end, and his neck extended at the other.

Bertram scrutinised the unit, his eyes settling on the bristles, and he screamed. Forgetting to move slowly, he leapt from the basket to hide.

To everyone's dismay, the scream woke up Molly, who went off again. Like a spring uncoiling, she let out a long, low cry, which got higher and higher as it went. They all groaned, and fled for the garden, getting stuck in the cat flap in their eagerness to escape.

Molly was the second cat that came back that week. The other was Reg, homed six years earlier. His owner no longer wanted him, as he was old. He had not seen a vet since he had left the cattery. Blood dripped from his mouth, as his teeth desperately needed attention.

'So you've left him in this state because you couldn't be bothered to have him health-checked? I can only hope that the same never happens to you,' Sally snatched away the basket. Whatever she said would never change things.

'Is it any wonder that I dislike humans?' she muttered walking away, not trusting herself to say any more, and risking Rochelle's sending her into the house for being rude to people.

Reg was immediately sent to the vets, and had all his teeth removed. With a course of antibiotics he was soon looking not only fatter, but certainly cleaner. He had apparently been in agony for years, making it impossible for him to eat. Certainly, Reg couldn't manage to clean his coat. The pain at last subsiding, he looked younger and smiled all the time. A big gummy one with his tongue hanging out; he did look strange.

Chapter Twenty-Three

Every day, the cats watched the progress of the birds with interest. Two days after arriving, they had gingerly ventured out of the shed. Sally fed them chicken feed, which they ignored.

'They don't know what it is,' she told Chicken Man.

She gave them a white powder instead, which they had been fed at the battery farm, and they pecked without enthusiasm.

Bungay looked at the food with disgust, and much preferred the mixed corn. He had come from a different place, as Sally told Rochelle, a roundabout in Norfolk. Chickens had lived there wild for many years. No one knew how they originated. A kindly man went daily to feed them. Then the council wanted them moved; so the nearby townsfolk signed a petition to stop them being taken. Soon afterwards, the chickens started to die through poisoning. The sad residents relented and contacted the chicken rescue and the birds were removed from their home.

Bungay, named after the roundabout, marched around looking disheartened at his new flock. He had hoped for a dynamic gang of ladies. This lot didn't have much go at all. He nudged a few with his head; not receiving any response he tottered off to have a doodle instead. Being a small bird it was not a loud one, thankfully. He soon became known as Half-cock or Little Doodle by the amused cats.

Later that day, Sally brought some sweet corn and the birds showed a mild interest. Bungay helped by picking up a piece and showing it to them, explaining what it was with little clucks.

That night, just before it got dark, Sally locked them securely away. Within three days the chickens had ventured further afield. One of them had a little scratch at the concrete. The others watched with interest. Another tried, and then the next. Then they tried the corn, deciding they liked it. They walked off round the yard, their legs too weak to go far. The sun was shining and warm on their bare bodies. They had never seen the sun before, and, at first, it confused them. The darkening day confused them even more. But bravely taking life in their stride, they accepted these new wonders. Bungay helped to supervise them; as night-time started to descend, he called them into the shed to bed down.

It was on the third night that Sally ran out in a panic. 'I forgot to put the hens away,' she called frantically to Chicken Man.

He came dashing out armed with two torches. They both ran round the yard searching every nook and cranny for the hens.

'Oh no,' cried Sally, near to tears. 'What am I going to do? The poor things, I've lost them. It's all my fault.'

'Calm down, we'll find them,' Chicken Man reassured her, attempting to hide his own anxiety.

The cats were confused, as they watched them both running round the yard. The scene was far more interesting than their night-time bath.

'But they're in bed,' Pansy said unnecessarily.

'We know that, but it seems they don't,' chuckled Comfort.

It was four hours later that Sally, in desperation, shone the torch into the shed. She received lots of grumbles from the hens at disturbing them from their dreams.

'How odd, they're in bed!' She scratched her head, and they both went off into the house.

'Even I knew that,' Pansy declared. 'Chickens always take themselves to bed at a certain time. Humans are funny.'

The next day Mathew strolled down the yard to tell them about a telephone call which Sally had received from Billy Bank Robber. None of them could believe what he told them.

A corpse of a cat had been found buried amongst a bundle of towels at the old cattery. They had left them behind in the linen cupboard as Billy thought them useful. It was some time before he emptied the cupboard and the cat was found. When he told Sally it was a long-coated ginger she knew it was Gus, the cat that Sylvia had homed.

'But how had she killed him?' Comfort asked, her face stiff with shock. 'Why would she do something so evil again? Surely murdering Twix was bad enough.' She shook her head, not understanding; neither had Sally according to Mathew.

'I don't understand it either. Humans can be so cruel. Worse still, they blame animals for being evil,' Mathew said sadly, remembering his own abuse.

'It seems that the result of what Sylvia has done has followed Sally. The story is so unbelievable that only the humans who were there believe it, and us of course. As far as some people are concerned, she made the whole thing up.

'Sally says they have never talked to the other people involved in the saga to clarify the story. To them Sylvia was a kind, caring person; why would they believe it? The story was something only seen in films or read in books.' Mathew sat down and washed his paw to contemplate the situation. He had never seen a film or read a book; he didn't feel he wanted to if they had lots of Sylvias in them.

Trevor ambled up, with his shoulders hunched; he was feeling the heavy gloom too. He had almost lost his appetite over it, he told them.

'Really! 'Mathew said with a little grin. 'I hadn't noticed.' He turned back to the crowd that had gathered to listen.

'It's the poor cat I keep thinking about,' Comfort told them. 'What if people believe that he was left behind in the move?'

'But no cat was,' Pansy said. 'We know that every one of us was accounted for.'

'Plus, Sally went back afterwards to clear out the unit. A cat would have been spotted. Why would a cat jump in a cupboard and push itself between loads of towels to die? The door was not locked, so it could have come out.' Trevor puzzled, before he went off to examine a dark spot, in the hopes that Rochelle had dropped a biscuit. Once he got to it, he realised that it was the same dark spot he had scrutinised earlier.

They watched him and had a grin, lightening the mood a little.

'The dead cat was put there deliberately, wasn't it, Mathew?' Domino's eyes clouded over sadly, not understanding how wicked Sylvia was.

Mathew shook his head, feeling as gloomy as the rest of them. He walked off to have a nap in the office, hoping things would be brighter when he awoke.

Very soon, the birds had grown in confidence, and were strutting around the yard as if they had lived there for years. The cats thought them great fun. Every morning, when their shed door opened they tore down the yard to be the first to the corn. The cats began to have biscuit wagers on which bird would win. This was usually small, nimble Bronte, who seemed to be a 'race hen', as she sped past them all. Bungay, with his short legs, was always last, as he flapped and wobbled a distance from the end. He was now delighted that his ladies were more vigorous. After corn, the cockerel always performed a strange ritual dance. This amused the cats immensely, as they fought for a good place from which to watch.

He would ruffle up his feathers, pull back his head, and side shuffle around one bird. Sometimes he tried to fly on her back; being so short, he slid off again.

'Good job,' laughed Sally, 'we don't want any babies. Especially when there are so many of you already unwanted.'

Bungay was not amused, as he sat down to work out other tactics. Sally laughed again at the disgruntled cockerel, as she decided he looked like a policeman's helmet when sitting.

They dutifully laid eggs, which Sally refused to eat after seeing one hen swallow a large slug and some cat poo. However, she did marvel at the creation of an egg.

'How amazing that their bodies process such a thing?' she said to Rochelle, holding up a perfectly shaped, oval egg, in the office one day. 'They eat a certain amount of grit in their food, crinkly seashells or chippings, and this comes out. They even have their own individual colour, either brown or white, for each hen.'

'I've never really thought about it before,' Rochelle said, as she rustled through the filing cabinet looking for some lost forms.

The hens turned out to be extremely intelligent, much to everyone's amazement, as rumours had circulated amongst the cats that they were dim. They most certainly were not.

Sally observed them, fascinated; she had always wanted to keep chickens. They clucked away in their own language, and seemed to understand what each pronounced cluck meant. If their corn bowl was low, they sent a spokes-bird to tell Sally. If one of them was missing or in trouble, the spokes-bird would, again, tell her. She began to understand bits of their language.

How the cats loved hen stories, and longed each day for Trevor or Mathew to relay one or two.

'They try and get into the house,' Trevor told them, not pleased, as they always tried to eat his breakfast. 'Chicken Man doesn't allow them in, though, because they poo everywhere.'

It was true: the hens loved being inside. They soon learned that Sally was a soft touch. Whenever Chicken Man went out they watched until his car disappeared through the gates, innocently pecking the ground so he did not suspect anything. Once he was gone, they flew for the back door, all flapping to gain speed and be the first.

Once inside Bronte ran around, vacuuming any stray crumbs, even beating Trevor to them. Rhoda snuggled on an armchair with the cats. The two Julies climbed on top of the wicker bookcase for a gossip and a snooze.

Scarlet jumped into the front room window to watch the traffic.

Amelia and Bungay were in a close relationship, and never left each other's sides. They sat together, preening each other's feathers. She was twice the size of him; they certainly looked an odd couple, but apparently they didn't care about the gossip.

The last bird, Dixie, was attached to Sally so loved to climb on her lap. There she sat and scrutinised with bird-fascination all the things in the house, especially the computer with its black thing that darts around the screen. Dixie watched with her head on one side. As Sally typed, she pecked the screen trying to catch it. It was a frustrating game, as, no matter how hard she tried, she never succeeded.

By the time Chicken Man returned, the hens were back in the yard looking innocent again. Sally ran around with a cloth and a mop until the poo had disappeared.

Soon, Squeaky Molly had lost a small amount of weight. With the help of a pillow to prop her head she could comfortably lie down.

'She needs exercise,' Sally announced one day. 'I'm sure she would come to no harm walking around the yard. She's still too fat to get under the gate, and climbing over the high fences would be impossible for her.'

So Molly was let out to wander around, much to the relief of the cats. She soon developed a routine of greeting humans as they visited. For each one, Molly let out a long piercing meow and rolled over to invite a belly rub. After everyone went home at night, she wandered up to Sally's house and called through the cat flap. She was still a little too weighty to go through. Trevor and Mathew were relieved: they didn't want her inside, causing a disturbance with her high-pitched decibels.

Every morning, Sally walked her round her car and up and down the yard. Within a month, she almost broke into a run, which was more a little skip. When let out, she would grin at the other cats, put her tail and nose in the air, and march off.

'See, I'm special,' she told them. 'Not like you lot. I bet Sally ends up letting me live in her house. I already sometimes sleep on her bed.'

'We don't care,' Domino sneered, wiggling her tail at Molly.

'I can't even compete with Chicken Man,' Trevor was moaning one day, as he and Mathew strolled down the yard. Molly, also having her stroll, yowled a long, piercing one at them. Both cringing, they rushed past, trying to pretend that they had not seen her.

'No one likes a nagging cat,' Trevor called back at her, once they were a safe distance away.

Mathew cat-smiled, dismissing the irritating female. 'Just because he can spray further than you.'

Trevor twisted his head. 'That's not fair,' he huffed.

'I didn't think humans sprayed.' Pansy, hearing the conversation, was surprised.

'Oh, Chicken Man does,' Mathew told her. 'Well, according to Sally; I think it was an accident. He got up in the night to use the litter tray. And instead of going in the tray room he sprayed from the top of the stairs to the bottom. It even went all over the television. Sally, hearing the splashing, went to investigate. He seemed to be still asleep. Much later, in the early hours of the morning, he went to look at his spray. I guess he wanted to measure, to make sure he had really beaten Trevor. With no blanket on he tried to clean it up before Sally moaned at him, like she does when Trevor does it. Anyway he slid, and ended up lying on his back in a puddle of wee.

'The commotion woke up a very disgruntled Trevor. He was so dismayed to find that Chicken Man had more distance than him, he half-heartedly sprayed up the television too. But, deflated by the competition, it came out more of a pathetic sprinkle, which further ruined his credibility. He will never be viewed in the same light by the other cats again.' Mathew looked serious and genuinely sorry for his friend.

'Once the hens hear about the failed spray, my credibility will be ruined further, as they are terrible gossips. They always do 'add-ons' to make their stories more interesting. Oh, life is so unfair!' Trevor said, feeling even more deflated.

'Goodness, what did Sally say about the television?' Comfort asked, walking up and giving Pansy a nose rub.

'Not much, she just went into fits of giggles that lasted for hours. In fact, every time she looked at him she did it again. She told him it served him right for drinking too much. But goodness knows why drinking too much made him compete with Trevor,' Mathew shrugged.

'Been on the catnip I guess,' Comfort nodded thoughtfully, sort of making sense of it all.

Trevor's heart sank further as he noted the hens sitting close by. Worse still, they stopped their usual clucking in order to absorb all the details. Once they had the story complete, they ran off to tell everyone they could that Chicken Man 'sprayed up the telly.' Adding, with glee, that Trevor had 'saggy sprinkles'.

Amelia and Bungay watched, shaking their heads at their childish ways.

Just as Trevor thought that his day could not deteriorate any further, the hens skidded to a halt in front of two mean, jowly toms. They began clucking an extended, much exaggerated story of Trevor's slack sprinkles. The two toms began whispering and smirking in his direction.

'Whatever happened to bad-tempered Minnie?' Comfort asked, changing the subject and noting Trevor's discomfort.

'Oh…err…she's still around, strange little thing. She never grew much, and the bits that did grow don't look right. She's a bit fat and only has one eye now,' Trevor told her, in an attempt to cast his mind from his depression and the two toms.

'She mostly lives in the airing cupboard, and, when she's cross, puffs and crabs.'

'Good grief, does she really? How odd!' Domino added, wandering in on the conversation.

'I don't think I've ever done a puff with a crab,' Pansy mused.

'Fancy living in a cupboard! What a strange cat!' Domino added, curling her whiskers.

'Yes,' explained Mathew. 'She feels the cold, and it's warm in there. Someone accidentally shut her in one day. The poor thing was trying to push the door open for ages. When Sally finally realised and opened it, Minnie came tumbling out, as she was pushing the door at the time. She was very cross, and could only produce saggy crabs and puffs for three days after that. In the end, she demanded that Jane find her another home, somewhere without incompetent people.'

'Oh, dear!' said Comfort, trying to visualise Minnie tumbling out of the cupboard. It was difficult, and all she ended up with was a spinning top.

'Sometimes she comes down and sits with us, though,' continued Mathew, ponderously. 'She calls us rude names, and is dreadfully grumpy. She's happy enough, though. She always rushes to the fridge when it opens for cheese, which she adores. Sally plays chase with her, which is her favourite game,' he laughed. 'When the cat is in a particularly bad mood, Sally calls her Texas Chainsaw Minnie.'

'Oh,' said Comfort, her eyes glazing vacantly.

A fine shower of rain started to fall, which soon turned into big glups of water that splashed on to the concrete. Rochelle rushed out of the office, and began grabbing recently washed beds. The cats sped off indoors, before they got too wet, as they hate rain. On her way, Pansy waved her tail at Marvin, before she went in. Mathew and Trevor ran into the office. They could not decide which bed to use, so they settled for the office chair, both clambering on together, bits of each hanging over the edges.

The rain fell all day without relenting, and, at times, became heavier. Big puddles formed on the concrete, threatening to overspill and flood the yard.

'It's almost time to wait for dinner,' Mathew yawned, trying to be heard over the noise of the rain on the roof. 'We could just squeeze in a quick nap.'

Trevor agreed that they had about an hour before wait time. This was usually another hour before the event.

Marvin, from the feral unit, looked glumly out of the window. It was getting near to dinner time, he thought to himself, his tummy agreeing by giving a slight rumble. The rain still fell in great waves, and the wind carried it across the yard. The patting of it on the roof was noisy, preventing him from taking his usual nap. He stood looking around dismally at the wet ground. He noted the hens looking glumly out at the water.

They sat hunched, sheltering under the room edge that jutted out to offer protection. They also hated rain, although the natural oil on their feathers protected their bodies to a certain extent. Very soon they would need to face the wet, and make a run for their bed.

Marvin decided to brave the rain and go outside. From there, he had a better view of Sally's back door. He shivered, as water plopped in big blobs on to his body, soaking into his thick, long fur. It was cold as it reached his skin. Still he refused to relent and go inside, like more sensible cats. It ran down his neck and back round to his belly. Shivering, he shook his coat. It did not help; it just sent the water further around his body.

'She's late,' he grumbled to himself. After half an hour his coat was drenched. The cat flap behind him started to clatter, as twenty other cats came through it one by one, and stood around Marvin, cringing as the water penetrated their fur and found their bodies.

'What's the hold-up? I'm starving,' Mummy grumbled.

'She's probably on the phone,' Marvin guessed, as a possible explanation, without taking his eyes from the door.

Suddenly, it sprang open, and Sally came out clutching a large, silver bowl.

'Assume positions!' barked Marvin. 'She's on her way!'

Mummy, Tabby and White Kitten and Beauty ran up ladders to reach a high shelf. The large roof protected them from the rain. Mummy rushed to the right, and the other two to the left. The Old Colonel, with his tongue hanging out, looked from side to side, trying to decide where to eat his food today. Unlike the others, he liked to change position every so often.

The other seventeen furry bodies flew to the cat flap and tried to access it at once, landing on top of one another, while some stuck at the sides. Many heads wedged into the hole, pushing and heaving to be the first to their allocated spots.

'No, no!' Marvin shouted, raising his eyes in irritation. 'One at a time, and in single file.'

They stopped pushing and slowly allowed their bodies to fall to the ground. Having the grace to look embarrassed, they shuffled into an orderly queue, the largest first, down to the smallest at the back. They filed gracefully through the cat flap.

Once inside, Marvin joined them, giving his coat another shake, spraying the others, who looked none too pleased. When finished, he looked like a punk, with his spiky fur. Marching to his bowl, he sat down to wait patiently for his food. Having a few minutes before it arrived, he took the opportunity to wash his paws and tail. It was hopeless, as he gave each a half-hearted lick to dry off some of the water.

Giving up, Marvin looked around to check that the cats were in the right place. A few of the naughty young ones were batting each other around the ears. Being bored with the rain caused them to be fretful and mischievous. For some odd reason, they had all decided they wanted the same bowl. Rhubarb wanted the yellow one, and so did Lacy. Piper, being awkward, wanted yellow too. Everyone knew that he always had a red bowl. Snapper, feeling left out, sitting alone by his blue one, suddenly decided to go for yellow too. So a real kerfuffle was taking place behind Marvin.

'Young cats,' commanded Marvin, 'STOP at once!'

Six paws stopped in mid-air. Snapper and Piper were being clever, using both back paws to bat. They lost their balance at the same time, landing on Lacy who was now flat on the ground.

'If you look hard enough, there are two yellow bowls out. Piper, go back to your red bowl, and Snapper, to blue.'

They both slunk off to their appropriate bowls.

'Now, Rhubarb, come over here next to me. There is a yellow one just here.'

Lacy smirked and soon stopped, as Marvin gave her a penetrating look.

'But I want this yellow bowl. I was here first. Besides, Marvin, you eat quickly and then you pinch the food in the next bowl,' Rhubarb grumbled. He stuck out his bottom lip and stretched forward his neck to assume an extended sulk.

'Rubbish!' Marvin felt offended at such an accusation. He did have a little nibble at surrounding bowls, it was true. But he could never decide what he fancied for dinner that day. So, after he'd eaten his, he tried some of everyone else's. Nothing wrong with that, he thought. He didn't eat it all, just a nibble.

Just then, the door opened, and Sally came in with a pile of cat food sachets. Their composure forgotten, the ferals began to weave around each other, each one being careful not to drift too far from their chosen bowls. They froze when Sally stooped and gathered up the dishes. She had a dreadful memory so everyone ended up with different colours. They did not seem to mind, as they gobbled the contents.

Chapter Twenty-Four

Trevor rushed up the yard, and yowled a greeting to Comfort as he passed. 'The blue comb's gone again. Can't stop,' his voice was stressed as he shouted to her.

She was sitting in the garden daydreaming when he flashed past.

Trevor was late. He was always a punctual cat, so it was unusual. Sally had overslept, which meant that he had to gobble his breakfast in record time to meet Rochelle as she arrived. He did this every morning, yowling to her that he was hungry and Sally had not fed him. He yowled and yowled until Rochelle relented and gave him breakfast number two.

After that he waited to greet the volunteers, who gave him a good scratch as they came into work. When Chrissie arrived, he yowled that both Rochelle and Sally had forgotten to feed him and he was near starvation; he must eat soon, as his blood sugar was dangerously low. Feeling sorry for him, Chrissie fed him his favourite biscuits. Leonie, who never arrived before 10.30 am, was his next candidate. She always went into the office to make a cup of tea before starting work, so was the next person to offer a scratch and stroke. He could snuggle on her lap for the next hour while she drank it.

His routine was tiring; after a long morning, he chose one of the two big soft beds in the office for a nap. He did this before Mathew arrived, so he had first choice. Testing each bed with his paw for softness, he had just settled as Comfort called in the window.

'What do you mean, "the blue comb has gone again"?' she asked, hoping that it wasn't going to be a spooky answer.

'That's why Sally was late with breakfast. Every time she puts it down it moves and disappears. So she couldn't straighten her fur. It's driving her mad, and me, I might add. Each time it disappears for at least three weeks. Then it turns up in the place she originally left it. It's not only the comb, either. Everything she puts down goes. Sally's in tears sometimes, thinking that she's going off her head. Her car keys, money, ornaments, jewellery, clothes, tools: the list is endless. It's so frustrating.'

'Poor Sally, how dreadful. Why does it happen, Trevor?' Comfort asked.

'I don't know, neither does she. But something in the house is not right, and I don't like it.' He shuddered, made his apologies and shut his eyes. He must get his sleep, to prepare himself for lunch.

Thursdays and Saturdays were busy days for Trevor. Iris had recently started to come into the office twice a week to help Sally with computer work. He loved to sit on the keyboard and watch what she was doing. It was fun pushing out his legs and knocking the papers on the floor. If he was bored, and if he had time during his busy schedule, he popped outside the gate and hunted down a mouse for the girls, just to show his appreciation of the good life he now lived. If he got a big one, he might leave it in Rochelle's bag so that she could nibble it on her way home.

One night he had managed six, and Sally was up most of the night catching them. She was up and down the yard in the early hours, putting them outside the gate, hoping that they found their way back home. Trevor enjoyed the game until, stopped in his tracks, the cat flap was locked at five p.m. each day. It was not opened again until nine a.m. the following morning. No matter how much he yowled and stomped, Sally would not relent.

Both Rochelle and Sally stood in the office, with doubt clouding their faces. 'It's true; you need to read more about it.' The visitor, Claire, laughed at their confused expressions.

'It's not that we don't believe you. It had never occurred to us before, and it needs some digesting.'

Sylvester and Roly nodded and agreed. 'It's about time someone educated humans on cats,' Sylvester whispered and looked back at the ladies through the window.

'Cats are obligate carnivores, which mean the nutrients they require to survive come from the bodies of other smaller animals. They have small intestines, which makes them meat-eaters. They need small bones, organs, blood and raw flesh to thrive. Even a few birds' feathers.'

'Yuck,' Sally said, looking green, as she was a vegetarian.

'Why don't you google the cat-food industry and find the truth?' Claire handed over a card for a raw meat company that produced a ready-made complete diet for cats and dogs.

'Maybe she's right,' Sally pondered, after Claire had left. 'I always wondered why the ferals are so much healthier than domestic cats, and why they shake off illness.'

'I hope that means we get live birds and mice now,' Roly licked his lips, a judder creeping up his body.

'I jolly well hope so – oh what fun,' Sylvester grinned.

It was a glorious day, which put everyone in a good mood. Even the ladies who cleaned stripped off their jumpers and wore pleasant summer tops. It was almost time for the large summer fête that was held each year. In earlier times, it had been held at the shop; now it was at the shelter. Large gazebos would be erected in the yard. Items were priced, and kind volunteers baked cakes and made craft items to sell. Many of the charity's supporters came along to meet up and buy goods. It was a great day, but hard work, and much preparation.

Some of the cats loved the visitors. Ones like Comfort grimaced and hid, beginning a sulk a week before in anticipation of a herd of humans invading their home.

Molly objected too, because, when the big day arrived, she was not allowed to walk around the yard. All day she squeaked in protest, causing the others to be bad-tempered.

Trevor loved the fête; his job was to sit at the end of the drive and escort each visitor through the gate. He told them about the shelter, in particular about his life and years as a stray.

'They love my stories,' he proudly told Mathew the night before, as he had an extra special wash, paying particular attention to his nether regions.

Mathew had a long bath too. He was grumbling at Trevor who kept poking him in the ear with his back leg. 'I get lots of cuddles on fête day,' he said, as he proceeded to untangle Trevor's leg, yet again, from his long coat.

'You do indeed. It seems to me that there are lots of Mathews. Every person who walks around appears to be carrying yet another.'

'I like to give everyone a fair share of me,' Mathew smirked.

The day arrived, and was a big success. So many people came, and gave generously to the charity, in support of their hard work. It was overwhelming and touching to see such wonderful dedication. Sally was proud of the progress, and marvelled at the days when she had stood alone in her plight. So many people had now joined, and projected such a fantastic atmosphere. Long gone were the days of spitefulness and power-crazy people who held sinister, hidden agendas. The supporters of The Scratching Post were sincere, genuine, honest and so giving, because they believed in the charity and what it represented.

'If I thought humans were weird before, then it is nothing to what I do now,' Trevor relayed to Mathew, as they sat at the edge of the shelter boundary watching. Mathew nodded as he looked on, not wanting to miss any of the action. Three chairs were set on the drive in a half-circle. Pam, Sally and another of the lovely volunteers, Ginny, sat there in anticipation. Eddie and Chris, Sally's friend, held an enormous bucket, or rather bin, filled with ice water. The two boys moved positions, as a crowd had gathered. They edged to the safety of a bush as the bucket was lifted and the iced water poured over the screaming ladies. At least Sally screamed; the other two just clenched their bodies and showed more dignity. Once soaked, the ladies plopped off leaving large puddles as they went into the house to change clothes.

Mathew shrugged, nonplussed, and went off to find someone to cuddle him. He spotted Iris on the tombola and knew she was always an easy target. Trevor walked over to the garden of the main unit.

Weaving in and out of the people's legs, careful not to be trod on. He saw the long black and white fur sticking out from an igloo bed, and called to Comfort.

'I really am not happy,' she told him, sticking out her nose just enough to converse. 'All these people! I wish they would go home.'

'Oh, I don't know,' Trevor responded, sitting down to straighten some dishevelled fur. 'I like all the attention, and goodness me, have I clocked up some tasty treats! I've hidden them in the old chicken run.'

'That's what I like about you, Trevor, you're so shallow,' Sylvester called down, twisting over to his missing leg side so that his belly could bask in the sun.

'That's not fair; I'm just sociable. Everyone likes me,' he objected, hurt at the insinuation.

He left the garden as Comfort pulled herself back into the bed in case she was spotted. He went into the house, to see what was happening there. Maybe he could even work out why the ladies wanted to have iced water thrown over them. Trevor slopped into the bedroom just off the conservatory. He found the three ladies standing half-naked in their underwear.

'We must have raised a lot of money doing that,' Ginny was saying.

'I hope so, that freezing water has got to be worth it,' Sally grumbled, giving an exaggerated shiver.

Ginny left, after giving Trevor a stroke and scratch. He, in return, gave her an appreciative yowl.

'Come on,' Pam said to Sally. 'I'll buy you a drink to warm you up.'

The two friends left arm in arm to pop next door to the pub.

Very soon after the chat about raw meat with Claire, Sally and Rochelle sat in the office discussing it again. This time a few more of the cats gathered to hear the results.

'It's true,' Rochelle was saying. 'There are so many studies to show that cats need raw meat to thrive. It must be specially prepared, though, to include all the ingredients essential for a cat's diet. The company Claire recommends provides such a food. We could become an agent, and give it a trial.'

'I was horrified when I read about cat food; it made so much sense. I guess that people will argue about the risk of salmonella, but human grade meat, which this is, has been tested for it. Worse still, I ventured off into other areas of cat welfare. It's a minefield, and people need to research the facts. One thing I did learn is that you never stop learning about cats. It's bad enough trying to promote neutering, without including other areas of cat welfare,' Sally said dismally, knowing it was an endless battle. 'It makes you wonder why strays suffer so much starvation, if all they need to do is live on mice or birds,' she pondered.

'I guess that, being brought up in a domestic environment, they're not used to fending for themselves. Plus rat poisons put a damper on catching their own prey. They must lose their natural instincts, by eating the usual cat food. Like children and junk foods: they get a taste for it and then know no different,' Rochelle answered. 'I guess some of the ropy ferals we bring in live in areas where rat poisons are put down. Still, let's get some in and give it a go. We could sell it to help pay for some of our supplies,' Rochelle brightened.

'Yes, we can't feed them on it completely, or it will be damaging when we home them. But at least we can see how it improves sick cats' health,' Sally agreed.

The cats, listening, were both excited and deflated at the same time.

'No live prey,' Roly's mouth drooped at the edges.

'Yes but the new food sounds far nicer than the tins of food we get now,' Sylvester said brightening.

Reg was disappointed, too, but reasoned that he would have a job with livestock without any teeth. Sucking a mouse could take a lot of effort, and he would surely starve before consuming it.

The food arrived, and the more poorly cats were fed on it. It worked on any with stomach problems; it either cleared them immediately or at least eased them. Most food allergies, which seem

249

rife in cats nowadays, were healed, and kittens simply thrived on the raw meat and grew into strong healthy cats.

Many visitors to the centre who tried their cats on the food reported improvements in their health, more energy and shinier coats.

It was not always easy to encourage them to eat it. They had long since lost the taste after years on processed foods. But after a few attempts they adapted. The kittens, not yet ruined by junk food, appreciated it the most. They became miniature lions when fed, grabbing a mouthful and running off growling as they consumed the offering with relish.

'Chicken Man's moved out,' Trevor told them one day. 'He's not coming back.'

'Really!' Comfort looked confused. 'Has Sally rehomed him, then?'

'Yes,' Trevor told them. 'I'm not sure why. I guess it's because he sprays; she has threatened the same with me when I do. I heard her telling Jane that the amount of gossip she hears about herself makes her feel like she lives in a fish bowl at times. And the extended version is far more interesting than the real one.'

'Oh dear,' Pansy mused. 'I wouldn't like to swim round in a fish bowl.'

Sylvester whispered that Sally was in the office speaking to Jane. A few cats ran up to listen. Comfort stayed on the ground, not wanting Sally to feel even more watched. She knew what it was like, and did sympathise. However, being nosy, she waited patiently to know what was said.

'I can't believe a few people have left the charity because my relationship has ended. How can people judge me by my private life and not my work? It's so unfair,' Sally was saying to Jane.

'Well you know what some people are like. Just hold up your head and ignore it,' Jane wisely advised again.

'But I've never left a job because my manager's or a colleague's marriage has broken down. People are strange creatures. They work on the assumption of what they believe they know, and judge you on it,' Sally said sadly. 'Worse still, they judge by a measuring stick formed by their own life experience. Then, when you do not fit into that measurement, you are judged. It's a sad world when people cannot be smart enough to be non-judgemental.'

Sylvester nodded. 'That's true,' he whispered to the others who shared his shelf. 'People judge me by this leg all the time, thinking that I'm inadequate. But it's not true. I'm just like any other cat, except that I need a neck scratch.'

Molly had a new routine; in nice weather she sat outside the gates while they were open. Here she could hide in the undergrowth and bathe by a large, dirty pond, as the staff called it. No one ever went there, so Molly found solitude. Her favourite place was on a large rock by the water's edge, where she lounged and snoozed. If the gates shut at two o'clock, Molly never worried as Sally would call to her in the late afternoon for dinner. She would waddle to the gate, and push her paw under. It was their secret code, to let Sally know she was there. The gate opened, and Molly would stroll confidently back in, pleased with herself.

Sally always told her that she was clever, which, she figured, made her even more special. Most of the time, though, if the sun was too hot, she went home before the gates closed. Life was good, and Molly was contented. She was still overweight, but the fat that had gone made all the difference to her life.

It was one of those days when Molly knew that the ladies would soon be going home. She lifted one eyelid, while debating whether to go in, as Sally had driven out earlier. It was a big decision, but Molly was very comfy and didn't want to move yet. She decided to wait for Sally, knowing that she would never be gone long. She settled back down, and wriggled on the rock to scratch an itch. It was hard, but warm and comforting. A gentle breeze rippled her fur, helping to cool the hot skin under it. She never heard the dog approach and, being fat, certainly could not even run fast. Lifting her eye at the rustling through the weeds, she did not have time to scream. The dog bit into her neck and eye killing her instantly. Her body rolled from the rock down the other side near the water's edge.

Sally came home an hour later and noted that Molly was not in the yard. Smiling, she called to her, and waited for the black paw to appear under the gate. When it didn't, she went with Trevor, who had come to greet her, to search the rock. There was no sign of Molly, so she texted Rochelle who confirmed she was definitely there earlier.

'But she is not now,' Sally texted back.

After another hour, she was so worried. Going back outside the gate she searched again.

Trevor wasn't; he was marvelling at how peaceful it was without the fat cat around. Mathew strolled up, wondering where they had got to.

'We're looking for Squeaky Molly, she's missing,' Trevor explained.

They both followed Sally outside the gate again. Mathew, jumping on the rock, spotted her first. He gave a nudge to Trevor who yowled loudly for Sally to come. There was Molly's body, lying near the water's edge. Sally was shocked and in tears, as she picked her up and carried her back inside the gates.

Trevor told the cats later that day that it had been a dog that escaped its enclosure from a house nearby. Sally had called the police, who were not obliged by law to take it seriously, as it was just a cat.

The others hung their heads sadly for the loss of one of their own.

'I guess if it had been a child they would have done something. But next time it could be,' Comfort stated.

'Dogs shouldn't be kept locked up in that way, and treated so abysmally. The human who owns that dog must use it for hunting or fighting. Why else would it have killed defenceless Molly? She was only sunbathing,' Pansy said, feeling sorry for the cat and wishing that she had not disliked her.

A little plaque was hung outside the gate so that no one could ever forget the beautiful, fat cat named Molly.

Chapter Twenty-Five

They often saw Furby showing off, by running along the rooftops of the opposite buildings, her tail flying at one end and her nose pointed in arrogance at the other.

Pansy, after Molly's tragic end, had made an oath not to dislike other cats, and always to be understanding and tolerant at all times.

Comfort reminded her of this, as she sneered at Snobby Princess.

'I know, but that one is so up her tail, I can't help it.' Pansy justified herself, as she lifted her head and turned it sideways, with her nose pointed and whiskers puckered. This stance was a code amongst cats to show distaste amongst each other.

Furby still used made-up Sally words. No one had ever bothered correcting her.

Comfort felt sorry that Snobby was ostracised by a language that made them laugh. But she thought that Sally was daft for catering to her constant demands. In contrast, Comfort, like the rest of them, thought it was great fun to watch Furby and laugh at her. The incidents entertained them long into the night, as they relayed details to each other.

The last had happened only the Sunday before. They had watched with amusement as Furby had curled herself around Sally's legs, nudging and raising their eyes in anticipation of a later gossip.

'Bank bank,' Furby mewed.

Sally stopped what she was doing, and ran off to find the softest blanket she could.

'Your other's in the wash,' she had offered as a guilty shamefaced explanation of why a second-rate blanket was produced instead of 'bank bank'.

Laying it on the grass, she gave it a pat of reassurance, gripping her bottom lip with her teeth in anticipation of rejection.

Flub Flub, which was Sally's silly pet name for Furby, wiggled her whiskers and tentatively put forward one paw. She gave a tap and a stroke, to assess the texture of the blanket. The wrinkling of her cheeks meant that it had passed the first test. Lowering her head Furby gave several long, meditative sniffs.

Sally let out her held breath as Furby climbed on. It was a sign of acceptance.

'Mmmm,' she purred, stooping and grasping a piece of cloth in her mouth. She turned her head around to study each leg in turn. This was essential, as wrong positioning could cause a wobbly suck. Two of the paws were slightly off-balance. She edged them from side to side until perfection was reached. Furby, satisfied, could now begin without any interruptions or hitches. Pointing her head upwards, and elevating the blanket that hung from her bottom jaw, she sucked.

Once her sucks were in rhythm, her legs joined in, all four moving consecutively to dig and dag the blanket.

Sally, pleased that Snobby Princess was happy, carried on with her chores.

Inside the main unit, Bernard and Bertram sat perched on their shelf, discussing tactics. Still under attack from the spiky animal, they were stressed. It had become a routine each morning to study the unit until it was found. Today, it had shimmied to the other side of the room. This should have made them feel safer. But it didn't; the animal was only trying to give them a false sense of security, before attacking. When they spotted its location, they both let out long, threatening hisses, bristling their fur and crossing their eyes for extra effect. They never dared lower their guard for one moment. They never worked out how the animal moved. The only clue was that sometimes one of the ladies walked it around the floor for exercise.

'I cannot see why the volunteers are not aware of the dangers,' Bertram puzzled. 'It could easily attack, by spiking their ankles or chewing their knees. You mark my words Bernard, that thing will have one of them eventually. And I hope they don't come running to us for protection. We've got our own problems to deal with. '

Bernard nodded in agreement; he was working on a new plan which, hopefully, would end the animal's days for good.

Today was the day he had decided to put his ideas into action. As the animal was near the door, he would stroll into the garden looking the other way, thus giving no clue to his intended attack, and taking it by surprise. Now was a good time, as it was asleep, with its long tail high and erect. That tail looks lethal, he thought, reassessing the details once again for any last-minute changes. He sat back, tucking his paws beneath his chest, to contemplate. He must have nodded off, because when he awoke the animal had moved again and was nowhere to be seen.

Bernard's eyes darted around the unit. He cautiously crept into the garden, but still could not find it.

'Our attacks and constant threatening have successfully eliminated the problem. The animal has vacated the premises,' he announced to Bertram a while later.

They both stood up and did fives and added a little twist of victory.

It was not until later that day that Bernard thought to ask the others about the disappearance of the dangerous animal. The cats looked in surprise as he walked forward, gave a little cough and carefully phrased his question. He was an older cat, so knew the risks which they had been under if the animal had been provoked too much. However he did not want to alarm them by letting on. Had they realised how he had protected them and kept them safe? He supposed not; but he was not offended, as it was his duty as an elder.

Sylvester opened his mouth to answer, trying hard not to smirk. When Comfort gave him a kick and a 'don't you dare' glare, he clamped his teeth together and washed his bottom instead.

'It was the no-nonsense Rochelle,' Comfort said, not wanting to demoralise him. She kept her whiskers in a civilised pose to look more serious. 'She rushed in while you were asleep. She bravely grabbed it by the tail, and hoisted it outside. You can see it out of the window; it's hiding by the wall. But it's safe there, and won't hurt you.'

Sally walked into the office, looking thoughtful, and Sylvester pricked up his ears to listen for any interesting gossip.

'We're in big financial trouble, Rochelle. I don't know how much longer the charity'll survive. We've been 'teetering' on the edge for so long.'

Rochelle looked concerned and worried. 'What can we do? More fundraising?'

'It doesn't seem to make any difference. We always spend more than what comes in. Most of the cats that come to us need dental work and, as they're so run down, expensive treatment. We take on more cats than we can afford, and homing them is so slow. Sadly, I think we are going to have to make Leonie redundant.'

'I'll work for no wages,' she kindly offered.

'Oh Rochelle, I can't let you do that; you already do so many voluntary hours. So does Chrissie, bless her, and Pam in the shop. You all work so hard for a pittance of a wage,' Sally bit her lip with guilt.

'Oh gawd,' Rochelle grimaced. 'But, being practical, you can't keep a job when we can't afford it. There are easily enough volunteers to cover the work.'

Sally sighed, 'I know; it's horrible. I hate to do that to someone. But people give money to help the cats. I'm sending out an appeal for help to our supporters. They've been so wonderful in the past. I'll warn Leonie that she may need to look for another job though. At least it helps to give her notice, to sort out something else. After all this work, I can't just let the charity fade away.'

Rochelle agreed. 'What would the cats do if there was no charity to help them?' she sighed.

Domino poked her head out of her basket on one of the outside shelves. Pansy, disturbed by the movement, sat up.

'What's wrong?' she asked.

'It's Sally, she's looking at her watch, waiting for Leonie.'

'Any particular reason?'

'She may need to leave,' Domino explained.

Comfort's head popped up from between them both. She squinted at her two friends. 'What's happening?'

They explained to her, and she took on the same gloomy expression.

They waited, in anticipation of Leonie's arrival. Finally she did, and Sally stood while she made her a cup of tea and had a rest at the desk while she drank it. Exhaling a deep breath she gave her the bad news.

Sylvester cringed as Leonie burst into tears, 'I love working here,' she sobbed.

'I know you do, and I'm so sorry. The worry is phenomenal. We spend so much each month. Every cat needs vaccinating, microchipping, health checking etc. It costs us over £15,000 a month to keep the charity afloat. We have got to make cutbacks somewhere. Rochelle has agreed to work for no money. Chrissie only works six to eight shifts a month. You are the only worker we can lose.'

Sally walked away, feeling bad. What a horrible position to be in! The cats were miserable, as a black cloud settled over the shelter. They sat quietly for the rest of the day, worried that their home was at risk.

'I can't keep him any longer. Every day I'm picking up dead birds,' a visitor ranted in the office. In her hand she was grasping a cat carrier.

Inside Roly could see a doleful tom peering through the gated front.

'I've tried everything to stop him, even a good firm smack. I can't stand it a moment longer.'

'Cats do that because they think they are feeding you. It's a gift. You should never smack him for cat behaviour, or at all,' Rochelle was explaining.

Sally had just strolled into the office when she heard the conversation. 'Are you a vegetarian then?' she asked the lady.

'No, what has that got to do with it?'

'Oh, I thought by your reaction you didn't eat meat. So when you sit to eat your roast chicken, it's OK for me to come and slap you round the chops?' she smiled sarcastically.

The woman gaped at Sally and didn't know what to say.

'The best way to stop him is to control the times when he's let out. Keep him in at night; that way, he'll not hunt mice and other nocturnal animals, or the birds that eat breakfast in the early morning. Keep him in late afternoon, when they feed again. This'll control the hunting,' she advised.

A look of 'Oh no, how do I get out of this,' crossed the lady's face. Being assertive, and not able to think up a further excuse, she took the plunge, and stood her ground instead. 'No, I don't want him,' she said, and turned away.

The tom was unneutered so was obviously not valued, cared for or loved. All the pen spaces were full; there was no choice but to release him in an outside run. He hunched himself into a corner, and looked dejectedly out through the wire. Rejection and hurt clouded his usually bright eyes.

'Don't worry,' Sally told him in passing. 'Someone will come along who'll love you.' She smiled at the tom as he looked at her, the words not helping to ease his fear.

The next day, while sitting and chatting to Rochelle, Sally received a call from Jane, reporting that a litter of eight-week-old kittens had been found at the bottom of a wheelie bin. As well as that, someone had thrown a mother cat and five kittens from the window of a car while it was moving.

'It's the same old story, Mum, isn't it? The neutering of cats is too much effort for some. I guess people believe that they can sell the kittens and make money. Then they find that there is an explosion in the cat population, and they have no chance, so the kittens are dumped. The pressure on cat rescue charities is phenomenal.'

'Yes,' agreed Jane. 'Every time the phone rings, my heart sinks. It doesn't stop ringing, so my heart dances all day. Every call is another report of an abandoned or unwanted cat. There's no way we can squeeze any more in. The reported cats are left destitute,' she sighed.

'The appeal for money has worked,' Mathew told them excitedly. 'So many supporters have come forward to help. Sally was saying it didn't pull the charity out of trouble completely but, with added fundraising, it will help keep them level for a while. At least Sally can allow Leonie more time to find another job.'

'I heard her tell one volunteer that she was not going. That Sally would have to force her out,' Comfort told them, shaking her head with disapproval.

It was a few weeks later when Trevor strutted down the yard, mumbling to himself and looking most perplexed.

'I'm not staying a moment longer,' he muttered. 'Enough is enough. First I have to endure all the building dust and cement. No heating and now this. How much can a cat be expected to take?'

'What's wrong, Trevor?' Pansy called to the disgruntled tabby, his tooth appearing more prominent with distress.

'I'm moving out,' he shouted back, most upset.

'Moving out.? Goodness, why?'

'There are things floating about.'

'Errr...?'

'Floating about. Things. You know.'

But Pansy didn't know. 'What on earth is he on about?' she asked Old Tom, a long-legged, skinny ginger who had recently arrived.

His elderly owner had cried as he had handed him in. He loved the cat, who was his only companion. He was forced to move into smaller premises that didn't allow pets. The charity was finding this more and more. Very few rented houses and flats allowed pets nowadays. With the problem of overbreeding, this also created another horrendous obstacle.

'No idea,' Old Tom shrugged and went back to digging his blanket.

'Really, Pansy, will you take note?' Trevor told her. 'I'm extremely upset, and you sit there looking confused,' he sat for a few minutes to scratch his ear and take a breather.

'Well, pardon me,' said Pansy offended, 'But I don't know what you're talking about.'

'There are things in there,' he jutted his chin towards the house to highlight the topic of his distress, 'and I, for one, am not stopping any longer.'

'Do you mean ghosts?'

'Yes, of course. Things walk about upstairs. When I go and investigate, there's nothing there. Last night was the final straw. Someone was knocking on the ceiling from the loft. It made my fur stand up, and I couldn't sleep after that.'

'Maybe there's someone up there,' suggested Old Tom, helpfully.

'You would think so, but there is no loft.'

Both Old Tom's and Pansy's fur stood on end in alarm.

'Things constantly get moved, or disappear completely. Sally lost five large ornaments one day. And do not even mention the blue comb, because it's gone again. The cupboard? Well, don't mention that either.'

'What about the cupboard?' both Pansy and Old Tom asked, looking behind them to make sure that no entities were hovering.

'Oh, OK, then I'll tell you. When we're sitting watching television, it opens by itself.'

'Maybe the wind blows it,' Old Tom suggested, again trying to be helpful.

'It is a latch lock. A long, black hook thing. It lifts and the door opens. We sit there gaping at it and holding our breath. Then it slowly shuts again, the latch lifting and re-hooking back into its hold.'

They stayed silent, trying to absorb this, and imagining a lock lifting on its own.

'One night, someone put their hand on Sally's head. She felt the fingers and everything. There was no one there. I was asleep on her lap at the time. I had to run to the litter tray, it frightened me so much. It was not pleasant, I can tell you. On top of that an old clock suddenly chimed on its own. It had not worked for years, and the chiming mechanism is wrapped with packing.'

'Crikey, I hope our food bowls don't start to float about. I think I'd wee myself if they did,' Pansy shuddered at the thought.

'Well, I'm sorry you're leaving, Trevor. Will you become a stray again?' Old Tom looked so concerned that his bottom lip hung. He liked the funny-looking tabby.

'No way, I'm moving into the office. Mathew is coming, too. It's taking him longer to eat his breakfast.'

'What about the girls?'

'They're remaining. Furby spends most of her time in the garden. Dunno about Minnie: she just tells everyone to bugger off, even the ghosts. Pippa, Sally's other cat, stays close to her, and sleeps so much she never notices.'

'What will Sally do, living alone with ghosts?' Old Tom asked.

'I dunno; like Minnie, she tells them to bugger off or ignores them. But I hear she is having a sort of clearing done to get rid of them. I know it won't help much, but it might keep Sally sane.'

'Them?' Pansy asked, her fur spiking a few more millimetres.

'Sally said there are many of them, not just one. Some of them are good, and others not. She believes this place is built on an ancient graveyard, but cannot find any information to back her theory.'

Pansy shuddered, as an image popped into her head of lots of white sheets with cut-out eyes floating around the house, wooing.

Matthew strolled up and joined them, sitting next to Trevor. 'Good morning, everyone,' he said.

'How are you today?' Comfort asked, strolling into the garden, and wondering why everyone was looking serious.

'Pardon?' Mathew screwed his face up at her.

'How are you today?' she said more loudly, giving paw signals and facial expressions.

'Forget it,' Trevor said, 'he's gone deaf. It's the brain injury from his accident. The vet told Sally that it's killing him,' his voice faltered as he spoke. Trevor swallowed; he loved his mate, and would be heartbroken when he went. He lowered his voice, even though Mathew could not hear him. 'The vet didn't think it would be too long.'

Mathew turned as he spotted Rochelle and rushed off for a cuddle. She scooped him up and he sank his head into her shoulder and began dig-dagging, oblivious to the sadness of his friends.

Trevor, jealousy diluting his sorrow, raised his eyes and ran over to be cuddled too.

'Poor Mathew,' Comfort said glumly.

Soon the story of the ghosts was around the yard, with the help of the chickens. One of the two Julies, with her comb still flopped over her eye, was the worst.

'There is a poltergeist in the house,' she clucked to the others. The other Julie clucked with her.

Bronte, not knowing what one of those was, pecked at the concrete and did not cluck.

So Trevor and Mathew moved into the office to live. They loved the life; the staff and volunteers spoilt them. Even visitors to the centre began to know the two boys. They soon became the mascots of the charity. One was never far from the other, as they were so close that they were inseparable.

Chapter Twenty-Six

After Chrissie placed a cardboard box in the main unit, Roly had a fantastic idea. He took a while to plan the details, and, of course, make a few simple calculations. When no one was looking, he sneaked inside the box. Making sure the lid completely hid him, Roly crouched patiently. He knew that, in five minutes' time, Comfort would stroll past on her way to the garden. At the precise time when he figured she would be level with the box, he sprang up. Comfort was so startled she flew into the air, twisting and hissing with her claws at the ready. On landing, she bopped Roly round the ear and walked off in a huff.

Pansy was next; not seeing what had happened to Comfort, she leapt so high that she almost landed on top of Roly. Cross Pansy chastised the naughty cat, before going out to grumble to Comfort.

Bernard was the next victim; he was an added extra, on his way to check that the brush had not reappeared, as he did every day. When Roly jumped out at him, Bernard thought it was the brush. He arched his spine and crossed his eyes, spitting and hissing as he levitated up, and again on his way down. Spraying Roly with saliva and many rude words, he also cuffed him around the ear. Feeling faint, Bernard turned round and went to bed. The brush search would have to wait until his heart had stopped thumping.

The next passer-by was Old Tom who, being slightly deaf, did not hear Roly. How disappointing, he thought.

He was in fits of giggles, and having so much fun. When Sylvester came by to use the toilet, Roly burst from the box taking him by complete surprise. As the others had, he took off upwards and, like Bernard, landed with spiked fur, a big hiss and very protruding claws on his three legs. Roly was beside himself now, his tummy aching from laughing. Sylvester was most annoyed. To teach him a lesson, he jumped on to the box trapping him inside. When the girls came back, he was still in there. A pitiful meow could be heard from inside.

'I'm sorry, please let me out,' Roly pleaded.

Reg, giving a gummy grin, watched, pleased that he had not been one of Roly's victims. He had recently had some luck, and grinned more than ever. Angela and Terry, two of the charity's hard-working, loyal volunteers, had offered him a home. They were coming to collect him the following day. He could not wait, and had been dreaming of snuggling on his own chair and beside a fire ever since. Apparently the humans had an enormous garden for him to explore, and where he could sunbathe. Oh, life was good, he marvelled. A sudden spring had developed in his steps. He had heard that they had other elderly cats which they had homed from the charity, offering them retirement in their golden years. Reg did not mind sharing with them. All he wanted was a place of safety, lots of strokes and love.

'Only if you promise to behave,' Sylvester was telling Roly.

At the threat of his wetting himself, he relented, and a guilty Roly popped out of the box.

'How odd, I've never seen that before,' Sally said, rubbing her chin.

Five human heads gaped through the pen door in disbelief at the new cat. There he sat, upright on his bottom, with his back legs in the air. As Chrissie scratched his neck he thumped his back legs. When she stopped scratching, he cowered in his bed.

'Charlie Happy Feet,' Rochelle laughed.

They agreed that he definitely was.

Charlie had recently been brought to the cattery, having lived outside for many years. He was soon moved to the main unit, to be with the others. Charlie adored other cats and made lots of new friends. He loved being out in the garden lounging on a shelf.

'What is he doing?' Comfort asked one day as Rochelle scratched him.

'I'm not sure,' Pansy looked on vacantly. 'I've never seen such a thing before.'

As Rochelle scratched Charlie again perched on his bottom with his back feet sticking up. Only this time, as she scratched, he thumped himself along the shelf. Once at the end he swivelled round and thumped all the way back again.

'Well I never,' said Domino, going out to take a closer look. 'Do you think he is ill? Or maybe his bottom itches.'

Charlie was such a delightful cat. He had been a stray for many years. He was assumed to be feral, as no one could get near him. A charity somewhere along the line had trapped and neutered the small, stocky black and white male. They knew this as his ear tip was cut off. This sounds dreadful, but charities had no other way of recognising from a distance if a timid cat was neutered. If it was female, there were even fewer clues. The only certain way of establishing this was by removing the ear-tip while being neutered.

Because of the numbers of stray cats, some rescues had no option but to neuter and put the cat back. This at least saved more breeding. It was hopeless without the public neutering their own cats, but at least they were trying to do something. Battling not only with over-population, but with ignorant members of the public, was a depressing, monotonous job for charities that worked so hard, not only on educating people but also on neutering, wherever they could.

So Charlie was neutered and put back outside to live, after a person to feed him was found. Sadly, the person moved, and Charlie was left destitute. Having been re-trapped by Samantha, who was a volunteer at the Shelter, he came into care.

The other cats soon became attached to the cheerful Charlie, and Charlie loved everyone. Each morning he went to every cat and rubbed noses with them. He snuggled next to Comfort each night and washed her ears, reminding her so much of Flick.

'Sally, you must curb your temper with people,' Jane chastised over the phone while she was in the office.

Sally cringed; she was in for a good nagging. She tried to divert her attention to Charlie who was looking through the mesh window at her. It did not work, as Jane's voice penetrated any diversions.

'How can I stop being sarcastic when you have such stupid people out there? I can't understand why they're so oblivious to the horrible things that go on in this world.'

'I agree,' Jane said. 'There are people fighting for every cause to raise awareness. We must just hope that one day things will change. I understand that, but you were rude to a man who brought his cat in.'

'Yes I was. I get so annoyed that these people, when they want a cat, go to a pet shop or breeder to get one, then, when they no longer want it, they call us. So why not support us in the first place by rehoming from a rescue centre? Some charities are forced into the position of having to destroy cats because of overload and lack of homes. I know we're a throw-away society, but to destroy unwanted animals and breed more to fit people's requirements is taking it too far.

'When they bring us their cats, they don't even offer a donation. We are left to worm, flea, vaccinate and microchip them. If we are lucky, they hand us five pounds or less to help us out. They don't seem to realise that it's us helping them, not the other way round,' Sally ranted.

'I know,' Jane agreed.

'I'm so glad I moved out,' Trevor was telling everyone, 'Sally has a new dog.'

Comfort was excited. 'Is it like Candy?' she asked hopefully.

'Nothing like her; it's dark brown. A bit like the battery hens – weird.'

'Goodness, in what way?' Pansy was alarmed.

'It crawls along on its belly, even though it has long legs. When Sally talks to it, it wets itself.'

'How odd,' Comfort mused. 'Doesn't it know how to go to the normal toilet? Sally needs a big litter tray.'

Trevor flicked his eyes irritated. 'Every night, when Sally takes it into the garden for toileting, it crawls under a large bush and cowers there trembling. Then Sally has to crawl under, scoop it up and crawl out again. Last night she accidently let it go after an hour to retrieve it, and it scuttled under again. Today Sally was out there with a saw, cutting down the bush.'

'Well really, why on earth would it want to live under a bush?' Pansy was confused. But then again, if she had had a bush when times had been rough in her life, she might have crawled under it herself. What's it called?' she asked.

'Cire, it's from a place called Spain. You wouldn't know that, 'cos you've not travelled, as I have.'

'Gosh Trevor, do you mean that there are places other than here?' Pansy was amazed by such an incredible, brain-expanding thought.

'Oh course. I've worked on a ship as chief rat-catcher. I supervised the other cats on how to hunt. We went to many other places.'

'Wow!' Pansy wandered off to have a stare at something which would help her to process the information.

'Tell us more about the dog,' Comfort wanted to know.

'Sally says that no one knows what life it had before coming here. But she thinks that it was horrific for the dog to be in such a state. There are people in Spain trying to help the animals, and find homes for them. But it's like dropping a pebble in the sea. Unless humans change their views and ways, nothing will change. Well that's what Sally says. Goodness knows why dropping a pebble in the sea has anything to do with much.' He paused to ponder before continuing, 'A charity called 'Little Pods' rescued the strange dog, and sent her to Sally. She says they are such good people.'

Soon after, much to Trevor's disgust, Sally homed another dog as a friend for Cire. His name was Jack, and he was also from Spain and the same charity. He loved people, and greeted everyone with a waggie tail and a big grin. His life had been dreadful also, but he did not have the same soul-destroyed look as Cire.

The cats had seen Jack a few times, but still not Cire. They longed to meet the funny dog, but she was still far too nervous to venture down the yard. Some days they spotted a long nose poking round the gate.

However, encouraged by Jack's boldness, Cire soon followed. One afternoon, the two dogs rushed along together. Cire liked cats, so she went and did dart through the wire at them. With her long nose, she could produce a good one. The cats, not understanding dart, were a little perplexed to see the long-legged brown dog pointing her nose at them. They thought her skinny with a big bark.

'What is she doing?' asked Sylvester through the office window to Trevor. He jumped up to the opening to take a look.

'Dart,' he shrugged and went back to his bed.

'What?'

'It's a Spanish introduction thing. She's trying to size you up, I guess. But I think it means she likes you. You wait till she does horse, and cuts shapes. That really is serious business.'

'Oh,' said Sylvester, flatly. He didn't want to ask, but, as he was a cat, curiosity got the better of him.

'I give up, what's "horse" and "shapes"?'

Trevor felt pleased that he had asked. It made him seem very knowledgeable. He arrogantly lifted his head and glanced over his shoulder before answering.

'Horse,' he began, 'is where they wave their heads around in slow motion. When you have lived and done as much as I have, you will understand horse.'

He widened his jowls which, with such thin ones, did not widen much at all.

Sylvester jumped from his shelf, and went to the wire to hiss at the dog. It had little effect as Cire just wagged her tail at him. So he did a dart back, by pointing his nose in the air. Having a short one, it was not very good, but Cire got the message and, excited at the response, turned her head to one side and clapped her teeth. After three claps, she turned her head to the other side, and clapped the other way. Sylvester, interpreting this as an act of aggression, hissed again and ran back to his shelf for safety.

The other dog, Jack, did not dart at them. After running around the yard, to assess it for stray food, he came to the wire to join Cire. He was not as brown, more of a sandy colour, with shaggy fur and a fat belly. He limped on one back leg, and while one ear stood to attention, the other lazily stayed flat. This gave him a wonky, unbalanced look, but very endearing. After having a gape at them, causing the cats to bristle and arch, they bounded off, chasing each other round and round the yard.

The chickens clucked in protest, when they had to flutter aside to allow them to pass. Cire, wagging her tail and grinning widely, grabbed Jack's leg and ran off with it. Jack, being smaller, had no choice but to hop along beside her. When she slowed, he nibbled her nose and mouth.

Round and round they went, until they were tired. They stopped and Cire, being taller, lifted her back legs over Jack, and rested on him. They became an odd cross-shape of one dog with two heads and tails.

'Why does Jack limp?' asked Comfort when she next saw Trevor.

'He has a pellet stuck in his back leg. Sally thinks someone may have tried to shoot him in his bottom. Half his ear was cut, so it won't stand up,' he explained.

'How dreadful,' remarked Charlie, as he was preparing himself for a thump along the shelf. He soon changed his mind when he noted that the wood was damp. Not only would his bottom get grubby but he could not slide adequately on wet wood.

'I know how he feels,' Sylvester added, listening in. 'My leg still gives me gyp, even though it's missing.'

Now Cire was not so nervous, she showed herself to be a cheerful dog, who always had a smile for every other animal. Humans were a different matter; the dog shouted obscenities at everyone she saw. This often made the cats jump in alarm and perform an immediate attack stance.

'I wish that dog would stop doing that,' moaned Sylvester at Cire's latest outburst. 'I was just having a doze. For goodness' sake, what's she doing now?' he asked, straining his eyes through the wire in the direction of the strange dog.

'Laaaa laaaa, loooo, looooo. Oooooo, Ooooo,' the dog chanted, lifting her head in different directions as she made the peculiar noises.

Trevor gave a sniff of distaste. 'She's getting her bark ready for the next victim. Wait for it!'

The dog rushed forward to the gate and let out the most enormous bark she could, startling them and a visitor.

'See,' Trevor smirked and flattened his ears against the onslaught of decibels.

Cire came back grinning, 'I enjoyed that.'

Seeing the cats staring, she took her cue and sprang in the air, landing stiffly with her legs in a running position and her head pointing to the left. After a pause she sprang again, landing with her legs level but crouched and her head pointing at the ground. Then she did it again, this time creating a half-sitting position with her head pointed into the air. The dog kept doing this, each time producing a new stance. After a while she ran off as 'can't clean windows Dave' came to clean the windows. Cire had saved her biggest bark for him, waiting until he climbed his ladder before producing it.

'Don't tell me,' Sylvester said to Trevor with his face screwed in confusion, 'cutting shapes.'

'You got it!' Trevor grinned, and nudged the sleeping Mathew, to see if he fancied a stroll.

Jack was a different character. He proved to be an expert thief, and was often seen running by with something he had stolen. Sally's garden was full of discarded tins and packets, cushions and items of clothing.

It became a good game to guess what he had stolen each day. Rochelle or Chrissie often came running out of the storeroom chasing Jack and trying to retrieve a newly-opened tin of special food. Jack just ran off, wagging his tail and laughing.

'What on earth has he got there?' Old Tom asked one day, screwing up his eyes to make sense of the item.

'Goodness knows, it looks like Sally's knickers.' Roly had seen knickers before, so he was an expert.

Jack dropped them in the middle of the yard, and went back for the matching bra. Visitors stepped over them, too embarrassed to ask why the underwear was discarded there. When she noticed, Sally reddened, scooped them up and stuffed them under her top.

'She is trying to warm them before putting them on,' Roly guessed. 'I bet her bottom's cold without them.' The others nodded, satisfied with the explanation of Sally's oddness.

Charlie, having had a brainwave, wondered how he could acquire a pair of knickers. They would be fantastic to wear when the shelves in the garden were damp. He could keep his bottom clean and slide with ease. He would discuss this with the others tonight, while they were having their bath.

When Amelia became ill, Sally was at a loss as to what to do. The other chickens felt depressed and concerned. They snuggled next to her, trying to offer comfort. Bungay was beside himself with worry. He sat by her side giving little nudges with his head. She didn't move, just sat hunched and lifeless. Sally read everything she could about chickens, and concluded that Amelia was egg-bound. She boiled water and took her indoors. Bungay followed, praying that it would work, and his lady could be saved.

Sally placed her in a wire cat basket, and, covering it with a towel, tried to steam Amelia.

It didn't work; the stuck egg would not dislodge. Admitting defeat, Amelia was taken to the vet's and put to sleep. The others mourned for weeks, hardly eating or clucking. Bungay sat with his head hanging, and not a doodle could be heard.

'How can anyone think that chickens have no feelings?' Sally said, looking sadly at the grieving flock, and trying to think of a way to console the cockerel. In the end she went to the hen rescue and homed two more. These were named Lucinda and Feathers. She found introductions to the other chickens difficult. The formed group rejected the newcomers, pecking and chasing them with no compassion.

'That must be where the word hen-pecked comes from,' observed Chrissie when they found the two hens hiding behind the car. Sally, not knowing what to do, separated them until she could solve the problem.

Chapter Twenty-Seven

'That's terrible!' Sally was upset. 'How can people make such dreadful assumptions?'

'What?' said Rochelle, coming into the office.

'A member of the public said that they refuse to put money in our collection boxes, because I buy expensive jewellery with it.'

'Why would someone say such a thing?' Rochelle puzzled.

'Apparently one of the ladies who was collecting was wearing a designer watch. I can't believe how spiteful people can be; derogatory rumours affect the charity,' Sally said, wondering how she could possibly put it right. 'That's it,' she announced. 'Anyone out collecting must remove jewellery, wear tatty clothes and have holes in their shoes. Oh, and a dirty woolly hat!' Although everyone laughed the comment was horrible.

'The person also said that when we were at the other cattery, the cats were left for days without anyone going to them. That's even worse.' Sally looked mortified and was not sure that she wanted to hear any more rumours.

'I'm guessing that's because I went at five a.m. and left for the shop before nine a.m., before any of the farm people arrived; no one saw me. I really don't believe how wicked some people are. There's nothing we can do about it, just hope that our supporters are smart enough to know it's not true.'

The other cats had been no help to Charlie about his knicker problem. In fact they were on the verge of insulting.

'Whoever has seen a cat wearing knickers?' Roly had smirked to the others, once Charlie had finished explaining.

'Pants,' Comfort piped up.

'Sorry?' Charlie questioned.

'Pants. Males wear pants, not knickers.'

'Oh. Where do I get pants from?'

Pansy, feeling sorry for Charlie, suggested making some from cleaning rags kept in the cupboard.

'Mmmmm,' Charlie murmured and lay down to sleep on the idea.

The time had flown by, and it was almost Christmas again. The weather was surprisingly warm, for December. Comfort told the new arrivals about the treats they would get. Unlike the early days of the charity, many people offered to help at holiday time. Sally was able to enjoy some of the celebrations, marvelling at the luxury of some time off.

Trevor told everyone that Jane and Eddie were visiting. 'You'll like them; Jane gives good strokes and Eddie won't sit still. They're tight with the treats though.'

Old Tom looked on, with pouting ginger lips. Being elderly, they always stuck out that way. He had had a bad night, with the girls moaning at him. He couldn't help having bony legs that got in everyone's way. Comfort had complained that his foot stuck in her ear. Pansy had grumbled that he was pushing on her bladder, causing her to go to the toilet three times.

'I heard Sally say that she is a super nagger. A bit like Squeaky Molly's meows, they get longer and louder as they go,' he said, worried that she might nag about his long legs, as the girls did.

'Jane doesn't nag,' Comfort assured him, 'only at Sally, when she has been naughty.'

Old Tom was feeling particularly sad today, and missing his Dad dreadfully. They had been together for many years, ever since Old Tom was a little tom. He had looked after his Dad, and comforted him when his wife had died, keeping him company on long, lonely evenings. Becoming frail and more disabled, his Dad was forced to move. How he had sobbed when Old Tom was taken to the shelter. They missed and grieved for each other dreadfully.

Thoughts of Christmas made Old Tom more melancholy. Last year they had hung a few decorations to make their home look festive. On the big day, they shared a turkey and many other nice treats. Then they both snuggled in front of the television, and snoozed through most of the programmes. Now his Dad spent long, lonely evenings and Christmas alone, with no one to speak to, or even get out of bed for, each morning. How Old Tom grieved too, knowing no one would ever offer him a home. He had long legs, pouting lips and was old; he would never share a turkey with anyone ever again.

They gaped at Jane as she went round talking to the cats. Comfort looked on, with her lip caught on her tooth.

'Hello, Comfort! How are you?' Jane asked politely.

'What is she doing?' Pansy whispered.

'Dunno,' shrugged Comfort, attempting to unhook her lip from her tooth and have a straight mouth for the special visit.

At that moment, Sally, after handing Eddie a list of DIY jobs, and watching him head for his car to retrieve his toolbox, came into the unit.

'Mum, what are you doing?' she asked.

'I was just having a chat to Comfort, she has put on a lot of weight,' Jane said reaching out her hand to allow a sniff.

'But she's over here, in the basket. That's a fluffy cat bed, empty at that. You really do need your cataracts done.'

Sally took Jane into the garden to meet Charlie Happy Feet. They both stopped. He was not only thumping his way up and down the shelf, but was sliding on a piece of cloth. Sally scratched her head, and tried to retract her hanging jaw.

'Well I never, how peculiar,' Jane burst into fits of uncontrollable giggles and more giggles, until tears ran down her face.

Sally pulled her camera phone from her pocket and tried to video the strange cat through her own giggles.

After they controlled themselves, they walked to the house.

Jane, who had a bird phobia, screamed and grabbed Sally's arm as a hen brushed her legs. 'Can't you lock the chickens away when I visit?' she moaned.

Sally laughed, 'Mum, it's Mathew tapping your leg for a cuddle.'

Jane laughed too, and scooped up the big, fluffy cat. He put his paws round her neck and began to purr.

Trevor, seeing that his friend was getting more attention than him, was cross at almost missing out. He had been delayed by advising Eddie on how to deal with the flooding problem outside one of the exercise runs. The two of them had their heads pushed together, mulling over the problem. Or rather Eddie was crouched down rubbing his chin while Trevor headbutted him.

'I know,' Eddie piped up excitedly as he walked over to the women, with Trevor in close pursuit.

'What happened about Leonie?' Jane asked, ignoring Eddie and his flooding floors, which were boring.

'The pens should have been raised slightly, to allow the water to drain away,' he told them with enthusiasm.

'I did tell them that when they were building them. But who listens to a cat,' Trevor yowled, shaking his head and sucking in his breath as he had seen some of the workmen do. He would have liked to tuck his front paws behind his back too, but didn't think he could manage that without toppling over.

'I didn't have the heart to make her redundant, not near Christmas,' Sally said, looking more worried than usual as she scooped up the yowling Trevor. 'She has a daughter, and it would have been a dreadful thing to do.'

'If we drill holes in the concrete down to the earth, it should help,' Eddie interrupted, in hopes that the two women would show at least a mild interest.

'Yes, I agree. It would be nasty,' Jane solemnly nodded.

'I think I'm too soft to run a charity. The financial worry is terrible: all the sleepless nights wondering how we will cope. But whatever, I can't justify doing that to someone. I just wish she could find another job,' Sally smiled sadly. 'But I am guessing that it is difficult to find something like this job. Although our wages are low, we are easy going.'

Jane looked thoughtful.

'The holes may need re-drilling, because they will eventually get blocked,' Eddie tried vainly again.

'I agree,' Trevor yowled. 'I'm an expert at drainage and can help by weeing in there to make sure you have drilled enough holes, or they are deep enough.'

'Trevor, I wish you wouldn't screech in my ear,' Sally grimaced.

'Honestly,' he yowled again, 'you women want jobs done, but show no interest in how us males get from A to B.'

Eddie gave up too, and began to walk back to the unit to have another look.

Trevor, feeling most disgruntled at the lack of response, wriggled free from Sally's grasp and followed. 'Us males must stick together,' he yowled, running to keep up with him.

A few days later, Comfort, Domino and Pansy shut their eyes and cringed as Sally opened the gates and reversed the car. They had seen the box outside in the driveway, and had guessed that there was another discarded cat inside. They heard the car hit it, as it could not be seen from inside the car. Luckily Sally heard the small thudding noise and stopped to look.

The cardboard box was sellotaped up. Feeling sick at the possible consequences of hitting it full on, she picked it up and went into the office. Inside was a layer of cats that could not move. A large tomcat was on the top. Underneath him were four large kittens. Beneath them was a mother cat and a litter of five tiny kittens. None of them could move. The box was damp, suggesting that it had been left there all night. The security cameras would let them know who had been so wicked.

Comfort, Domino and Pansy were quiet and thoughtful for the rest of the day. How cheap their lives were, cast away when humans had something else to occupy them.

It was an important day for the hens and Bungay. It had taken four days of careful planning to arrange it.

Despite the frosty morning he strode out of the hen house extra early, long before anyone else even considered it day. The ground was cold and damp against his soft pads. The frozen grass was crisp and crunchy as he walked, fluffing his black feathers. Bungay gave his bottom a brisk shake. The shake vibrated up the length of his small body, eliminating the remains of sleep that still engulfed him.

There were no hens awake yet to indulge him in a shuffle, so he did it alone. First lifting his left wing slightly, he bustled to one side in a semicircle, closing his eyes while he did so, to imagine a hen within his circle. Then, lifting his right wing, he went the other way. It was not as satisfying as having a real hen to shuffle with, but it would have to do, he mused. Pulling back his head into his neck, he took a deep breath. Then, jerking it full length Bungay let out a well-practised 'cock-a-doodle-do.'

He smirked as he heard Sally and the two dogs groan from inside the house. None of them were early risers. To Bungay, everyone should appreciate the mornings, absorbing the glorious daybreak. But sadly, most thought four a.m. far too early, even more so in the winter. All except the cockerel next door, who, on hearing Bungay's doodle, did one of his own.

He heard the hens shuffling about, and knew it would not be long before the first popped out of the door ready to face the day. He began to preen his wings, combing each feather carefully, wanting to look his best if he was to settle the dispute amicably.

His mind drifted back to when the trouble had begun, trying hard to recall all the details as precisely as he possibly could. He needed to be clear in his own mind if he were to chair the meeting professionally, as was his duty. All squawks and clucks must be kept under control. It was a huge responsibility for him.

It was no good; he could not visualise the events that had taken place one week earlier. An idea struck him which might solve the problem. After another shake, and a few more doodles, he headed to the spot where the incident had happened.

'Arrr,' he breathed; it had worked – the images came flooding back in an instant. There it was; all seven hens and himself on an area of dirt, having a peck around. The two new hens, Lucinda and Feathers, were now accepted as part of the flock. That was with Bungay's help, as he had chastised anyone who bullied them.

As the ladies scratched at the ground, he dozed nearby, careful to listen for any discord that might erupt. He could hear the large feet scratching expertly over the dirt in a worm and bug dance, a movement perfected by birds, and very difficult for any other animal to imitate. He himself had trained many young chicks in his day.

'Scratch, scratch jump, scratch, scratch jump,' he had chanted to the clumsy youngsters until they too were experts.

The adults had the art to perfection, despite having never seen dirt, or a bug for that matter, before coming to live at the rescue centre.

This particular day none of them were in luck; well, except Dixie, who seemed to have bigger feet than the rest. She carefully rooted out a beetle.

Bronte, instead of keeping in the dance circle, had unhurriedly scratched her way to a nearby bush. Bungay remembered seeing her from the corner of his eye. On reaching it, she had stuck her head inside; it disappeared amongst the greenery. She had always been a sneaky bird, Bungay smirked. He had taken little notice when her head popped out a short time later. Suspicion was, however, aroused when she took a slight peep to either side of herself. Sure that none of the others were looking, Bronte began side shuffling along the bush edge. Thinking back now, he realised how unusual it was to do this. But at the time, he had dismissed the thought, and shut his lids to continue his doze.

Suddenly, an enormous commotion had erupted, scaring him half to death, and almost making him topple forward, banging his beak in fright.

'It's a worm, it's a worm!' chanted the two Julies.

The devious Bronte had been trying to hide it. In her fluster at being discovered, they had seen it sticking out from the corners of her beak. It was a funny coloured worm, long and white, probably pale through shock.

Bungay's eyes had sprung open to a cloud of dust, flapping wings and rotating legs. Bronte, in her attempt to hide it, was caught shuffling around the back of the bush to eat her delicacy without the others knowing.

Bronte used the kerfuffle to flap her wings and take off down the yard, a line of hens in her wake. Bungay, still dozy from his nap, lifted himself up and joined in the chase, flapping his wings to build up speed and keep up with his long-legged ladies.

Bronte, in her panic, almost dropped the white anaemic worm, but re-caught it, as it almost found the ground. With speed and tactics on her side, she diverted around the car, confusing them as they ran past. Dixie, being small and nimble, not to mention her big feet, skidded round easily, sticking out her wing to balance herself. As Bronte looked back, to see if anyone was gaining on her, Dixie took the opportunity to fly at Bronte and make a grab for the worm. Bronte screamed, and stuck out her head, to make more length between Dixie and her worm. She did not see that Feathers had snuck around the other side of the car.

Very clever, Bungay smiled, and then shook himself; he must not be seen to be prejudiced.

Poor Bronte, in shock at seeing the hen in front of her, dropped the worm, and Feathers scooped it up. The transition of worm allowed the others to gather around them both. After a quick assessment of the worm owner the two Julies, Scarlet and Dixie, along with the now very cross Bronte, flew at Feathers to steal the bounty. A loud clacking of beaks could be heard just as Bungay reached them.

'Ladies, ladies,' he doodled, attempting to calm flayed tempers.

Feathers, trying to keep hold of the long, white worm, turned her head from side to side and up and down to confuse them, while finding a gap in which to run and get away.

'LADIES!' Bungay screeched so loud that his crown vibrated.

They froze, and Feathers dropped the worm. They eagerly lowered their vision, hoping that the unfortunate creature was wriggling their way. To everyone's dismay, it was not a worm at all, but a twig. Just to confirm the fact, Bungay walked over and poked it with his beak. After all, it could be a worm with concussion, he thought. After several pokes and a few nips he looked up at the fourteen eager eyes staring hopefully.

'Definitely a twig,' he announced.

The eyes turned with raw hostility to Bronte, who seemed to not only have shrunk, but also to have reddened.

'Well, really!' huffed the two Julies.

'I'll never cluck to you again, Bronte,' snapped Feathers. 'I thought it was a big juicy worm, and all it is, is a dried salad.' She turned her back to the others, feeling rather deflated.

Dixie pushed her beak towards the sky and blew a chicken raspberry at Bronte, before skulking off into a corner to be alone.

'I never said it was a worm,' Bronte defended herself, having a half-hearted scratch at the concrete to divert attention from her. She stared at a loose stone and gave it a little push with her beak. 'I was just lifting it up to look when you all started chasing me. I suddenly found myself in one of those horrible dreams where you run and don't get anywhere. It spooked me so much I just took off.'

'Huh,' they all said in disgust, not accepting her reason for getting them excited and then letting them down again.

'Well, how would you like six beaks pointed in your direction? It was not pleasant, I can tell you. It can turn even the brightest day into dark terror.'

They all began clucking in argument.

Bungay couldn't hear himself think, as accusations flew in every direction. It was Dixie's fault as, when they were running, she had almost tripped Julie One up. It was Feathers who sneakily ran round the car. Then it was Bronte's fault, for not only hiding a twig, but also screaming and rippling their calm day. On and on the row raged, until the clacking of beaks got physical again.

It stopped abruptly when Sally walked from the back door with a green truncheon in her hand.

'Cucumber!' Bungay called, hoping to divert attention. It did, as they flew over to look.

That had happened a week ago and, since none of the birds were talking, Bungay had been forced to call the meeting to put an end to the dispute.

He stretched his wings and gave a few more flaps, now ready to face the day.

The meeting was to take place outside the main unit. If it was raining they would have to move to one of the pen units where the overhanging roof would protect them.

The cats, hearing the gossip and sensing the heavy atmosphere hanging like a big black cloud over the hens, were looking forward to the meeting. They hoped it wouldn't rain, so that they could listen in and nudge each other in certain places.

'It makes a change for the hens to be having troubles and us to be gossiping about them,' Sylvester smiled. 'Fancy having a row over a worm!'

'Well, I guess,' Comfort reasoned, after batting Roly around the ear for pinching her catnip mouse the day before, 'that it's similar to our rowing over a mouse.' Then, when she realised that this made her no better than the hens, she went quiet.

'That's different,' Sylvester argued, giving Roly a bat too. 'A mouse is interesting and fun. A worm is slimy and boring.'

'Not to a chicken,' Comfort reasoned.

'Ow!' Roly cringed, pulling his ears backwards for protection. 'That hurt.'

'Serves you right,' Comfort flicked her nose in the air and went into the garden for some air. The weather was cold, but, with her thick coat, she never minded too much.

Her thoughts flickered to when the cats had first seen the chickens do their ritual dance to find bugs; it was so fascinating. They had watched intently as the hens dug their nails into the dirt. First one foot, then the other, in swift movements, and then jumping backwards, as they scrutinised for any worms or bugs they might have disturbed.

Roly had dug a fluffy mouse into the litter tray, and tried to retrieve it using the same tactic. He soon gave up, after falling twice on his bottom, making them giggle. When Sylvester offered a far more interesting game of the ground touch, he left the mouse. He later found it soggy, where Old Tom had accidentally weed on it.

Chapter Twenty-Eight

The meeting of the hens had begun, much to the delight of the cats, outside the main unit.

Bungay stared in despair as the group of hens clacked and beak-banged. His head was about to explode any moment, if they didn't stop.

'Ladies, please!' Bungay yelled. 'I cannot hear myself doodle, let alone think.'

They stopped in mid-combat, and gave a few shoves with their wings and bottoms instead. On seeing Bungay's penetrating glare, they each shook themselves and puffed their feathers, adding volume to their size.

Roly and Sylvester, delighted that they could listen in, sat high on the top shelf, with their noses pressed against the wire. They chuckled, delighting in the strife.

'They are hilarious,' Sylvester said, not daring to take his eyes from the gathering and miss any action.

Bungay gave a cough to indicate the start of the agenda. 'Ground rule Number One,' he looked around importantly, making sure they were paying attention. They were, and looking intensely his way.

'No pecking or non-constructive clucks. Number Two,' he gave another little cough, to stall for time because he could not think of a Number Two. 'Well, just behave.'

They grunted in agreement, turning to each other and nodding, before remembering they were not talking. After a small embarrassed shuffle they sat one by one.

'Oh yes, Number Three. Each one of you will have a turn to cluck. But I do not want to go over old ground, or old worms.' He gave a chuckle at his little joke. On seeing the intense expressions he stopped. 'We must work out a way to move on. Right, who's first?'

No one spoke as he scrutinised each red face. His eyesight was not as sharp as it once was; he was an old bird now. The hens stared at him, not murmuring.

'Okay, can I suggest that, in future, worms and bugs are shared amongst the group? We spend the day gathering. Then, near bedtime, they are dropped into a bowl and we take one each. That way, every hen and cockerel has a fair share.'

'What if there are not enough to go round?' asked Feathers, looking most perplexed at having to share her booty. 'Mind you,' she considered, 'I don't mind having a share of the others. That Dixie always discovers lots of bugs. So maybe it's not a bad idea after all.'

'Well, then we cut them in half. Half a worm or bug is better than none,' Bungay reasoned.

They were absently weighing up the suggestion when a high-pitched screech interrupted.

'Ladies!' Sally called, in the voice she adopted for hen alerting. She emptied a tin of sweet corn over the ground. Lifting their feathers, they sped off clacking down the yard. Bungay flapped at the back trying to keep up.

'End of meeting,' he panted.

'Well, I guess that's it then,' declared Comfort, who, along with the others, was pressed against the wire.

In the early hours of the next morning, even before Bungay was awake, Old Tom let out a blood-curdling scream. Whatever it was had frightened him so much that his mouth had widened, and his pink tongue was trembling, along with his long legs. The unit was on red alert within seconds. Not knowing why, they were all pointing different ways. With stiff bodies and tails, their eyes darted around trying to see what had disturbed the old cat.

'There's a man in the yard!' he screamed again.

In the sparse moonlight, they could just make out the silhouette of a man.

'That's outrageous,' Domino screeched. 'He has no fur or cat bed on.'

Sure enough the man was almost naked; a belt was strapped round his waist with objects sticking out at various angles. In his hands he carried a drill and a piece of wood.

'Good grief,' Pansy's eyes widened so much her forehead disappeared. 'He's trying to steal the building opposite.'

They gaped across not daring to breathe. The man proceeded to plug in his drill, and began to fix the piece of wood to the wall. He scratched his head and behind a few times, while completing the task. The noise of the drill was so loud, in the dead of night, that it vibrated the walls.

The cats were stressed; they had never seen such a thing before. No one except Sally ever came into the yard at night and even she didn't often in the early hours. How grateful they were when she appeared, wrapped in a long green dressing gown and pink fluffy slippers flopping along. The two dogs at her side both did a double take and grinned.

Sally looked perplexed at the scene of an almost naked man holding a drill to the wall. A big smirk spread across her face, assuring the cats he was not dangerous.

'Now come on, Chris, it's the middle of the night; you're naked, except for a tool belt. Put down the drill and go to bed.'

'I'm putting up a shelf,' the man bumbled, most indignant at the interruption.

'Chris, you're sleepwalking. Now come on back to bed.' Sally removed the drill and wood from him and laid them down, then gave him a push towards the house. He obeyed instructions and sloped off, his tools rattling away as he disappeared into the darkness.

Jack ran over and cocked his leg up a plant pot near the unit. Comfort ran into the garden to have a word. 'Who's that man?' she asked the dog.

Taking a long sniff at his wee before looking up Jack answered, 'He is a friend of Sally's who's staying for a while. There is so much maintenance here that he has offered to help with it. He's going to dig up the lawn in the garden for her.' Jack ran off to have a sniff at Cire's wee.

'He's a strange man walking about in the cold with nothing on but a bunch of tools,' Pansy was saying as she negotiated the cat flap with Old Tom.

'Yes definitely,' Cire agreed running over to sniff Jack's wee. 'He walks around while asleep. Yesterday he brought Sally a cup of tea at one o'clock in the morning. She was not very pleased, I can tell you. Then she found him in the kitchen cooking. We didn't mind, 'cos after Sally shooed him back to bed, me and Jack had a tidy feast.'

'Why is he digging up the lawn?' Domino puzzled giving a long yawn. 'She's not long had it laid.'

'I dunno, she doesn't like it. I think a new unit will be built in its place.'

'Oh no, not more cats!' Comfort exclaimed.

Excitement over, she disappeared through the hole in the wall to find her cosy bed.

Bernard and Bertram were on the other side, both still wide-eyed and on rear alert. They were waving their heads and sniffing the air for a signal to attack.

'It's OK, chaps, nothing to worry about. Just some naked man. He's gone now,' Sylvester assured the brothers. Performing a snake, with their bellies scraping the floor, they slithered back to their basket.

The next day, Sally went into the office to see Rochelle. She looked so worried that even Domino jumped on the shelf to listen.

'Finances are looking so grim. We're just about keeping things afloat.' She sat on an office chair, so Domino could only see the back of her head. 'Our supporters have been fantastic; we can't possibly ask for help again.'

'We'll think of more fundraising ideas,' Rochelle suggested. She already supervised a fantastic Facebook page which generated so much support.

The cold weather hit them in late January. A thick icy frost covered the ground, which, with the freezing air, did not relent. The volunteers, chickens and dogs, slipped and slid dangerously as they tried to walk from unit to unit. A plastic shelter was built in the garden, so that the chickens had a place to eat and stand without frozen feet.

No cat braved the garden. They stayed inside, huddled near the heaters.

'The units are warmer than the house,' Sally shivered, rubbing her hands together to ease some movement back into her fingers. The two dogs hated the cold; sniffing around the yard was impossible.

'The walls inside the house have hurricanes coming through,' Cire exaggerated, to sympathetic Comfort and Pansy, as she stood in the little entrance while Sally fed them that night.

'Brrrr! Sounds horrendous!' shivered Pansy, ruffling her coat with the shiver to offer understanding of Cire's predicament. 'We've got two big heaters in here. You're welcome to come and sit by them,' she kindly offered.

'I'm not having them in here,' grumbled Bertram to Bernard, 'they'll pinch the heat.'

'Boys! that's so mean,' Comfort chastised as she overheard them.

'It's OK, we snuggle next to Sally and so it's bearable. Going for a wee is horrible though. Rooting through the bin bags is not so much fun in the cold,' Cire confessed.

It was a much-loved hobby of the two dogs, Jack being the brains behind the safe-cracking. This really annoyed Sally, as each day she looked despondently at the ripped rubbish bags and the piles of tins and packets scattered around the garden. Inside, the house was worse. It did not matter how hard she tried, Jack always outwitted her. Every morning Sally awoke to rooms filled with smelly packets and other unmentionables ripped into thousands of tiny shreds.

Every time she thought she had solved the problem Jack, the master criminal, grinned as he cleverly un-solved it.

How many times had the cats watched Sally drag 'yet another' large bin from her car saying, 'Right, Jack you won't get in this one!'

How wrong she was as, the following night, Jack, or Macavity, as Sally sometimes called him, stood on the footplate of the bin while Cire stuck her nose in to retrieve the tasty morsels. In the morning the living room looked like the usual landfill, with not even a peep of the rug on show.

Sally stared hopelessly at the mess, while Jack and Cire looked in different directions, innocent expressions pasted on their faces.

'Goodness, how on earth did that get there, Jack?' Cire, curled in a 'c' shape and looked under her tail.

'No idea, Cire do you know? Maybe the ghost did it,' Jack's lips were poised in perfect sympathy for Sally, while she collected the debris.

The problem was finally solved by Sally keeping refuse at the back of the kitchen work surfaces until bin collection day. It was most embarrassing when visitors called.

The long winter was never-ending, as January turned to February, but finally March arrived, with a promise that spring might be on its way.

'Even with this cold weather, there has been no lull in kittens being born,' Sally griped one day when in the office.

'Tell me about it,' Samantha said dismally. Almost every night she was out trapping cats to neuter them. Not only for them, but also for other charities or for any cats she heard of which needed help. Sadly there was no space to fit them all in rescue charities so, if they were being fed, she had no option but to return them to the site. It was hard, laborious work, and often heart-breaking.

'One road I counted over thirty-five abandoned, starving pregnant cats.'

'What are we going to do?' Rochelle sighed, as they all did daily.

'It's just hopeless, isn't it?' Sally closed her eyes, to embrace the image of a deserted island where there were no people.

'No, it's not!' Samantha smiled. 'We keep going and one day, you never know, we may make a breakthrough.'

'I admire your optimism,' Sally grimaced.

'We should take pictures of the pregnant cats and publicise them. People may listen if we show them.' Rochelle brightened at the thought of doing something positive.

'I hope they're not bringing thirty-five pregnant females in here,' Sylvester whinged to Roly. 'All those hormonal queens would be unbearable.'

'Well, if they do, I'm staying up here,' Roly agreed.

'Me too,' said Charlie, assessing the worn hole in his rag pants.

By May, the spring arrived, and so did more mums and babies. The shelter was bursting at the seams with them. Most went to foster homes, until they were old enough to be homed. It seemed that more stray mum cats than ever were reported giving birth and walking away from litters of kittens. Their constant struggle for survival meant that they knew they could not rear a litter. Many deaths of baby kittens were reported. Many were dumped, anywhere people could think of, including rivers and skips, when they were unable to rehome their own excess.

The charity tried dismally to save what they could. One foster lady, Carol, was hand-rearing twelve new-born kittens so far.

'Goodness knows how she's coping,' Sally sympathised. 'I struggle with one newborn. Bottle feeding all night every two hours and all day must be shattering.

Sally threw bread pudding out to the hens and Bungay. 'I don't think all the kittens are abandoned by the mothers though. People are finding the nests and removing them, assuming the mother has disappeared. The poor thing has more often than not gone to find food. Sometimes that journey for a morsel can take up to eight hours. When she returns, her babies are gone. It's heart-breaking how they grieve. The mother can search for weeks for her babies. Then they become pregnant again and the horrendous cycle repeats itself.'

'I agree,' Pansy nodded, cringing, as she watched the chickens peck at the pudding. They had such sweet beaks, she thought.

Comfort did too; she was an old cat now, and the thought of kittens filled her with horror. One thing older cats dislike is youngsters bouncing over them. Especially females who had 'done their day' with their own litters of tearaways. Strangely, the tomcats were far more maternal and amenable towards youngsters. 'I wouldn't have the patience,' she confessed to Pansy.

'The homes are so slow coming. Most people home kittens from internet sites or friends and family. Some are being advertised at only four weeks. How cruel,' Sally shook her head despairingly.

When Jane called, asking if they could take yet another litter of kittens, they groaned, even the cats. The owner of the cat had thrown her out six months earlier. A kind neighbour had been feeding her, and allowing her to live in her shed. When the cat had given birth, the lady took her indoors and agreed to foster until they could squeeze her in.

The cats screwed their faces to the wire of the window while Leonie completed the intake form.

'It's another black one with five black kittens,' reported Roly to the others.

'Just like Elsa and her monsters,' Comfort laughed, pleased that they would be in another unit.

A week later, the cats in the main unit heard Leonie call out. Sally, who was just coming out of the office at the time, went to see what was wrong.

Moments later Leonie was in the office and a volunteer was washing her blood-soaked hand.

'I only went out of the unit for a minute to retrieve a tin of cat food from Jack,' Leonie cried. 'I had let the mother cat out to clean her pen. When I went back, the cat was standing in front of her kittens and flew at me.'

Jack, who stood nearby, sunk his tail, pulling it between his back legs so it snuggled close to his stomach.

'I guess you didn't think to close the pen door before opening the outer one,' Sally said, coming into the office behind Leonie. 'The mother cat must have seen the dog as you opened the door and then smelt it on your hands and thought it could get to her kittens. We all know that working with rescue cats is a risk. Some have been ill-treated and can be unpredictable.'

The volunteer took Leonie to hospital.

'Leonie was bitten at half past eleven. She had not even started work. Most of the other volunteers have already finished and gone,' Sally said, looking at Rochelle who looked away and didn't reply.

Pansy watched them go. 'Fancy the cat's attacking like that.'

'I guess she was protecting her kittens,' Comfort said, watching with Pansy before going over to a plate of biscuits for a snack. She picked up a few, and dropped them again, changing her mind. Just lately she had lost her appetite.

'Yes,' Pansy agreed, her eyes blinking in concern, 'I heard that Leonie is badly hurt.'

Later the next day, when the cattery was closed, most of the cats were half way through a nap when the gate bell rang. Old Tom and Comfort jumped. Sally must have pressed the gates' button because they slowly and creakily swung open, exposing a man clasping a cardboard box.

The two dogs bounded through the yard barking, and Sally walked behind them. They bounced around as she peered in the box.

The cats, although disturbed by the barking, were glad of it. They felt safe and protected against any burglars that might try to break in. They knew there were security cameras that recorded any intrusion, and, of course, a security alarm; but, not understanding what that meant, they thought the dogs were a better deterrent.

'What's in there?' Roly asked, standing on his back paws and lengthening himself. He still was not tall enough to see.

'Now, how would I know? My psychic powers are out of power,' Sylvester despaired.

Roly, ignoring the sarcasm, ran up the ladders to the top shelf. 'It's two tiny black kittens,' he shouted down.

'Not more of them,' Comfort despaired.

'One's dying,' he called again. 'Don't look good for the other.'

'Oh no,' squeaked Domino.

'The mother has abandoned them,' the man was saying.

Sally sighed. 'How do you know.'

The man explained that he had found them in his garden a week earlier. The mother cat is still around with an older kitten. She does not go to the nest.

'We'll get someone to trap her, to save her from having more offspring,' Sally told him taking the box. 'If you had called earlier, we could have neutered her before she became pregnant in the first place,' she could not help but point out.

It wasn't until a week later that Comfort had the opportunity to ask Cire how the kittens were doing.

'One died a few hours after it came in, but the other is still going strong. Sally has called her Blackberry, because of her shiny little toes. I cuddle and wash her sometimes,' Cire told them, with a gooey expression, 'she is a dear little thing.'

'I do believe you're broody, Cire,' laughed Comfort.

'Oh, I love cute kittens,' she cooed, reminding Comfort of Marmite all those years ago.

The conversation was interrupted by Sally's ranting voice coming from the office. Nosy Roly ran to the window. He enjoyed his role as reporter.

'I despair!' Sally screeched. 'People are so blasé. Her cat has kittens. The kittens have kittens. The original cat has more kittens. She can't cope, so can we take them. We now have over one hundred and fifty kittens to home and two thousand cats reported as abandoned. Goodness knows how many of them are pregnant! And that stupid woman has forgotten to have her cat neutered for two years. The next person who reports a litter of kittens I will go round to their house and strangle them. We home about thirty cats a month. We have no chance of getting through that lot. Not to mention all the ones waiting for help.'

A little black head suddenly popped out of her pocket and squealed. Sally pulled her out and kissed the top of Blackberry's head.

'Do you know what? I think you grow'd again with that nap,' she told the kitten, who was delighted to know that she was marginally bigger than just an hour ago. Popping her back into the pocket, Sally turned from the office and slunk back to the house, feeling slightly better for letting off stream.

On her way to the house, Sally stopped and looked at the squashed dog in the cat trap. She laughed, while lifting the door and freeing Jack.

'You pig! I'm trying to catch a loose feral cat. So far I've trapped two chickens, Trevor, Mathew and now you. Goodness knows how you squashed in there.' The grateful dog wriggled free, looking embarrassed, especially as Cire kept smirking at him for the next two days.

'It's so wearing keeping the charity afloat,' Sally whinged to Jane during one conversation.

'It'll get easier,' Jane consoled.

'I don't think so. Not now. The larger the charity becomes, the more the work escalates. I barely get time to bathe.' That was ironic; Sally had hardly had time to bathe in the past ten years. 'Sometimes I would rather stack shelves in a supermarket,' she sighed.

'Rubbish!' her Mum stated.

But in a way, it wasn't. Sally had given up eleven long, hard years of her life working to build The Scratching Post. Plus the many long years with the charity before. She was exhausted, and longed for time to herself to do other things. The interests she had loved had long since been given up for endless work. Her precious interests, all gone, along with the friends she had lost touch with, as well as all the social occasions she had declined because there was never a lull in the relentless workload.

She grimaced as she looked at her broken nails, that had once been filed to perfection and polished every week, and thought of the make-up, sitting disregarded in a drawer, because she never had time to apply it; and her clothes, which she had loved to design and put together. Each day Sally threw on the nearest thing to hand. Rarely did they match or flatter her.

Any spare time she ever did have was a few moments snatched here and there; even then, it was at the cost of getting behind with work.

She cast her mind back to eating any food with the phone propped under her chin, or trying to decorate while sorting out another problem. Bathing with the phone again glued in the crook of her neck. Even watching television with an endless stream of calls, or visitors to the cattery after hours. The rare evenings out, texting or emailing people in an attempt to sort out one saga after another, each time believing that tomorrow would be different, and that there would be time to herself. After the next fundraiser maybe, or 'get this out the way,' and then she could take a few hours off. Even simple tasks like vacuuming the carpet could take between four to six hours, with endless interruptions in between.

Sally thought of her husband, hearing his voice on a glorious sunny day. 'Come on, Sally, please. Just this once have a day off. We can go out anywhere you want. London, the seaside. It's been two years now without a break.'

Sally had looked away from his pleading eyes. 'I'm sorry, but I can't. There is just no way anyone will cover for me. Last time I tried, everyone cancelled at the last minute. Besides, the fête is coming up, and I'm so behind with the advertising and pricing. I'm so sorry.'

Off he had gone for a day out alone, sad and dejected.

The preparation for the yearly fête had started months before. Then, the work started on the day at four a.m., and finished after the clearing up at eleven p.m., well after people had even forgotten that it had existed.

Sally thought of her friend Sonya. 'Sally, please just take a break. We could go shopping like other friends, or go for a bite to eat somewhere.'

She had declined, as there was always too much to do.

Yes, she was tired, and so was her mother, who had now given over fifty years of her life to rescue work. In all that time, Sally only remembered her having a few days break, unless she was ill.

At that point, Blackberry mewed from her snug pocket; her thoughts were broken and forgotten. It was time for her feed.

'Tomorrow I'll have a few hours off,' she smiled and gave the kitten a kiss. 'I do believe you grow'd another bit with that sleep, Blackberry. If you keep sleeping, I will have a tiger in my pocket, at this rate.' The innocent kitten wriggled with pride and glowed, oblivious to anything other than her next feed.

'When you came in, you were only half my hand. Now you're almost a whole hand.'

Cire looked up, and studied the baby. It was true; soon she would be big enough to play with.

'Goodness, is that Blackberry? She looks so much bigger,' Iris said peering at the kitten.

Sally was holding the black bundle in one hand, with her other hand in a claw, wiggling her fingers.

'Honestly,' the kitten squeaked to Cire indignantly, 'don't humans realise that I'm far to grown-up to play spider now?'

'I know,' Cire agreed, 'you just have to humour them.' She flicked her eyes conspiratorially. 'You're nutcracker size now.'

It was true. When on the floor, Blackberry could produce an almost perfect nutcracker. Although her back legs were still a little wobbly, she could easily lift herself on to them and wave her front legs almost to perfection. Soon she knew that she would be at platter-puss stage, and she felt very grown up.

Cire was proud, too; to her, Blackberry was like her own pup.

'Another cat ruined by Sally's silly words,' Comfort stated.

'Yes,' said Cire, running outside to get ready for a bark. 'We already have nake.'

'Nake?' Domino puzzled.

'Yes, poor Blackberry is terrified of snakes. She saw Sally's computer lead move the other day. Thinking it was a snake she did a big fluff and spit, then stuck her head under a cushion. I didn't have the heart to explain to her that her bum was still on show. Every time Blackberry sees something long and thin she screams, 'Nake-nake!' then runs and hides.'

'Oh no! That's terrible! Already she cannot speak properly. She'll end up like Snobby.' Comfort shook her head, 'That poor kitten.'

'I cannot believe it's almost the end of the year. Where does time go?' Pansy said one evening, while having her bath, or rather washing the now elderly Comfort, who struggled to clean herself adequately these days, making her think of old Summer, all those years ago. So both Pansy and Domino, after their own bathing, took one side each.

Some of the volunteers also brushed her, much to the old lady's disgust. But she had to admit, she was happier when clean.

'Do you know that it's been eleven years since the charity started?' Comfort told them, as she did most days and nights.

'Yes, I think we're all getting old. Mathew must be ancient, at least twenty.' Domino was depressed at the thought. For even she must be over middle age by now.

'I'm never going to the shop again,' Jack was saying, one Monday, as he jumped from the car and cocked his leg up one tyre to relieve himself. He stayed silent, with his eyes half-closed, while he concentrated on his flow.

Cire jumped out after him, and ran up and down to see whether she could find some potential barking victims. To her disappointment, it was dark and late, so there was no one there apart from the cats.

'I've never been so embarrassed in all my life,' Jack said, once his wee had finished dribbling, and he had given himself a shake.

'What happened, Jack?' called Pansy, popping her head out of the outside litter tray.

'I've had two dreadful experiences lately, and I don't need to talk about them and make them larger in my head.'

Cire ran over. 'Take no notice. He's upset with Sally.'

'Why?' Domino asked, popping her head out of the tray beside Pansy.

'Sally told everyone in the charity shop that he weed on the kitchen floor. Now he says he is never going to the shop again.'

Jack sloped over his shoulders hunched. 'I'm never going to the shop again. Everyone knows. Sally might as well have published it on Headbook.'

'Facebook, you turnip,' Cire laughed.

'Oh,' Domino and Pansy gave each other long looks before turning back to the dogs. 'I'm sure the humans didn't take any notice,' Pansy consoled, not really understanding what the problem was.

'What was the other bad experience?' Domino asked, remembering that he had had two incidents.

'Well,' explained Cire, 'we went to Eddie and Jane's at the weekend. And Sally was explaining to Eddie that she had heard the best way to eat a pomegranate is to keep squeezing it until it is soft. Then make a hole and drink it. We were happily snoozing while he was squeezing and halfway through '*EastEnders*' it exploded. Well, you should have seen us go. Eddie leapt from the chair so fast his glasses took off and bopped him on his nose on their way down. Jane screamed and spilt her tea over her lap. I jumped so high that I landed on the back of the sofa, and Daisy dog ran round in a circle, barking, in case they were under attack.

'The nine cats were so startled that they took off in different directions; three hid under one basket. Four flew through the air and ended up wedged in the tiny gap of the patio door opening. The other two jumped up and down three times because they couldn't decide what to do. Jack, in the confusion and commotion, weed himself.

'And what did Sally do? Well, we were so disgusted with her. She just sat there giggling. Then she had the audacity to put her arms over her head when old Elsa flew over it with bits of pomegranate stuck over her coat. In fact we all had bits of horrible sticky pips stuck to us. It's such a terrible disgrace. We were so upset that we refused to go there again, and none of us spoke to Sally for ages. Well, at least until food time.'

'That's terrible. I never heard of anything so bad in all my life,' Pansy tutted loudly to show empathy.

'Me neither,' agreed Domino. 'Did you tell them about Snobby?'

'Oh yes, I didn't tell you what happened with Princess this morning, while you were in the car,' Pansy wiggled excitedly; how she enjoyed a good gossip. She was getting as bad as the chickens in her old age, and sometimes worse.

'What?' Cire and Jack said together, both pushing their noses to the wire of the enclosure to hear better.

'Well, Sally, as you know, was running late and you two were already in the car waiting. Old Snobby decided that she was hungry again – greedy thing, 'cos she had had breakfast. So Sally ran back to the house, and grabbed a sachet for her. Well, Snobby just twisted her nose in the air. So Sally ran back for a different one, and what did she do? Yes, twisted her nose, and, this time, her tail in the air. So Sally ran back again and found a different food. And she did it again.'

'That's terrible! Especially being trapped in the car. We could have scoffed the ones she didn't want,' Cire said, huffiness sneaking up her paws.

'Well, Sally grabbed another, and then another and another. Each time Snobby did the same. In desperation, she took the really expensive food Rochelle was saving for sick cats and opened that. And yes, you guessed it, she ate it. I tell you, us cats sat in a line watching with our eyes and whiskers pointed to the sky for ages. Even the hens and Half-cock had their beaks pointed upwards in disgust. I'm never going to speak to her again.' Pansy huffed and licked her toe for a few strokes.

'You don't speak to her, anyway,' Domino pointed out.

'Well I... I'm never going to look at her again,' Pansy grumbled, putting her toe back to the floor.

'I'm so embarrassed that I weed over a popping pomegranate,' Jack said.

'That's nothing,' Cire, told them, her lips puckering into an 'o ie'. 'When Sally goes to the litter tray in the middle of the night, Snobby gets out of her bed and demands to be fed. What's worse is that she gets precisely what she wants. Have you ever heard of such a thing?'

'No, I've not, and I think it's diabolical. We don't get fed at four am,' Pansy huffed, glad that she had something to gripe about to the others at bedtime.

'Anyway, what's a pomegranate?' Domino asked when Jack and Cire had run off.

'I've no idea,' puzzled Pansy and lifted her toe again. 'We'll ask Trevor; he knows everything.'

'Jack is in further disgrace,' Cire shouted to the cats on her way past for her morning bark. By the time she came back, a large crowd had gathered to listen to her story.

Cire felt a little overwhelmed, as all eyes bore into her, in anticipation of a good gossip. Even the chickens and Bungay had gathered by the wire to listen.

Now she wished she had not mentioned it; her head was still thumping from last night. Jack had laughed all night at her. Sally had poured herself a large glass of Bailey's that she had received as a present. When she was not looking, Cire had sneaked on the sofa behind her, and stuck her tongue in the glass. She liked the taste, so she lapped the whole lot. Sally was cross when she saw what was happening. Cire suddenly felt very strange, as the room started spinning. Her legs went wobbly, and, as hard as she tried, she could not stand up.

'I feel sick,' she slurred. 'Call a vet, I've gone funny!' But of course Sally did not understand. 'Now you will get a headache,' she told the naughty dog. 'Your legs look like Bambi.' Sally had kindly looked after her, getting her a blanket and some water. Then she tucked her up on the sofa telling her she won't do that again.

She was right, Cire wouldn't. She had woken with a pounding head, just as Sally predicted. Her barks were just not as productive as usual today, and not even the postman had jumped. Had she been damaged forever?

'Well, come on Cire, what happened?' Sylvester, who was perched on his shelf, prompted.

Cire looked at them and began to tell her tale. 'Well this morning, Jack went out of the dog flap, to wee, like he usually does. Sally was in the bathroom having a wash, when a man knocked on the door. She wasn't pleased, as she was undressed. But putting on her dressing gown she opened it.

"Is that your dog,'' the man pointed, and there was Jack running along the pavement. Sally, in her panic, shouted to him, but because of the car noises he couldn't hear her. So she had to run into the street to chase him. There was a line of traffic outside of people on their way to work.'

'Naughty Jack,' they gasped, knowing how dangerous cars were.

'Sally took off down the road with her Isaac Newton hair, as she calls it, before it's brushed. No fur to cover her except a worn dressing gown and silly fluffy slippers. He got a telling-off when she got him indoors, I can tell you. Sally told him she had never been so humiliated! His tail went floppy for at least five minutes.'

'I can't see what the fuss was,' clucked Feathers. 'I get up and charge through the yard every day before I've had a preen. Mind you, I have my feathers on.'

'Me neither,' Comfort puzzled, 'but I think humans are more vain than us,' she chuckled to herself on her way to bed.

Chapter Twenty-Nine

It was late one night when Sally stood in the middle of the Shelter yard, staring dreamily upwards. She marvelled at the wonderfully clear sky that appeared, as a canopy of black silk with hundreds of gleaming crystals sprinkled far beyond her sight. The enormous, silver luminous moon hung weightless, just above the silhouetted trees that outlined the vast forest. There were no street lights to dilute the fabulous sight, and most nights she stood in wonder at such mysterious beauty. Most nights here felt full of mystique, but for some reason, tonight the air was full of magic.

Chris came up behind her, and put his arm around her shoulder, kissing the top of her head affectionately. She smiled and snuggled against his chest.

'Happy?' he asked, smiling back, his eyes full of warmth and love.

'How could I not be,' she answered with as much warmth in her voice. She curled her arm around his waist and they both stared up at the wondrous, mysterious moon with its sparkling stars shimmering around it.

'I need a large sum of money to buy a larger site,' Sally said thoughtfully, 'so we can help more animals.'

Chris laughed. 'Do you ever give up?'

The cats in the main unit were unaware of Sally standing nearby. They were cosy and snug in the large basket by the window. There were so many of them that bits of bodies hung over the plastic edges.

Many hours before, they had completed their bath, and now they were deep in sleep: Old Tom with his front legs around Pansy and his back tucked under Domino; Roly, stretched along the side, very squashed, with three heads snoring away on top of him; Sylvester on top of them. Only the tip of Charlie's tail could be seen, poking out in the middle of the mismatch of different coloured bodies. Under the pile, with only a pink nose on show, was Edward, a newcomer to the group. Cuddled next to him, Comfort was so squashed by Pansy and Domino that her fur was flat.

Her eyes sprang open, and she disentangled herself from the heap. She jumped out of the basket, causing many moans and groans of protest. Comfort shook her coat and pushed her face against the window, squinting through the glass.

'What's wrong?' Pansy asked in concern, dislodging herself too, and looking at Domino to see the same worry creasing her brow.

'Did you hear that? Someone was calling me. It sounded... like...' Comfort hesitated, not wanting to sound silly. 'It sounded like Flick.' Comfort's heart was racing as she strained to see through the glass.

The other cats awoke and blinked at her.

'It was a dream, Comfort. Please calm down and try to rest.' Pansy was so worried about her. She did not seem well. She was becoming forgetful, and twice now had been found sleeping in the toilet tray.

'It's OK. I'm just getting senile in my old age,' she reassured her friends, climbing back between the entwined bodies. 'I'm old and silly; you're probably right, it was nothing, just a dream. Go back to sleep.'

It took Pansy a long time for sleep to come; she lay for ages, thinking about Comfort. She couldn't get comfortable; Old Tom's bony legs kept digging in her back. Her friend was not her usual self. If anything happened to her, what would they do?

Comfort had not been well for some time. Much to her horror, she had been taken to the vet's, and had had blood tests. To her relief, they had been OK, which was surprising for an old cat like her. She must be over eighteen years old now. She was at least eight years old, if not more, when she came into care, how time had flown. Now her bones were aching, and she was tired all the time. The vet had given her three lots of antibiotics, but they made no difference. Comfort knew, deep down, that death, for her, was drawing closer. Nothing could be done. She would miss this place, the only home she had known for many years. She would miss her friends, as she did all the ones that had gone.

Comfort had not thought about her old home, where she had been young with her Mum and siblings, for a long time. She had been born on a nursery, where humans grew vegetables. Her mother had struggled to care for the five kittens, and two of Comfort's brothers had died. The humans never thought to feed them; they lived on rats and mice. But she had been happy, not even considering how the adult cats, her parents, aunts and uncles struggled. Not until she became an adult herself.

She was pregnant at just five months old. Far too young to give birth; little more than a kitten, she had two beautiful babies. How proud she was, washing and showing them off to the others, who cooed and told her how clever she was. Four days later they had died. How sad she had felt, leaving their tiny bodies in her nest as she walked away.

She was too young to understand, and was soon pregnant again. The next time, she had given birth to five kittens and reared them all.

At just four weeks old, a male human had taken them from her. She was frantic, as she searched, but had never found them.

Life was a struggle, hunting to feed herself. The winters were harsh and cruel, the wind whipping at their bodies. All twenty cats would huddle together against the onslaught to keep warm. When the snow and ice came, it was even harder to find food. The older cats died when their teeth became loose, as they could no longer hunt to survive. Most were only seven or eight years old, the hardness of their life making them appear older.

Then, one day, the humans disappeared altogether and the place was deserted. Big machines came and started smashing up their homes. The cats ran for their lives in fear and confusion, leaving Comfort, who froze in terror amongst the rubble. After that day, she never saw her family again. She searched, as she had for her babies. But not a cat, or even a mouse, was found anywhere.

Hunger forced her to leave, in search of food. It was the only home she had known, and the world was a scary place. Strange cats chased and bullied her. She became pregnant, and wondered how on earth she would care for a brood when she could not even care for herself.

One day she met a friendly dog named Rufus, who was concerned at the dishevelled state of her matted coat.

'Follow me home,' the gentle dog offered. 'My Mum's a soft touch; she will take care of you.'

Not knowing what else to do, Comfort followed until they reached a garden. Rufus was led into a house, so she could not follow. She sat in the garden and stared at the window where, after a while, Rufus on his back legs stared out at her. Much to Comfort's alarm, he began to wuff, looking around at his owner and back at her.

A lady with kind brown eyes appeared at the window, following Rufus's gaze. Her eyes fell on the filthy, matted cat as her hand patted the dog's head.

'Oh Rufus, you've brought home another stray, have you?' she smiled at both Comfort and Rufus.

Turning from the window, the lady disappeared. Opening the front door, she placed a plate of sardines on the step, and returned to the window, to watch the little cat devour the contents, her body shaking in desperation of hunger.

Comfort stayed in the garden, hoping to receive more food. She made a nest under a large bush and hid, appearing at five p.m. each day for food.

A week after finding her new home, Comfort was trapped in a large cage. It was hard admitting that she had been complacent. But hunger still dominated her and, although it had been odd, her meal being placed in a big basket, she had not thought about it too much. Hunger does funny things to one's body, causing pain and weakness. So trapped she was, and how frightening was the whole experience! She was taken to a vet and spayed. It was a relief; she could not rear any more kittens, her body was too tired and worn out.

Then she had come here to live. How wonderful it was to have a soft, warm bed and regular food.

With the thoughts of her younger days, Comfort fell into a restless sleep. Her dreams were strange and so real, she believed them true. She dreamed of Flick. His warm paw touched her head and she opened her eyes, looking up at him with surprise.

'You came back?'

'Yes, Comfort, how could I ever forget you?'

'But you've been gone so long,' she gently chastised, elated to see him at last.

'I know. I tried. After a month, we were released from the barn we were confined in. I tried to smell the cattery, but couldn't find a way back. Eventually I worked it out and left. I walked and walked for weeks, until I was so close that I could sense you, still waiting. I was weak from hunger, and my paws were sore and bleeding. I wasn't thinking, and stepped out in front of a car.'

'Oh no!' Comfort was dismayed. 'But you were OK?'

'No, Comfort, I died instantly.'

'You're dead?'

'Yes, and soon it will be your time too, old cat. I want you to know that I'm waiting for you. We all are.'

Comfort looked, and there behind Flick was a crowd of cats. The first she spotted was a black, glowing face, the image of Flick's. He was grinning cheekily at her. 'Mac,' she breathed in disbelief.

Another black cat nudged him out of the way with her leg. 'Move over, thug!' she hissed, but with humour rather than malice.

'Summer, oh Summer, you look so wonderful.'

'Don't forget me.' Comfort looked at the next cat, a stunning, skinny grey female; and next to her stood a majestic, handsome ginger.

'Sky and Jacob, you're together,' she said, delighted that they had found each other.

A young tabby and white pushed himself through to the front.

'Oh Twix, you're safe.'

'And me too,' squeaked a voice near the back, and a black face popped out from the crowd. Comfort laughed delighted, 'Squeaky Molly, you look fantastic and slim.'

'Comfort, it's me!' She turned her head and saw the most magnificent orange cat she had ever seen. Despite his perfect features and physique, she instantly recognised him. Joy flooded her heart; it was her dear friend Banjo.

'Oh Banjo, you've died.'

'Yes, Comfort. I was adored by my owners. I passed away peacefully in my sleep. But I never forgot my old friends, especially you. And now it's time; we've come to take you home.'

Comfort looked behind them, astonished and bewildered by what she saw. Her mouth fell open, and her eyes widened. Her vision rose upwards and upwards again, until it reached the invisible ceiling.

Dominating the room was the most beautiful thing she had ever seen. No words could convey or explain what exactly it was. All she could think was that it was some sort of alien or entity. It definitely was not a being of this world, not at least one she had ever encountered before. The being did not seem to be male or female, human or animal. The colours it emanated were so intense, crisp and dazzling, that they could never be compared to the dull, grey earth. They were so bright that Comfort had to avert her eyes and squint. The brilliance radiated so far that it illuminated not only the room, but the whole Shelter. Its exquisite features, not an earth face, still and unmoving, seemed to smile, injecting the room with joy and happiness. Its aura was so immense and powerful – if it had not been so magnificent, it could almost have been feared, through lack of understanding of it. Love vibrated out and engulfed the little black and white cat, touching her both inside and out. Its unmoving arms stretched out and embraced her. She felt the warmth and love glowing through her body, along with hope and peace. Happiness as she had never known before. Comfort knew it was an angel.

Flick's voice penetrated her trance. 'Look who I have here, Comfort.' She turned her head to him, her mouth agog. Two pretty fluffy kittens ran forward towards her.

'My babies!' she cried, reaching out her paws to them. Just behind were five other kittens, wobbling on tiny, thin legs, with round pop bellies. 'And you're my lost babies.'

'I've been looking after them. They're waiting for their mother. How I have missed you. After tonight, we'll never be parted again,' he breathed, the emotion of his long wait clear in his voice.

With those last words, Flick and the others vanished. Comfort jumped out of the basket, startling Pansy again who had just drifted into a deep sleep. She ran round, calling out names, begging Flick and her friends to come back, but she could no longer see him, or any of them.

'Comfort, what's wrong?' Pansy asked anxiously.

'It was Flick. He was here. And my friends and my babies. He touched my head.'

Her legs buckled, and she crumpled to the floor, as pain struck her stomach. She let out a long, agonising wail.

'Comfort, please don't do that,' Pansy begged.

Sally heard the wail from where she stood with Chris. Comfort rarely made any noise; she went to see what was wrong. Finding her on the floor, she lifted and cuddled her to her chest. The first cuddle that Comfort had ever allowed.

'It's time old lady isn't it?' She kissed the top of her head, as a great wave of sadness swept into her heart.

'We've been together a long time now. I remember you all. The ones that have been homed and the ones that have died. How many cats have there been? Hundreds, thousands even. I bet you remember them too don't you?'

The fluffy cat looked up at Sally, her eyes filled with knowing. She understood, and, at that point, Sally and Comfort became the closest that two beings from different species could become. They both knew that this was not the end; it was the beginning. And Comfort was not scared, why would she be? Flick and her friends were waiting for her.

They watched helplessly from the window, as Sally carried Comfort to her car and drove through the large gates to the midnight vet. How they would miss their dear friend! Cats cannot cry tears, but Pansy stood and let out a long painful howl. She couldn't see the cat, whose face was so black that his features were barely visible, standing close.

Flick smiled sympathetically at Comfort's friends. He did not want them to feel the pain of loss, but it was his time now; he had waited so long to be reunited with her, as she had waited for him.

The cats in the unit stared at Pansy, not knowing what to do. Then Old Tom stood on his wobbly back legs. He raised his head, and let out a long pitiful wail, too. Domino, Roly, Bernard and Bertram and Sylvester, and even the new cat, Edward, watched, and then they stood. Slowly they reached out their necks and wailed along with them.

Trevor from the office snapped his head up, as the blood- curdling noise shuddered through his body. He nudged Mathew, and mentally portrayed what was happening.

'No, not Comfort,' Mathew cried.

Trevor looked distraught, as they both stood and wailed.

Then, in all the units, the cats asleep or in mid-wash froze and time stood still. They climbed to their feet, lifted their heads, and the whole cattery erupted.

Cire and Jack heard the noise from the house; even Furby and Minnie stood. At first Cire barked; she soon stopped and let out a long wolf howl, joined seconds later by Jack.

The angel hovered over the middle of the yard. Hearing the noise of pain it spread its arms, projecting warmth and love, injecting hope to them all.

A magnificent glow of light spread from its body, creeping slowly over the whole Shelter, stretching far wider until it flooded out into the forest. Throwing back its head, and closing its eyes, the angel shimmered and a fine silver dust sprinkled and fell from its body. Rays of other colours shone through the silver spreading goodness; messages of reassurance and hope.

The dogs and chickens, rabbits and foxes nearby awoke, or stopped and froze, hearing the noise. They looked to the sky and saw the lights of colour raining down, engulfing them with peace that filled their bodies and hearts. Then an incredible thing happened. They all stood, their gazes lowered in respect for the end of an era. Each then threw back their heads and howled.

They howled for the battle to make things right for them to live a life on earth alongside humans and not at the mercy of them. For they knew they were defeated unless humans changed their ideas and accepted them as fellow beings that shared the earth. It was humans' choice, not their own; they had no choice.

They stood for themselves, each for their own species, for their struggle and suffering. They stood for justice, not only for all beings, humans and animals, that suffer at the hands of others, but for the planet they were so privileged to live on, but which was being destroyed through ignorance. They stood for what is right.

They stood and howled for a beautiful, insignificant, little black and white cat called Comfort.